VERDICT OF GOLD

FROST BOUND DUOLOGY: BOOK TWO

ABIGAIL L. WILKES

ALSO BY ABIGAIL L. WILKES

Seconds

Color of Ash

Judgment of Frost: Frost Bound Duology Book One

For the Bob Father, the one responsible for my love of a particular gladiator movie and many other good stories.

CONTENTS

Mount Rachav

Lake Kefa

To the Ravine and UR

The Pens and Field

Old Judge's hut

Death's Wall

Doram

Eder

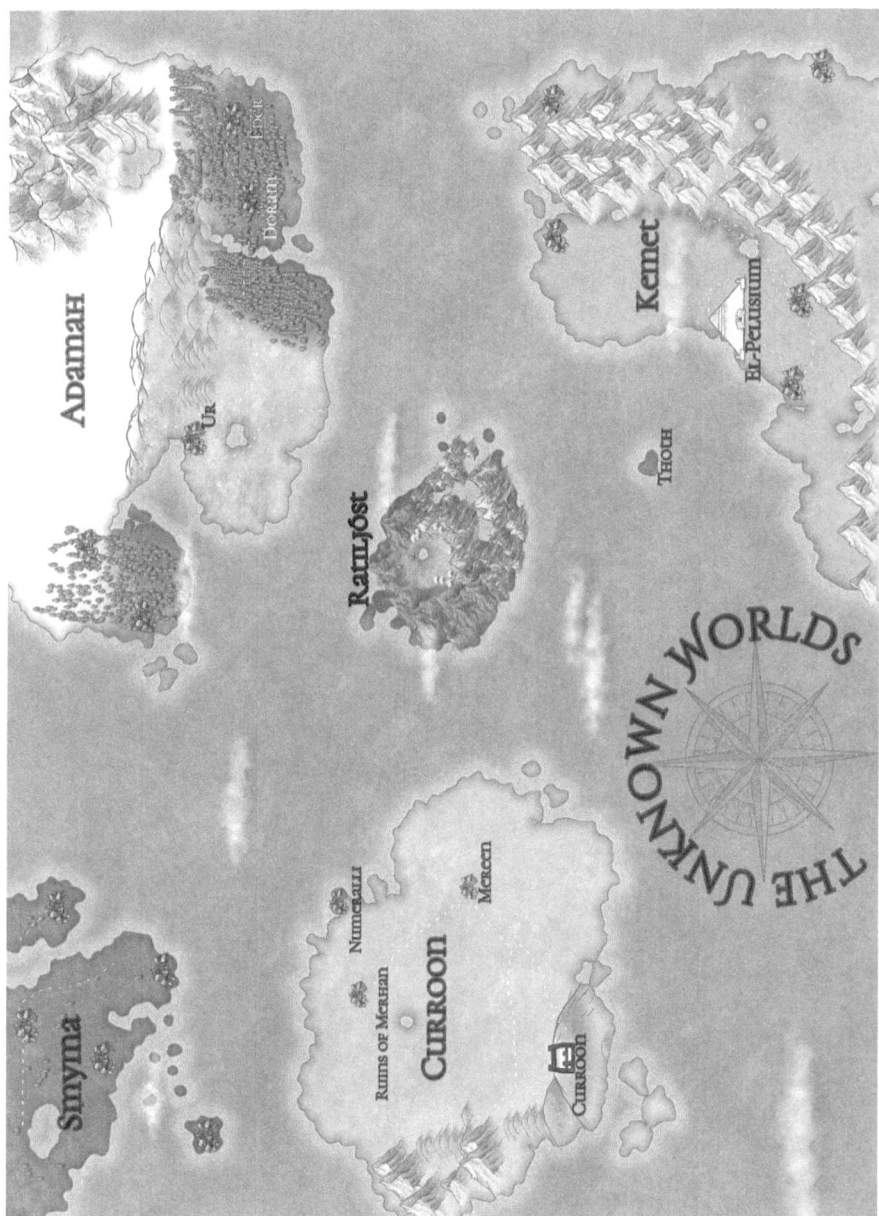

PART I

The sea is no kinder than the wind or the rain. The sea will eat what it is given and give back nothing, but the sort of nothing it returns is sometimes worth more than everything on land.

-Old Smyman proverb

SOMEWHERE IN MEMORY

Shoshanna strode through the maple rows of Doram, strapping the wooden shaft of the everlasting torch to her thigh, then cursed under her breath. She'd left her dagger at home. There wasn't time to go back across the village to get it. Not with the Yocheved marching on them.

Someone jostled past her, bumping her shoulder.

"Sorry, Commander," the soldier mumbled as he sheathed his own knives.

"Tell the others to move on." Shoshanna waved him forward. "The Yocheved have already reached the waterfall."

The man nodded and jogged toward the other leather-wrapped squad members on the far side of the rows where they gathered alongside two war-elk. They carried an array of weapons, but Shoshanna's was the only everlasting torch. If it took pressing the hidden trigger and igniting the torch to eradicate the Yocheved, she'd do it in a heartbeat.

She started to follow the soldier, the familiar heat of the torch soothing her strides.

4 | VERDICT OF GOLD

A firm hand gripped her elbow, accompanied by a low, raspy voice. "Are you sure you can trust that Ederian scout?" Itzaak.

She turned. Her husband's gray eyes were darker than usual, worried. The breeze ruffled his black curls as he stepped closer.

"Why would he lie? We need to go before the Yocheved get to Doram. They'll massacre everyone."

"It just doesn't feel right, Sho"

She ran a hand through his soft curls and allowed herself to breathe in the moment with Itzaak before they charged ahead. He had a way of stilling her need to move, even if there wasn't time for this now.

"Don't go into the woods," he pressed. "It doesn't feel right. I don't trust the Ederians, Reuben. He's been looking for a way to lord over Doram ever since they made him Chief." Itzaak's thick brows furrowed, casting shadows in his usually clear gray eyes.

She laughed, tugging one curl harder than she meant. "You worry over nothing. If the scouts say there is trouble at the pools, to the pools I will go. The trees can't hurt me. Or the Yocheved."

"I'm serious. It's not all a joke. You've been lucky so far. It won't always be that way, love. Don't go into the woods, please."

"If there is nothing happening, we will come right back. But if there is, we're running out of time." Shoshanna reluctantly pulled her hands away from his hair and started to turn away.

"Sho, please. I don't like it."

"Unfortunately, we do have to go." A streak of annoyance overrode her affection for him. Itzaak never challenged her openly. A few of the nearest squad members watching them looked away hastily. Shoshanna's cheeks burned. She looked back to find a hurt look in Itzaak's eyes. Maybe she needed to take it easier on him. There had been several sleepless nights since they heard the Yocheved were roaming the outskirts of Doram. Shoshanna gently took his arm and pulled him nearer.

"Eder wants the Yocheved away from the tribes as much as we do. I trust the scout, even if I don't trust this new kid chief they have."

"Sho," Itzaak lowered his voice, "do you ever wonder if the Doramites have it all wrong?"

"You *are* a Doramite now. I don't care what my father says. We married at the old Judges' rock just so that fool couldn't deny your grafting into the tribe. May he be cursed out of the Summerlands for his rejection of you."

"What if the Summerlands aren't real? What if it isn't about the Spirit of the Forest, but someone else? This Eloah—"

"This is not the time. We're heading to a fight. The squad must know where their souls are going if this goes badly, though it won't." Nothing ever did. They were the best squad in history. "Why are you bringing this up again? It was funny the first time, but we were in the privacy of our own home. You yourself said these are childhood myths."

"But my mother said that all myths hold a nugget of truth—"

"You aren't a child any longer, my love," Shoshanna insisted, striving to keep her voice level. Her patience had been plentiful when she thought he was joking about this Eloah before, but now they were in the heat of preparing for a possible battle. "We have more important things to do right now. The fate of Doram depends on it."

He stared at her, an incomprehensible emotion welling in his gray eyes. "Sho, promise me we can discuss this later."

"I can't promise anything until this battle is over." She turned away from him, and into the clamor of the fighting squad. Knives glinted, men breathed out nerves, elk stamped. But Itzaak remained silent as he joined her, his face strangely sorrowful.

Shoshanna jolted awake, sweat slicking her back, the last

conversation with her husband this side of death still ringing in her ears.

1

THE COST OF REMEMBERING

Shoshanna

The ghost of the vivid dream followed her into the dawn, no matter how hard she tried to think of anything else, as she hiked up the grassy knoll on the continent of Curroon.

"Forgive me, Itzaak," she whispered.

His answer didn't come. The knee-high grass shushed around her legs. Even at dawn, the warm wind rippled through this plain, unlike the frozen land back in Adamah. Back home.

Home. A thing Shoshanna no longer had. Reuben, her former master, had made sure of that when he wiped out her memory with a potion. He'd stolen who she was and made it impossible for her to find it again. His men had destroyed her everlasting torch the same day he destroyed her life. And while her hands had remembered how to use an everlasting torch the day she burned the pavilion in Eder, her mind was not as quick to piece together all her memories.

The argument with Itzaak about Eloah... she shivered under the rising sun. They'd never continued that conversation. What would she have said, anyway? Eloah wasn't real, though Itzaak knew the truth of the afterlife better than she did now.

She'd had the whole month, sailing from Adamah to Curroon, to dwell on it. Had Izaak found the Summerlands? Or nothing at all?

She wouldn't know until she left this life. If only she could find herself again before that day. The journey to Curroon had also proved how difficult that task was going to be.

Shoshanna clenched her fingers around the smooth stone in her palm, her thumb pressing against the 'x' carved in the end—the rock from her old dagger which had started her on the path of remembering her lost eighteen years. The rock she'd murdered for. She knew it was green, though her cursed half-sight left everything in varying shades of gray, black and white.

The rising sun bit into her eyes as she pushed through the last of the grass and stepped onto the dirt road leading up to the pass in the distance. The grassland ran straight up to the abrupt edge of a rock plateau. What she sought sat at the top. She hadn't waited for the others to wake. She needed to move now. To scout. To be alone. They couldn't understand. Especially Avner. At least the others tried—or pretended to try.

He'd stopped pretending on the second week of the sea voyage. His suspicious glares made it obvious. Things were easier that way. After what she'd done as Nuri, she couldn't fault him for not trusting her.

She didn't trust herself.

Pebbles crunched under her sandals as she made her way into the road. Nuri never would have made so much noise.

"I'm not Nuri any longer," Shoshanna whispered.

The grassland didn't listen. It didn't care. No matter what torture she'd undergone the last two decades, time moved on. The world moved on. And most importantly, the *frost* moved on, now certainly covering all Adamah. Her homeland. Desperation to fix it, and all she'd done wrong, consumed her.

Kill my past.

Stop the frost.

Save my people.

Each desire—no, need—pumped through her veins like the life force driving her up the rocky pass to the town which supposedly sat at the top. The town hiding Yor—one of the missing tribes. Find them. Unite them. Stop the frost.

Redeem myself.

Shoshanna bit back a scoff. Redemption was impossible when she didn't even know who she was supposed to be anymore.

So, she'd scout the next step in their mission. One moment at a time. One job after the next.

Bile rose in the back of her throat. Reuben used to give her one job at a time. Missions. Scouting. All to form her for his purpose, and yet she still followed the same disciplined pattern.

"But not for *Reuben*," she whispered as softly as the shushing grass behind her. "For me." For Itzaak. She pressed the stone in her hand harder, imprinting the 'x' into her palm, just as she longed to imprint her murdered husband into her soul. Make up for the years she'd forgotten him.

His ghostly voice remained silent. She hadn't heard Itzaak since they left the ship back in the harbor a week ago, as if he'd stayed behind with the only other villagers who had fled Doram when the frost arrived.

But why should he accompany her? She'd abandoned him, even though she hadn't wanted to, without knowing she had done so.

Shoshanna fled up the pass, the prairie dropping away behind her. *Finally,* her blood seemed to say. She'd longed to run like this since the moment she stepped foot on the ship. Of course, it hadn't provided the opportunity, and she couldn't have just run away from Tevye and Chava. They'd given her a chance to be Shoshanna again, even if Avner's dark looks didn't. She'd stay loyal to them, find out what was up this pass, and return.

Or I could run. And not come back. But to what? Be a mercenary again? Find a new master?

She scratched a fingernail against the pommel stone before popping it back into her pocket. No.

She'd fulfill this mission. Ensure this town of Curroon was safe—and that it held the object of Yor.

A stale breeze ruffled the sleeves of her shirt as she ran, and a far-off chill took her bones. Still unused to feeling temperatures, Shoshanna shivered. A splotch of darker gray held the horizon above the pass, though it had been clear when she ascended. A storm would end this mission before she found anything.

A scream echoed far away. She shivered again. The gray rolled closer, but too close to the ground. Fog? It grew closer with each stride, and so did her unease. A grating sound came from within the mist, and Shoshanna slid to a stop.

Her breath came quicker. The scream didn't come again, but the grating sound grew louder.

Shoshanna took one step back.

The fog came closer.

She glanced around, but the rocky trail offered no shelter.

Curses and ash. She shouldn't even need to hide. It was just fog.

An unearthly yowl ripped through the air on the growing wind. Lightning flashed, not in the sky, but *within* the puffs of gray rising along the road. She backed up again, only to draw in a sharp breath as the strange screaming rose once more, closer this time. Her ears burned. The tendrils of mist crept within inches of her sandals.

Nuri wouldn't fear this. Nuri would venture forward for discovery.

"I am *not* Nuri," Shoshanna whispered, even as the rising wind threw her words back into her face.

But neither was she a coward. Steeling herself, Shoshanna stepped into the fog, and everything vanished from sight.

2

MADWOMAN

Avner

Curroon's warmth was a lie. Too warm. Too safe. Avner knew enough of the world—slave pens, death matches, cruelty—to know nothing was safe. They might be thousands of miles from the frost as it ate its way across Adamah, his homeland, but Avner wouldn't rest easy. He wound a thin cord pulled from his leather belt through his fingers as he sat the last watch of the night.

Chava lay in the grass to the left, her booted feet just peeking through the golden grass. Tevye slept nearby, the fingers of his maimed hand sticking out at strange angles beside him. Though the paste could never cure it, he hadn't let the injury slow him down on their month-long voyage from Adamah to the plains of Curroon.

One month. Weeks Avner had spent looking over his shoulder, dreading the sight of frost creeping over the water behind them, though it had never shown. Endless hours spent keeping tabs on Nuri—no, Shoshanna—in case she showed signs of her old, murderous self.

And she had, just not in the ways Avner expected. Dark stares, the shifting rash, fingers dancing across the knife she'd bought. Avner couldn't shake the feeling that Shoshanna could kill him, Chava, and Tevye in the time it took a frog to croak. The grasslands were deserted. No one would know of the murder. She'd be free to collect the artifacts of the missing tribes herself. Her willingness to join the mission to stop the frost by finding the remaining artifacts of the missing tribes had seemed convenient at first, but what would Shoshanna do with the power promised by the prophecy to the one who reunited the tribes of Adamah?

Avner wound the cord tighter, cinching it around his palm. He could strangle Shoshanna before the others awoke. She slept within the grass to the right and out of sight, far enough from the others so that the grass would block her struggle from view. All Avner needed to do was slip the cord around her neck...

"What are you doing?" Tevye's voice was like a crack of stray thunder, though he only whispered.

Avner started and dropped the cord.

"I'm keeping watch."

"On the grass where Shoshanna is sleeping?"

"That's not..."

Tevye stared at him, deadpan.

"She's killed more men than either of us combined and doubled," Aver said in a whisper and thrust his hand toward the still grasses.

Tevye crouched further down. "That was *Nuri*. She is Shoshanna now."

At first, when Nuri had suddenly remembered she was

Doram's lost hero, Avner had wanted to believe she *could* be Shoshanna again, but the longer he spent with her in the close quarters of the ship's hold, the more he realized that wasn't true. Whatever she'd done as Nuri had made going back to Shoshanna, hero of Doram, impossible. She was a murderer, not a hero.

"Av, I know that look," Tevye muttered.

"Bah," Avner scoffed. "I *know* she isn't Shoshanna, just as I know I'm not a pacifist any longer and couldn't be if I wanted to. Haven't you seen the way she fondles that knife she traded her cuff for in the harbor when we arrived? She prizes the knife. She's *tender* with it."

Tevye frowned.

Avner took the moment to press his point. "And none of us have weapons, apart from the slingshot you made, since we traded the ones we had to the ship's captain for passage." The absence left a strange twist in his gut. He didn't like wanting a weapon or needing one. Sure, Chava had the staff of Doram, but it was a priceless artifact. Not exactly what he wanted to wield in battle. They'd only escaped Doram with the clothes on their backs and couldn't spare anything in a trade for more weapons.

Avner shoved the thoughts back. "How do we know Shoshanna won't slit our throats and steal my bracelet?"

"Shoshanna could have done that weeks ago. She wants to help."

"She's a madwoman. You can't expect her to make logical decisions," Avner hit back.

"Some used to say that of Chava. Do you want to strangle her as well?" Tevye ripped the cord out of Avner's hand and threw it far into the grass.

"That's different. Chava didn't drink a potion that wiped away her memories and made her a monster."

"Didn't she though?" Tevye's words filled the warm breeze with fire.

Avner choked back any argument. Chava *had* taken Reuben's forgetting potion, only it hadn't worked. She and Tevye might attribute that to their deity, Eloah, but more likely it had been a weak batch of potion.

Chava's feet wriggled out of the grass, followed by her knees and her right hand. Three intersecting pale purple rings glowed softly in the pre-dawn light—the pointless marriage mark they shared. Before Avner could rip his gaze from the unwelcome reminder, Chava's face popped out of the grass. Her red curls tumbled over her face, and she pulled them out of the way with a freckled hand. She shot Avner and Tevye a smile. Chava was still, well, *Chava*—incessant about her deity, stubborn, and clumsy—but the weeks at sea had forged an unlikely camaraderie between them.

"Curroon today? The town, I mean." The town bore the same name as the continent, but was the hardest town to reach on the land mass, being situated at the top of a plateau only accessible via a rocky pass.

Tevye stood up and parted the waist-high grass where Shoshanna slept. Would he mention Avner's murderous thoughts? Shame tinged Avner's cheeks with heat. Could he really have murdered Shoshanna while she slept? Murder fell inside the purview of being a gibborim again, something he was trying to leave behind.

But this knowledge didn't shake the unease he felt at Shoshanna's continued presence.

"Shoshanna isn't here," Tevye said, frowning.

Avner shot to his feet and leaned over Tevye's shoulder. The grass where Shoshanna had lain was pressed down, but empty. His pulse spiked. He'd been right about her!

"Av, the fact that she's missing proves she didn't want to kill us. Or she could have already," Tevye said, exasperated.

"But it does prove she's not trustworthy."

Tevye sighed and turned away.

"Maybe she went out to scout?" Chava offered, shouldering her pack of provisions with one hand, and hefting the staff of Doram with the other—one of the two artifacts of the missing tribes they had in their possession. At least if Shoshanna did come back to attack them, Chava could shoot supernatural light and heat out of the staff. Maybe that knowledge would keep Shoshanna from risking it.

When Avner looked around, there was only grass in every direction. The sun lit the yellow strands a brighter gold, almost the color of his abnormal blood. But the plains were calm and uninhabited, like much of Curroon, apart from the cities. If Shoshanna had taken it upon herself to scout, what did she think she'd find out here in the wilderness?

Maybe she'd just tired of them and left. Gone off to be a lone assassin again as she had when she worked for Reuben under the influence of the potion. Avner breathed easier at the thought, but his hand traced the beads on his wrist. This, they hoped, was the second artifact they possessed. Tevye believed the runes on the beads proved the bracelet was from the Nameless Tribe, but it had yet to be confirmed.

Hoping for it to be so easy was foolish. But Avner couldn't help it. The faster they found the rest of the artifacts, the faster they could save his homeland from the frost, redeeming a chunk of his soul in the process.

And it would all be easier without Shoshanna's menacing looks. Yet, not knowing where she was left an unsettled knot in his stomach. Someone like her, the deadliest gibborim in history and an ex-spy, wasn't someone he wanted out of sight.

The wind whipped past faster, churning through the grass. Avner wheeled around, but no lean-muscled woman with a half-burned face appeared.

"I'm *sure* she is scouting the way ahead," Chava eyed him as if she knew exactly what he was thinking. Heat tickled Avner's cheeks.

"Sure," he mumbled. He'd learned when to pick battles with Chava, and now was not the time. Chava could never truly understand the way he felt about Shoshanna. Chava had been raised in Eder, not Doram, and couldn't feel the deep sting of Shoshanna's crimes against his people, even if they had been done under the influence of Reuben's potion.

"Let's get moving then. It should still be several hours' hike to the city of Curroon." Tevye grabbed his own pack and led the way back to the narrow, overgrown trail.

Avner refused the urge to look around again for Shoshanna and fell into line behind Chava and Tevye. Despite his unease, he relished the sun warming his scalp and his back. Here in the balmy grasslands of this new continent, the frost could almost be a bad dream. The warmth and the crystal-blue sky denied that lethal ice had invaded the land a thousand miles away. It was tempting to forget about Doram's plight and settle here under the sun in Curroon. Surely, they could find a safe little village and make a new life farming, or whatever they did here. Avner would never have to think about his past or this seemingly impossible mission to thaw Adamah again.

But he couldn't live with himself if he did. He could barely live with himself now. He'd be adding thousands more people to the list of those he'd killed, though not directly. No, the only way forward was to resist the temptation to be comfortable and save the people he'd grown up amongst. Illa, his adoptive mother, would have wanted that. Same with Silas, his murdered brother. Their memories insisted that Avner try to save their homeland. There wasn't another option. Though he had failed to save his family, he would save Doram.

Avner clenched his fists as he walked. How many Doramites knew just how fatal the frost was now? Had any survived its deadly grip? The swirls of ice crawling across the ground from the pools to Doram would never leave Avner's memory.

The grass beside him rustled, and he glanced up, pulse racing. He expected to see Shoshanna's cinnamon-flecked brown eyes, but Tevye fell back beside him instead. Avner cursed inwardly. His paranoia would get the better of him.

"I'll admit I didn't like the cryptic warning of the man back at the harbor to stay away from 'that demented city Curroon'." Tevye's one green eye shone.

"It doesn't matter if that merchant's warning means anything or not," Avner said to Tevye. "We must go to the city of Curroon to get an artifact of Yor. We only have one—"

"Maybe two," Tevye pressed, looking at Avner's bracelet.

"—maybe two," Avner conceded, "but it's still not enough. Reuben has more, if he's still alive."

At the mention of her brother, Chava stumbled over a rock and staggered to the side before righting herself and leading on.

Avner couldn't hide a faint smile. Her clumsiness had

grown from annoying to mildly entertaining in the last month. Tevye's gaze bore into him yet again, and Avner hastily looked away from Chava.

A rocky ridge jutted out of the plains in the distance, as if someone had cut the land away with a rusty knife. The plateau rose hundreds of feet above them, while only grass and desert ran back the way they came. Curroon sat on this plateau, or so the merchant had claimed. Avner had faced the gibborim arena and the frost and lived. What danger could one town possibly hold?

"Come on, I think that's the pass the merchant mentioned." Avner veered toward it, the grass brushing against his leather pants. The ground rose sharply as they hit the bottom of the pass, and after an hour's hike, the winding gravel path led them up to the top. Sweat streamed down Avner's back, and he thought wistfully of the chilly wind from Lake Kefa, where he'd fought for a year before escaping the life of a gibborim. But he would never want to return to that life. This heat was blissful, and he gladly accepted it.

"What is that?" Chava asked behind Avner.

He slowed down, glad of the respite from the constant upward climb. He inhaled sharply. The road ascended a hundred yards away into a thick wall of fog, or mist. Nothing was visible within the gray clouds.

"I've seen fog," Tevye mused as he stepped up beside Avner, "but never that thick. Do you think the pass continues much further?"

"I'm not sure. The merchant didn't mention how far the town was." Avner frowned. Something about this fog...

"There aren't any clouds nearby," Chava said, catching up with him.

She was right. The brilliant sky showed in all directions, except at the top of the pass. The longer Avner stared at the fog, the more it seethed. Thick swirls of silver wound through the dense fog as if it were *alive*.

Impossible.

"Maybe this sort of fog is natural here?" Tevye offered.

"I doubt it." Avner mused. "This land is arid. There shouldn't be that much moisture in the air."

Chava chuckled nervously beside him. "A naturalist now, are you?"

"No. Just observant... what's that?"

A dark shape flitted through the fog and came closer. Tevye pulled out the slingshot he'd made on the journey, and Chava raised the staff in front of her. Again, Avner cursed at the lack of weapons. If they were going to have to pass through this fog to get to Curroon, Chava's light from the staff would help, and Tevye could throw a mean stone, but what if more than one danger hid in the gray mist? Bandits could be taking advantage of the cover it provided, among other threats. Wild dogs, militia, any number of things.

"Should we wait here for the fog to pass?' he asked.

"It's just a cloud." Despite her words, Chava didn't lower the staff. But maybe she was right.

His paranoia *was* getting the better of him. The closer they came, the thinner the fog seemed.

Just as Avner started to relax, the dark shape flickered in the fog again. He picked up a stone. Tevye grabbed two and fitted them to the slingshot. Chava muttered something to herself.

The calm breeze became a stronger gust, catching the edges of the fog, and pulling it into thin wisps. The dark figure in the fog came into focus. Human. Avner stopped, flinging his arm out to keep Chava from going forward. The staff knocked into his elbow, causing his eyes to water. The wind tore through the fog, dissipating it into the air, and leaving nothing but clear, blue sky.

And Shoshanna staggered down the road toward them, blood splattered over her pants and streaking her cheeks.

3

DEMENTED CITY

Avner

Avner raised the rock, but Chava pushed past his arm and ran to Shoshanna just as the woman collapsed onto the ground. Chava's frantic fingers roved over the splatters of blood on the sweat-soaked shirt, searching for a wound.

Shoshanna's face was glazed with sweat and her hair was disheveled, leaving her entirely different from how she'd looked last night before she vanished.

"What happened, Shoshanna?" Chava pulled Shoshanna's bleeding palms into her lap.

Shoshanna stared at the ground with her strange, shimmering, cinnamon-flecked eyes.

"Where were you?" Avner asked, his hand clenched around the rock.

Chava glared at him.

"It's a valid question," Tevye said, though not unkindly.

"You don't have to be on his side about it." Chava

muttered, laying a careful hand on Shoshanna's arm, just above her left wrist where a flaming sun encircling a 'z' had been branded. Shoshanna kept it covered with a scrap of cloth, but Avner couldn't wipe its image from his mind. Shoshanna clearly wasn't comfortable with this reminder of her dead husband or the missing tribe he'd been the last member of. Her fever-glazed eyes met Avner's.

"Scouting," she croaked.

Chava's glare intensified.

"I'm not going to apologize for being wary of her. We all know what she's capable of," Avner shot back.

Chava opened her mouth, her gaze fiery, but Shoshanna cut her off.

"I—couldn't—sleep."

As little as he trusted her, Avner knew that to be true. He'd woken many times during the crossing from Adamah to find her pacing the ship's deck, muttering under her breath.

Chava placed a hand on Shoshanna's forehead and frowned. "Feverish. She wasn't sick last night—drop the rock, Avner." Chava demanded without looking up at him.

"I don't like it—" he began.

Tevye's good hand rested on Avner's arm. "She's not going to hurt you in this condition, mate."

Gritting his teeth, Avner let the rock drop to the road with a crack. Being wounded didn't make Shoshanna any less of a threat, but Avner also didn't want to turn his only two friends against him.

"The fog..." Shoshanna trailed off, and while she *did* look feverish, her strange eyes seemed clear. "The fog did it."

"*Fog* made you sick?" Chava shared a concerned glance with Tevye.

Avner glanced back up the pass, but there was no sign of the unsettling gray mist. They knew Shoshanna had been altered by the potion, so why should they believe anything she said about the fog?

"I-I'm not sure. But there was noise. Terrible. Screeching." Shoshanna's right hand settled over her branded wrist and her fingers clenched white. "From the fog. Evil. Wrong."

Shoshanna's usual reticence only made her description more chilling. Despite the heat, a trickle of ice crept up Avner's back. Chava believed in the supernatural, as did Tevye. Though Avner wanted to deny a force beyond himself, his blood and his unnatural marriage to Chava spoke of things he couldn't control or understand.

But that didn't mean he had to cower before them. The fog only proved Shoshanna hadn't run off to come back and murder them all. While he still couldn't trust her, it gave him time to get rid of her on his own terms without resorting to murder.

"Did you find Curroon? The town, I mean," Avner said curtly, stepping around her.

"Didn't make it that far," Shoshanna said as she stood up with Chava's help. "The fog came. I fell on the rocks, but the pain kept me awake." Her shredded palms took on a new meaning.

"Shoshanna, your ears..." Chava raised a finger to the woman's right ear.

Shoshanna wiped it with the back of her hand, and it came away bloody. She blinked. Even without seeing in color, she knew what it was.

Avner shivered, then cursed himself inwardly. He wouldn't give in to any fear.

"Did you hit your head?" Chava asked Shoshanna, her voice heavy with concern.

She shook her head, still frowning at the blood. But what did it matter? The fog was gone, and the way was now clear.

"We must be close. Let's move." Avner pressed on. Footsteps behind him told him the others had followed.

"Do you think what she said about the fog is true?" Tevye asked as he caught up.

"It doesn't matter. That's not why we are here, and it is gone." Avner wouldn't admit to the unease still gripping him. That wouldn't help them get the artifact of Yor.

"Av, you can keep pretending the supernatural doesn't exist, but eventually it's going to catch up to you. You can't outrun Eloah. I couldn't"

Avner remained silent. He liked Tevye. Respected him. This argument wasn't worth ruining their friendship over. Tevye sighed but didn't say any more. Chava helped Shoshanna up behind them, whispering encouragement, as if they were friends.

When would she see that such a thing was impossible?

AN HOUR later they crested the top of the pass, and the ground flattened out once again. There was no sign of the strange fog.

Avner refrained from letting out a sigh of relief. Shoshanna was wrong. Mad. The fog had been perfectly normal and natural. There must just be more moisture in Curroon than Avner thought. He only knew what one week on this continent had taught him so far.

Just beyond the top of the pass, a city spread out before

them, covering the plateau with houses and the first signs of civilization. Heat waves danced across the adobe walls and shimmered off leather yurts. A large pavilion stood to their right, while streets lined with clay houses ran off toward the low-lying hills at the western edge. Colorful awnings flapping in the breeze broke up the monotony of the brown landscape.

They'd found Curroon, and hopefully the descendants of Yor.

"He was always right about the tribes," Shoshanna murmured behind Avner.

"My brother, you mean?" Chava asked.

Shoshanna frowned, no doubt thinking of her former master. Here, at least, Avner could pity her. He'd been owned by the same man, and he didn't want to dwell on it either.

He took in Curroon. The town was twice as large as one of the tribes back in Adamah. Where would such people keep an ancient treasure or artifact?

"Let's head to the village center. If we heard of Allambee Yanathan across the sea, someone must know the name here." Avner moved toward the town, his sandals crunching over the gravel. The name was all they had to go on, thanks to Reuben, so by the ashes they'd find the Yanathans.

"What if they don't want to give the artifact up? You saw what Reuben and Dalea did to keep or find artifacts." Tevye matched Avner's pace.

"I won't let that happen here."

Shoshanna snorted behind Avner. Disagreeable about everything. Hopefully this Allambee Yanathan would be more cooperative, or their mission to reunite the tribes would be dead before it truly got started.

WHILE THE TOWN looked large enough to house thousands of inhabitants, silence and emptiness prevailed in the streets. Colorful shutters were fastened tight, giving no clue to whether the locals were home. A chicken clucked and strutted across an empty road, hopping over an overturned clay pitcher, obviously dropped in haste. Street after street was the same. Silence. Deserted wares. Shuttered windows and closed doors without a person in sight. A cart stuck with its wheel in a rut, the donkey harnessed to it braying in desperation.

Chava shot Avner a nervous glance. He returned it. What was going on?

"The fog," Shoshanna whispered to Avner's right.

"You think it scared them all inside? Surely they know it is gone now," Tevye said, surveying the wreckage of what must have been the market. Dozens of merchants' stalls lined the adobe walls of the square, showcasing an assortment of nuts, fabrics, clay pitchers, and even odd little carved statues. Avner wouldn't have been surprised to find something like the crystals the Doramites used back home to connect with their Spirit of the Forest. But maybe these Curroonians weren't superstitious.

Yet their goods were scattered on the ground, many broken and ruined. Deserted in a hurry, it seemed. But why?

A door creaked somewhere down a nearby alley. Chava jumped, twirling around and almost knocking Avner off his feet with the staff of Doram.

"Easy," he said.

"Someone's coming!" She pointed with the staff toward the opposite side of the market.

A woman in purple robes staggered down the road, gripping her basket tightly. She tripped, her shoulder hitting the nearest wall, then stood straight again, panting. Her gaze went straight to their party, and she froze.

Avner raised a hand in greeting.

The woman stood straighter and clutched her basket tighter. She turned, looking down the street she'd come from. Red lines ran out of her ear.

Chava drew in a breath, and Avner's heart pounded faster. Chava glanced at Shoshanna's ears, paling.

"The blood can't mean anything," Avner muttered, trying to calm his nerves.

"*You* are the one who should understand that blood means something. How can you dismiss it so quickly?" Chava shot back.

"Because I *don't know* what my blood means."

What *did* the blood on the woman's ears mean? And what was this place? The woman vanished back down the road before they had a chance to ask for answers.

"Maybe that merchant in the harbor was right about this place," Tevye said, his tone dark.

"Even if he was, we *must* find Yor's artifact." Avner turned away from the road where the woman had vanished. His hopes rose again as a few more locals wandered into the market, nearly as dazed as the first woman.

An orange-robed man staggered over to the stall selling nuts, frowning at the wreckage of his merchandise strewn on the ground. A plump woman followed, her silk robes swishing as she hurried to the counter displaying ugly statues.

"Should we ask one of them about an artifact?" Chava asked, though she looked doubtful.

"Apparently, it's them or no one." Tevye led the way, stepping around a broken statue and over a pile of rumpled red cloth.

Avner pushed past Shoshanna and joined Tevye and Chava at the merchant's stall. The woman's eyes narrowed as her gaze went to their blood-free ears.

"Hi, can you tell us what is going on?" Chava asked her. "Where is everyone?"

"Still home if they know what's good for them."

"Because of the fog?" Chava pressed.

"Well, the Orroroo hasn't struck in years, has it?" the woman snapped, picking up another ugly idol with trembling fingers. "At least no one pilfered the market like last time."

None of her ramblings made sense to Avner, but Chava apparently managed to pick out the one essential word.

"Orroroo?" she asked.

"The *fog*. I thought you were one of *them*, but if you don't know about the fog, then you can't be, unless you're just stupid." The woman grabbed a rag off the counter and scrubbed at the dried blood under her ears. "That one—" she jabbed a finger at Shoshanna's bloody ears, "—knows about the Orroroo. Ask her."

Shoshanna stared daggers. After all, the fog wasn't the real question here. Avner cleared his throat.

"We're looking for someone. Allambee Yanathan."

"Heard of him?" Chava leaned across the counter, knocking a statue over with the end of Doram's staff. It hit the packed dirt and cracked in two.

"Hey! Watch it! You better pay for this!" The woman snatched up the broken pieces and shot Chava a dark glare. "I hope you know what kind of luck you've placed on yourself by doing that, especially with the Orroroo striking today."

"Eloah doesn't operate on luck," Chava said, straightening away from the counter. "Do you know this Allambee or not?"

"I do not care to give you any information until you pay for this." The merchant woman set the fragments on the counter along with the bloody rag.

"So, you know him?" Avner stepped forward, urging Chava back with one hand. They didn't need her to make this worse than she already had. Then he dug into his pouch and showed the merchant the few copper coins they had, a gift of thanks from the fifty Doramites who'd escaped the ice with them. Hopefully, those poor souls were smart enough to head elsewhere in Curroon, and not to this rude and mysterious city.

The merchant eyed Avner's coins and sniffed.

"That's not even half what this idol costs."

"It's all we have."

Her tan features contorted. "Travelers. Bah! Never have the correct currency or change. Why do you even bother to come up here if you can't afford anything and you don't know about the fog?"

These repeated mentions of the fog kept a knot of unease in Avner's gut, but unless it showed itself again, he could afford to ignore the strange mist.

"We told you, we are just looking for Allambee Yanathan, or anyone with that last name, for that matter," Chava said.

The woman scoffed. "Well, that'd be the disgraced Commander, wouldn't it? I don't need to be paid for that sort of common knowledge." But she scraped the coins out of Avner's extended hand all the same.

"Who?" Chava asked.

"She means my husband," a voice said loudly. A lean woman with dark hair twisted into twin buns at the base of her neck stood among a group of people filtering into the market. But while all the others wore worried expressions on their faces, some even feverish, this woman stood tall and forbidding, her loose linen shirt snapping in the breeze. Her golden-brown eyes took in each member of Avner's party, narrowing when they landed on Tevye's maimed hand and Shoshanna's burned face. The newcomer stepped closer. Unlike the merchant at the stall, this woman's ears weren't bleeding. Or she'd already washed them off.

"I don't need your patronage here, Leewana Yanathan," the merchant mumbled, shifting her gaze to the ground.

Leewana's narrowed eyes glanced at the idols on her counter.

"You have nothing I need." The words were loaded with unspoken meaning. Leewana turned to Chava again, "But why are you looking for my family?"

"It's complicated, but you may have something we need. Something we must have so we can save our homeland."

Leewana took a step back and motioned for them to follow.

"Come with me, and better to be quiet until we reach my home."

Shoshanna mumbled something, but then stepped after her with Tevye on her heels.

"This had better lead to something, or I'll be inclined to heed that warning about this place and get out of here," Avner muttered to Chava as he followed them. There were many ways a town could be dangerous besides supernatural fog and bleeding ears. If tensions were high between the two women who'd bothered to talk to them, what else could be brewing?

"Maybe, but Eloah will protect us." Chava said.

The newcomer, Leewana, slid to a jarring halt and whipped back around, her eyes wide.

"Don't say His name out here. Do you understand? Not until we are safely inside."

Tevye shot Chava a questioning glance. Avner had grown accustomed to them prattling on about their god, but he was still far from enjoying it. They'd grown wise enough to stop trying to include him or Shoshanna, but it wasn't particularly comforting to have only that woman on his side.

But this was stranger than all that. Why did Leewana fear mentioning the deity's name?

Chava nodded in response to Leewana's stern command. When no one said anything else, Leewana took off at a light jog down the street. More and more people were coming out of their houses, some looking feverish.

Tearing his gaze from this strange sight, Avner followed Leewana. They needed this woman's information, but he couldn't stop a chill from creeping down his spine. Just what had they gotten themselves into in this town?

4

STRANGERS

Avner

Leewana's plain adobe house sat at the far edge of the town, bordering a meadow filled with sagebrush. The sight of this humble dwelling comforted him. It was the closest thing to the cabins of Doram that Avner had seen since arriving in this land. Away from tight streets and bleeding ears, the air was calm, almost serene. It nearly felt like the peace of the trees back in Adamah, before they were locked in the eerie, frozen silence.

Their host opened the wooden door of the flat-roofed home and stepped inside. Avner hesitated only a moment before following. Shoshanna followed as well, her hand hovering by the slim knife in her belt.

"Let's not give these people any reason to hate us," Chava whispered. "She's our only lead."

Shoshanna jerked her hand off the knife as they stepped into the bright interior. The sunlight from the one window cast warm rays over Avner's feet. Shoshanna muttered something under her breath but didn't touch her knife again. Tevye and Chava filed in behind them, sliding along the tapestry-covered wall, since there wasn't anywhere else to stand in the small space. A few pillows lay in a semi-circle as a sort of lounge area, but the only other furniture was a low shelf holding a few scrolls and jars of food.

A man stepped out of the only adjoining room, his gray eyes catching the sunlight. Chava gripped the staff tighter at the sight of the scar marring the man's nose. His left arm ended unnaturally just past his elbow, and the stump hung from his sleeveless shirt. The merchant woman had referred to him as the disgraced commander, and clearly he had seen combat. But a man with such extensive injuries should probably be called a hero, not a disgrace.

Leewana moved into the ring of pillows and motioned to the newcomer. "My husband, Colebee Yanathan."

Husband. So, marriage wasn't a dead tradition here. Avner couldn't keep his gaze from dropping to the man's hand, then Leewana's, but they bore no mark like the one on his own hand. Heat rose in his cheeks as he caught Chava doing the same. Her eyes flicked up to his, and she looked hastily away.

"Who are your guests, Lee?" Colebee met his wife in the center of the crowded room. Even the huts of Doram were more spacious than this.

"They are searching for a descendant of Allambee Yanathan, though I've yet to figure out why. But more importantly, they *publicly* invoked Eloah's name." Leewana's dark eyes flashed.

A fleeting look of joy passed over Colebee's features before he gripped his wife's hand.

"Leewana will have told you the dangers of that, I'm sure."

"No, she just warned us not to speak of Him." Tevye extended his hand. "Seems you've seen your share of fighting, eh?"

Colebee shrugged. "Eloah has been gracious to me, though I don't deserve it."

Avner couldn't help himself. He scoffed.

"You know Eloah?" Chava spoke with excitement and took a step closer to their hosts.

"Yes, we know Him and follow Him, but most of the town does not," Leewana said. "There was a time when you'd be burned at the stake for professing belief, and while that time passed years ago, it is still not safe. At least, not since the new Free One Commander started driving out any Polys."

"Polys?"

"It's what they call followers of Eloah. If they catch wind that you are Polys, your welcome here will be over."

Avner suppressed another scoff. Naturally, this deity was already causing them trouble in a new land.

Colebee said, "As good as it is to hear of fellow believers from so far away, why were you seeking my great-great grandfather—"

"Father!" A child's voice squealed outside the open window, and brown fingers gripped the open frame. Soon, a head full of curls popped into view. A girl no older than ten, with golden eyes and a brilliant smile, took in the visitors.

"Oh! Hi. I didn't know we were having people over."

"Alira," Colebee scolded "I told you to play outside until supper. Where are your brothers?"

The girl pouted. "Out in the meadow, chasing roo critters, but they won't let me play!"

"You're the oldest, and they won't let you play?" Colebee raised a brow.

"Well, I don't want to play. They can be such a pain sometimes, especially Pan."

Avner's mind flashed back to childhood memories of playing with Mikhail and Silas. Cheerful laughter. Ridiculous dares. Sparring illegally in the woods.

He clenched his fist. Thoughts of his brothers only brought back to the forefront their whole reason for coming here.

"Colebee, Leewana, we need to ask you for a favor," Avner said.

"Go on, Alira. Find your brothers." Leewana shooed her daughter back out the window. "I'll find you when it is time to come back inside."

Alira dropped out of sight. Leewana sighed and turned back to face their party.

"What does this favor have to do with Allambee Yanathan?"

Tevye met Avner's intense gaze. They'd feared this part from the beginning. Their hosts were going to think they were insane. Chava placed a warm hand on Avner's shoulder and took the lead.

"I'm not sure what you know over here, but back in Adamah, a deadly frost has covered the entire continent. We had to flee just to stay alive. There is only one way to thaw our homeland and save those who stayed. We must gather artifacts from the six tribes of Adamah and reunite them. So far, we have two." She held out the staff.

"Chava," Avner warned. She shouldn't reveal the staff to strangers.

"They follow Eloah—"

Avner cut in, "We think your ancestor descended from the tribe of Yor. If that is true, any family heirloom you have could be the artifact we need."

"We have heard of this frost in letters from other Members, but I had not realized that it covered the whole of Adamah. How do you know you need the artifacts?" Colebee stared at the staff and ran his hand through his hair.

Well, he hadn't called them crazy and demanded they leave. Avner felt a flicker of hope.

"There is a prophecy," Chava said, "But more importantly, Eloah told me to unite the tribes. I'm certain this is the way to do it."

Avner wanted to elbow her.

"Hm. I may have something. Wait here." Colebee turned and retreated into the other room.

Chava shifted beside Avner, frowning at him. Shoshanna stiffened at her movement. She hadn't said a word since they entered Leewana's house, and her face was like stone. A vein ticked away in her temple, and she stared at Chava so intently, the skin on the back of Avner's neck crawled. He'd ask her what was wrong, but he was afraid to alert their hosts to the woman's madness.

Colebee returned, clutching a black stone dagger in his hand. Intricate carvings were etched on the blade, swirling and twisting all the way to the tip. The knife could have been any age, but was in good condition.

"This has been handed down for generations. My father gave it to me the day I joined the Free Ones." Colebee frowned. Whatever a Free One was, he clearly regretted that choice. "His father gave it to him on his own Choosing Day, like his father before him, and so did each man in my ancestry, including Allambee Yanathan. It's never seen combat.

The obsidian blade is too brittle, but it's been well-maintained for generations. If this isn't your artifact, I don't know what is." He held out the blade, the intense glare of the setting sun catching it and bringing out specks of silver and light in the dark stone.

Avner reached for the knife and turned it over in his hands, examining the etching.

"How can we know for sure?"

"These markings," Tevye pointed to the intricate carvings. "If you look close enough, the flowers are composed of words. See?" He ran a dirty fingernail across the blade.

Avner squinted. Sure enough, the delicate petals *were* made of words! But it wasn't a language he knew. However, if Tevye recognized it, that was all the confirmation he needed. How fortunate they were to have one of the greatest linguists in the world with them on this mission.

"Is it Yorite?"

Tevye studied it for a moment longer, lips moving soundlessly. Finally, he nodded. "It's a blessing for the lineage of the Yanathan who was the original founding member of clan Yor."

"Ha!" Chava shook the staff.

Avner's knees went weak with relief. It'd been so easy!

"Aren't you going to ask them if they mind that we steal their precious heirloom?" Shoshanna spoke for the first time, her voice tense.

Leewana jumped. No doubt, she'd forgotten the woman was there. Shoshanna's wandering rash, though smaller than it had been when she was Nuri, still lay across her nose. Combined with her strange, cinnamon-flecked eyes and the nasty burn on her left cheek, she looked like a nightmare.

She had to know what she looked like, but there was nothing to be done about it, and it wasn't her fault.

Chava smiled at her across the room.

Shoshanna continued to frown.

But she was right about the dagger. Avner turned toward their hosts.

"Do you mind if we keep this knife? I know it is a family heirloom, but—"

"If it can help you on this task from Eloah, you are more than welcome to it," Colebee said with a smile. "I've never used it for anything anyway. I nearly forgot I had it, until you mentioned heirlooms. Since my own children won't be joining the Free Ones, there's no need to save it. What is the point of a knife you couldn't fight with?" He chuckled and handed over a smooth leather sleeve for the knife.

Chava accepted the sleeve, then spoke up in a rush.

"The merchant woman said you were a disgraced commander. Why?"

Avner groaned, and even Tevye frowned. Chava glared at them.

Colebee chuckled again.

"I chose Eloah over my previous sect, the Free Ones, and walked away from the most coveted position among them. I bet you can see why I would." He met his wife's gaze, and they exchanged smiles.

Avner felt an inexplicable pang of envy. The Yanathans looked at each other as if they'd walk over fire for one another. As if the sun didn't rise if they weren't together. As if they *loved* each other.

Avner refused to look at Chava. Shoshanna's face, on the other hand, wore a look of disgust. Before any of them could ask where she was going, she opened the door and fled into the oncoming evening.

Chava started to follow, but Avner grabbed her wrist and gave it a light squeeze.

"Don't," he whispered. "She doesn't know who she is. I wouldn't trust her alone out there."

"If we don't trust her now, she will never be Shoshanna again," Chava argued.

"Just leave her alone for now, all right ?" Avner released her arm.

"Fine." Chava handed him the leather sleeve.

Avner slid the knife into the sleeve and attached it to his belt. This had all been too easy. It couldn't last, could it?

5

A HAUNTING OF TWO MEN

Shoshanna

Shoshanna's very soul ached. Twenty-six of her men dead. Itzaak was the only one still alive. His face was white but resolved. She wouldn't let him die. Not when he hadn't wanted to come on this foolish mission.

The two Ederian warriors flanking him dragged him closer to the pile of bodies.

"No!" Shoshanna screamed.

"Tsk, tsk, is that any way to talk to your hosts?" Reuben, the kid chief of Eder strode closer, holding her everlasting torch. She hadn't even gotten a chance to unstrap it from her leg before she was ambushed.

Rage and regret burned through her.

"Don't touch that," she snapped.

"I don't think you're in a position to be making demands. I, however, am." Reuben raised the torch. "Show me how to use this, and I'll let your man live."

Shoshanna's gaze flitted to Itzaak. There was a hard look in his eyes, and his jaw was set. She knew what he wanted.

"Never," she whispered to Reuben. "I won't help you after the treachery you pulled today."

"I guess you don't love him as much as the spies reported. Pity." Reuben lazily tossed the torch on the pile of corpses. "Eder won't need these torches after today anyway." He turned his gaze back on her, delighted. Predatory.

Shoshanna wrenched her arms harder, screaming. The Ederians held her tighter, the rope around her neck choking her.

"No, Sho! Don't struggle. Save yourself—" Itzaak cut off, doubled over from a blow.

Shoshanna shook herself free from the memory before her mind showed her the one thing she didn't want to witness ever again. She gasped for breath as she jogged a hundred paces out into the meadow behind the Yanathan's house. Forgetting had been as easy as taking Reuben's potion, but remembering stripped her soul bare over and over every day as she stared at Chava and remembered what the woman's brother had done to her. As Shoshanna watched Avner, remembering both her time as a gibborim, and the thousands of times she had caused injury to her own people. Seeing Tevye so close, knowing that as Reuben's slave, he'd interpreted runes on an artifact as she, Reuben's Right and closest confidant, had watched.

Shoshanna stopped at the edge of the scraggly bushes. The horizon glowed with a fierce sunset she couldn't put color to, though it must be there, and the croaking of frogs echoed on every side. It should be peaceful.

But she'd never feel peace again.

She shouldn't have let Chava get to her. The woman didn't even know the effect she had on Shoshanna. And it wasn't like she resembled her brother, apart from her smile. Reuben *always* smiled wider than anyone Shoshanna knew, and nothing would wipe away her old desire to see it, not even being on the other side of the world.

Her fingers trembled and she stretched them taut, but it didn't help.

A fresh bout of fever burned through her, though not as hot as before. Shoshanna cursed as her legs shook. The horizon wavered. Shadows lengthened, clouds collided, and the sun dipped lower. She blinked, trying to distinguish what was real from this strange fever-vision.

A figure moved on the horizon, a dark form against the receding glow of the sun. The light breeze ruffled his curly, dark hair. Shoshanna instinctively took a step forward. Itzaak? The sage crackled under her soft boots as she took another step, holding her breath for a better glimpse of the man on the horizon.

The figure turned to face her, and his eyes twinkled. Even in her cursed gray vision, his eyes were exactly the right color. His soft smile seemed to say *I love you.*

Shoshanna's knees buckled and she staggered forward just in time to stop herself from collapsing.

"Itzaak," she gasped. The dream from the previous night rose before her again, and sobs welled up in her chest. If only she'd known he was going to his death. Would she have waited to hear all he had to say? Even if it was about Eloah? She hadn't remembered that bit about him until the dream. Would he have become like Chava, devout and insufferable, if he'd lived?

She wouldn't have minded, if he breathed again. She kept her eyes on the figure on the horizon. He could stand there forever, and she'd savor every moment, impossible and imaginary as they were. It didn't matter that he was dead and she was seeing things. This was as close to her husband as she'd ever get again. She hadn't felt the touch of his rough hands, or truly heard his raspy voice in eighteen years. When her skin had been smooth, not covered in a cursed rash or scars. When her eyes had danced with merriment and adventure, not with flecks from the potion that had stolen her true self.

Even if Itzaak were alive, he wouldn't recognize her and wouldn't want her. That fact hurt to the marrow of her bones, and it had kept her awake countless nights on the voyage here.

The wind shifted, and Itzaak's curls flattened. His bright eyes became dull, and he shrank several inches, until the figure on the horizon was no longer Shoshanna's dead husband but the only other man who'd ever been central to her life.

Reuben.

Her breath returned full force, slamming against her lungs, spurring her heart to twice its usual rhythm. Nuri would have controlled herself, but she wasn't that woman any longer. Shoshanna staggered back, but caught herself mid-step. Just like Itzaak, Reuben didn't want her.

"And I don't want you," she whispered to his ghostly form, but the words tasted like lies and ash. Thoughts of someone else had kept her awake on the boat. Reuben had been part of Shoshanna for so long, the missions, the meetings, the camaraderie. The implications of not knowing how to distance herself from him, even thousands of miles away, terrified her. If she missed Reuben, could she ever really leave Nuri behind?

Her fingers closed around the cool hilt of her cheap

dagger. If only Reuben were here, then she could kill him and have vengeance.

Is that what you want? Itzaak's raspy voice whispered.

Shoshanna pulled the dagger out of her belt. The last ray of sun glinted off the blade before plunging below the horizon, just as she longed to plunge the blade into Reuben's heart. And yet a longing tugged at her. To really see him. To share sikerah and talk for hours, long into the night. To run a mission again and feel the adrenaline and exhilaration pulsing through her veins as Reuben flashed her that luminous smile—

The figure wavered and faded with the last light on the horizon.

Shouts coming from the town echoed over the meadow, and Shoshanna whirled around, the dagger still extended. Sweat slicked her palms and beaded down her face. She wiped her forehead on her cotton sleeve, then glanced back at the horizon. The sun was gone, and so was the vision of Reuben. Still, her breathing didn't level out. What had this fever done to her?

The shouts grew louder. Ignoring her trembling muscles, Shoshanna dropped back into a crouch. She approached the Yanathan's home again just as a crowd advanced on the door. Maybe Leewana had been right about them not being welcome after all. Shoshanna ducked behind the adobe wall and crept forward just enough to peer around the corner. There were at least twenty-five Curroonians thronging in front of the house. Some carried torches, the flames casting flickering shadows across the road. A man stood in the front, wearing a wide headband, leather breeches, and little else. Shoshanna had seen enough fighters to know this man was of the highest caliber. Or he thought he was.

"Colebee!" the man yelled, his arms crossed over his chest. "We know who you have in there. Send them out so we can give them a proper Curroon welcome."

There was a shuffling sound from inside the house. Shoshanna gripped the dagger tighter. She slid into the narrow alley between houses, her shoulders catching on the rough walls. More frantic shuffling came from the Yanathans'. The door creaked open just as Shoshanna slid along the last ten feet of shadows. She hovered on the edge of the gray torchlight, just inches from exposure.

"Ah, Birrani, good to see you." Colebee's calm voice came from the door.

"*Commander* Birrani. I'd think you'd still remember what it's like to address the Commander of the Free Ones' Squad, even after all these years since you went soft," the other man sneered.

"I will never forget," Colebee said with obvious restraint.

Birrani snorted. "Yet you've forgotten the danger of the Polys. Of the Orroroo."

A nervous round of whispers echoed throughout the crowd. *Orroroo.* What the merchant had called the fog. Sweat pricked Shoshanna's palms. These people were right to fear the mist. She feared little, but the screeching noise that had reverberated in the fog would never leave her memory. The sound of death. Pain and destruction. A supernatural force hungry for souls to feed upon. If they made it out of this, she'd ask their hosts about the fog.

"We may not be savage enough to burn Polys anymore," Birrani continued, "but they've brainwashed one too many Free Ones in the last year. Monos too. Proper, civil ones who loved their philosophy before your kind filled them with fantasies and lies."

"What is he saying?" Chava's voice drifted through the cracks of the shutters above Shoshanna's head.

"We want your *guests* to leave." Birrani's ultimatum was the only answer. "I don't believe it's a coincidence that they showed up, then vanished into thin air, just as the Orroroo came. This town can't handle another four Polys."

He spoke as if the Polys controlled the fog, but that was impossible.

They needed to leave this forsaken place.

Shoshanna counted the people in the crowd as well as she could from her shadowed vantage point. The woman closest to her had streaks of blood coming from her ears. Only a handful of the men and women held weapons. Two spears, five torches, and four knives sheathed on belts. The ones with spears also had some contraption hanging from their belts that she didn't recognize, but the foot-long wooden shaft was the closest thing she'd seen to an ever-lasting torch since she'd burned the last remaining one in Doram. Her torch from her memory minutes ago didn't count. It was burned. Gone.

Her breath came faster, and though she knew it wouldn't, it felt as though her pulse thundered loud enough to give her position away. She flattened further against the wall, keeping the strange weapon in the man's belt in view. These people wouldn't know about the everlasting torch, but she knew enough to be wary.

The Commander was still out of Shoshanna's line of sight, so no telling what weapons he had hidden on him.

"The visitors haven't harmed anyone and have no intention of doing so. They are my guests, as you said. I will not send them out into the night." Colebee's voice rang stronger this time.

Shoshanna snorted. She was the only one here who could save them, though Avner and Tevye would be of some use against the crowd.

"If you will not send them away, we will arrest them for—"

"For what?" Leewana's voice joined in, firm and biting. "They haven't even tried to 'brainwash' anyone."

Birrani chuckled darkly. "Leewana Yanathan. Always coming to her husband's rescue. Do you want to end up like your twin? Maybe we shouldn't have abandoned the old ways."

Silence settled like a heavy blanket over the crowd. Some shared looks heavy with meaning. The man closest to Shoshanna's hiding place took one step back, his fingers gripping the shaft of his spear. Whoever Leewana's twin was, mentioning them had clearly made the people nervous. Shoshanna prepared to move. A nervous crowd was dangerous.

"We've proved before that Members of the Way aren't dangerous. We can do so again, if needed," Leewana offered.

"Ha! Dangerous doesn't matter. You could be as docile as kittens, and I still wouldn't trust what you can do to innocent minds. But you *aren't* docile. You're two ex-Free Ones raising a brood of Polys. Nothing is more dangerous."

"We don't want any trouble," Avner said.

"Oho! This one does look dangerous," Birrani stepped back into Shoshanna's line of sight. His hand went to the strange weapon hanging on his belt.

Shoshanna lifted off her heels, settling her full weight on her toes. Feverish chills washed over her, and she cursed silently, holding out the knife. She refused to let whatever the fog had done to her stop her now.

"Are you always this aggressive to your visitors?" Avner asked. "We plan on leaving at first light. Is that good enough for you?"

Birrani unclipped the weapon. Someone behind him shuffled nervously and pulled their knives out. This was it. Either Shoshanna could let the bad happen, or she could *be* the bad. Birrani said something, but the crunching of gravel under her feet drowned it out. Someone yelled a warning, but it was too late. She reached the commander in three strides, pressed the blade to his throat, and yanked his head back.

"Shoshanna, no!" Chava's frantic cry rang out over the crowd.

"Think you can scare us out of here?" Shoshanna growled into Birrani's ear. "You don't even know who we are or what we can do."

Her grip on his hair weakened for a fraction of a second as another chill swept her body. Then she tightened her grip, shoving the fever to the back of her mind. Birrani didn't notice her slip-up and was either skilled enough not to fear her, or foolish enough not to have good sense.

He flung the strange weapon up to clip her in the head. Shoshanna yanked the knife away, ducking the blow and leaving a thin line of blood on his dark throat. The weapon smacked into the man behind him who raised his own strange weapon. A deafening *bang* exploded over the crowd. Someone screamed and dropped. Speckles of blood covered Shoshanna's moccasins, and she jumped away from the convulsing man whose hand had been demolished by a one-inch metal ball.

Cannons. Shoshanna had heard of this mystery, but could never fathom how it worked. Deadly, and as impossible as the everlasting torch. She took a step closer to get a better look, and the gathered mob gave her the room, whispering to one another.

"...heathen..."

"lunatic..."

"That's what we get for allowing travelers."

Someone scrambled over to the fallen comrade and hefted his arm up over their shoulder.

"Get him back to the Keep, quickly!" Birrani snapped. He held a hand to his throat, a thin trickle of blood seeping between his fingers and running down the backs of his knuckles. "What your *guest* has done is treason, Colebee."

Shoshanna scoffed as two of the spear-wielding men advanced, despite the rest of the crowd hanging back.

"It's not treason if I never swore loyalty to you," she spat and raised the knife at Birrani, ignoring the guards. She'd taken on twice as many and come out on top. Her muscles tensed with eagerness, and expectation. The voyage across the sea had been too calm. Even with the fever, her body longed to be used as it knew best, both as Shoshanna, and as Nuri.

But Shoshanna never longed to kill, Itzaak whispered.

"I don't long to kill," she whispered back. "I long for release."

Birrani's eyes narrowed, and he dropped his hand from his neck. "Arrest her. We will see what a trial says about your motives."

"Commander, please, she doesn't know our laws," Colebee protested, stepping out into the mob from the false safety of his threshold. The light of the torches only accentuated the grizzled appearance of his scar.

"I am quite sure that trying to slit someone's throat is considered a crime in any country."

"We will let a trial determine that. I will hold her here until the proper measures are taken to hold a trial. It will take an hour, maybe two?"

Birrani wiped his bloody hand on his leather breeches. "You think I'm a fool? If that madwoman stays here, so do two of my best men. One to guard the door, and one for the window."

"I'd expect nothing less." Colebee stepped back and motioned for Shoshanna to come back inside the small house. Avner, Chava, Leewana, and Tevye stood in the doorway.

Colebee waved her forward again, and Shoshanna obliged, stopping at the nearest guard and wiping her dirty blade across his loose, canvas sleeve. He jerked away, but the mark was already there.

Shoving the blade back in her belt, Shoshanna pushed Avner out of the way and stepped into the house. Colebee followed, slamming the door shut behind them. The flickering torches beyond could still be seen through the cracks, until two forms moved closer and blocked them out. The guards.

"You're such a fool!" Leewana whirled on Shoshanna. "What possessed you to do that? In the name of all things right and true, you could have gotten us all killed. We had just told you how volatile this town is, and they're already on edge from the Orroroo." She stepped so close that her hot rage was almost tangible, but she did not elaborate on what the fog was.

Shoshanna said nothing, clenching her clammy palms as another chill washed over her.

Avner shot her a dark glare. "Did you really have to do that? We had the artifact, and we could have left without any trouble."

A twinge of guilt tugged at Shoshanna. She'd vowed on the boat to figure out who she was again, but throwing Nuri's clothes into the sea hadn't changed her instinct to attack first, ask questions later.

But you want to be someone else, don't you? Itzaak asked, always so persistent.

"Yes," she murmured in response, a bit of her fighting streak dying down for the moment.

"Then *why* did you have to attack that man?" Chava asked before turning to Colebee. "What are we going to do now? Wait for this trial and hope they let Shoshanna go?"

Colebee shook his head as he retreated into the only other room. "No," he called back. "It's not safe. They've been looking for a reason to imprison or punish one of us for months now. I'm sure they won't spare your friend."

Avner scowled. While Chava, Tevye, and Avner could claim friendship, Shoshanna was simply bound with them to a foolhardy mission to fulfill a prophecy. Even she knew it.

Leewana picked up a satchel off the low shelf, and began stuffing various packages of dried food into it.

"You need to leave, and now," Colebee said as he emerged from the other room, another woven bag in hand. He took one look at his wife and froze. "What are you doing?"

"I'm going with them. They won't survive out there without someone who knows this place." She slid her bag over her shoulder.

"Lee, *you've* hardly been out there," Colebee sputtered.

"Twice is more than enough. Besides, I know the culture.

They don't have the first clue where to look for Lorinyans. They'll be snatched up by morning if they go alone."

Snatched up? Slavers? Chava had mentioned that Curroon was a land of slavers when they first started on their journey, but Shoshanna had run into slavers back in Adamah and always escaped. These Lorinyans couldn't be any worse.

Colebee tossed a bag to Tevye, and said, "No, Leewana, I forbid it. You have children. You are staying here."

She stared him down for a moment, her eyes flashing. Colebee stood his ground, muscles tensed and jaw set. What a marriage it must be. Shoshanna was going to have to fight her way out of this hovel.

But then Leewana wilted. "Fine. I will let the *only* other followers of Eloah who've ever visited our town leave alone and unprotected."

Colebee flinched but said, "Thank you."

"Watch for spear tips in the moonlight," Leewana said to Avner and Chava. "Don't go up to any traveling caravans. And don't eat the plants growing right off the road. You'll spend all night throwing up." She handed her bag to Chava.

"Thank you for everything," the woman said in earnest, her red curls bouncing.

Colebee pulled back the rug occupying the main space to reveal a small trap door. He pulled up the wooden planks, and a deep dark hole stared up at them.

"Now go through the tunnel and back down the pass as quickly as you can." Leewana lit a candle and set it at the bottom of the three-foot drop into the tunnel, illuminating earth and pale roots. "They won't pursue you once you get off the plateau. Not even Birrani cares that much."

Chava slung the satchel across her shoulder and jumped

in the hole up to her waist. She grabbed the candle in her right hand and dropped onto her stomach before slithering out of sight. Tevye and Avner followed.

Shoshanna spared a moment for Leewana. The guilt she felt still warred against her instinct that she'd been correct to attack the Commander. But Itzaak was right. She'd never put off the person Reuben had made her if she always struck first.

Steeling herself, Shoshanna said, "I'm sorry."

Leewana looked taken aback, but before she could respond, Shoshanna dropped into the hole just as Tevye's feet wriggled away into the darkness. Shoshanna crawled on her belly after her companions, turning her head to the side to avoid the puffs of dust kicked up by Tevye's sandals.

Shoshanna's breathing echoed in the semi-darkness, the musty scent of rich dirt pressing in around her as she crawled. The last fifteen minutes of activity *had* weakened her, loath as she was to admit it. Cursed fever. She pulled at the ground faster, willing the weakness to leave.

The earth was more firmly packed now, and Shoshanna dared to look up again. Chava's light flickered weakly, then vanished as she pulled herself out of the tunnel. Shoshanna slid out after the men, but refused to meet anyone's gaze, looking instead over the darkened landscape covered in sage.

Itzaak and Reuben weren't there any longer.

Something in Shoshanna's weak soul broke. This night had proved how little she knew of who she was, and how quickly it could ruin everything.

6

SPEAR TIPS IN THE MOONLIGHT

Avner

"That woman is going to get us all killed," Avner mumbled under his breath to Tevye as they jogged down the rocky pass in the meager moonlight. Chava ran ahead of them, her satchel swaying against her hips. For some reason, this sight brought a strange sensation to Avner's gut.

He was hungry, that was all. He hadn't eaten since that morning.

Tevye glanced back to where Shoshanna jogged a hundred paces behind them.

"It's impossible to know what is going on in that head of hers because I don't think she even knows."

"That is what makes her so dangerous," Avner said, running his fingers over the soft leather sleeve that held the knife of Yor..

"Though if those men hadn't come searching for Chava

and me for being Polys, or whatever they call followers of Eloah, then Shoshanna wouldn't have had to attack."

"So, you're saying it's your fault?" He had meant it as a joke, but found that the words rang true. Their Eloah was causing more trouble than anyone so far on this journey, and Avner didn't even believe in him. He would have stated as much to Birrani, but hadn't figured the man would care.

Tevye's look of concern didn't fail to show in the moonlight. "Av, if you want to talk about—"

"No, that is the last thing I want to talk about. We have the artifact of Yor, and relatively speaking, it was easy. We don't need your deity to help us. We can do this ourselves."

All they'd had to do was ask, and they now had half the artifacts of the missing tribes. Chava still carried the staff close, and Avner wore the Nameless Tribe bracelet from the nomad his mother had tried to save. As old as they were, the rune-covered beads still glinted in the moonlight. If the bracelet was from the Nameless Tribe, they now had three artifacts out of six, same as Reuben. Maybe this wasn't impossible. Maybe beating Reuben to another three artifacts, or getting them back from him, could happen.

"Mate—" Tevye began.

Shoshanna cut him off with a hiss. When had she caught up? Avner spun around to ask what she was doing, but her hand flew up in a stiff warning. She nodded toward the bottom of the pass, just a few feet away now. Rippling grass ran right up to the road, dull gray in the night.

Chava doubled back. "What's going on? Why did you stop?"

"Spear tips in the moonlight," Shoshanna whispered.

Avner's pulse quickened. Leewana had been afraid for them, but she didn't know who they were, or what they could do even with so few weapons. Chava was the only one who wasn't a trained gibborim, but she had the staff. The four of them could take care of themselves. Still, Avner reached for the knife of Yor. Ashes! They should have worked harder at procuring ways to defend themselves back at the harbor or in Curroon's market.

Tevye pulled out his slingshot and took a few steps forward off the trail and into the grass. Avner held his breath, then when nothing happened, he exhaled. The night remained calm, the grass was still, and the silence settled over them thick and full. There wasn't anyone out here with them.

"Let's keep going. Just keep an eye out." Avner met Tevye at the bottom.

"I did see something out there," Shoshanna insisted.

"And you also made us flee from Curroon when we could have spent the night and had supper," Avner shot back.

"I apologized for that." Her voice was oddly small. Avner whipped around to meet her piercing gaze. A sheen of sweat still covered her face. The fog fever.

"You what?"

"Apologized. To Leewana."

"Good. She was nice. Hopefully, that Commander doesn't give them any more grief," Chava said as she met the rest of them at the base of the Pass. "Let's get going. I don't like how still and quiet it is out here," she finished in a whisper.

Avner didn't either. "Keep whatever weapons you have close. I'll lead. Shoshanna—"

"I'll take the rear," she cut in. Did she suspect that Avner wanted her further away? She'd held that knife to Birrani's throat easily enough, even with the fever.

His pulse quickened as he gripped the knife of Yor, but Shoshanna didn't even glance at it. She let the rest of them pass and fell in line behind them, her own blade in hand. Avner let out a sigh of relief.

A rock cracked somewhere in the night.

"Avner—" Chava began but didn't get a chance to finish. Something glinted in the moonlight twenty paces away, followed by swishing grass and scattering pebbles.

"Run!" Tevye yelled.

Avner caught Chava's warm hand and yanked her around. "Come on, with me!"

But a figure—no *five* figures—cut them off from returning to the pass. All shirtless, all wearing black pants and bearing spears.

Spear tips in the moonlight.

Avner's blood ran cold. Chava leveled the staff at the attackers with trembling hands, but Shoshanna stood in the way, knife up and shoulders rigid.

"Av—" Tevye's voice cracked out over the still night behind them, only to cut off with a groan.

Avner spun back, wrenching his hand out of Chava's in time to see Tevye drop to the ground with a thud and a hulking man bend over him, chains clinking. *Slavers.* This was the danger Leewana wanted to protect them from. So dangerous that Colebee hadn't let her.

Avner stepped back, expecting to bump into Chava, but his shoulder met the open air as her scream rent the night.

"Chava!" He spun around, longing for a staff like the one he'd used in the arena. He jumped forward, his knife slashing toward the slaver who held Chava's arm. She flailed with Doram's staff, but the man was blocked by her own body as he dragged her back into the waiting group of slavers in the grass.

"Shoshanna, do something!" Avner shouted as he sprang after Chava, but more men closed in, blocking Shoshanna from sight. Avner ducked under a swinging spear, the *whir* of air over his head telling how close he was to ending up like Tevye.

"Avner!" Chava's cry carried over the growls, scuffling of feet, and grunts of exertion.

Avner popped back up and spun around, but at least ten slavers surrounded Shoshanna and Chava. She held the staff aloft, her pale fingers glowing in the moonlight, a sign of the precious artifact in her grasp. Tevye was gone, but wagons stood out against the moonlit grasslands a hundred paces away.

Another slaver came at Avner with chains trailing this time. He glanced back at Chava, but she was gone.

Chains clinked and pain spiked in Avner's foot. He roared and grabbed the chain before the slaver could fling it again. The cold iron bit into his palms as Avner ripped it out of the man's hands and swung it back before he had a chance to react. The chain cracked into the slaver's skull, leaving a massive wound across the man's bald head. He staggered back, tripped on a rock bordering the road and toppled backward.

Another slaver emerged from the mass of bald heads and skin, drawing a jagged sword from his belt. A growl Avner would have recognized anywhere rent the night as Shoshanna burst out of the horde of slavers, scattering three of them in front of her. Her knife sang through the air and sank into the back of the man advancing on Avner. Shoshanna tackled him to the ground, ripped her knife back out and slit his throat. Splatters of blood flew across Avner's face, and he winced at the sudden heat.

Another group of slavers rose out of the grass and Avner took a shaky step back. There could be hundreds of them lying in wait out there. One of the newcomers advanced on Avner while the others moved toward Shoshanna. She screamed, her blade flying and her feverish eyes glistening like a mad dog's in the night. Then she vanished under a pile of arms and flailing spear shafts.

Shoshanna *was* weakened. She couldn't save them.

For the first time since becoming a gibborim, Avner turned and ran. Adrenaline raged through his exhausted muscles, driving him to a cluster of rocks less than fifty yards away. Avner planted his hand on top of the rough boulder and vaulted behind it.

Someone barked something in a tangled language he didn't understand, but no sounds of pursuit followed. The blood thundering through his ears drowned out any sound, but a glimpse through the rocks showed the slavers dragging Shoshanna back to the wagons. Chava's fierce red hair shone like a freshly lit bonfire, but a ring of bare heads surrounded her. There would be no way to get to her now. The night covered any sign of Tevye.

Avner sagged behind the rocks, letting his heart slow down to a normal pace, gripping the knife of Yor to his chest. Any thought of easily finding the rest of the artifacts vanished from his mind. *Chava.*

Avner raised his clenched fist to his mouth and bit into it to stifle a scream of frustration.

The night settled back to silence. The very efficient band of roving slavers had vanished in the dark. A frog croaked nearby.

His muscles shaking from the rush of adrenaline, Avner braced himself on the rock and stood up. The grasslands and the pass were deserted. Forcing his legs to remain upright, Avner crossed back to the path where the disturbed gravel was the only testimony to the horror of the night.

"Ashes," he breathed, all other words catching in his throat.

The staff of Doram lay in the middle of the road, overlooked by the slavers who surely had much finer weapons back in their wagons. Avner's fingers closed around the smooth shaft as it had hundreds of times around another, similar staff out on the ice. But this time he almost felt Chava's unnatural heat still radiating off the wood.

Avner was alone.

7

LEFTOVERS

Shoshanna

Weakness. Failure. Twin aspects of the ambush last night and the ambush from two decades ago. The same screaming and frantic fighting. The acidic stench of blood, and the tang of bile in the back of Shoshanna's throat. Telltale signs of repeating the greatest failure in her life. She remembered too much now. The swish, the clunk, the cry tearing her throat beyond use for days as Itzaak's head was separated from his body.

A vision of Reuben stood out from the line of shirtless slavers as they marched their captives along the road they'd cut through the grass. Reuben's self-satisfied smile glinted just beyond the slaver who held the chains fastened around Shoshanna's wrists, just as it had the day Reuben killed her husband. She yanked her hands further apart with a clank of metal, hoping the pressure and pain in her wrists would squeeze Reuben out of sight, but he didn't fade. He *couldn't* be there, could he? She was seeing things. The fever still held her.

The implications of that stung worse than the cold iron on Shoshanna's wrists. A simple *fever* brought on by fog had crippled her, making her too weak to fight out of the attack. What hope did she have of returning to the true Shoshanna if she could no longer fight like her?

Shoshanna groped for the stone in her pocket, not to use as a weapon, but to hold onto *anything* that would ground her. The slavers had already relieved her of her knife. She had nothing else but the stone she'd murdered Mikhail's woman for. She released it and squeezed the fabric covering her brand.

And she had the brand. It would never leave, even if she refused to look at that permanent reminder of her failures. She needed to get a new cuff, as this scrap of cloth wouldn't last to cover the brand until she died, even though death seemed nearer than ever before.

The unknown language rang out as a slaver shouted something. The line stopped where the wagons towered ahead, cages made of steel bars were molded into wooden bases on wheels. The slavers in Adamah rarely used such contraptions, as they were too unwieldy in the forests and ravines. But then, the slavers there worked in smaller groups, not a disciplined horde like this one. Adamah slavers waited until you were alone, then crept in and took your freedom at the end of their knives. If you were armed, escape was easy.

But the creak of hinges opening a well-constructed door into a moving prison defied the notion that escape would be as simple here. Five slave wagons stood in a circle in the middle of the plain, most already housing a rag-tag group of prisoners. Dirt-and-tear-stained faces glared at the slavers with open hatred which wouldn't do the captives any good out here. A woman in a tattered dress stared hard at her hands in her lap, as if that might make this misfortune vanish. Several men with open wounds on their faces sat at the back of the closest wagon, and a slaver pointed a spear at them as the door opened. The men scowled back, but didn't try to make for the open door, since impalement would be the only way out.

"In," the nearest slaver barked at Shoshanna. The butt of a spear prodded her back.

She grasped the bars above her, her chain jangling, and heaved herself up. Every muscle in her body screamed to twist the chain around the spear, yank it out of the man's grasp and stab him clean through. Shoshanna could do it. Nuri wouldn't hesitate to, but then she would never have allowed this to happen in the first place.

But the cursed fever had sapped all her energy, and killing the slaver would only secure Shoshanna's death. Gritting her teeth, she jumped the last step into the wagon. A glance over her shoulder proved Reuben wasn't there. Just another figment of her mind. Her hand went to the fabric tied around her brand, but she pulled it back before she could feel the ridges of the flaming 'z'.

Chava's unbound curls bobbed as she scrambled up into the wagon. There was a shallow cut across her freckled cheek. She grumbled under her breath as the slaver jabbed her with the spear again to make her move further into the cart.

"I'm going," she snapped, and staggered toward Shoshanna.

More chains clanked as Tevye's head emerged above the wagon steps, followed by the rest of him. He looked slightly bruised and battered, his hair sticking out at all angles, but he was not bleeding. The door clanged shut with the same force that had ripped away their freedom. A slaver slid a latch shut and locked it, then returned to the other men behind the wagon. Someone yelled in their guttural language, and with a jolt, the wagon moved. Chava lost her footing and fell against one of the men sitting at the back. Tevye sprang forward in time to pull her back before the large man's fist found Chava's nose.

"Watch it," the slave growled.

"It was an accident," Tevye said calmly. "I figure we've made enough enemies out there without any more in here."

The man clenched his fist but didn't try to stand up as the wagon jolted along the ruts in the makeshift road.

"Why can't they take the real road?" Chava grumbled as she sank onto the bench that ran along the side of the cage. The woman in tatters glanced up, her eyes bright as stars against her dirty face, but wide with fear. She scooted away from Chava, her hands trembling. Shoshanna held back a scoff. The fool made herself an easy target for slavers to beat with a countenance like that.

"The road gets us to Mereen twice as fast," a teen-aged lad said. He bore a black eye, but didn't seem much worse for wear. He raised a brow at Shoshanna's stare. "They took me yesterday from the smithy I indentured at. The Lorinyans are getting bolder. Coming into outlying settlements and not waiting for us to wander into the grasslands."

Shoshanna grunted in disinterest and sat down hard as the wagon jolted over another bump. The wind had finally cooled her fever, and Shoshanna breathed deeper. At least she could sit and save her strength, and maybe keep the sickness away.

"Mereen, you say?" Tevye sat beside Chava and leaned across to the boy. "We docked not far from there when we first arrived."

One of the men in the back scoffed. "That's where the slave market is, you dolt."

Slave market. The words shivered down Shoshanna's spine, and Tevye's face went white. He'd been to one. That was where Reuben had bought him over two years ago. Shoshanna, however, had skipped the slave market, as Reuben had wiped her memory in Doram and taken her straight to his gibborim pens. Chava, on the other hand...

"You can't be serious," she protested, as if the man had any reason to joke. "I-I don't have any skills worth selling."

"Don't you?" The man took one long, roving look over Chava's body and a cruel smile spread over his face.

Chava blushed and pulled further away, bumping into Tevye.

"I hate to say it, Chava, but the man's right," Tevye said, frowning "These Lorinyans don't care if you've a marketable skill or not. They'll find one for you. I've seen it. Women sold to warm a bed. Children sold to sweep floors. Men sold to be—" he cut off, swallowing, as if it hurt to say it.

Chava didn't miss a beat. "Gibborim, you mean? But surely, they don't have those here."

Shoshanna couldn't stifle a dry laugh. Although Chava had been right about the tribes, and about her brother, she could still be so naïve.

"Everyone wants glory and riches, and gibborim are the

quickest way to get them. That's why Reuben—" It was Shoshanna's turn to break off, choking on *his* name.

The pity in Chava's eyes only made it worse. Shoshanna dug her fingernails into the rough bench beneath her, forcing herself to hold Chava's gaze and hating her for it. Hating her brother, hating how this woman was connected to all of it.

Chava saved her by saying, "But what about Avner? I don't think they got him, or he'd be here too. Won't he come after us?"

"Nah, lassie. I don't think he will. We're in a cage surrounded by lethal fighters. What could one man do against all of them?" Tevye whispered, his voice barely audible over the creaking of wheels and the jangling of chains. "No, I'm afraid you're about to see what a slave market looks like."

"Or in two weeks anyway," the lad said. "Until then, hold tight and try not to let them jostle the brains out of you."

Shoshanna didn't need help losing her brains, as her recent visions of Itzaak and Reuben had demonstrated. She'd lost so much of her mind already, and going back to the arena wouldn't help make it any better. Images of men lying dead at her feet overwhelmed all her thoughts

'I give you the deadliest gibborim in all Adamah!' Reuben's voice rang out loud enough to be real, but he wasn't there, and she wasn't on Lake Kefa.

"Shoshanna? You're bleeding." Chava's voice broke into her thoughts.

She glanced down. Blood trickled from where she gripped the splinter-ridden bench too tightly.

"I can't do it again," she muttered, not to anyone there, but to Itzaak. He'd know. He'd understand. Her breathing constricted in her chest, coming in thin spurts, making her head light.

"If you were taken so easy, no way they will sell you as a gibborim," the man in the back sneered. "You're leftovers. They'll sell you to a labor farm and you'll die there."

Shoshanna couldn't bring herself to contradict him. Leftovers. That was all she was.

8

OF FOG AND MYSTERIES

Avner

Avner slid into the tunnel leading to the Yanathan's house and made it down faster than he remembered leaving. The flight back up the pass had been similar. He couldn't remember anything but the last glance at Chava's shining hair as the slavers hauled her away. He gritted his teeth as he crawled through the darkness. He'd get her back. Though Tevye was the better friend, Chava's face haunted him.

Pain wracked Avner's skull as his head struck the trap door sooner than he expected. The sound echoed in the house above. He rammed the wood with his shoulder and the plank moved out of the hole. There were scuffling sounds nearby, and candlelight flared above him, illuminating Colebee's wide eyes. His shirt was untucked as if he'd just tumbled out of bed.

"What in the name of all things right and true are you doing here?"

"The Lorinyans took my friends." The term still didn't apply to Shoshanna, but that didn't matter now.

Colebee's jaw tightened, and he handed the candle to the girl who'd tried to scramble in through the window the day before. Right. They had several children. Guilt tugged at Avner for putting them in jeopardy, but he had no better choice.

Colebee offered his hand and pulled Avner out of the hole. Avner kept a firm grip on Doram's staff. He still had all three artifacts and wouldn't lose them now.

Colebee turned toward his daughter. "Go, wake your mother."

She nodded, her curls flying every which way. Just like Chava's, only dark. Avner clenched his fist. What was happening to Chava now? Were the slavers beating his friends, or saving them to look their best for the market? There was no doubt that was where they'd be taking them, though Avner had no clue where the slave markets were.

"I'm already awake." Leewana emerged from the bedroom, her dark hair no longer in buns, but piling around her face. She took the torch from the girl and put it in a holder on the wall. "Alira, go back to sleep. Don't wake your brothers."

"But Mama—"

"Listen to your mother, Alira," Colebee said, his voice firm.

Alira scowled, crossed her arms, and stomped off to the bedroom. A curtain fell shut, but Avner had a feeling it wouldn't be enough to keep her from staying awake and listening. A strange pang tugged at his chest. His last conversation with his mother had involved talk of grandchildren for her, and he'd shrugged it off as ludicrous because he was still a gibborim then, destined to die on the ice.

But now? Would he have a chance at a family if he managed to free the others and reverse the frost? After all, at twenty-three he was still young. The faint hope lingered until Chava's face flashed in his mind. They were married, and yet the thought of living together as man and wife seemed impossible, even if he'd grown used to having her nearby. He shook his head to clear all the nonsense away. Avner wouldn't have children. He wouldn't be a father. After all he'd done, it was better that way.

"What happened?" Leewana asked as she rubbed the sleep from her face with a damp towel.

"Lorinyans took his friends," Colebee said. His expression testified to the seriousness of the situation.

She let the washcloth fall back into the washbowl, sending droplets of water over the red-stone walls.

"I *told* you I should have gone with them!" Leewana raised a finger at her husband. "I knew this would happen!"

But Colebee didn't back down. "And you'd be captured right now if I hadn't stopped you. Avner, how did you get away?"

"Sheer luck, I think. We took a few down, but by the time I decided to run for it, they already had the others and didn't bother chasing me." For the hundredth time, Avner cursed himself for not grabbing Chava, or Tevye, and running for it sooner. Shoshanna had suspected they were being watched minutes before the Lorinyans made their move. They might have been able to make a break for it.

"I came here because I didn't know where else to go, or who else to ask..." he trailed off, unable to put the question into words. These two had children to care for, and they knew the dangers more intimately than he.

Leewana found the words for him. "You want our help getting your friends back?"

Avner nodded. Colebee stared at him, clenching and unclenching his hand.

Avner held his hands up, the torchlight glinting off the knife of Yor.

"I know what I'm asking, but I can't leave them. Tevye has saved my life many times, and Chava... she is..." Ashes and dust, why did he even try to explain what she was to him when he really didn't know ?

"Do you love her?" Leewana asked, crossing her arms.

The question stung.

"No, I don't."

She pinned him with a fierce gaze that demanded an answer, but he didn't have one to give.

Instead, he said, "What matters is freeing them. I can't stop the frost without them."

"I will go with you, as I should have done to begin with," Leewana said.

"No, Lee, I forbid it!" Colebee crossed over to her.

She snatched up a faded red belt hanging from a hook by the door and wrapped it on. She stepped around her husband, pulling a long knife off the shelf by the window. "You know if I don't go, his friends will never be free again. They'll die as slaves, when we could have stopped it."

Colebee stared at the belt around his wife's waist, his left eyelid twitching. Finally, he looked up and said, "You don't know that—"

She whirled on him as she shoved the knife sheath into the belt. "I *do* know, because not fifteen minutes ago while I slept, Eloah told me they'd all die in the arena! A vision as terrifying as any dream I've ever had, but as real as the pain I felt when Pan burned."

Colebee took a step back at that, his mouth slightly ajar.

Leewana continued with fire in her words, "Why do you think I was already awake when he arrived? I was coming to tell you we had to follow them. Would you hold me back from doing His will?"

For once, Avner could have thanked the deity, if it got Leewana to help him. He held his breath as Colebee stared Leewana down. The torch flickered brighter and popped, sending a spark onto the threadbare rug, but neither of them moved to stamp it out. It slowly lost its glow, leaving behind a black burn mark on the faded weaving.

A child coughed behind the curtain, followed by someone shushing them. Apparently more than one of the Yanathan's offspring was eavesdropping.

"What about the children?" Colebee whispered.

For a moment, a look of pain passed over Leewana's face. "I trust Eloah, and you, to protect them. Once Avner is gone, there will be no danger for them. I'll return as soon as I can. A month, maybe a bit longer. Surely you can keep them alive that long." She gave a small smile.

The tension between them broke, and Avner breathed out in relief as Colebee sighed and delicately touched Leewana's arm.

"Yes, I can." He pulled her into an embrace. "May Eloah go with you."

"He will," she murmured.

Avner averted his eyes, his cheeks burning. To be so near to such open displays of affection between husband and wife... His own parents had not been in love, his passion with Dalea hadn't lasted long enough to mean much, and his relationship with Chava would never make others blush.

Avner cleared his throat. "Can we leave now?"

"Yes, I'm not waiting for Birrani and the others to figure out you've returned. I'm guessing the Lorinyans have at least six hours on us by now. They will have put them in wagons, and while I hear it's a difficult ride, they move quicker than you'd think." Leewana tightened her belt, planted a swift kiss on Colebee's cheek, and slipped behind the curtain.

"Mama! Where are you going? Why do you have a sword?" It was a boy's voice.

"And why do you have your old belt on? I thought you didn't want to wear it anymore," Alira chimed in.

"Shh." Leewana lowered her voice to a whisper as she said her goodbyes.

Avner glanced away, though it was impossible not to eavesdrop in the small house.

Colebee's steady gray gaze drilled him. "You'll watch over my wife?"

"Of course."

"I mean it. Think back to anyone you've ever cared for and remember what you would have done to protect them. Extend that same concern to Leewana." His words thrummed with intensity, but his voice didn't break. He took a step closer.

Avner nodded and held out a hand. "I promise I will." He'd have done anything to protect Silas and his mother. Now Tevye and Chava. Leewana would fit right in.

Colebee grabbed Avner's hand in his. "Thank you," he said gruffly. "Eloah grant you aid."

Avner pulled his hand away, not bothering to explain

that he didn't believe in the deity. The curtain rustled and Leewana stepped out again, wiping her eyes.

"And I told myself I wouldn't cry," she mumbled.

Colebee chuckled. "You wouldn't be a mother if you didn't. Now, I want to hear the plan before you run headlong into danger."

"They will take them to Mereen. It's the only slave market of value, even though it is a long trek," Leewana explained.

The name was familiar. "We docked not too far from there."

"I'm not surprised. It's gone from a floundering port city to a thriving trade center in one short year, and not for a good reason." Leewana grabbed a stick resting near the fire grate and scratched a square into the dirt floor beside the rug. "Our biggest problem is what happens if we don't catch your friends before they make it inside the city wall. It's impenetrable."

"Why does a market need such intense fortifications?" The market in Ur—the largest trade hub in Adamah—was not so protected.

"Because of the kind of slave they deal with most often." Colebee said, the torchlight giving an eerie glow to the scar on his somber face. He took the stick from his wife and drew a circle in the far corner of the square.

The skin on Avner's neck prickled. There had to be several kinds of slaves to bother building an impregnable wall around, right? Not all dangerous slaves were fighters. They could be worth more, like linguists, or clerics. It would make sense for slave-masters with valuable slaves to want them behind walls. He had to stop jumping to the worst conclusion.

Colebee pointed to the circle he'd drawn. "This is the arena."

A chill went down Avner's back. No, surely not here.

"Arena," he echoed, though his voice seemed distant.

"For the gibborim," Colebee said, his face dark.

Gibborim.

The word seemed to stab through Avner's chest. He took a shuddering breath and traced the scar through his leather pants on his thigh. He'd received the mark from Leaf, one of Reuben's Pack members, during his first training session over a year ago.

"Gibborim?" Thankfully, his voice didn't shake, but it was thin, strained.

"Slave fighters. Have you heard of them?" Leewana asked.

He held back a dry chuckle as memories of the last year flooded his mind. Blue B, his highest rank, might still be cinched tight against his arm, with Zira's blood splattered on it.

"I've heard of them," Avner muttered. Would that he hadn't. How much would be different? Would Reuben have reunited the tribes with Shoshanna's help as Nuri by now? Would Avner's mother and brothers still be alive? Would Dalea be the mother of Avner's children, and Silas still Judge of Doram? If Mikhail hadn't betrayed Silas, then Avner's life would be as it was supposed to be, not this jumbled mess. Avner wouldn't have killed dozens in the arena, or ever broken his Oath of Do No Harm.

For a moment, the vision of that sweet alternate world stung so badly, he could scarcely breathe.

"So, you know what monsters gibborim are?" Colebee's question broke into his thoughts.

Avner jerked his hand off his arm where Zira's rank used to be tied.

"Y-yes. They were common in many places in Adamah. I didn't think you had them."

"Their exodus from Adamah is probably why there has been such an increase here." Colebee scowled, not seeming to pick up on Avner's discomfort.

He could tell them what he really was, all he'd done on the ice, but it wouldn't increase the chances of saving anyone, and speaking of it, especially with Chava and Tevye in harm's way, was the last thing Avner wanted. Certainly not if Colebee thought gibborim were monsters.

And they were, weren't they? Wasn't that why Avner was fleeing his old self?

Leewana pulled the rug the rest of the way off the trap door. "We will run hard and sleep little, and will catch the caravan before they enter Mereen. I will pray we do, otherwise this mission is over before it begins, and your friends may die in the arena."

"Or before. I've heard gibborim are ruthless even outside the arena. They are merciless savages who've been trained to no longer feel the pain of their own souls." Colebee's words bit hard.

Avner pushed his confession of being a gibborim further down. He couldn't tell this man who he was when he'd just tasked him with protecting his wife.

Leewana sat at the edge of the tunnel, her feet dangling into the hole. "I hope you're not tired of crawling. The guards are still outside. No one wanted a trial at this hour, apparently. They'll wait until morning to bother us."

"Are you sure you want to wear that?" Colebee stared at her red belt.

"Why keep it hanging on the wall all these years if I'm never to wear it?"

"Yes, but why now?"

"Eloah brought me out of darkness with it on once before. He will do so again." Her tone was determined, and she offered no other explanation for the mysterious belt. She jumped down into the hole.

Avner stowed his knife back in his belt and followed her, the staff thunking against the dirt tunnel wall as he climbed in.

"Eloah be with you both," Colebee said from behind, then the trap door dropped into place.

Avner made it through with only a few bumps this time. Leewana's feet wriggled out of view, and Avner followed her out, the grass tickling his feet through the gaps in his sandals. He let out a pent-up breath and turned toward Leewana. She wrapped her hair into the two buns she'd worn the evening before and dropped into a crouch. Her eyes closed and her lips moved soundlessly, as if speaking to someone who wasn't there.

While he had no idea what she was saying, a chill ran up Avner's spine. The movements were so like what he'd seen Chava and Tevye do. They never explained what it meant, but the ritual obviously involved their god, just as Doramites used to chant over their useless crystals.

Leewana spread her hands over the earth, running the grass through her dark fingers. "Please," she murmured.

Avner looked away from his new companion, stifling the urge to tell her that this wasn't the time. Another moment passed, then she stood up and moved past him.

"Follow me." Leewana broke into a jog.

Avner needed no second urging. It had been too long

already. As she'd said, the caravan could be hours away now, doing who knew what to his friends. To Chava. He ground his teeth together. He shouldn't single her out as if she mattered more. He just felt the duty to protect her as a friend, and because she was a woman. That was all. Not to mention how much better Tevye and Shoshanna would fare in captivity with their skills.

Fog settling on the far side of the meadow was beginning to overshadow the clear light of the moon, but that was a blessing. Harder for Birrani to see them. Avner followed Leewana, but before they had moved more than fifty yards, she stiffened, and he nearly ran into her.

"What is it?" Avner asked.

"He's answered! It's the Orroroo," she whispered almost reverently.

"The fever fog?" From the way everyone feared it, it didn't make sense for her to be excited.

She cast him a sidelong glance, and her awe turned to surprise.

"You can't hear it?"

"No? What am I supposed to be hearing?"

"The most beautiful song you've ever heard. Like mango nectar on a hot summer day, sticky and lusciously sweet." She closed her eyes as if trying to taste it.

Avner still didn't hear anything apart from the chirping of insects hiding in the underbrush, a sound so like home, like Doram, his heart ached for it. But this wasn't why he was here. They needed to move.

"I don't see what this has to do with getting my friends back."

"It's a sign from Eloah. He will cover our escape." Leewana opened her eyes and took off again, slipping around the larger clumps of sage and between the smaller ones.

Avner kept up, confusion roiling in his mind. The fog covered the ground thicker now, so that only the larger plants and shrubs were visible. Everyone in town feared this strange mist, so why would Leewana think it was from Eloah? Even when Avner had seen the fog on the pass, something had been...*off* about it.

Avner stumbled in the thick fog and tripped on a shrub, the brittle branches scratching against his legs and tearing through his leather pants.

"Can you hear the song now?" Leewana kept going, dodging the obstacles in their path with practiced skill.

"No—wait..." Avner stopped moving, and the crackling of shrubs stopped. Something grated on his senses, like a dagger being scraped across rocks. He shivered, but the sound only grew worse.

"Th-this isn't a song. It's a curse," he muttered.

Leewana stopped ten paces ahead and spun around, face tense and eyes wide. "You don't hear a song? You hear a terrible scratching?"

"Scratching is definitely a better word—ah!" Avner cut off with a gasp and grabbed his ears as a sudden, sharp pain throbbed in them. It was all he could do to keep upright.

"No, no, no... but your group, you follow Eloah!"

"Ashes and dust," Avner breathed, but the words came slowly. He fell to his knees, more sharp branches jabbing through his pants. Bright flecks of golden-red blood glowed in the night as the sticks ripped his skin.

Leewana gasped, but there wasn't a moment to explain the curse of his golden blood. Back in the town, someone yelled.

"They've seen us!" Hands clutched his armpits and tried to heave him upright. "Come on, I need your help, or we won't even make it to the pass."

"I–I can't! What...is...this fog?" Avner's labored breathing came harder than before, and his golden blood swirled before him as the whole world shook. "I c-can't stand," he mumbled uselessly.

"You're telling me you escaped the Lorinyans, but you can't run through some dizziness? Come on!" Leewana tugged with a surprising amount of force.

Avner stumbled up, closing his eyes, hoping the dizziness would subside. It did, but only slightly. The screeching sound morphed into a terrible wailing song, doubling the pain in his ears. It couldn't be what Leewana referenced with mangos and sweet nectar. She was insane to think this was beautiful! Avner staggered forward, her arms around his shoulders. For the first time since leaving the arena, he wished to be there instead of here. At least on the ice he could control what happened, but this... His stomach heaved and he almost vomited on Leewana's sandals.

"Keep it together for another few minutes and we will be out of this," she said breathlessly as they pushed forward. "I promise, it will pass. Birrani can't see us. The fog is too thick, and he's probably unconscious now anyway. He will feel it like you do."

Her mumblings didn't make any sense, but they helped Avner stay lucid. He shouldn't have come back to this town. He should have set off after the others alone. At least he wouldn't be under the influence of some monstrous fog. His incomplete and pained thoughts struggled to connect, but one thing made it through. *This* was why the townspeople feared the fog.

"How?" he wheezed.

"I'll explain when you're free of this," Leewana gasped, straining to bear part of his weight..

Avner gradually started walking on his own, and their pace increased until the ground turned to loose rubble. The screeching still rang in his ears, and moisture trickled down his lobes and the side of his neck. Ashes, his ears were *bleeding*! Just like the Curroonians they'd seen earlier.

They staggered another dozen yards, Leewana's silence allowing the resounding song to take over. Each breath Avner took came harder, shallower. His body ached, almost as with a fever. But that was impossible. He wasn't sick! Or hadn't been ten minutes ago.

Still, Shoshanna had come down with a mysterious fever after escaping the fog on the pass.

Avner shoved the crazy thought from his mind as each second brought on a fresh wave of chills and nausea. He gasped for air, but it wouldn't come. His legs shook beneath him, and his foot caught on something firm on the ground. Lurching out of Leewana's grip, he fell to the rock-covered ground, more glowing blood dotting his palms as pebbles bit into them. He hadn't died in the arena, but he just might here.

"*Why* didn't you tell me you don't believe in Eloah?" Leewana demanded angrily.

When his head stopped spinning, Avner took a deep breath and rolled over. Leewana's tense form was bending over him, the stars bright behind her. Her words sunk in.

"How do you know I don't believe in El—Eloah?" Avner wheezed, as he dug one elbow into the ground and pushed halfway up, his body still shaking from the effects of the fog.

"I prayed for Eloah to cover our escape, but only because

I didn't know about *you!* We almost didn't make it," she seethed, her eyes blazing again.

Avner sat up the rest of the way, blinked to clear his vision, and said, "You're not making any sense."

Leewana took a step back and breathed deeply. Behind her, the fog still hung over the meadow and the town as if it were there to stay. Avner scrambled up, ready to flee if it came nearer, but Leewana guessed his thought.

"It doesn't work that way. It won't go past the town limits unless I ask it to. Come on, let's get going before they recover and come after us." Leewana grabbed his hand and yanked him up.

Avner staggered back, one hand on his feverish forehead, and leaning on the staff of Doram with the other. What in the name of freedom had she done to him?

"Do you need help, or can you walk?" she asked, one arm already wrapping around his shoulders to help him.

"I'm f-fine." Or he would be once he got moving.

Leewana glared at him but removed her arm and took off down the pass. Avner started off slower. Each step brought another wave of nausea, but he fought it down. Leewana offered no explanation for how the fog could do this to him. Avner shivered through a burst of chills and picked up his pace as they gradually faded. Maybe choosing Leewana for his new traveling companion hadn't been so wise after all.

9

MEREEN

Chava

Apart from breaks for the prisoners to relieve themselves and to change out the drivers, the carts carried them for nearly two weeks before they showed any sign of slowing down. Further up the line, canvas-covered wagons carried the Lorinyans who slept in shifts, while the others marched silently behind the slaves. Other slaves walked with them, their chains sounding like death settling closer, one clink at a time. Chava couldn't complain about her sore rump, or her wrists rubbed raw by the chafing iron when the slaves outside were being forced to walk. These switched in shifts as well, trading with the slaves in the other wagons, but sparing those in Chava's. She wondered at this, but why complain about the one comfort she had?

The slavers provided half-rotten fruit and water daily, leaving her stomach growling most of the day. At least she was alive. Though presently, sitting under the sweltering sun in their exposed wagon, Chava was sure that going home to be with Eloah was far preferable. She blew air out over her scorched chin, only to suck it back in with a hiss. Blazes, it hurt!

"You're as red as an over-ripe berry," Tevye chuckled.

"You won't be joking in a few hours when we reach Mereen and you're sold to the labor farms," one of the men at the back of their wagon said, scowling..

"I've been to a slave market before. I'm not shaking in my sandals." Tevye leveled him with a flat look.

The man winced as he wiped the sweat from his sunburned forehead. "Even you won't be chuckling once we pass the gates."

"I expect not—"

"Ho!" A Lorinyan shouted somewhere further up the line, his voice rising over the snorting of horses, the whimpers of slaves, and the pounding of dozens of feet on packed, dry ground. The wagon jerked to a slower crawl and Chava slid off the bench, careening into Shoshanna on the opposite side.

The woman peeled her off and gently pushed her back. Shoshanna's speckled eyes flashed a warning, but she kept silent. She hadn't shown any signs of fever since their enslavement began. At least this was something to be thankful for.

"Chava, we're there," Tevye said.

She looked over her shoulder and her heart started to race. Red stone walls jutted into the sky a hundred paces away, looking more menacing with each roll of the wagon wheels. Muttering broke out among the others in their wagon. The only friendly one, the lad they'd met on their first night, gaped as the wagon rolled closer to a large arch surrounded by intricate stonework. The wall cut the blazing sun out, and a blessedly cool shade soothed Chava's burned skin. The voices of the Lorinyans and slaves echoed off the walls of the short tunnel before they jolted into the sun again. Chava squinted and winced, trying in vain to block the intense blaze with her sunburned hand.

Tevye whistled low beside her.

"So, this is the true Mereen."

The harbor where they had docked had been at least a mile from the main town, and they'd never caught a glimpse of *this*.

Chava dropped her arm. The sound of voices and the bustling ruckus of a market spread out before them. She'd thought Curroon was the largest market she'd ever seen, but this... She caught her breath. This was *massive*.

Hundreds of people milled about an open area the size of Eder itself. Countless slaves huddled inside cages lining the interior of the stone walls. Finely dressed men and women thronged between them. Coins jingled as money— and lives—traded hands. Dogs barked, people screamed, slavers laughed. A cacophony of chaos. Chava forced down a shudder.

As the wagon pulled further into the market, at least two dozen armed guards watched over the inner side. The market had clearly once been a town, but slave stalls now stood over the ruins of old foundations, and the town well swarmed with thirsty marketgoers instead of mothers carrying water pitchers. The only children present were sitting in a slave pen with tear lines staining their filthy cheeks.

Chava's nails dug into her palms.

Where was Avner? Why hadn't he tried to free them? She fought back another wave of anxiety. Didn't he care that they were going to be sold as slaves? She'd known ever since she married him that it would never be an actual marriage, but didn't he see her as a friend after the last few months? Surely that was enough to warrant at least an attempt at a rescue. She'd grown accustomed to his constant presence. She gripped the edge of the seat tighter. Was he all right, or had he been apprehended after them? Did he worry about her at all as she did him?

"Where are you, Avner?" she whispered.

"Your Judge isn't coming," Shoshanna's voice rasped as she stared straight ahead, the veins in her neck popping tight and her hands clenching the bench beneath her.

She'd said Judge, not Avner. Were they losing her back to who Reuben had made her? No doubt this place reminded her of things she'd rather forget. She'd gotten quieter with each passing day.

Before Chava could respond to Shoshanna, the wagon rolled to a stop alongside other wagons. The cage door creaked open.

"Out," a bare-chested slaver barked.

Tevye moved first.

"It's never good to ignore them," he whispered as he tugged Chava's sleeve.

Chava let him lead but stayed close as she jumped out of the wagon. Her chains rattled against each other, and she hissed as they scraped the open skin on her wrists. At this rate, she'd beg to be sold first if it meant they'd take the things off sooner.

Shoshanna thudded to the parched ground behind her,

her eyes strangely vacant. If she returned to being Nuri before they escaped, would all be lost?

Chava whispered, "Shoshanna, you've come so far and remembered so much. Don't let this city take that from you."

The woman's fingers clenched around the fabric covering her brand. She blinked, and clarity seemed to return. "I'm never going back to that, girl. Never."

Chava nodded, though her heart continued to pound hard.

"This way. March!" The Lorinyan waved his spear toward a gap in the chaos before them. The line of slaves filed into it, and he arranged them into two rows against the stone wall. The sun radiated off it, sending searing heat down Chava's back. She groaned. Her skin couldn't take much more of this. In Eder, even when the weather was warm, there was plenty of shade and a refreshing breeze.

"If this is anything like the slave market in Ur, they'll lead the buyer's past. Stand straight. It doesn't help to make them think you are undesirable," Tevye whispered to her.

"But wouldn't I rather no one buys me?"

"Only if you want to go to the labor farms."

Chava nodded nervously. This was it. They were going to be sold like common animals to the highest bidder. Men and women shuffled in behind her, and the lad from the wagon bumped into her.

"S-sorry," he murmured, his face downcast.

"It's okay," she said kindly. Eloah was with her, a constant presence. If only she had a clue as to Avner's location.

The lad nodded, but his shoulders trembled. The crowd thinned out in front of their group of two dozen slaves. More waited their turn back in the wagons. The Lorinyans probably sold them off in batches, then waited until the end of the day to count their profits. Unease swept over Chava, but she fought it back as a group of merchants, or buyers, veered toward the slaves.

The sun glowed off the long, blonde hair of the man in the front. His eyes were the lightest shade of blue Chava had ever seen. He blinked as he approached, the color fading even more to a milky blue so pale they were almost white. A white shirt tucked into his breeches billowed around his lean frame. He looked neither Curroonian nor from Adamah. She'd heard of the blonde people from Smyma, sailors by trade, as this man's sun-kissed skin attested to.

But the man behind him stole Chava's attention. Was that—

"Dov," Tevye grunted. "What in blazes is he doing here?"

Chava silently wondered the same thing as Dov strode closer, his enormous frame as commanding as ever. He was dressed far better than they were in their ruined clothes. Dark stubble covered his previously bald head. According to Avner, Dov had left the moment they'd escaped the gibborim pens, intent on finding a new life as a trainer. Maybe this was where he'd found it, though he couldn't have arrived much sooner than they.

Shoshanna stiffened, fists clenching. How would she view this turn of events? She'd been Dov's master, and now the roles were reversed.

The golden-haired man swaggered up to them, his lips pursed in concentration. He studied the men they'd shared a wagon with, only to click his tongue and turn away to the lad. The boy looked down, and even his tall shoulders seemed to shrink under the intense scrutiny.

"They are all so...unimpressive," the buyer said, waving his arm dismissively.

"There's more in the pens on the far side of the market, but I'm telling you, the Lorinyans always have the best stock," Dov countered as he stepped close enough that Chava could have spit on him.

And she almost did. What business did he have advising a slave owner on new purchases?

"What about the Yocheved you spoke so highly of?" The buyer pressed, still sniffing in discontent.

"You won't find them in the market. Their gibborim fight professionally, not as slaves. They had nowhere else to go once Adamah frosted over." Dov's face clouded. Chava knew Dov wouldn't have forgotten the ways of the Yocheved in the arena.

Tevye shifted beside her and Dov caught the movement. His eyes flared wide, and his jaw dropped.

"What? A beetle fly in your mouth?" The buyer asked.

"No, sir, it's just, I know that slave and—" Dov's gaze swept the line, pausing on Chava, "—and that one." His look of surprise turned into a sly smile as he pointed at her with a scarred hand and arm. The marks of a burn curled up to his elbow and disappeared into his sleeve. Must have been from the explosion at the pens when they escaped with the spark stone dust Chava had given Avner.

Shoshanna spat forcefully, the wad speckling the cracked, pale earth a deeper brown. "What are you doing here, Dov?"

He flinched at her voice and stared at her again. A vein popped tight in his large neck. Of course, he wouldn't have recognized Shoshanna right away without the short, spiked hair Nuri used to wear.

"You know that one too, I presume?" The buyer said with curiosity. "She looks interesting. What luck that I hired a slave advisor, and he knows three in this very market. What kind of slaves are they?"

Dov shifted, cleared his throat, and ripped his gaze away from Shoshanna's murderous glare. "Gibborim."

"Ah!" The man rubbed his hands together, his sleeves flapping. "What a marvelous set of circumstances, considering that is what I came to purchase today. Tell me, are they any good? That one seems inadequate." He frowned at Chava.

Dov snorted. "No, not at all. She wasn't a gibborim—more like a gibborim's pet. She'd be better at warming beds than fighting in the arena."

"How dare you—" Chava began, but a Lorinyan's spear whacked across her forehead and specks of light exploded in her vision. Tevye held her upright.

"Feisty, though, wouldn't you say?" The buyer's voice filtered through the stabs of pain.

"She isn't worth the trouble or money, Sir."

"Fine," the buyer sighed, as if he'd been excited by the challenge. "What about the two gibborim? It's rare to find experienced ones at market. I'll need them to best these Yocheved."

"Well, Tevye is a cripple." Dov motioned to his maimed arm.

"I can see that," the man said, amused.

"But he's mighty wicked with a slingshot and fork. He lasted two years competing in Adamah before escaping; one year included his injury."

The blonde man whistled low. "*Two years*? Blood and ashes, I could use longevity like that. Okay, I'll take him. Never mind the cost."

Chava caught Tevye's fierce jaw and burning eyes. Had

he expected Dov, a former comrade, to go easy on him? The man had no morals or scruples. Still, Chava reached for Tevye's good hand. She couldn't let them take Tevye away from her. He was the only other person in this forsaken place who knew Eloah. His hand felt like stone, but before Chava could beg Dov to change his master's mind, the buyer stepped closer to Shoshanna.

"What of the woman? Lots of scars means she's lived through her fair share of matches. Muscle to match, and a gaze to kill. Did she also fight for two years?"

Shoshanna snorted but didn't lash out as the man moved within striking distance. Perhaps she had a shred of self-preservation after all.

"Seven years," Dov said warily.

"Even bloodier ashes! Seven!" The buyer flashed a gleaming smile. "That's unheard of. If I can put her in matches, the fame, Dov, the fame!"

"I wouldn't. She's unstable. Addled. Her eyes prove it. She'll gut you the first chance she gets and leave your rotting corpse for the birds. If you buy her, you'll never know a night's peace as long as she lives. She'd need constant guards."

The buyer's smile broadened. "Excellent. Sounds like just the gibborim I need."

"Sir, I just said—"

"You've indicated what kind of fighter she is in the arena. This is what I do, Dov. I wouldn't be the finest gibborim master this side of Ratiljóst if I didn't have an eye for good stock."

Dov looked as if he was about to protest again, but the buyer waved his arm, and a Lorinyan produced a ledger.

Whatever the cost of Chava's companions, the buyer didn't balk as he handed over a bag of coins.

No, no, no! Chava couldn't be left without them! Desperation overrode the inner calm of Eloah's presence, even though she knew she shouldn't let it. She yanked Tevye's sleeve and hissed, "You can't let them separate us!"

A Lorinyan moved to pull him out of the line.

Tevye shouted, "We're a team! A team! If you buy us, you buy the redhead, too."

Dov rolled his eyes. "Like I said, she's never fought. He's lying."

"And I believe you," the buyer said as he tucked the rest of his money away in the folds of his wide leather belt. "Though, what *is* that?" He pointed a suntanned finger at Chava's hand grasping Tevye's arm.

Her marriage mark. It glowed purple, as usual, with an undertone of gold throughout. She rarely thought of it any longer since it meant little to Avner, even though it sometimes warmed in his presence.

Dov chuckled under his breath. "That may be the only thing worth mentioning about Chava."

The buyer came closer to her, the scent of salt and sweet perfume wafting through the hot air. "What is it?"

"She's bound to another gibborim, though I don't see him here."

"And you won't. Avner's too smart to be caught up in all this again," Chava lashed out, a thrill of pride running through her. *If* he was still free. Maybe it was better that he never tried to rescue them. A gibborim master like this wouldn't have hesitated to snatch up a prize like Avner, no matter the cost, as he said.

"Bound? As in property of?" The buyer raised one pale eyebrow.

"Something like that. She used ancient magic to save his life and tied hers to his," Dov said. "It's a pity he isn't here. If you were looking for a prize, it'd be him, what with his glowing blood."

The buyer inhaled sharply and grabbed Chava's hand, his skin smooth against her own. His hands were soft, smelling of moisturizers. She tried to pull away despite the pain in her raw wrists, but he held on, staring at the mark with such intensity he might have been trying to burn it off. "Did this gibborim with glowing blood used to be a pacifist by any chance?"

"Actually, he did. How did you know?" Dov asked, crossing his arms over his chest.

"Do you really think I could train the best gibborim in the world without having heard of the pacifist gibborim in Adamah with glowing blood? I'd always wanted to make it there to fight him, but the frost prevented me. As you say, he'd be a prize worth having." The man stroked the marriage mark.

Chava shuddered and tried to pull away again, but he let her hand drop and she over-balanced, almost falling into the lad behind her.

"I'll take her too." The buyer offered more coins to the Lorinyan.

Chava let out a captive breath. She might be sold as a slave, but at least she wouldn't be alone. Tevye shot her a tentative smile and she returned it.

"But sir, why? She's madder than the other woman!" Dov said, letting his arms drop.

"Because if I ever get the golden-blooded gibborim, I

want the set." He stepped back as the Lorinyan yanked Tevye out of the lineup.

When he came for Chava, she didn't protest, though Shoshanna growled low behind them as she was sorted out. Even knowing she wouldn't be separated from her friends, Chava bit her lip to keep from voicing her fears.

She had been bought as half of a pair she didn't feel a part of, yet all she wanted was to see the other half before she died in the arena without him.

10

TRUTH OWED

Avner

Avner's new traveling companion had been silent since they fled from the cursed fog in Curroon. They'd crossed grasslands and desert, and now a rocky mix of both. Each day was the same. Jog, walk, run. Bed down in the grass and consume their scant provisions. Sleep four hours and repeat it all in silence. Leewana had yet to comment any further on what happened with the fog, though he'd been fever-free since day two of their journey. No matter how many times he'd tried to get the answer out of her, she only glared and kept running.

Now Leewana's back bounced in front of him as she led the way over the shifting terrain, hopping from one stone to the next. Something about her from this angle reminded him of Rivka, one of his few gibborim friends who'd braved the frost to find her missing sons after they escaped. If he'd believed in Eloah, Avner might have sent a prayer asking for her success, but settled for muttering a hope under his breath.

Avner stopped short as a shape enlarged on the horizon. Walls with black specks moving in front of them.

"Is that Mereen?" he asked, forgetting Leewana wouldn't speak with him.

She slowed down and sank behind a cluster of bushes fifty paces from the main road which they still hadn't dared to use. Avner joined her, peeking through the branches to get a better understanding of where the Lorinyans had taken his friends. He clenched the branch so tight, a bit of it broke off in his hand.

"We're too late, aren't we?"

No caravan of slave wagons mingled outside the sandstone wall, though smaller groups of merchants and their wares entered the massive arched entrance. They'd followed the wagon trail carefully, and it was impossible for them to have passed the slavers somewhere on the journey here. A group that large couldn't just vanish.

"They will be inside, if not already sold." Leewana said, as if she'd been speaking with him this entire time.

Avner broke off another branch and dropped on his rear. "I *won't* give up on them."

Leewana studied him, her golden-brown eyes intense. "Do you have a plan?"

He'd been going over one for days, ever since they left the grasslands behind and the fever had cleared enough for him to think straight again, but he still didn't like it. Avner met her stare head-on.

"If they're so stringent about who is allowed inside, what sort of proof do they ask?"

"Either a ticket to the matches or certificates of invitation to compete as a gibborim team."

"Can't we just say we are looking to buy slaves?"

"They'd inquire about what sort of stock you are looking for. Even if they were to let two low-level people like us in, I've heard they escort buyers to the pens to ensure they purchase something."

"So, we will purchase my friends back."

She shook her head. "We don't have the money for that. Even if they are sold cheap, it would be more than either of us have, especially for all three."

"Then how do we get in?" Avner tossed away the broken branches.

Leewana's fingers ran over her faded red belt, a mystery she still hadn't explained. "The only way I see is to pretend to be a master and slave going to auction. But that still won't help us buy your friends, and we risk someone wanting to buy you, which would put us in a tricky situation."

"I'm guessing this isn't the town to be in a tricky situation." Avner didn't want to propose his own idea, but it still ran through his mind, all other options seeming too impossible. He didn't comment on Leewana's immediate assumption that he'd play the slave. He knew the part intimately.

"Red means a tournament is happening this week. Our first stroke of luck." Leewana pointed to a red flag on the top of the wall, flapping in the warm breeze.

Avner's pulse quickened, and he rose into a crouch. "What about the tickets you mentioned? Can we go as spectators?"

"I hear tickets were cheap last year, but now... Even the sale of my house wouldn't cover one ticket, let alone two."

Avner resisted breaking another branch. "So how is this a stroke of luck?"

"We can try to attach ourselves to a traveling gibborim crew and hope no one notices. There will be more traffic than usual this week."

"And if someone notices?" he asked, his hope sinking again.

Leewana frowned. "We're imprisoned for impersonating gaming officials or for entering without a ticket. They take all of this seriously here."

"Many commoners snuck in to watch us in Adamah." The words flowed out naturally, and he realized his mistake too late.

Leewana's face lost a bit of its color, and she sat back, eyeing him carefully. "*Us?*"

Curses and ash! What was he supposed to say now? He sat back down and remained silent. Would Leewana think of him as her husband did? A monster with no soul? Or would she listen and understand his past, since she clearly had one of her own?

He eyed her faded belt, but the fog was the more critical concern.

Steeling himself to divulge his ugly history, Avner said, "I'll tell you about my past if you explain about that fog."

Leewana sighed. She glanced again at the city. The thin line of people and carts entering didn't veer from the path. No one glanced at the two of them hiding in the shrubs. She turned back to him, a look of resignation on her face.

"The fog only affects those who don't believe in Eloah. To them, it's torture to their dead souls, but for me, and others like me, it's sweet nourishment. That's how I knew you didn't believe in Eloah. And I guess I shouldn't have been so upset. You never mentioned him, while your friends did."

The faint heat of a blush blended with the warmth of the sun on Avner's cheeks, though he knew he shouldn't feel ashamed for not believing in something that went against logic. But how could he comprehend what Leewana was saying?

"You mean the fog is supernatural, and you can control it to hurt those who don't believe in your Eloah?"

"No. Eloah controls it and uses it to press those who don't believe. I can do nothing with the fog without him. It's a sign of how he's turned our souls from the darkness within us to the light and freedom he brings. If you don't know the truth about him, you can't see the fog for what it truly is. You're blind. But now that I know about you. I won't call it again."

"Thanks." Not that Avner understood any of this, just as he didn't understand Chava's power when using the staff of Doram. He glanced at where it lay among the brush. Maybe there was a supernatural power in the world that Avner had never tapped into, but that didn't mean it was connected to Eloah.

"So, you were a gibborim?" Leewana pressed.

He owed her an explanation. She'd taken him this far, after all. Avner ran a dusty hand down his face, then traced one of the scars on his arm.

"Yes, I was a gibborim." The admission tore at his heart, and sitting here, so close to where others were fighting in the arena, it felt as if that part of him still existed. For once, it made sense how put-off Shoshanna was by Chava's presence, or his and Tevye's. No one should be forced to spend time with reminders of the evil deeds of their past.

"You fought in the arena?" Leewana paled.

"That is what gibborim do," he shot back, heat burning up his neck.

"Sorry," Leewana held up her hands. "You probably heard what my husband thinks of gibborim. You don't seem like that."

"A monster, you mean?" Avner gritted his teeth.

Leewana had the good sense to look away. He stopped short of telling her he *was* a monster.

"We all have monsters within us," she whispered, again touching her red belt. "That is why we need Eloah."

Even though she mentioned the deity, her words were a cool balm to his anger. She didn't curse him for being a monster, but admitted she was equally bad. What could this mother and wife have done that was so evil?

Leewana sighed. "I see it on your face. The question you don't need to ask. I chose a false freedom I thought this belt would give me by joining the fighting squad. When my brother was burned alive for believing in Eloah, I trapped myself in anger instead of choosing the path he wanted for me. Anger only led me to murder my best friend."

Avner stared. Though he wanted to press into the whole 'burning alive' thing, he kept the question simple. "And what path did your brother want for you?"

"Love." A small smile pulled at the corner of Leewana's mouth.

Not the response he expected. He'd be furious if someone burned anyone he cared about.

"I'm sorry about your brother," Avner said earnestly. "I didn't mean to be so harsh about being a gibborim. Being here, knowing what's going on in this city, and to my friends..." He trailed off. His plan increasingly appeared to be their only path to Chava, Tevye, and Shoshanna.

"You want to say you're a gibborim again, don't you?"

"I want nothing less, but it is the only way to get in. You'll be the gibborim master. You'll say the rest of your team died in a match somewhere else, and you need to enter me into the matches to earn enough money to buy more gibborim."

Leewana nodded. "It's a good plan, but you'll have to teach me how to act like a gibborim master."

Avner snorted. "That's the easy part. Act like you own the very air everyone else breathes, and cast judgements on every slave you see. Don't be kind to me, but also don't abuse me. Most masters want to keep their own stock in good condition." Reuben had. Avner's last encounter with this felt like a lifetime ago, not just two months.

"Are you sure you can do this? Return to that life, even for a charade?"

Avner snapped another twig in his palm. "I have to." For Chava, for Tevye. Shoshanna though... Maybe this was their chance to leave her behind.

The plan filled him with hope. He needed only to face the city and come out with his friends, minus the murderess. There would be no need for him to fight, or even go into the arena.

PURPLE CLOTH PURCHASED from a merchant outside the city walls. Rusted chains salvaged from junk in an alley beside the market. These were the only tools they procured for their charade. Avner hoped it would be enough, since all Leewana's warnings were proving accurate.

"Only gibborim teams and ticketed spectators allowed past this point. State your business." The hulking guard at the inner gate glared down at them, much like his companion at the outer gate had before letting them pass into the turmoil and chaos of the market.

The same market that had been devoid of Chava, Tevye or Shoshanna. Sold, just as Leewana feared, unless they were in the pens inside the arena proper. If so, breaking them out under the vigilant gaze of Lorinyans would be tough, but if not... Avner avoided dwelling on that possibility.

Leewana stood in front of Avner, her shoulders thrust back, and the purple cloth wrapped into a turban around her head. Avner hoped the cloth was enough to make her seem wealthy, as a gibborim merchant should be.

She yanked on the thick chains securing his wrists and he stifled a hiss. The chains were a necessity, but that didn't make them pleasant.

"I'm a gibborim master with my one surviving gibborim, come to fight to secure a larger team," Leewana said without wavering. Whoever she'd been before settling down, it showed through now.

The guard gave her a once-over, but when his gaze shifted to Avner, any doubt in his eyes disappeared.

"Aye, I see that. Go on, then." He waved them through.

Leewana yanked the chains and Avner stumbled forward, startled. She didn't have to play the part *this* well. But he wouldn't complain, since her act was working. They crossed from the hustle of the primary market into the smaller market before the arena. Large red-stone columns rose a hundred paces away, guarding the intricately-carved doors to what must be the arena. Avner looked away, not wanting to imagine the blood spilled beyond.

"There are more pens over there," Leewana whispered, and she tugged the chain more gently this time.

Avner followed willingly, eager to glimpse Chava or Tevye. The pens here weren't as full as the main ones, as fewer slaves were good options for gibborim. Lines of stone-faced men greeted them inside the pens, along with the occasional muscular woman. A flicker of red flashed between two dirty men in half-tunics, and Avner rushed to the bars. Leewana let out a sharp hiss. *Idiot!* A slave wouldn't run to the pens, but shy away, or be indifferent altogether. Forcing his rising nerves back down, Avner let Leewana approach the bars before him, while his gaze swept the slaves for another glimpse of Chava.

But it wasn't her. A red-haired lad slouched toward the back, his spirit broken as well as his arm. He'd die in his first match. Avner yanked his gaze away, his thudding heart betraying how disappointed he was that it wasn't Chava.

"Are they here?" Leewana whispered over his shoulder.

Avner looked again, but none of the slaves had an eye patch, and none were the unmistakable form of Shoshanna.

"No," he whispered back, trying to salvage his crashing hopes. What would they do now? What if whoever bought his friends had already taken them out of Mereen? He'd never track them down.

"So, they caught you too, Judge?" The familiar nickname came from a deep voice behind them.

Avner wheeled around, his chains clanking as he pulled Leewana with him. Dov stood ten paces away, unsurprised, as if he'd been expecting Avner, even this far away from Eder. He held a canteen in his burn-scarred hand.

"Chava claimed you weren't foolish enough to be caught, yet here you are. And already bought, by the looks of it." His gaze moved to the chains.

Avner almost broke his façade, ready to release the small pin they'd inserted so he could loosen the chains, and grab Dov by the shoulders. But at the last second, Avner lowered his hands like the contrite slave he should be.

"Where did you see them? Are they sold?" Avner kept his voice as level as possible. Never mind what Dov was doing here in Mereen, or how on earth he hadn't frozen to death.

"I'm assuming you mean Tevye and Chava. You surely aren't interested in Nuri."

Avner almost said no, but if Dov had seen her...

"Her too," he admitted. "She's helping us to stop the frost."

Dov threw his large head back and laughed. When he looked at Avner again, he wiped tears from his eyes. "You think that madwomen will help you do anything? She'll gut you as soon as look at you."

Avner knew this well, but now wasn't the time to let that worry distract him. He stepped as close as he dared.

"Just tell me, Dov. Did you see who bought them?"

"No one other than the gibborim master of all gibborim masters. Felix." He rolled the man's name off his tongue as if it meant something.

But Avner stared at his ex-comrade-in-arms, at a loss. "Am I supposed to know who that is?"

Dov shrugged. "I suppose not, but you will if you stay here long enough. If Reuben thought he was the best gibborim master, this man puts him to shame. He's a slaver from Smyma whose entire career is built on adding the greatest gibborim to his stock. Not just winning, but having only gibborim with massive reputations. Five times as many gibborim masters vie to fight his team as ever did Reuben's. A king among gibborim masters if there was one."

"Do you know him?" Leewana said, drawing Dov's attention for the first time. "You speak as if you worship the man."

Dov raised a brow. "This little thing thinks she can own the famous golden-blooded pacifist gibborim? You'd be better off selling him to Felix, who'd know how to put him to use."

"No one owns me anymore," Avner hissed.

A new light came into Dov's dark eyes. "Ah. So, this is a ruse to get close to your friends."

Leewana groaned.

Avner ignored her. Revealing their plan may have been a fatal mistake, but there was nowhere else to turn.

"Dov, doesn't it mean anything that we used to fight together? Tell me where I can find this Felix and help me get them out."

Dov scoffed. "You don't just get them out of here, or away from Felix, Judge. They are to fight in the games tomorrow. I understand why you'd want to free Tevye. He's a good man, if even a little too good. He saved my life his fair share of times, but it's not worth risking your own neck to get him back. My advice? Take your pretty new friend and start a new life as a free man. Chava isn't worth it. Nuri is so far from worth it, you'd be as mad as her to save her. And Tevye? He will do all right in the arena. He knows it. I could tell when I looked him in the eye."

Dov had looked Tevye in the eye here in this pit of hell, and refused to save him. Avner clenched his fist.

"Judge, I'm trying to be a friend." Dov raised his hands. "I've got my freedom and won't risk it for anyone. You should do the same. We were lucky enough to escape that frost, so don't die here in this desert."

Avner scoffed. How could Dov pretend to care about him when he so willingly left the others to die? He shouldn't even be here!

"How did you escape Adamah?"

Dov shrugged. "There was another, smaller boat in a cove around from the one I'm assuming you got on. Mostly nomads and members of the Clan, so Reuben must not have known it was there. Anyway, they took me on in exchange for helping to sail the thing, and brought me here. I met Felix right off when he was in the market looking for a gibborim advisor. Who better than a former gibborim?"

"You *helped* sell our friends to him?"

Dov shrugged. "Better to him than to the labor farms. As I said, take my advice and leave them. There's a whole world out there. Don't waste it." He gave Leewana another interested look, then turned and walked into the throng of gibborim masters, his large back melting into the crowd as it had so long ago in the snow of Adamah.

"I'm understanding both more and less of you, golden-blooded pacifist gibborim," Leewana said. "I noticed your blood. What does it mean?"

"Nothing," Avner mumbled. There was too much to tell. Too much to explain and not enough answers yet. He closed his eyes to the sight of men chained up like animals, but he couldn't block the groans, clanging metal, or rough cries. Sounds of gibborim training, or new weapons being forged so they might impale each other.

Avner opened his eyes to the great arena doors. Intricately-carved wood with large, magnificent brass hinges and handles, hiding the gruesome horror they held on the other side.

Tomorrow Chava, Tevye, and Shoshanna would be there.

"What are we going to do?" Leewana asked, his chains still in her grasp.

Avner exhaled, shivering... "Looks like I'm to be a true gibborim one more time."

11

TOKENS OF LUCK

Chava

R ed stone walls enclosed them deep within the
tunnels under the market above. Felix's guards had
led them through a myriad of halls, as if he wanted to ensure
they couldn't escape. If so, his plan had worked.

Chava was hopelessly lost.

Each cell they passed seemed just like dozens of others,
and every left turn soon ended in a 'T' leading to another
section of cells and torch-lit walls. The lack of sunlight after
the days of being carted across grassland was maddening,
and Chava longed to use the staff of Doram for light.

Except she'd left the staff for Avner. She could only trust
he'd found it and kept it safe.

"We're below the arena now," Tevye whispered
behind her.

"What?"

"Listen. You can hear the thrumming."

Chava strained to hear what he spoke of, but the

stamping of the guards' boots drowned out almost everything else.

Then she heard it.

A distant roar, rising and falling.

"That'll be the crowds."

"Quiet!" The guard barked.

Tevye didn't speak again. Chava winced at the chains
digging against her wrists as they reached the bottom of a
stone stairway and started up another. Shoshanna must still
be following, but Chava couldn't bear to see the pain etched
on the woman's face at their predicament, so she didn't turn
to check. She couldn't have slipped away in these catacombs
of death.

Their party climbed at least two dozen stairs, and Chava
was panting by the time they reached the top. She stepped
off the last step, half expecting the sun to flare into her eyes.

It didn't. They were still surrounded by the torch-lit walls
of a large room. Weapons lined the walls in bins like the
ones back in Eder's gibborim pens. Wooden doors were
centered on each wall. One of them creaked open and Felix
strode out, his golden hair tied at the base of his neck and a
smile brightening his pale eyes.

Chava hated that smile even more than she'd ever hated
Reuben's.

"Ah! My new prizes. Thank you, Gaul, for delivering
them to me." Felix nodded at the guard. "Now, if you'd
please go find them some weapons for a bit of a test to see
what I've purchased."

Gaul moved off into the far corner with the weapon bins
as two other guards emerged from the doorway behind
Felix. Of course, he wouldn't give them the slightest chance
to try something. Not that Chava had the skill to fight her

way out of an underground prison, with or without a weapon.

Felix chuckled, catching her thought. "Oh, no, my dear. You won't leave my possession until I see fit. Which, as of now, isn't until I have secured your more valuable half. Even then, I think I'll keep you both. I'm curious to see what these marks do when they're near each other."

He stepped up to her and reached for her hand as he had in the market. Chava jumped back.

He grabbed it anyway. "At least your spirit will help you stay alive in the arena, even if you don't know how to fight."

"If you want her alive, then why put her in the arena?" Tevye spat out.

"Interesting how this slave thinks he can demand answers from me, isn't it?" Felix asked the nearest guard.

The large man didn't bother to interject an opinion. Chava doubted Felix was one to entertain even solicited advice. The guard and his companion approached. Felix dropped her hand, and she had no option but to endure a rough pat down from the guards.

"No need to fret. They are just looking for anything the Lorinyans may not have confiscated," Felix said, amused.

"We have nothing." Chava had ensured that when she left the staff for Avner. He already had the knife and the bracelet. Nothing else mattered.

Shoshanna snarled as a guard snatched something out of her belt pouch. The green pommel stone shone as it caught the torchlight. Shoshanna tried to grab it back. The guard ducked, but Shoshanna's foot caught him in the chest. He staggered, dropping the stone.

She snatched it up before it had rolled two inches. She spun back to the guard and kicked him to the floor.

Shoshanna cinched her arm tight around his neck, the green stone pressing against his Adam's apple. The guard's boots scuffed against the stone floor, his limbs flailing uselessly as she choked the life out of him.

"Shoshanna!" Chava's protest was half-hearted. While the man deserved it, attacking Felix and his men wouldn't get them out of this mess.

Felix's laugh boomed through the underground chamber. He clapped, and the guard who'd inspected Chava stepped away from her. The butt of his sword hilt cracked against Shoshanna's head. She dropped away from her victim, but didn't release the green stone.

The guard she'd been strangling rolled over, hacking, and pushed himself up on trembling forearms. His comrade moved toward Shoshanna, who held onto her stone as if it alone preserved her life force.

Maybe in a way it did. She didn't know Eloah. Perhaps she found her comfort in a rock. At that moment, Chava suddenly understood. She stepped forward.

"Wait!"

Felix held up a hand and the guard stopped his advance while the one on the floor staggered to his feet.

"Do you wish to add to this show?"

"It's a good fortune charm," Chava said in a rush. "The rock. It's the only reason she made it seven years as a gibborim in Adamah."

Shoshanna's eyelids barely fluttered, but Chava could have sworn a look of gratitude flashed over her features.

The guard took another step closer, his rapier gleaming. Shoshanna snarled again and clutched the rock tightly to her chest.

"Stop," Felix commanded. "Let her keep the rock. She

will need the fortune in the arena. Besides, I imagine selling replicas of the '*Deranged Gibborim*'s' good luck token will bring in quite a fortune on its own. Ah! What a delicious idea!"

The guards backed away from Shoshanna, but she didn't relax. Gaul returned and gripped Tevye's bound hands. He yanked him toward a bucket of wooden swords. Chava started.

"Where are you taking him?"

"I like this," Felix said gleefully. "You're concerned for one another, yes?" His pale eyes flashed as he looked from Tevye, struggling in the guard's grip, to Chava, and then Shoshanna still sulking off to the side.

"You'll fight better if you care enough to protect each other." Felix clapped his hands again. "Yes! Perfect. You— deranged woman—will protect the redhead with your life. If she dies in the arena, you die. One of my archers will shoot you down the moment the golden gibborim's woman falls. Understand?"

Shoshanna glowered at him as she tucked the green stone back into her belt. Chava couldn't imagine she enjoyed being ordered about, but her own shoulders relaxed a bit. Chava's chances were better with Shoshanna guarding her.

"I'd say it is an excellent plan!" Felix chuckled, his giddiness a sharp contrast to the dim room and the dire circumstances. The smile gracing his face was enough to make him *almost* attractive.

Chava scoffed. He was horrible enough. He didn't need to look *agreeable*.

"You're insane," Tevye muttered.

"Yet I'm the one who owns you." Felix motioned to Gaul. The guard handed Tevye a gleaming, two-foot-long pronged spike like the fork he used to fight with in Reuben's arena.

Chava met Tevye's grim gaze. *Dov.* He must have told Felix their history. Leveraging their lives to ensure his own success.

"You will spar two on two, the third resting until their turn, for thirty minutes. After your ordeal in the grasslands, I won't waste your limited strength sparring since you fight in the morning. You, woman," Felix turned toward Chava. "Do you have *any* skills worth considering or do I have to trust your scarred friend to keep you alive?"

She could tell him Mikhail had trained her to snare rabbits, but she'd rather not turn that into snaring people. Instead, she leveled Felix with a flat look.

"I'll take that as a no."

"Felix!" The shout echoed down the hall he'd come from, along with the pounding of sandals on stone. Dov charged into the chamber and skidded to a stop, his hands on his knees as he caught his breath.

"Good ashes, man, what happened?" Felix turned toward him.

Dov glanced up, still panting. "He's here."

"Who?"

"Avner."

Felix stared blankly at him. Tevye dropped the prong with a clang.

Chava inhaled sharply. *No!* Her hope that Avner would come for them dashed against the stone floor. Avner didn't realize his reputation and how desirable he was to gibborim masters in Mereen. To Felix. How could one man stand up to Felix's resources?

Felix caught Tevye's reaction, then his gaze slid to Chava. She tried to force a calm expression, but it was too late.

Felix's smile widened with realization. "Avner is the golden-blooded pacifist gibborim."

"Yes. And he's in the market right now looking for *them*." Dov flung a large hand in Chava and Shoshanna's direction.

"What good fortune. It is decided then."

"What is?" Chava asked, dreading the answer.

"The scarred woman will protect you. You will stay to the side, but in full view of this Avner."

"I'll guard her too," Tevye picked the prong back up and crossed over to Chava, Gaul on his heels.

Felix shook his head. "No, I need you to join the rest of the team, killing off the opposing gibborim, or I won't win the match. I *always* win. Nothing about this match will be different, apart from drawing in the golden gibborim."

Tevye paled just like Chava. This was all to get Avner. A trap, and one she'd help spring against her will.

If she didn't die first.

Felix and Dov moved off to one side, Felix's bejeweled hand, such a contrast to his simple clothes, resting on the man's large shoulder. Dov nodded as Felix spoke, though the stone walls muted their voices as they discussed their plan to capture Avner.

But he wouldn't dare to come into the arena stands, would he? Even though he didn't know about the trap, he, like Shoshanna, wouldn't want to relive his past or be anywhere near the reminders of it.

Chava could only hope that was true.

Gaul shoved a training sword into her hands without unlocking her chains. *Eloah, please keep Avner away!*

Shoshanna's face remained stone-like as the guard

shoved a wooden sword into her hand. The other guards closed into a triangle formation, Gaul in the center, the training sword flashing toward Tevye. He blocked with his prong, and the session began.

The half-hour may have passed quickly, or achingly slow. Chava couldn't be sure. All she knew was that by the time she was deposited into a cell off the main chamber, her limbs shook with fatigue, and the vision of Avner draped in chains wouldn't leave her mind. Shoshanna sank to the ground opposite her, her head hanging between her knees and her slumped shoulders. Tevye sat beside her, staring silently into the dim corner.

Shoshanna finally raised her head. Her flecked eyes met Chava's and there was no encouragement in those irises, only death.

For them, and for Avner if Felix's trap closed in on him.

12

LIVING NIGHTMARE

Shoshanna

"I give you a new gibborim—a woman! But not just any woman, for she is a ferocious, battle-hardened warrior. She comes to us bound under madness after surviving the captivity of the nomads. Now she will fight for a chance at eternal glory. I give you... NURI!" Reuben's voice rang out across the ice, his arms flared wide before the dozens of spectators who had come to see his newest prize.

Nuri gripped her twin blades and stepped over the line of crushed leaves on the ice and into the fighting ring. She planned to finish her first one-on-one arena match within two minutes.

The dream—or memory—which tormented her sleep still haunted Shoshanna as she waited on the dark side of the arena doors. Would this match mirror that first one? She'd finished her opponent in one minute, not two. Reuben had never filled the crowd in on what made her a battle-hardened warrior or how she'd come to be mad, but they'd loved her all the same. Would anyone have protested if they had known the truth?

Shoshanna switched her weight from one foot to the other, testing how the sand shifted with her movement. Even this simple action grated against every muscle, defying her not to partake in something she'd vowed to never do again. But she'd never imagined becoming a slave again, and the situation was not something she could simply erase.

Tevye stood as still as stone on her right side, facing the luxuriously ornate wooden door separating the gibborim from the arena. He held a slingshot, and the prong hung in his belt. If he hated being cast back into the position he'd left behind, he didn't voice it.

Chava stood at Shoshanna's other shoulder, moving restlessly. Her mass of wild hair had been pulled into a rough braid by one of Felix's servants, while Chava continued to protest that she didn't have any fighting skills. Their brief spar yesterday had proved it. Shoshanna knew the girl would fall first.

If she let her.

But when she looked at Chava, she only saw Reuben. Shoshanna drew a thin breath and shoved the thought of him away. After all, it was only because of her former master that she had the skills needed to survive today. Perhaps she should thank him.

You're one of a kind, Nuri! To survive seven years as a gibborim... It's unheard of! His voice, filled with wonder, resonated in her mind, even though it wasn't real like the nervous whispering of the three other gibborim they were paired with.

"Go away," Shoshanna whispered to Reuben's ghost, though part of her longed to turn and see if he was hiding in the tunnels leading back to the cells and talk to him about the match ahead. Outline a plan to neutralize the strongest competitor, using Reuben's knowledge gained from another master.

Shoshanna swallowed the lump in her throat. Reuben would never chat with her again. She took a deep breath, rolling her neck from side to side. If this was going to happen, couldn't they get it over with?

Tevye muttered something similar.

Chava looked at him sharply. "Eloah is with us, Tevye."

He nodded, short and curt. "Aye, that he is."

Their deity *wasn't* with them, but cutting down their hope seemed foolish now. They would need every ounce of hope they could muster the moment this door opened. If Shoshanna was to obey her new master's wishes and protect Chava at all costs, she'd need every scrap of luck and concentration she had. She glanced at Tevye. His stoic face said he knew the same. Felix was a fool to trust Chava's life to the arena if he valued her so much.

But he's trusting her to you, Shoshanna, Itzaak whispered.

And if she didn't save Chava, Shoshanna would die.

The heavy hinges creaked, and the massive door inched open. A voice roared beyond it.

"—unusual guests from the land of Adamah! Combined, they have over nine years of experience in the arena, a feat itself worthy of eternal glory!"

More like eternal shame.

Sunlight flared in the widening crack of the slowly opening door. She gripped the smooth hilts of the knives she'd been given. This Felix possessed fine weapons, even for his gibborim. He cared about the show, about the reputation. She'd shred both, then shred him, the moment she had the chance, for forcing her to relive the memory of her first match. Dov was right about her, and Felix should have listened to him.

She caught her breath at the Nuri-like thought. Shouldn't she strive to think like Shoshanna?

There wasn't time to answer the question. The white sunlight gleamed in her face, and the roar of a waiting crowd crashed over her. Her eyes snapped open to an arena swimming in light, surrounded by massive columns and rows of spectators seated beyond. It was impressive, even in her colorless vision, and so unlike Lake Kefa with its heavy snow clouds, and torches blazing against the ice.

"Warriors!" The announcer's voice rang out again. "May you fight valiantly as you fight to the death in this black match!"

"Black?" Tevye said, aghast. "Is this Felix trying to get us all killed in our first fight for him?"

"I'm testing you." Felix emerged from the doorway's shadows. He smiled and held out his bejeweled hands, the sun catching two gems the size of his fingernails. Shoshanna didn't need color to know how opulent they were compared to what he had worn in the market yesterday. He was here to show off.

"If you live through this, you truly are what Dov claims. If you don't, I don't need to bother to feed you any longer, and can look to the next gibborim."

"But what of Chava?" Tevye cut in. The fool.

Felix's eyes glistened as he took in the woman. "If the golden-blooded gibborim's woman dies in this arena, he will only have more reason to seek me out, won't he?"

Chava choked on what sounded like a squeak.

"Your death isn't my preference, of course," he added, as

if that made his words less offensive. "I'd prefer the set of you, but a vengeful gibborim coming to find me is better than just you. I'm choosing to trust Dov's assessment of your friends and believe you will *all* make it out." Felix clapped. "Now, out you go. Show me what you can do."

Tevye clenched his jaw and walked into the sun, the roar of the crowd erupting louder. Chava adjusted the heavy ax in her grip and followed him out. Shoshanna pushed past them and entered the arena. The noise of the crowd washed over her, just as it had on the ice. She shuddered, drawing the knives closer to her chest, as if that might shelter her in a bubble of safety that her opponents, her master, or the crowd couldn't break through.

The announcer shouted something again, and a door on the opposite end of the stone ring opened. Six dark shapes emerged, their weapons gleaming wickedly. Chava's shadow fell over her, followed by their three other companions, men Shoshanna hadn't bothered to meet. They'd be dead in a matter of minutes, anyway.

Her blood pounded in her ears, urging her to turn and run, to overcome her disdain for begging, and plead for her freedom back.

But a gong sounded loud and clear, signaling that flight was no longer an option. The doors clanged shut on either side of the arena.

The match had begun.

"Chava, get to the side and stay there! I'll keep them off you," Tevye shouted as he fitted a stone from his pouch into the sling shot. He raised, aimed, and let the strap fly. The stone sang through the air and smacked into the forehead of the unlucky first opponent. He dropped into the sand, and the gibborim behind him jumped over his prone form with little hesitation.

The chaos was so familiar, and so hated, that Shoshanna froze. Her body refused to engage as the others raged and screamed around her. Something flashed in her side-vision, but it could have been Chava's hair or someone's body. The world begged to black out, the edges of her vision flickering darker as they used to before she'd remembered who she was. Shoshanna wheezed, covering her face, as her body refused to cooperate. She was going to die here, frozen by her past like the fool she was.

"Shoshanna! Take him out before he gets to Chava!" Tevye's voice cracked through to her numb mind.

A whoosh of air warned of a sword flying toward her. Instinct and muscle memory overrode her anxiety. Her mind broke free from the grip of the past as her opponent prepared to stab her. Shoshanna ducked the whirring blade, spun to the side and popped back up, her knives flying before her. They sank, one after another, into the attacker's torso, a malnourished man whose eyes widened with relief as he left this world.

Someone yelled behind her. Chava. Shoshanna tore away from her victim as the first man Tevye hit sprang back up. She dodged right to avoid tripping over him and whipped her knives across his throat. He fell, gurgling in his flowing blood. Not seeing any color was a relief for a change, as she didn't need the sight of bright blood to make things worse. Her fingers tightened around the hilts of her knives as she pummeled into Chava's would-be attacker, a female gibborim whose eyes were wild with the fight. Her whip snaked back as she staggered to the side, and Chava careened into the sand, her ankle still wrapped in the weapon. The ax lay a foot away, useless.

The woman's fingers clawed at Shoshanna's neck, digging into her rash, but Shoshanna ignored the pain and stabbed the knife in the woman's chest, pinning her to the sand.

Three down, three to go.

Chava yelled again and Shoshanna jumped up in time to catch the next gibborim in the gut with her foot. The dark-haired man staggered back, gasping at the impact. His face whipped up, his gray eyed-gaze piercing her.

"Avner?"

Dov hadn't mentioned Avner *fighting* in the tournament.

Avner ran toward Chava. "Move! One of them has a crossbow!"

Shoshanna didn't stop to ask what in the blazes he was doing there, but spun and dragged Chava two feet to the side. A crossbow bolt sank into the sand where she'd been lying.

"Roll!"

Shoshanna didn't need Avner's instruction. She rolled, pulling Chava with her, as three more bolts hit the sand behind them. Avner hissed as one of them glanced off him, golden blood spilling from his shoulder.

The crowd gasped along with Shoshanna. She could *see* his blood! She looked at her hands, but the blood coating them was still dark gray. Chava's hair—gray. Avner's blood on the sand—gold.

What the...

The crowd's stunned silence fell over the arena, matching Shoshanna's shock. But before she could take a breath to clear her confusion, the silence shattered and steadily crescendoed into a wild chant Shoshanna couldn't make out.

The Judge jumped up, glowing blood trickling down from the wound in his shoulder to pool into the sand at his feet. Shoshanna couldn't look away. She was so used to her cursed gray sight. The gold tore through it—unnatural, beautiful.

"Tevye! Take him out!" the Judge yelled.

The Judge. In here, that was who he was. Not Avner, but the gibborim he used to be.

Tevye, standing fifty paces away, jerked around at the sound of the Judge's voice. Hope gleamed in his eye, but his face shared Shoshanna's confusion. If the Judge had come to free them, he was going about it entirely wrong.

Tevye raised his slingshot, but before he could launch a stone, one of the other remaining gibborim lunged out of the shadows of the wall, his face streaked with blood, and his hands clenched around twin axes.

He'd reach Chava first and cut her down as she struggled to stand up. The Judge saw him coming and launched himself between them.

"Chava! Get back!" he screamed in desperation.

Silence held the crowd as they no doubt wondered why an opposing team member was trying to protect his enemy. Then a collective shocked gasp swept the stands as the Judge's sword sank into the man's belly. The twin axes jerked overhead, and the man stood frozen, choking. The Judge withdrew the sword and the man dropped to the ground. Clearly, the Judge didn't need a staff to kill.

Four down. One on their side, one left to kill. All three of the other gibborim on her own team were dead as well.

Shoshanna ripped her gaze away from the Judge's golden blood burning through her dark world and spun, knives ready. An adrenaline Nuri used to love pulsed through her, and a half-satisfied, half-horrified groan escaped between her clenched teeth. Ecstasy and torture all in one breath. The crowd stared down, twice as large as any she'd fought in front of before, putting her in her rightful place. They didn't know her, but they knew this was where she belonged.

That's not true, Itzaak whispered in the back of her mind. *You belonged with me.*

But he was dead. So did that mean she needed to die?

The remaining gibborim hadn't seen the Judge take down their teammate, and seemed to think they were still on the same side, waving for him to attack. He shouted something unintelligible.

"Chava, don't let that man near you until we finish this," the Judge breathed heavily.

Chava nodded and grabbed the ax, though doing so almost made her tip over. Tevye refitted his slingshot and let it fly. Their remaining opponent dodged it, and shot another bolt from his crossbow at Tevye who narrowly missed being impaled by dropping behind the woman's dead body.

"Let's end this," Shoshanna said under her breath. She broke into a sprint.

A resounding gong cut her off. A voice, amplified by a cone, boomed from the upper stands.

"There seems to be confusion about which side the golden-blooded gibborim is on. His team's owner is demanding back-up to make up for the loss he caused. We will now pause for one minute to allow the additional gibborim to be made ready."

Shoshanna slid to a halt, sand spraying in an arc in front

of her. The other man stood ten paces away, eyes narrowed, his crossbow pointed at her. Let him have back-up. It wouldn't do any good.

13

A DIFFERENT KIND OF GIBBORIM

Avner

He was back in the arena, though it was so different from the ice he was used to.

Pausing for backup? Nothing like that had ever happened back on Lake Kefa, and Reuben would have been ashamed to allow it. But this magnificent arena, surrounded by two layers of red stone and massive columns, proved the gibborim masters of Mereen expected something else entirely.

Avner fought to catch his raging breath, drawing in the hot air, only to choke on the coppery tang of blood that came with it. Chava stood beside him, the ax clutched to her chest, but to her credit, she didn't shake.

"What are you doing here?" she demanded breathlessly, as if he hadn't just risked life and limb to save her.

Avner scoffed, adrenaline thundering through him. "I'm saving you! But I guess you couldn't bother to be grateful for that, could you?"

"Grateful? You're a slave like the rest of us and I'm supposed to be thankful?" Her arms sagged under the weight of the massive ax. What had the gibborim master been thinking to give her that?

The opposing gibborim didn't lower his crossbow, the bolt trained between Avner's eyes. Avner would take him out first. The success of taking down a gibborim warmed his core. Being here wasn't good for him, but there'd been no alternatives. He wasn't sure what good he was doing, apart from ensuring the others still lived.

"Chava, stay back while we finish this," he said.

Chava bristled under his command. "I'm not worthless out here, you know."

"Yet I had to thrust myself back into this life to save you!" Avner whirled on her, taking his eyes off the gibborim with the crossbow.

"I didn't ask you to do that! In fact, I was glad Eloah had spared you from this!" She dropped the ax, letting it thud into the sand. Her face was burned by the sun, and a few blisters bubbled on the red skin of her neck.

Avner's temper cooled, but before he could say anything else, the announcer's voice split the arena again.

"Aaand here they come!"

The door on the far side creaked open, releasing three more gibborim. Four on four, since Chava's other teammates were dead. As fair as it would get. A strange rush of air swept through the arena, and sand swirled around the group of new gibborim in a spiral. But no, that couldn't be right... Avner inhaled sharply. The sand *kept swirling* around the group, even as the wind moved off. It hung suspended in the air, as if held there. A woman gibborim standing within the sand held her arm up, sweating, almost as if *she* was the one keeping the sand around them.

Impossible.

"What in the..." Chava trailed off.

"Looks like we have a Manipulator in this new batch!" The announcer roared.

The crowd screamed wildly.

Avner didn't have a chance to dwell on what that meant. Something shrieked past his ear, and he dropped just in time to see the crossbowman reloading. He hadn't waited for the command to resume fighting. Chava yelled something unintelligible behind him, but Avner couldn't reach her before the next bolt sank into her hand. She screamed, the sound ripping straight into his chest.

"You idiot, Chava! Get out of the way!" He yelled, adrenaline and panic driving him forward. He shouldn't care this much that she'd been hurt, but he launched straight into the crossbowman and tackled him to the ground, impaling him with the sword before the man had a moment to fight back. Avner jumped off his body and met the next gibborim head on.

Sand danced around the woman. Her eyes were slightly slanted like his, but were a luminescent pale green. They widened as she took in the blood glowing on his shoulder.

"I've heard of you—"

Avner didn't give her time to finish. He cut his sword to the side. The sand fell to the ground as the woman jumped back. She thrust her hands forward, and a blast of air whirled into Avner, stealing his breath for several seconds.

What was this woman?

She raised her hand again, and Avner did the same with his sword. Her supernatural air couldn't stop steel. He jumped forward. Sand flew into his face and up his nose. He stabbed the sword blindly, but wasn't rewarded with any contact. Curses and ash!

The crowd screamed even louder.

Wiping the sand from his eyes, he spun around again to face the woman standing behind him now, one hand out and the other gripping a gleaming saber. As she raised her free hand, another gust of wind, ten times stronger than natural, slammed into Avner. The intense force made it impossible for him to take in oxygen. Avner tried to push his way out of the barrage, but the wind pressed even harder, cutting off his air. The woman's eyes glowed a fiercer green as she stepped closer, her hand out, shoving the wind up Avner's nose and into his mouth.

His lungs screamed for air. His eyes watered. He was going to suffocate on this cursed sand...

A blur of red smashed into the woman. The wind cut off and Avner fell to his knees, pulling in blessed air. Chava's shouts rang out and Avner glanced up to see her flying backward as the wind answered the gibborim's unnatural call. Chava hit the ground and lay still, though her chest still rose and fell. The roar of the crowd couldn't get any higher. They *loved* this show.

Avner gritted his teeth. He needed to remove this woman before she did any real damage. He stepped toward her as she raised both hands. Sand shot into the air, twisting into a funnel, and moved straight for Tevye, who'd stepped away from his opponent to reload his slingshot. The sand hit him, drowning out Avner's warning yell.

He'd be suffocated by the sand, or worse, eaten by it.

Avner ran for the woman. He'd take her out and end this now. Tevye's scream cut through the roar of the wind and sand. A bloody leg stuck out of the pillar of revolving sand as it raised Tevye into the air. Five feet, ten, then twenty. The woman continued to raise her hand as her malicious smile widened.

She was going to let him drop. Tevye was going to fall to his death. Avner slid to a halt just as the woman raised her other hand at him. More sand shot straight for him. Avner ducked, but the sand tore through his skin, anyway. Impossible. Brutal. Avner screamed. The roar of the wind and stinging bite of the sand devoured him.

Until it stopped without warning. Burning sunlight replaced the burning sand. Avner inhaled and looked up. The woman stood still, one hand still elevating Tevye in the pillar of sand. Was he even alive inside it?

"I was ordered not to kill you," the woman said between heavy breaths. "But I can kill *him*." She closed her palm.

"No!" Avner pushed up and sprinted toward the pillar.

Avner's heart dropped as Tevye plummeted down with the sand. Something cracked as he landed on another unlucky gibborim. Though Avner wanted nothing more than to run and see if Tevye still lived, he couldn't risk it while the woman remained standing.

She'd admitted her weakness. Letting Avner live.

He spun toward her and attacked before she could raise her hand again. She parried his sword with the edge of her dagger, though it was only half the size of his weapon and wouldn't protect her for long.

Avner hesitated, his sword falling away.

She jerked away. Cursing, Avner followed, cutting his sword into her path. The woman fell, screaming, trying to grasp her missing arm.

The screams from the crowd shifted to a unified groan,

like some wounded animal. Avner scoffed. He'd taken down their favorite. He ignored the pleasure of his excellent strike and stuffed it deep down with his worry for Chava. This wasn't who he wanted to be, and he wouldn't return to it now out of desperation. But at least this gibborim couldn't use her unearthly power anymore.

"Av!" Tevye's voice rang out over the chaos.

Avner's heart leapt, and he glanced back to where Tevye had fallen. The gibborim who'd broken his fall lay still at an awkward angle, dead. Tevye stood several feet away, facing off with the final opposing gibborim.

Before Avner could step up to help, Shoshanna came flying out of who-knew-where, jumped over Chava who was cradling her hand, slit the sand-woman's throat, and sank a knife into Tevye's opponent's neck. The man jerked and toppled into a pile of immobile limbs. Shoshanna landed on the other side of him, panting, a wicked gleam in her speckled eyes. She would always be the deadliest gibborim in history, no matter who she became next.

Silence settled over the arena, baited and expectant. Avner gulped for breath. They'd won. But instead of cheering, the audience followed the gazes of the spectating gibborim masters in the dais far above as they moved toward the arena entrance.

Avner's blood pounded.

The mammoth gate creaked open once again, and a line of guards marched out. Avner spun around and ran for Chava. He only managed to brush her shoulder, his finger catching on her coarse wool tunic, before he was yanked off, the stench of man and sweat rolling over him.

"Avner!" Chava's yell followed him back into the darkness of the tunnels below the arena, and the door clanged shut.

14

THE GREATEST GIBBORIM MASTER
IN THE WORLD

Avner

The torches outside Avner's cell flickered in time with the voices rising and falling out of view. The arena's noise failed to penetrate the maze of tunnels down below. No one stood guard outside his cell, as each gibborim master was responsible for their own stock. The men who put Avner here had left without answering his questions about his friends. He had no idea what had happened to Chava, Tevye, and Shoshanna. Leewana, who was supposed to meet him after the match, hadn't come to fetch him yet.

Would he remain behind these bars? Would they let Leewana take him back after he'd massacred his own team in the arena? Would he spend the rest of his life as a slave?

Avner gripped the rough bench he was sitting on, trying to force his spiraling thoughts under control. He'd make it out. They had a plan. This wouldn't be the end of his freedom.

But his heart thudded treacherously fast.

Where was Chava? Maybe Tevye was caring for her injured hand now in their own cells. Shoshanna was probably grumbling about Chava's poor performance.

Avner gritted his teeth. His resentment of Shoshanna waned, but he didn't want it to. She may have helped to protect Chava in the arena, but that didn't redeem everything she'd done.

The distant voices cut off, and footsteps scuffed down the hall. Avner jerked off the bench, wincing at the sudden pain in his shoulder. Mereen gibborim masters had a salve for wounds, but it didn't take the pain away like Reuben's had. Avner didn't enjoy wishing for things he'd been given as a slave.

Leewana appeared around the corner, scowling.

"Are you a complete idiot?" She stopped three feet from the bars, the staff of Doram in one hand. They'd agreed she wouldn't let it out of her sight while he was fighting. "How did this contribute to saving your friends?"

"I don't recall you having any better suggestions."

Leewana pulled a key out of her belt. "You're lucky they are letting me take you back. As soon as the match was over, three game officials found me and demanded repayment for the men you killed on your own team. Their owner had only agreed to take you as part of his team to get profits from your share of the winnings, but now he's in debt and out *seven* gibborim!"

"I assumed you wouldn't care about their politics. And thank you for keeping the staff safe."

"Apparently it and this knife," she pulled the leather sleeve containing Yor's knife out of her bag and handed it over, "are the only things I can 'keep safe'. As for politics, I didn't care about them until they threatened to enslave us both to repay the debt." Metal clanked against metal as she inserted the key and opened the door. Avner's heart rate slowed down, but he wouldn't breathe easy again until he saw Tevye and Chava.

Minding his wounded shoulder, he accepted the knife of Yor and slipped its leather sleeve in his own belt, pulling his shirt down to hide it. He'd let Leewana carry the staff for now, as a gibborim walking around with one would look suspicious, especially if anyone knew who Avner was and what weapon he favored. Though the audience had seen his glowing blood, it seemed unlikely anyone would have heard of him way out here.

Avner stepped around the gate of his cell.

"At least I ensured they all lived through the match," he murmured more to himself than to Leewana. There *must* be a way out of here for all of them that didn't end in being dragged, lifeless, from the arena.

"That one friend of yours, Shoshanna? She didn't need any help in that arena. It seemed like second nature to her." Leewana led him down the longest corridor, where the air didn't smell as foul.

"She's not my friend, but yes, she was a gibborim once too."

"I understand the impulse to fight, to see it as the sole solution." Leewana's fingers stroked the faded belt. "But I'm free of that now, thank Eloah."

Booted footsteps stopped Avner from asking more, and brighter torchlight crept along the tunnel. Leewana held out a hand and they both stopped short.

"Remember, you're a gibborim master," Avner whispered. "You're allowed to be down here. And I'm allowed to be anywhere you are."

Leewana nodded, stiff-backed, as light filled the hall, revealing two men entering.

"You there! Owner of the golden-blooded gibborim."

Leewana squared her shoulders. "Yes?"

"Felix wants to see you. He proposes a way out of your debt," the guard said with a sneer. His turban almost touched the arched ceiling above them, and he moved his hand to the rapier in his belt. "I'd suggest going to see him, or we won't have any choice but to lock you and your slave back in the cells until this matter is sorted out."

His partner chuckled, as if nothing would be more entertaining.

"What is this Felix offering?" Avner asked, only to curse himself. He was supposed to be a slave, for ashes' sake! He shouldn't be asking questions.

The guard glared at Avner, but then his eyes went to the dried blood on his shoulder. "If I know anything about Felix, he will give your master much in exchange for you."

Avner met Leewana's gaze, and her eyes mirrored the same understanding dawning on him. Felix owned Tevye and Chava and was the formidable master Dov worked for. A new plan began to form, though he couldn't speak outright again.

So, he gave a small nod.

Leewana's eyes widened, and she leaned close so the guards wouldn't hear. "How does that help?"

Avner raised his brow and inclined his head an inch toward the guards. *Ashes, she'd better understand.*

She scowled at him, her dark face and features so unlike Chava's, but just as stubborn. Was it Avner's curse to only ever be surrounded by such women? He squared his shoulders. Leewana gave a shrug of resignation.

She faced the guards. "Take us to Felix."

THE MASTER of all gibborim masters had rooms on the upper level of the arena complex. The air here smelled of citrus and a spice Avner couldn't name. Leewana inhaled and made a face.

"Cardamom. It's expensive. Not that we needed further proof of Felix's insane wealth."

Avner agreed. Sheer purple curtains hung in the windows, shifting in and out with the breeze. Plants in brass pots stood in each corner beside padded chairs with gilded armrests and tables laden with assorted fruits. The arena stretched out in perfect view below. No doubt this was how Felix had witnessed Avner's blood. Now all signs of blood had been freshly raked from the sand, and all bodies had been carried off. The decadence of this arena clashed sharply with the death on the sand. At least the ice had been true to the brutality of the matches it held.

Dov stood next to the windows talking to the man who must be Felix. If he wasn't Smyman, Avner wasn't a trained gibborim. Blonde hair was rare enough that the few people Avner had met with it had always come from the land west of Adamah.

Felix lounged casually against the railing, his silk sleeve brushing the red stone, as if he hadn't just watched men and women massacred below. As if he were nothing more than another smiling silk merchant from Smyma.

But his dusty and practical sandals told another story. Felix trained gibborim and put in work usually reserved for his subordinates.

Avner hated everything about him.

Handing Dov a small coin pouch, Felix laid a hand on the shoulder of a boy standing beside him who couldn't be older than ten. Felix ruffled the boy's unruly brown curls and bent, whispering something in his ear. The boy's eyes reflected uncertainty. Felix's smile widened.

Dov yanked the boy's arm and escorted him past Avner to the door. Dov didn't meet Avner's glare. How dare he buy a *child?*

"Now isn't the time," Leewana hissed in his ear.

She was right. Tevye and the others mattered far more, even if Avner's heart ached for the lad. Dov and the boy vanished out the door Avner had come through.

"Ah! My good fellow master!" Felix held his hands wide toward Leewana. "I'm sorry, but I hadn't caught the name of the woman lucky enough to possess such a specimen as the man before us."

Leewana did not bow as Avner had advised her to do, but he couldn't blame her. Everything about the luxury of these apartments made his skin crawl.

"I am Namira, gibborim master to Numeralli," Leewana said without a flicker of doubt.

Felix raised one pale eyebrow. "I hadn't heard that Numeralli had joined in the gibborim trade. Too preoccupied with their imaginary Eloah deity."

"I am the first, hence my small team," she smiled so wryly Avner almost believed her.

But a whole town on this continent believed in Eloah, and everyone knew it. What kind of place was this?

"And how did you come to own the Golden Gibborim of Adamah?" Felix stepped closer, and the scent of cardamom came with him.

Heat burned up the nape of Avner's neck. He even had a nickname among other gibborim masters? Had Reuben known? Avner held back a scoff. Or had he started the rumors himself? Thankfully, he was probably dead from the frost.

"I traded my wagon to buy this gibborim not a week ago," Leewana said seamlessly, as they'd planned. "I hear you are looking to purchase him?"

"And *I* hear you are swimming in debt after your prized slave helped my team take out his own, plus their backups." Felix said with a smile, his eyes glittering as if he'd enjoyed every moment of the match.

"What are you offering?" Leewana's voice dripped with caution now, as would a gibborim master who feared being robbed blind after being cornered like a stray dog.

Felix brushed his shoulder length hair behind his ear and clapped his hands. Guards wearing the same breezy style of clothing appeared from the apartment's far doorway. Three figures stood between them.

Tevye's face was streaked with dirt, and Shoshanna's rash had disappeared into the burned skin, leaving her more murderous-looking than she'd been in the arena.

But it was the sight of Chava that drew Avner forward. She stood between them, her eyes wild with defiance and her hair in a tangled braid. He'd known she was alive after leaving the arena, but seeing her now...

Leewana hissed at him. He forced himself back, his fists clenched at his side. Chava's left hand hung at her side, bandaged and well-cared for, but Avner's nerves didn't settle. Her gaze fell on the staff of Doram in Leewana's grasp and relief swept over her freckled face. Avner tried to give her an encouraging smile, but he feared it was more of a grimace.

"I propose a trade," Felix said, sweeping his hands wide toward Avner, then his friends. "Two of my new stock for your famous one."

"Trade? How does this pay off my debts?" Leewana scoffed.

A trade wouldn't get Avner any closer to freeing any of them. He almost whispered as much to Leewana, but Felix interjected.

"You can sell the gibborim to pay it. It should be enough to cover that fool's low-bred stock the Golden Gibborim massacred."

"You said yourself this one gibborim is a prize." Leewana yanked Avner's sleeve and forced him to stand in front of her.

"If this slave is worth so much, I demand coin up front, as well as all three of these gibborim," Leewana said, her voice firm.

Felix threw his head back and laughed, the sound too jovial to come from someone who made a fantastical profit watching other men die. "You prove how new you are at this, Namira. Tell you what, since you amuse me and I don't want to crush your budding career so early, I'll take pity on you. I'll give you two of these gibborim, as well as pay off the debt you owe the other master. Deal?"

"Which two?" Leewana countered.

Avner drew in a breath, not daring to hope it would be Tevye and Chava. Maybe he'd finally be rid of Shoshanna and her murderous stares. Guilt rose within him, but he squashed it. They could let her rot for all she'd done, and she would probably think she deserved it. Even now, her strange gaze pierced him, as if she knew his thoughts.

"The crippled man and the killer woman. I will keep the redhead," Felix said.

"No," Avner breathed. Not Chava.

Felix stared at him for the first time, as if he'd been denying himself that pleasure until the latest possible moment. He raised a tanned hand and approached, a new look of hunger growing in his eyes.

"Ah, yes, you are bound to the red woman, aren't you? May I?" he asked Leewana without taking his eyes off Avner.

She grunted and he took it as permission. His callused palms, such a contrast to his jeweled fingers, slid over Avner's right hand, his thumb brushing across the marriage mark. The three intersecting rings still shone dark purple. Tingles followed everywhere the vile man's skin touched his, and Avner jerked back.

Felix clicked his tongue and turned to Chava. He snapped his fingers. "Come."

She scowled at him and crossed her arms over her chest, wincing as her wounded hand hit the other. A guard yanked Chava out of the line.

"I'm not a thing to be manhandled—"

The guard backhanded her. Chava cried out and her eyes watered.

"Stop it," Leewana hissed. "I won't have you abusing a slave, even if she isn't to be mine."

Felix raised a brow at that. "So, you agree to my terms?"

Leewana's dark golden eyes smoldered. "I haven't said that yet."

But it was clear she needed to agree as Felix pried Chava's uninjured hand from her side and stroked it as he had Avner's. "You two have some sort of servitude or connection to each other I can't quite figure out. But given time, I will."

Avner would see to it that opportunity never came. There was no way around this trade for now. At least Tevye would be free, even if that included Shoshanna. The woman could help keep the staff safe, and Avner could keep Chava in his sights and ensure she survived until a chance came for escape.

Leewana's fingers pinched his shoulder harder. Avner nodded, hoping she'd understand what he intended. Her hand fell away after another moment's hesitation.

"I accept your terms," she said, her voice heavy with uncertainty.

"Excellent!" Felix released Chava's hand and motioned for the guards to escort Tevye and Shoshanna over.

Avner took two steps closer. If he took a third, he'd be a slave again, after nearly two months of freedom. The knowledge weighed heavily on his shoulders, and his chest tightened, robbing him of air. This was all because of his blood. Because of some unsolvable mystery cursing him.

Tevye stepped up to him from the other side of the line and their gazes met. Suppose they fought their way out? Tevye's eyes narrowed, glancing at the first guard, then the second, then Felix, then to the corridor they'd come from. Shadows were framed against the wall. Broad shoulders and spears. Any hope of escape dissolved with the realization that they'd be apprehended less than a few steps away from Felix.

A post-deal escape route must exist. Avner had survived the impossible before. He could overcome this.

He took the third step, and a broad smile spread over

Felix's face. Avner almost turned and ran back to Leewana, but he gritted his teeth as Shoshanna and Tevye moved to her side. The deal was done, and his freedom was gone.

15

THE GOLDEN GIBBORIM

Avner

He was a slave again.

The icy claws of panic dug into Avner's chest, and he struggled to take his next breath. He made the mistake of meeting Chava's eyes. They glowed with an emotion he couldn't identify. He glanced away, his heart pounding.

"Excellent!" Felix snapped his fingers, and the guards joined Avner on either side.

A glance behind showed Tevye whispering with Leewana, but she waved him down. She lifted the staff an inch off the floor and waited, staring hard at Avner. He shook his head. There was no way to take it with him and ensure its safety. The bracelet, however, remained on his wrist. But the knife! He'd forgotten about it during the quick exchange. The leather sleeve pressed against his abdomen under his shirt. He should have handed it over before the meeting. *Ashes.* Felix would find it. Take it.

"And my debt?" Leewana asked Felix.

"Will be paid by sundown. I will send a messenger with the coin within the hour. I vow it."

Leewana gave a tense nod. "What are your plans for the Golden Gibborim? Even if he is no longer mine, I'd like to see him fight."

"The rumors of his presence here will spread. I'll take him abroad. El-Pelusium has a tournament in a month. We should make it if we leave tomorrow."

"You don't plan to stay and show him off here?" Leewana said, clearly surprised.

Felix shrugged. "I'd stay if I wasn't pressed for time to reach Kemet. We will be back. I'm confident the Golden Gibborim will survive until then."

Kemet? Avner hadn't dreamt this would lead them to his birthplace. Perhaps delaying escape until their arrival in Kemet might allow him to trace his origins.

But another thought brought him up short, even as the guards' gripped his arms.

The frost. He couldn't waste time searching for an answer to his blood—or his birth family. People back in Doram were dying.

Avner jerked his arm out of his captors' grip. "I'll cooperate. No need to hold me."

Felix chortled. "Do you hear this? The most famous gibborim in the land will cooperate!"

"I make a habit of not believing anything a gibborim says." The guard on Avner's left snickered beneath his mustache, and his fingers dug in tighter.

"Kemet?" Leewana asked, but she looked at Avner, not Felix.

Avner nodded, relief sweeping over him as understanding dawned on Tevye's face. He'd meet up with Tevye in Kemet, though ashes knew how.

Felix quipped something about "the land of the pyramid", but Leewana didn't respond. She hesitated one moment longer, looking at Avner as if expecting him to *not* cooperate and break free. When he didn't, she clenched and unclenched her hand, then turned on her heel and left. Shoshanna followed, not sparing them another glance. Avner cursed inwardly at her going free while he and Chava remained slaves.

Tevye waited for one more moment, clearly torn about leaving them.

Would you like to stay on my team, after all?" Felix asked him, amusement in his voice.

Tevye started. "No, of course not."

"Then leave."

He spun around and jogged out.

Chava stepped an inch closer to Avner. They were alone, and they were slaves. He felt Leewana's absence acutely after having her by his side, even if mostly silent, for the past eleven days. A snap of energy zapped between Chava's fingers and his own. Avner started. She looked away quickly. Felix crossed to a tray of food resting on the windowsill and popped a ripe grape into his mouth. Unable to tolerate Felix's chewing, Avner nearly seized a spear to silence him, but then Felix swallowed.

"Ah, glory. I can taste it!" He wiped grape juice from the corner of his mouth, then snapped his fingers at Avner. "You, my Golden Gibborim, what is your real name?"

"Avner," he bit out.

"Bleh. Boring, isn't it? I think we will stick with Golden Gibborim in the arena, what do you say?" Felix didn't give

Avner a chance to disagree. "Why does your blood glow? I've heard rumors varying from you were cursed as a child, to you traded your soul to your native god...."

"I don't believe in gods or souls."

Chava shifted beside him, and mumbled something under her breath, but this wasn't the moment to argue about her deity.

Felix choked on a laugh as he tried to swallow another grape. His eyes watered, and he wiped the tears away with the back of his bejeweled hand.

"A champion, and a jokester. So, is it the first option? Cursed as a child?"

"No."

Felix's expectant gaze deflated. "Come now, surely you know why your own blood glows."

"I don't."

"Has it always been golden?" Felix pressed.

The question caught Avner off guard.

"I-I can't remember anything from before I was seven. I suppose my blood could have been normal before that." If he hadn't been born with golden blood, what could have changed it?

"Why seven?" Felix took a swig from the brass cup beside the fruit platter.

Avner shouldn't have mentioned this. He had no reason to think his blood had ever been normal, and his new master was *not* the one he wanted to brainstorm with.

Still, he had no choice but to answer. "I was adopted from Kemet to a Doramite family at seven years of age."

Felix's eyes bulged. The cup clinked against the tray as he set it back down. "You are genetically Kemetian?"

"Yes." Avner cast Chava a questioning glance, but she only shook her head.

Felix turned away from the fruit platter and snapped his fingers. The guard nearest the door stepped closer, and Avner noticed his features for the first time. Narrow eyes, light skin, dark hair. Kemetian?

"Horem, read him, please." Felix waved toward Avner.

Read him? What did that mean? All thoughts of his blood's origins dissipated. Chava sidestepped closer, though Avner would have pushed her further away in case whatever *reading* this man meant to do was harmful.

The guard, Horem, didn't come any closer, but something changed in his eyes. They lost their focus, and the brown hue changed to a softly glowing amber.

Avner blinked, certain he was mistaken. Felix stood at rapt attention, focused on Avner. What was he supposed to be reading?

"Well?" Felix asked, his impatient gaze flicking back to Horem.

The man's eyes returned to a natural brown. Avner caught his breath. Just like the woman in the arena.

"I sense nothing." Horem frowned.

Felix's shoulder sagged.

"What was he trying to sense?" Chava asked.

It was Avner's turn to warn her off with a glare. Horem took his place by the doorway.

"The potential to manipulate." Felix turned back to the table and lifted his goblet again. But he hesitated and looked at Avner. "You can't manipulate, can you?"

The power the gibborim woman had. A chill tingled down Avner's spine. "No."

"I'm never wrong, sir," Horem said from his station.

Felix waved him into silence. "I know. I wish you were for once. I suppose it was too much to hope for. Both golden blooded and a manipulator."

"What is—" Chava began.

"A Kemetian who can control the elements. Quite valuable in the arena, even if you must pay for their services. And I swear, if you ask another question, I'm going to reconsider having the set of you," Felix drawled. "Manipulators are rare in the arena, as many masters don't find it worth the risk to their investment. Horem goes into the arena once a year for me, and while the profit for us both is enormous, I wouldn't risk him more often than that. Still, I believe you already saw a manipulator in the arena today. Did you forget already?"

Avner could have asked another dozen questions. How was such a thing possible? Why Kemetians? He kept quiet. They didn't need Felix to follow through on his threat.

But the man perked up again. He took another sip of his wine and smacked his lips. "Well! You're still Golden Gibborim. More than that wouldn't be fair. I would have liked to work up your entrances with the story of your blood. Make it a legend. But we'll make do with the mystery. It could be even more entertaining, I suppose." Felix paused, and his light eyes flashed. "Are you ready for glory, Avner?"

No. He wasn't. And judging by Chava's increasing paleness, she wasn't either. But for now, there was no way out of it.

16

NEVER AGAIN

Shoshanna

Freedom.

The air was ripe with wonderful freedom as Shoshanna and Tevye followed Leewana out into the sun of Mereen's market. The woman hadn't uttered a word to them as they fled Felix's chambers and the arena compound.

Not that Shoshanna could blame her. This situation was doubly cursed and could still kill everyone involved. Especially Chava and Avner. Even as the sun rippled over Shoshanna's back, relief didn't come. Avner had a death wish if he thought he could free Chava from Felix.

The sounds of goods and people being sold as they entered the marketplace dampened her rising spirits. Shoshanna scanned the stalls, fingering her fabric-covered brand. She needed another weapon.

"We're not stopping here," Leewana said over her shoulder as they cut through the den of slavers. "The harbor market offers everything needed for your sea voyage. I don't want Felix changing his mind and coming to buy you back. Or the game officials deciding to charge me more for what happened. They'll never find Namira of Numeralli once we leave this city."

"You're coming with us?" Tevye asked.

Leewana didn't answer as she stepped up to the gate. The guards held out a hand.

"Papers of purchase for the slaves."

"They're a free man and woman," Leewana said, her fingers clenching the staff of Doram. "I freed them after I purchased them."

"Then you'd still have the bills of sale, wouldn't you?"

Leewana glanced at Shoshanna. Did she think Shoshanna would be foolish enough to cut their way out of this just because she'd cut her way through the arena? At least a dozen guards stood around both sides of the gate, each with at least two more weapons than Shoshanna's zero.

The guard confronting them stepped forward, his eyes narrowing. "No one leaves this city without papers."

On second thought, maybe Shoshanna *would* fight her way out. She would not stay another night in this cursed place, and she *wouldn't* be captured again.

Tevye reached for her wrist, fingers brushing the dirty fabric covering her brand. She stiffened. No one other than the slavers had dared to touch her since Reuben, and even that was only a punch in the shoulder, aside from the night he freed her.

She shoved the memory away and shoved Tevye off her. That night would remain a distant memory.

"I traded the golden gibborim for these two, then freed them. I don't have papers because I already owned the golden gibborim." Leewana's voice was tense yet commanding. Good woman.

The guard nudged his nearest comrade, metal and leather armor clinking together.

"Didn't you say the woman who fought with the golden gibborim had a cursed rash?"

His friend's gaze raked over Shoshanna. "Yes, but on her face. Look, this one's got it on her hands."

"Well, I heard it moves."

The fool had heard too much. Shoshanna held back a shiver. Being subjected to scrutiny was one thing, but knowing people in this backward town were gossiping about her was far worse.

"Yes, it moves," Leewana snapped. "Now let us through."

"Why would you trade the most famous gibborim in the world for this diseased one and that crippled one?" The guard motioned to Tevye's maimed hand.

"If you've heard so much gossip, you'll know the golden gibborim turned on his own team. That liability is no longer my problem."

The second guard chortled. "Too right, you wouldn't want that. I heard it cost you more than he's worth to repay the damage."

"Let us through. I've told you my story," Leewana snapped.

The guard still hesitated, but a small boy pushed past Shoshanna and presented the guard with a letter bearing a wax seal Shoshanna couldn't make out.

"An urgent message from Felix," the boy said.

"Felix who?" the guard snapped.

"The man who bought the golden gibborim." Leewana

stepped closer, while Shoshanna stood filled with dread. What if Felix *had* double-crossed them?

Tevye edged away, eyeing the swords in the guards' belts. Shoshanna would almost trade one of her recovered memories for just one of them. *Almost.*

"I've heard of Felix," the second guard said in awe. "You better open that, mate."

His friend snapped the seal off the fine parchment. It landed on Shoshanna's sandal—a rose with crossing sabers in the center. She kicked it off, and a passing merchant's horse trampled it. Just as Shoshanna wished to do with her memories of this place.

"He's provided proof of your trade." The guard held the paper aloft.

The sun glinted off a splatter of dried gold blood. Again, Shoshanna's heart raced at the color she shouldn't be able to see. The gold shone against the gray parchment, as if beckoning her closer. She almost moved toward it, but caught herself. As confused as she was by the fact that she could *see* Avner's blood, it meant little if they couldn't get out of this forsaken town.

"There you have it. Let us through." Leewana moved toward the gateway.

The man stared at the glowing blood. "I could make a fortune on this."

"*We* could," the second guard hissed.

She shoved past them. Shoshanna followed, with Tevye close on her heels.

The guards didn't stop them. Their argument over the paper grew louder behind them. When had Avner's blood become such a commodity? Reuben had missed the opportunity to capitalize on Avner in Eder.

Shoshanna outpaced Leewana as they left the shadow of the high walls. A warm desert breeze didn't bring relief from the sun, but Shoshanna breathed in deep all the same. Now *this* was freedom.

"We need to get to Kemet," Tevye said.

Shoshanna had known this would end in trying to rescue Avner and Chava, but the prospect of crossing the ocean and braving another gibborim city was not at all appealing.

Leewana handed him the staff of Doram and motioned toward the harbor. "I'll pray Eloah grants you success."

"You're not coming?" Tevye pulled the staff close.

"I must return home. My husband was already worried about me coming this far. I can't be gone for another two months, and I certainly can't leave the continent. I know Eloah will go with you. He always has."

Good. They didn't need this stranger with them any longer, especially if she kept testifying to this deity.

But she helped free you, Itzaak whispered.

Shoshanna's cheek twitched. She scratched at the old burn scar. Fine, Itzaak was right. As always. She clenched her hand around the pommel stone in her pocket. It had become the replacement for his little ball of wood that Reuben stole.

"Thank you," Shoshanna whispered.

Leewana's dark gaze alighted on her. "I'd say 'anytime', but I'd rather never do that ever again."

"Agreed." Tevye pulled her into a hug and whispered something in Leewana's ear.

"Eloah sent me, so I came. Listen to him and teach Avner to do the same," she said as they pulled apart.

Tevye raised a brow. "Ah. You discovered his true loyalties?"

"Much to the danger of our mission," Leewana grumbled.

When it looked like Tevye might ask more, Shoshanna cleared her throat. There'd been enough of this. They needed to put this city behind them.

Tevye moved away from Leewana with one last wave. Shoshanna didn't look back at the woman, no matter what she owed her, because that would mean looking back at the cursed city which had made her the worst version of herself again. As she and Tevye hurried down the road to the harbor, Shoshanna swore under her breath.

Never again.

17

HIDEOUS FLOWERS

Avner

Light filtered down the stairs to the upper decks of Felix's ship, but no torches burned among the cages and cargo. Faint light showed the outlines of stacks of crates through the bars of their cage. The knife of Yor still pressed against Avner's belly beneath his shirt, but he didn't dare to hope that he'd be able to keep it. The cell was empty, without so much as a bench. Just metal bars spearing the floor and ceiling, with nowhere to hide the knife.

Avner's shoulder still ached, and he stifled a hiss as he turned toward Chava who sat on the floor at the other end of the empty cell. In the dim light, he could just make out her form and the edges of her red hair.

They were alone. That hadn't happened since his escape back in Eder, when she had taken the potion. The memory of the heat of her skin as he carried her through the frozen trees seemed to flow through his fingers. Avner clenched his fists, forcing the memory back.

"Where are his other gibborim?" he asked her.

"I don't know. He never let us near them until the match. He's probably got another hold to stow them in, since you are too precious to taint."

She scooted closer to him, stopping just inches from where he sat on the rough floor planks.

"What do we do about Doram's staff? I know Leewana follows Eloah, but it's hard to trust it in her hands." Chava's skin still gave off faint heat as her fingers pressed into the wood close to his own. A clean bandage was wrapped around her palm.

"I'm sure Tevye will take charge of the staff. He knows where Felix is taking us and will meet us in Kemet." How large was Kemet? He hadn't seen the place with adult eyes and couldn't remember anything about it. Would Tevye even be able to track them down if they escaped Felix's grip?

Chava reached lightly for his right wrist where the bracelet from the Nameless Tribe still held on. It had miraculously survived yet another match. He needed to be more careful with the bracelet if it could be an artifact of the Nameless Tribe.

Chava touched the rune-inscribed beads. "Do you still have the knife?" she asked.

"Yes." They'd been too busy rushing out of the city to search him. How long until Felix remedied that?

"Well, we aren't in a place to do anything with the knife now."

Yes, they were in a place he'd never imagined, and at a proximity Avner had never tried to achieve with her before. The memory of the old hut in the forest after he'd rescued her from taking Reuben's potion came back to him. Avner drew in a breath and pulled back. He now faced weeks alone with Chava on the journey to Kemet. Just him and the woman who'd married him to save his life.

Avner released his pent-up breath just as Chava stiffened, as if she too realized the situation for the first time. The tense silence lasted another few minutes, only disturbed by muffled shouting above deck and the rhythmic clapping of waves against the hull.

Finally, Chava exhaled, and whispered, "You were so angry with me in the arena. Don't you realize it wasn't my fault?"

Avner sat straighter, wincing as his wounded shoulder touched the bars. "Not your fault? If you hadn't been captured, I wouldn't be here." Once the words were out and couldn't be taken back, adrenaline and courage flowed through Avner. "I wouldn't have needed to enter the arena again. You can't understand what a year of that life does to you. The constant mental pressure to beat out your friends or watch them die. The rising hunger for death, for a good kill. The blistering desire to be the killer your master wants, all the while hating yourself for it, but not enough to stop." The words came swiftly, too powerful to stop now. "I had to throw myself back into that mindset, unleashing months of shuttered emotions and traumas to save *you*. I've reopened my soul to a darkness I'm afraid I'll never escape, and the worst part is, I think I'd like it."

He could feel Chava's breath, too close. Heat ran down his back.

He scrambled up, ignoring the pain pulling at his shoulder. "And you didn't even thank me for it."

"It wasn't just me, Avner. You had to save Shoshanna and Tevye, too." She frowned up at him.

"They can both take care of themselves. It was you, Chava, who I knew would die in the arena if I wasn't there."

"Why do you care if I die? You don't even like me!" Chava scoffed, standing up.

"Don't I?" he bit back, his voice rising. "Then why did I risk my sanity and my soul for you?"

She took a step back and blinked twice.

The words echoed back in Avner's own mind. *Don't I?* He hadn't meant to shout that.

Chava stared at him, her eyes wide. Golden. Beautiful.

Avner shook his head to clear his mind before he said more things he couldn't take back. He ran a hand down his face. "I-I just meant we've been through too much together to just toss our friendship aside, or to let you die," he stuttered.

"Well, well, have the lovers fallen out?" Dov's self-satisfied voice rang through the hold. He stood at the door of the cage, his arms crossed over his chest and a smug smile on his face.

Avner hadn't heard him come down the stairs.

"I'd forgotten how much fun it was to watch you two spew loving statements of hatred at each other."

Chava snorted.

"Do you need something?" Avner shot at him.

Dov dropped his hands and pulled a key out of his pocket. "You don't have to sound so hurt, Judge. I told you to take your freedom while you had it. If you'd listened to my wise advice, you wouldn't be here. Now I must do as my employer requests." Dov swung the door open.

"And what would that be?" Chava asked.

"So glad you asked!" Felix descended the steps, the light

from his torch illuminating the crates with fingers of flame and shadow.

Two sailors came down the steps as well, dressed in similar sea-faring attire as their master. One held a box and had a towel draped over his shoulder, while the other carried a bucket, slopping water onto the steps.

"I was so nervous about leaving the city without having done this, but there wasn't time." Felix moved into the hold and slid the torch into a ring on the nearest pillar.

Wood scraped against wood as Dov pulled the nearest crate into the open space between the cell and the steps. He motioned for Avner to sit on it.

Chava exchanged a glance with him, all thoughts of his recent admission to her fleeing to the far reaches of his mind. What was this about? Avner refused to let his nerves get to him as he stepped out of the cell and sank onto the crate. Chava started to follow, but Felix swung the cell gate shut before she could.

"I'd rather not deal with your emotions while they do this." He smiled apologetically.

Chava's sunburned hands tightened around the bars as she leaned against them. The two sailors moved in around Avner. The first one set the box he was holding on another crate and flipped the lid open, revealing small rolls of fabric, neatly stacked. Avner leaned closer as the sailor removed the first roll and handed it to Felix. The man's eyes shone with excitement.

Unease rippled through Avner. Dov's hands gripped his shoulders and forced him straight again as Felix turned toward the torch he'd hung on the pillar. He unrolled the fabric and something dropped into his extended hand.

"I was nervous I couldn't mark you while we were still in

the city. But thankfully, no harm done." Felix laid the piece of cloth across his forearm and picked up a short wooden stick with a metal nib. He held the nib in the flame of the torch.

The second sailor removed another package from the crate and opened it. A pot of ink. He uncorked the lid and held it out toward Felix.

"Mark him?" Chava's voice rose with worry. "Like a brand?"

Felix glanced at her, offended. "I'm not a savage, my dear! No, I *tattoo* my property."

Chava didn't look any less horrified, but Avner stifled a groan. He'd be marked as Felix's property for the rest of his life. Escaping Reuben's grip with memories was bad enough, but if they got away from Felix in Kemet, Avner wouldn't be able to escape this tattoo.

"Well, I don't want to spoil the surprise, so I'll leave you to it." Felix pulled the nib out of the flame and handed the tool to the sailor holding the ink. "Dov, do you have him? I don't want any mistakes."

Dov grunted. Felix turned and vanished up the stairs, but Avner's anxiety didn't leave with him. Avner could fight, but he wouldn't be able to take them all out. Felix would tattoo him eventually. Better to save his strength for the escape. Because they *would* escape. Perhaps he could burn the tattoo off later.

"Remove your shirt." The sailor demanded.

Avner was too aware of the knife of Yor pressing against his skin. He felt Chava's frantic eyes on him, but he didn't move, lest it give them away.

"Do we need to rip it off you?" Dov stepped around to Avner's front.

Avner clenched his fists. He hadn't liked Dov as a fellow gibborim. He loathed him as a master. But he had known this moment would come. Avner gritted his teeth and pulled his shirt over his head.

Dov yanked the leather sleeve out of Avner's waistband.

"Oho! What's this?" His eyes shone as he slid the sleeve off, revealing the dark, silver-flecked stone knife. Dov met Avner's gaze. "Thought you'd try to escape with *this*? It's a trinket."

"It's the object of Yor, Dov." Chava said from the cell. "Remember the frost? That *trinket* will save everyone back in Adamah."

Dov scoffed. "That frost isn't crossing the ocean. Everyone knows that. I don't care what happens to those idiots in Adamah." He slid the knife back into the sleeve and held it tight. "Start the tattooing."

Avner shot a meaningful glance at Chava. She nodded. They needed to monitor the knife in case Dov tried to keep it for himself. They couldn't afford to lose track of it.

Pain pricked Avner's left biceps.

"Don't move," the sailor ordered as he held the instrument against Avner's shoulder. The metal nib pricked his skin again, but it was the tattooist, not Avner, who gasped as golden blood seeped onto Avner's skin.

"It's not as great as everyone thinks," Dov grumbled.

The tattooist stared for a moment longer, then dipped the pen into the ink. Then into the fresh cuts, and back to the ink. Then back to Avner's arm. More golden blood oozed out. Over and over. Fists clenched, Avner refused to look at his arm for what felt like hours. Instead, he overcame the mildly annoying pain by thinking of ways to kill Felix once they were free. Strangling was too good for him. Perhaps stabbing. Or crushing his skull with a rock. Barbaric, just like his gibborim business. The time passed with Dov's grunting breaths behind him and Chava's frustrated sighs nearby.

Finally, the tattooist pulled the pen away and wiped Avner's arm with a cloth. He stepped back. Avner could resist no longer and looked down at the mark he'd bear forever unless he wounded himself to remove it.

A black outline of a flower was carved into his flesh, the petals left unfilled with ink. It was almost beautiful. Avner hated it.

His work done, the tattooist packed up his supplies and left.

"You'll get your petals filled in as you advance in the arena," Dov said. "Felix never sells a gibborim once they're marked, so you can look forward to building your career here. The man is more civilized than Reuben."

Flower petals instead of rank bands. Everything about using such a delicate and beautiful symbol to denote the rank of a killer was wrong.

"You're twisted," Chava muttered.

"Being twisted gets me further than being mad," Dov said as he moved toward the cage. "I'm going to let you out now. There're things to do."

"What sort of things?" Chava asked.

"Felix purchased the Golden Gibborim for a reason. He wants to see his money put to good use."

"We're on a boat. I can't very well fight in an arena," Avner said dryly, silently thanking fate that this was true. He stood up from the crate, refusing the urge to keep staring at his fresh mark of slavery.

Dov's grin was tinged with irony as he stuffed the knife of

Yor in his belt and unlocked the cage. Avner's assurance melted away. He stepped toward the stairs where a brighter torchlight flared down from above. It must be night now. He'd lost track of the time they'd spent in the dark hold.

Dov yanked Chava out of the cell and motioned to the stairs. "Go see what your new master has planned for you."

18

NOT TONIGHT. NOT EVER.

Avner

The dark water stretched endlessly in either direction, broken only by thousands of pinpricks of light and the pale form of the crescent moon dancing on the waves. The trees in Adamah had blocked these from view. Breathtaking was the only word for it.

"His arm sparkles like the stars above," Felix's voice broke the moment. Avner's new master stood in a ring of torches set in holes built into the deck of the ship, a good twenty feet in diameter. It took up most of the free deck space before the stairs leading to the upper deck. The ship was expensive, constructed of oiled mahogany wood, but not as large as the ship they'd fled Doram on.

Felix held a gleaming rapier, and his light blue shirt was stained a darker navy by patches of sweat. Apparently, he'd been busy while Avner was being marked. Felix handed the sword off to the man standing across the circle from him, and Avner's stomach dropped.

This man had to be a gibborim. He was shirtless, wearing only billowing cream pants. The flower tattoo stood out on the skin of his left shoulder, missing all but two petals. Avner refused the urge to look at his own fresh tattoo, glancing instead at Felix's guard, Horem, who stood at rapt attention beside the mast, a saber in his belt. But it was his long fingers, not the sword, that caused Avner to shiver. Was the man capable of drawing ocean water? Or commanding the wind to fill the sails? Maybe they would get to Kemet too fast, before Tevye and Shoshanna could meet them.

Escaping would be harder with a manipulator on Felix's side.

Felix stepped out of the ring of torches, pulled a towel off the rail surrounding the mast, and wiped his forehead. The boy Dov had escorted out of Felix's apartments back in Mereen stood nearby, holding a canteen. Felix snatched it from him and took a sizable drink, water dripping down his chin.

"He owns a *child*?" Chava whispered angrily.

Avner motioned for her to be quiet. Railing against all the things their new master did wrong wouldn't help their plight, even if Avner's own stomach churned at the sight of the child waiting on Felix. At least he was just a personal slave, not a gibborim.

But as Felix handed the canteen back to the boy and clapped him on the back, something about the twinkle in the man's eye as he assessed his "property" made Avner less sure. He had looked pleased when he gave Dov the money for the lad back in Mereen, as if this boy was better than any other deckhand. His long sleeves hid any tattoo, but surely Felix wouldn't be *that* cruel.

Felix's jeweled hand fell on the boy's shoulder, and he

said something to him. The boy's eyes widened, and he shook his head, his unruly hair bouncing.

Felix chuckled and stepped away.

Standing beside Avner, Chava exhaled murderous whispers. He wrapped his fingers around her arm and squeezed it, signaling her to be quiet. She obliged.

Dov held out the knife of Yor with one hand, keeping a firm grip on Chava with the other.

"I found this on him. Not sure how his previous owner missed it."

"Tried to smuggle a weapon on board?" Felix stepped away from the boy and accepted the knife, with a raised brow at Avner.

"Seems like he succeeded," Chava pointed out.

Felix chuckled and slid the knife out of its sleeve. The torchlight made the silver speckles in the black stone dance.

"A lovely piece! Though your choice of smuggled weapon is not very deadly. These engravings—simply marvelous." Felix placed the knife back in its sleeve and slid it through his belt.

Again, Avner caught Chava's gaze. Her golden eyes flashed with understanding. Luck permitting, they would recover the knife before making their escape in Kemet. *If* they could escape. Avner looked toward Horem, but the guard seemed as uninterested in him as ever.

Felix grabbed Avner's left wrist and yanked it upward.

"And what is this trinket? Had you been hiding it under your sleeve?" Felix rolled one bead from the Nameless Tribe bracelet under his thumb.

Chava caught her breath. Though his heart thundered, Avner shrugged.

"It's a good luck charm. I've had it since I became a gibborim."

"Ah. You credit this little thing with your success, just like your crazed friend? She had a charm too." Felix narrowed his eyes and studied the beads. "You Adamites are a superstitious lot, but all it did was get your land covered in death. Tribal ignorance is very self-destructive."

"I'm alive, aren't I?"

"True." Felix dropped his arm. "You may keep it."

Chava and Avner exhaled together. Finally, something in their favor.

"I almost brought you up hours ago before the tattooing, but convinced myself that waiting for absolute darkness would be far better," Felix said as he turned back to the ring of torches.

Avner couldn't help himself. "Why?"

Felix ogled him. "To better see your blood, of course! Did your old masters never try it? What fools, ha!" He flung the towel back to the ground. "Why have a golden-blooded gibborim if you don't at least *enjoy* it? Your renown in the arena is undeniable; however, your value extends far beyond that." He pushed up his sleeves, revealing well-muscled forearms. Maybe this man's claim of being the best gibborim master in the world had merit.

"Who is he fighting?" Chava asked.

"Gavin. He's only a level two," Felix gestured to the rose tattoo and its two filled-in petals, "but he will still fight hard enough for this to be amusing."

"So, I'm to put on a show for you?" Avner clenched his fists.

"For me and Moises." Felix pointed at the boy, then took Chava by her marked hand. The purple glowed stronger in the dark. "And for your woman. Fight him, or her blood is payment, even if there is nothing remarkable about it."

"You're a savage!" Chava wrenched her arm, but didn't get free.

"I'll do it." Avner held up his hands, trying to signal Chava to calm down, but heat rose along his neck again. Once again, he was thrust into an arena—albeit a small one —to save her. How had it come to this? A year ago, he'd been sworn to never harm another soul, and now all it took was one red-headed woman to make him bleed another human.

Felix's smile returned. "Excellent! Dov, watch over the woman—"

"My name is *Chava*," she cut in.

"My apologies, madam." Felix dropped her an exaggerated bow, and Chava blushed deeply. He rose again, his golden hair blowing free in the light evening breeze. "Avner, you are connected to a real beauty."

Hearing this man mention anything about Chava, especially the beauty Avner had tried to ignore, curdled something in his stomach. He extended a hand impatiently, eager for the night to end. "What weapon am I to use?"

Felix raised Chava's marked hand into the torch light. "I was going to ask how the marks came to be, but as with your blood, I'll feed the crowds a tale of mystery and witchcraft." Felix waved his free hand in a dramatic arc. "A wild woman tamed the golden gibborim, marking him as her own in some heathen ceremony! Ha! They will eat it up, traveling miles to see the beautiful witch and her slave." He finished with a flare of his oversized sleeve, his rings sparkling in the torchlight.

Avner glanced at Chava, but she was too busy glaring at Felix to notice. Felix wasn't wrong. She *was* beautiful. The firelight danced on her hair, sending streaks of red-gold through her curls. Gold like the day she saved him—A flash of golden light, warm fingers against Avner's. Pain receding, and a voice, whispering things that couldn't be true. *You are loved, Avner. Come to me and find rest.*

Avner blinked and staggered one step back. He'd never remembered the voice before. Just Chava's face, stained by tears he didn't comprehend. But now the voice slipped through the cracks of his hazy memory, just like the vision, or dream, from his childhood. A golden glow, a man's voice. Did those memories share a single voice? The day he sat beside a dying man as a child, and the day Chava sat by him while *he* died. Avner's breath came raggedly in the back of his throat. He hadn't thought of the dream from his youth in weeks, maybe even months. Which was probably why he hadn't seen its connection to the day Chava saved his life.

Or there wasn't a connection, and his weary mind was making things up.

"All right!" Felix stepped back, snapping his fingers. "I'm eager to see a rousing fight."

Dov forced Chava to sit on the deck. She grunted in protest as her rear-end thumped against the wood planking, but remained silent for once. Another sailor emerged from the lower deck holding a quarter staff still gleaming with fresh oil. The sight sent a spasm of desire through Avner, and he cursed it. He *wouldn't* get sucked back into this. Not tonight, not ever.

"We've heard the rumors of what you could do with just this, *Judge*," Felix said, his voice dripping with pleasure. "Dov claims it was marvelous to behold."

Avner scowled at Dov, who didn't bother to look ashamed for such a bold lie. He'd never come close to praising Avner when they were gibborim together. Avner reached for the staff, holding himself back so he didn't snatch it from the man too quickly. When his fingers closed around the wood, he stifled a groan of satisfaction. This staff, with its smooth grain and solid weight in his palm, was even better than the one he'd used in Eder.

"You look pleased. Good. Now show me what you can do." Felix sank onto a cushion beside Chava. He didn't offer her one.

The boy, Moises, refilled the canteen and stood beside Felix.

"If this goes well, I plan to use Chava as bait in the matches, with you fighting for her." Felix added. "A true show, rife with romance and glory. But if you're too slow, she could die, so you'd better be as good as they say."

Chava made an odd, strangled gagging sound, her eyes blazing. Avner's anger kindled again.

He raised the staff and faced his opponent. The man sneered at him, brandishing his rapier. Sword against staff, a common enough arrangement. Avner crouched low, the staff tight to his body, ready to spring at the first chance. The man stepped right, Avner went left. They circled each other for several rotations before the man slipped up. He broke the rhythm and flung himself forward, leading with his sword.

Avner's arm snapped up, his staff cracking against the man's shoulder. It should have been enough to make him drop the sword, but he held on, despite grunting in surprise. Avner whirled to the left, but the man sensed his intention and met him, his sword clacking against the staff and cutting off a brutal blow to his arm. Avner smiled grimly and yanked back, only to lurch forward as the boat hit an enormous wave. His opponent's legs were far more seaworthy, and he slashed his blade down just as Avner careened haphazardly into him. Pain, white hot and fierce, sliced into his left biceps where his rank used to be tied, and just below his new tattoo.

Bright golden-red blood pierced the darkness, even overcoming the light of the torches. Avner staggered back, but another strike didn't come as clapping echoed off the planks.

"It's marvelous!" Felix was on his feet again, his eyes reflecting the glow of the blood. "Quick, douse half the torches so I can see it better!"

The sailors who had brought the staff and cushion jumped to do his bidding. Without the torchlight, Avner's blood glowed brighter. Moises gasped, and even Chava echoed him. Avner refused to look at the pools of his golden blood. He wasn't a freak on display. If he had to be here, couldn't he at least do his job as gibborim?

Felix stared for another moment, then dropped back onto the pillow. "Gavin, don't slice Avner's tattoo off, or I'll take your arm."

Avner's opponent dropped a hasty bow, his features tensing with fear.

"Resume the match, please." Felix waved them on.

Avner lunged forward. His staff met steel. Five minutes later, he wiped Gavin down with a brutal sideswipe from the staff, and Felix declared him the winner with thunderous applause.

The night seemed to last for hours. Gibborim after gibborim with varying numbers of petals tattooed on their arms were brought from the other hold on the ship to challenge him. Only one other used a staff and was poorly trained at it. Avner flung him down in thirty seconds, despite it being his fourth match of the night. Sweat and gleaming blood poured off him. While no other fighter cut him as badly as the first man, Avner couldn't deny he was rusty in the arena.

He gritted his teeth and threw himself into the fifth match against a hulking man wielding the large ax Chava had used in Mereen. Avner's tattooed shoulder throbbed as he collided with the man's chest and thrust him to the deck. He cut the staff down onto the man's brow, beating him just as the sun hit the edge of the sea. Felix cheered, though Avner couldn't understand how the man had any voice or excitement left.

Avner glanced toward the stairs to the hold, yearning to be down there in the dark, away from Felix. Chava caught his gaze. For a moment, the thought of returning to the hold with Chava seemed blissful. Like a ray of light in the dark night they'd both endured.

"What a thrilling night!" Felix bounded off his pillow and clapped Avner on the back. "Dov, see that he gets salve on his wounds and a poultice for the tattoo. I want it to start healing before the bouts tomorrow night."

"You're making him do this *again*?" Chava asked as she staggered to her feet, clearly exhausted.

"Every night!" he cried with glee. "We still have two weeks until we reach Kemet. I could have Horem push us faster, but I want the extra time to get Avner ready. Granted, I'll have poor Moises scrubbing the blood twice as often, but at least the boy will be good at *something* when we berth."

The boy stared, wide-eyed, at the glowing blood splattered on the deck. Chava's knuckles were white as she clenched her fists and stared at Felix. If only loathing could kill.

Every night. Avner's knees shook with weakness, but he forced himself to stay upright. Dov ushered them back down to their cell, Avner gritting his teeth against the exhaustion biting his muscles. He collapsed to the cell floor once Dov had finished applying a healing paste and left.

Chava sank down several feet away and rested her head against the ship's wall.

He should scoot closer and say something. Encourage her. Point out she'd be safe because he'd keep fighting. He'd protect her as he hadn't been able to anyone else. But fatigue ate at his muscles, edging closer to his mind the longer his limbs rested. Avner's heavy eyes closed, only to jerk back open as he struggled to stay awake. But Chava was already asleep against the wall, her face still and peaceful. Smiling to himself despite the circumstances, Avner turned away and let sleep take him.

19

NEW OPPONENTS

Chava

Another night of matches was upon them, just like the dozen prior. Chava didn't even bother to throw a snarky comment at Dov this time as he escorted her up the steps to the deck. He'd gotten better at ignoring her looks, and she was just too tired to rail against him any longer. As she moved to the familiar space on the deck, she was relieved to see another pillow beside Felix's. *Finally.* She sank onto it, trying not to give him the satisfaction of letting out a groan.

"Well, this ought to be fun!" Felix rubbed his hands together, his purple sleeves flapping in the wind, and sat on his own cushion at the edge of the boat's "arena".

Avner stood facing Horem, the staff in his hands, and his tattoo finally healed. The empty petals showed off his tanned skin from days in the sun back in Curroon. Chava glanced at the manipulator who looked like a fair opponent even without a weapon. If this was Felix's idea of fun,

Chava *really* didn't want to spend another day in his possession.

They were still at least several days from Kemet, and Avner had finally fought every gibborim on board, including several of the sturdier deckhands. Which left the manipulator. Chava sat on her hands to keep from twisting her fingers in nervous anticipation.

Avner rolled his shoulders as he always did before a fight. Horem didn't warm up. He simply stood there, his eyes igniting into that freakish amber. Having seen this back in Mereen, it did nothing to settle Chava's nerves. *Eloah, what is this power?*

Maybe it was just genetic, as Felix seemed to think.

"Fight to first blood only. I want to avoid permanently harming either of my most valuable assets." Felix raised a hand.

Avner required a different strategy to win. Even Chava could anticipate his every move after watching so many matches over the course of the last ten days. Horem had stood guard for each of them, meaning he knew as much as anyone.

Avner didn't drop into a crouch as he usually did. Chava held her breath, dreading the moment Felix would drop his arm.

"Moises, you need to pay attention here, understand?" Felix regarded deck-boy with paternal affection, though Chava was sure he wasn't Moises' father.

Chava dug her fingertips into the decking. A *child* shouldn't be a slave! There hadn't been a moment to speak with Moises, but Chava had been praying that Eloah would provide one.

"Go!" The jewels on Felix's hand glinted in the candlelight, sending out flashes of aquamarine and indigo as his hand dropped to the deck.

Horem remained motionless, but a stream of water shot over the side of the deck and pelted Avner in the face. He stepped back, sputtering, the staff useless.

"This isn't fair," Chava muttered.

"I beg to differ, my dear." Without turning his eyes from the two men, Felix said, "This match is as fair as they come for your man."

More water sprayed from the deck. Avner sidestepped it —wait, no. The water spun in mid-air and followed him. It doused his face again.

"Do you really have to play with him like that, Horem?" Felix complained.

The guard gave a fleeting half-smile. Avner shot the end of the staff out. A gust of air shoved him back.

"This *really* isn't fair," Chava pressed.

Felix ignored her, leaning in toward the fight, if it could be called that. Avner kept spinning in circles, trying to escape the gusts of air or streams of water. How could this possibly bring about the drawing of blood? While Chava didn't wish Avner injury, the sooner this fight was over, the sooner she could be away from Felix.

Avner sidestepped another shot of water, but instead of trying to snap the staff at Horem again, he dropped to the floor and kicked out at the man's feet. Horem fell to the deck with a thud. Avner scrambled up, only to be met with a spiral of flame as the fire from the torches melded into one long, snake-like entity. It swirled around him, cutting off any hope of getting back to Horem.

Chava chewed on her upper lip. Not fair, so not fair!

Avner dropped back to the deck to escape the flames, but

they followed. Horem was on his feet again, his eyes flashing supernaturally. He might not kill Avner, but he could burn off several layers of skin. Chava glanced nervously at Felix. He wouldn't allow his prized gibborim to be ruined, would he?

"Come on, come on," he muttered as he pressed his jeweled fingers into his knees.

A small stream of water rose beside Chava, and shot toward the inferno above Avner. The water evaporated before it could douse the flames.

"Now, Moises, don't help Avner," Felix chided.

Chava twisted around, glancing at the boy and the open canteen in his hands. *No.* A stream of water drew back inside it, and Moises' eyes dulled from dark purple to brown.

Moises was a manipulator. *That* was why Felix wanted him to pay attention. He wasn't just a deck-boy, he was a future gibborim in training.

Avner's yell jerked Chava's attention back to the "arena". He leaped right, avoiding the flames. He twirled the staff over the back of his hand, gripped it in his fist like a spear, and threw it. The end struck Horem straight in the breastbone. The flames snapped out, sending the entire deck into an eerie darkness under a cloudy night sky.

Avner might have saved himself, but he'd lost his staff.

The ship pitched violently to the side and Chava fell over, her elbows cracking painfully into the wooden decking as she caught herself. There was a yell, followed by a groan. Small feet kicked past her face, and Chava reached for Moises as he tumbled across the deck. His brown eyes met hers, perfectly normal. She grasped his fingers, and they felt normal too, but those fingers had *manipulated*. She continued to cling to the boy, despite the vessel's renewed pitching. She'd save Moises, no matter what he could do, and no matter what Felix wanted him to be.

But the lurching of the vessel became more violent. Moises' fingers slipped out of hers and he rolled to the far side of the ship, stopping against the steps leading to the upper deck. Chava should crawl after him, but something warm and floral-scented pinned her ankles to the deck.

Felix.

Chava rolled and tried to scramble out from under him, but the ship tipped again as another wave hit it, sending Felix sprawling flat against her, nose to nose. His scent violated her as much as his chest pressing against hers. His eyes glinted with mischief.

Light flared over the deck again as the sailors re-lit the torches, revealing Avner standing again, fixing Felix and Chava with a dark look.

Chava's cheeks burned. She squirmed back, and Felix watched her go, his forearms pressed against the deck. She tried to calm her breathing. The smell of him clung to her clothes. She stood up, staggering into the mast as more waves rocked the ship. Ocean spray followed by rain cooled the heat of her skin. Maybe it would wash his stench off her.

Avner's staff rolled by with the motion of the ship, and Felix grabbed it before jumping up casually, as if he hadn't enjoyed what had just transpired.

"Continue." Felix tossed the staff to Avner.

He caught it, but his intense gaze didn't leave Chava. She felt herself blushing again, but indignation soon followed. *She* shouldn't be the one embarrassed by this! She certainly hadn't wanted Felix to touch her. She opened her mouth to say as much, but snapped it closed as Felix approached. He stood beside her, making no move to sit down, as his cushion had slid to the far side of the deck.

Fire flared again as Horem stole the flames from each torch. Chava clenched her fingers. She wanted this match to end more than any before. Strangely, the thought that she'd then be alone with Avner below deck took her breath away.

He still avoided coming within several feet of her in their cell, which only made her more aware of his proximity. The way he glanced at her when he thought she wasn't looking was more painful than he knew.

Felix's whoop drew her out of her ridiculous thoughts. Only Avner's feet remained visible as the fire surrounded him. The rain evaporated as soon as it came close to the inferno. Avner stepped forward, and the fire came with him. A glint of steel flashed in Horem's hand, but Avner couldn't see it.

"Watch out!" she cried.

Felix gripped her arm, and his eyes flashed a warning. "Do not interfere."

Chava jerked out of his grasp, her heart pounding, as golden blood ran onto the decking and mingled with the rain. Horem pulled his sword back out of his flames. Avner's staff dropped to the deck.

Felix clicked his tongue. "Shame. I was hoping he'd hold out longer, weren't you?"

For once, no.

The fire returned to the torches, revealing Avner, his rain-slicked hair clinging to his forehead, holding a bleeding hand. Horem walked away without waiting for applause.

Chava couldn't help herself. She spat at his retreating back.

Felix roared with laughter, then commanded, "All right, next up!"

"*Another* one?" Chava cried. There wasn't anyone left to fight.

"Moises!" Felix waved the boy over.

Avner's face fell, as did Chava's stomach. *No.*

Moises slunk over from where he still stood at the base of the steps, looking bashful and like a water-logged rat, but not frightened. He was a fool not to be. Avner had killed dozens of grown men.

"You can't be serious. I won't hurt a child." He stepped out of the ring of torches.

"Yes, you will. The boy needs the training, and I know you are the only one here, besides Horem, who won't kill him." Felix pressed one finger into Avner's breastbone and pushed him back in.

Chava's pulse raced as Moises approached the ring. Rain dripped off his curls, between his narrowed eyes, and down his nose. His gaze flashed to Felix. The man nodded, but didn't offer him any weapon. Moises stepped beside Avner, his eyes wide. He was so young. She took a step toward him, only to slip on the rain-slicked decking. Felix's hand steadied her elbow and lowered her back to the deck. She jerked away.

"The rules are the same." Felix turned back to Avner. "Fight to first blood."

"You're a barbarian," Chava spat out.

Felix frowned. "On the contrary, I'm known for being the gentleman of the gibborim masters. Clearly, you haven't seen enough of them."

"I've met two too many."

Felix chuckled and went to sit on his pillow, frowning

when he found it missing. He clicked his tongue and faced the arena, his arms crossed.

"Begin."

Avner stood still, his face drawn in some unknowable emotion. Moises raised his hands. Oh goodness. He was actually going to try to fight. Chava balled her fists, her breath locked in the back of her throat.

A thin stream of water shot from the puddles on the deck and squirted Avner in the face. Felix let loose a laugh. There *was* something laughable about such a weak show of manipulation against one of the greatest gibborim in the world.

Still, pride showed in Moises's expression and in his glowing purple eyes. He raised one hand higher. Nothing happened, though with the crashing waves, wind and rain whipping across the deck, it was hard to tell what he was going for. The ship rolled again and Moises staggered to the side, just barely catching himself on the rail. Avner didn't move. He was finally getting his sea legs.

"Come on, fight." Felix urged.

Would he punish Avner if he didn't?

Chava felt a chill that had nothing to do with the gathering storm. Would Felix beat *her* as he'd often threatened?

"First blood?" Avner asked tightly.

Felix nodded.

Avner raised his staff and locked gazes with Moises. The boy took a step back.

"Avner, no!" Chava begged.

He raised the staff and brought it down on his own foot. Hard. Blood ran from the broken skin, piercing the night with gold once more.

Chava laughed with relief. "First blood! Avner loses."

All eyes were on Felix.

He raised one brow, raindrops running off it to his long nose. "That's enough for tonight. Dov, get them below."

Rough hands dragged Chava upward, and she followed Dov back to the cell. Avner stepped inside after her, his face drawn with exhaustion, and his sodden pants plastered to his legs.

"Here." Dov held out a stack of fresh clothes for each of them and a woven blanket. "Felix says you'll need these with this weather coming in. He can't risk you falling ill."

Chava's cheeks burned, even though she knew Avner was gentleman enough not to watch as she changed. She accepted the clothes, but her face fell as she looked at the blanket. "There's only one."

"Take turns, or cuddle. I don't care." Dov dropped the blanket to the floor, swung the door shut and locked it.

20

NEW WEAKNESS

Avner

"Avner!" *His mother's voice shot through the trees.* "Come here!"

He spun to the left and pounded over the forest floor, clutching a basket to his chest. The mushrooms he'd collected tumbled out as he darted around a birch tree and slid to a halt to keep from running into his mother.

She wasn't alone in this dense section of forest. A man lay beneath a rotten tree, looking nearly as rotten himself. His skin barely hung onto his thin frame, clothed only in a dirty loincloth. His eyes were closed and his breathing labored.

"Who is he?" Avner asked. The man wasn't any Doramite he'd ever met.

"Quickly, hand me the water skin from your basket." His mother wrapped a strip of cloth around the man's bleeding shin.

Before Avner could obey, the man jolted upright and his brittle fingers snapped around Avner's wrist, yanking him closer.

"Hey!" Avner shouted. But his protest was overridden by the

man's words in a guttural language Avner didn't know. His mother pressed the stranger back down, but the man didn't release Avner. His fingers dug in, and his words ran together louder, fiercer.

Avner screamed and he couldn't stop the sound from intensifying, mirroring the man's widening eyes. Wider, darker, crueler, until Avner couldn't see his mother, or the trees, just the gaunt face of the stranger. The scream threatened to tear his throat apart, and to stop his heart—a blazing flash of light cut the nomad from view just as his words ended in a death rattle.

Avner jolted awake to cell bars silhouetted by sunlight from above the stairway. No forest, no river, and no sign of either his mother or the nomad. He was a grown man, not a ten-year-old.

He rolled onto his back, trying to force his thundering heart rate back to normal. The nightmare hadn't haunted him in so long. But his mother's face... he hadn't seen it so vividly since she visited him at the pens right before she passed to the Summer Lands. Or wherever she went once she died. Did those who believed in Eloah have their own afterlife?

But that would mean Eloah was real.

Avner groaned and brought a clammy hand to his forehead. He would not get another moment of sleep with those thoughts.

Chava exhaled in her sleep on the other side of the cell. She must have rolled with the ship's incessant movement— the bad weather hadn't let up during the day—for she now lay just past Avner's feet, her hair in a mess over her face. She inhaled, drawing a curl against her lips.

The ship rocked, and something pressed lightly against Avner's hip. The blanket Dov had left. Still folded. Neither of them had claimed it after their unspoken agreement to face in opposite directions as they changed into dry clothing. Avner had ignored the blanket, hoping Chava would take it, but she hadn't. Had she thought the same?

Now Avner picked the soft blanket up. It was tempting to throw it over his legs and try to doze off again. The air had cooled dramatically since yesterday. He unrolled the blanket and glanced at Chava again. Her arms were folded, and her cheek rested on her hands.

Avner leaned forward and draped the blanket over her. She might possess supernatural warmth, but she wasn't impervious to discomfort.

The ship rolled on the waves, and Chava flopped all the way against Avner's leg. By instinct, he jerked his legs away and Chava tumbled against the wooden floor.

Oh, curses and ash.

Chava groaned and sat up.

He froze. Her hair showered down around her face as she pushed up with her elbows. The blanket piled around her, and she sat up, rubbing her hip.

"This deck isn't very forgiving," she muttered, her voice heavy with sleep.

He forced himself to say, "I'll admit I don't know how you slept off your pallet like that. I wake up the moment I roll off mine."

"You could have woken me, or at least scooted me back onto it." She scowled as she went back to the thin pad, pausing as her gaze fell on the tangled blanket around her ankles. She looked at the empty floor where Dov had left the blanket, then at Avner.

He felt himself blushing, but he refused to look away. "It seemed the chivalrous thing to do."

Chava blinked at him. Avner waited for her to argue that she didn't feel the chill, but she pulled the blanket up. She froze for a moment, some untold emotion flickering across her face. It passed, and she wrapped the blanket tighter around herself.

"Thanks."

"Anytime." He cracked a smile. As if there would be other times when they were enslaved together and given one blanket to "cuddle" under.

Chava smirked. "Why are you awake, anyway?"

"I couldn't sleep."

She quirked an eyebrow.

He shouldn't feel ashamed to admit things like this to Chava, yet he avoided her gaze as he said, "I had a nightmare that has haunted me since I was a child."

She scooted closer along the wall, then rested her head back, her red curls spilling across her shoulders. "What is it about?"

"A memory." Giving truth to the dream sent a shudder down his spine. His bare skin went cold against the wood at his back. The fresh clothes hadn't included a shirt. Typical. He'd stopped begging Dov to give him a shirt days ago when it became clear Felix wanted to show off the tattoo even while Avner slept. He refused to look at the healed mark, instead focusing on Chava's bare feet.

They wiggled as she scooted closer still. Avner's skin tingled.

"A bad memory?" she asked.

"Yes, though it makes little sense. My mother is the only good part."

A smile touched Chava's lips. "Seeing her again must be

nice. I dream of my own mother sometimes, but never clearly."

Avner had almost forgotten she'd lost her mother as well, in a much more gruesome scenario. "Do you miss her?"

"Yes, but she's with Eloah, so I wouldn't want her back."

Her mention of the deity made him uneasy. Her words were too much like his own thoughts just after waking.

"But your dream, or memory. What happens in it?" Chava pressed.

"Nothing much happens. My mother and I found a dying nomad in the woods when I was a child. It's where she got the bracelet."

Chava's face softened. "I wouldn't write off seeing a man die as a child as nothing happening."

"My father was furious that we'd talked to an outsider, let alone touched him." Avner's hand twitched. He didn't want to remember the man who'd claimed to be his father but had never fulfilled the role.

Chava flinched. "Your father beat you for it, didn't he?"

"Yes," Avner said curtly.

"My father wasn't kind either. Though he seemed to save most of his anger for the day he killed my mother." She glanced down at her marked hand. "And for the mark like this he shared with her."

Shame burned up Avner's neck. He had sworn to cut his own mark off when he agreed to take the potion. Avner never told her that Reuben had planned to do the same to her.

"Sorry," he murmured.

"It's okay. I've made my peace with Eloah's plan." Chava said, not realizing he wasn't talking about her parents.

Still, Avner gave a wry chuckle. "We're cut from the same cloth, aren't we?"

"Orphans with tragic pasts? I'd say so." Yet a smile pulled at Chava's lips. "I don't think I've said it, Avner..." she trailed off, and the blush returned to her cheeks.

"What?"

She inhaled and sat up straighter.

"Thank you for trading away your freedom back in Mereen. I'm glad you're here." She spoke so quietly, the thumps and shouting above deck almost drowned out her words.

But Avner heard each one. His heart thudded harder, and he was suddenly far too aware that he wasn't wearing a shirt.

Footsteps padded on the stairs, and Avner jumped up, thankful for the excuse to interrupt whatever *this* moment was.

Moises came down the stairs, holding a tray with their usual breakfast, though it came at everyone else's dinner time.

"Hi." Moises approached the bars and held out the food. He appeared unaffected by his forced practice with Avner. Chava breathed out a sigh of relief as she and Avner gave the boy a once-over. Felix might be a monster, but at least he knew to treat his property well, as noted by the freshly pressed clothes the boy wore.

Avner took the strips of dried meat and fruits off the tray. "Thank you, Moises. And I'm sorry about last night."

The boy gave him a defiant scowl. "You didn't even give me a chance to fight."

"You don't want to fight me."

"But Felix says I must eventually, and in a proper fight.

Not one where you hurt yourself." He glanced down at Avner's injured foot. The wound was so small he hadn't bothered to wrap it. He'd be fine by tomorrow.

"How are you?" Chava asked Moises as she accepted her own food.

The boy glanced up the stairs, then back. "Felix is annoyed that I don't learn quicker."

Avner set his bowl of meat and fruit on the floor and put his arm through the bars. He squeezed Moises' shoulder, hoping his next words were true. "You don't need to learn what he's teaching. Stay strong. Felix won't hurt you. He values his slaves."

"I didn't mean to end up here," Moises said, looking more frustrated than fearful.

Avner smiled gently. "We didn't either. We hope to get away, and when we do, we'll take you."

"I promise." Chava set her hand on Moises's other shoulder.

The boy looked from one to the other. "He has your knife, doesn't he?"

Avner's hand dropped. They hadn't seen it since Felix confiscated it. "Yes."

"I could get it back for you. He keeps it in a drawer in his desk. It'd be easy."

Avner exchanged a look with Chava. They'd suspected that Felix was keeping the knife of Yor in his cabin, though that didn't make it any easier to retrieve.

"Thank you for the offer, Moises, but I don't want you getting caught," Chava said.

But Avner leaned closer to the bars, hope rising within him. "Does Felix leave you alone in his cabin often?"

"He's just a *boy*," Chava hissed beside him.

"I'm ten, so nearly a man," Moises insisted. Chava snorted, but the boy's excitement carried him on. "I could do it. Felix leaves me alone a lot, though Horem is usually outside the door."

"If you take the knife, there's nowhere to hide it," Chava pressed.

True enough. Avner's hope dimmed, but didn't die. "Moises, when we get close to land, do you think you can take the knife and bring it down here?"

The boy nodded, his curls bouncing around his ears. "Yes!"

"But only do it when we are about to berth—"

"And *only* if it's safe and Horem isn't watching," Chava cut in. Her marked hand grabbed the bars beside Avner's. Heat snapped between the purple rings.

Avner pulled his hand away, hissing at the discomfort.

Moises's eyes, so like Avner's, widened at Chava's mark. "You're magic."

"I'll tell you where it comes from when we escape," Chava said softly.

"I've seen power, but nothing like that, or your blood." He looked at Avner.

Avner held back a frown. His blood wasn't special, no matter what Felix thought.

Someone shouted above deck. Moises jumped and glanced over his shoulder. "He wants me back."

"Then don't give him reason to get angry at you," Chava said. "Just a while longer, and we *will* get away from Felix."

Moises turned and scampered back up the stairs.

Chava's soft demeanor vanished as she withdrew her hand and turned on Avner. "You can't ask a child to steal from Felix! He shouldn't be involved in this."

"It isn't stealing if the knife already belongs to us. He will be fine. I don't think Felix cares what Moises is up to half the time."

But the twinge of guilt working through him didn't fade under Chava's fierce, golden-eyed stare.

"I'll make sure it's safe," Avner offered.

"How? We're stuck in a cage, remember?"

"I don't need to be reminded," he pushed back, his annoyance rising.

Chava opened her mouth as if she was going to continue the argument, but her shoulders sagged instead. "Sorry, I'm just worrying when I should be trusting Eloah. If he wants Moises to help us, he will make it safe."

Her abrupt apology caught him off guard, replacing his own annoyance with confusion. Chava retreated to her mat, food in hand. Avner sat on his own and took a bite of his jerky. It was better than what Reuben had provided in Eder. Felix wasn't one to skimp on anything, even fuel for his gibborim.

Chava, however, made a face. "It's gross."

Avner couldn't keep from chuckling. "Gross? Its ginger and orange spices would be a delicacy in Doram."

"And I don't like it." Chava made a face as she took another bite. Her freckles formed dazzling patterns, lit up by her hair.

Avner choked on his food, his eyes watering as he coughed.

"What?" Chava lowered her food.

"Nothing." Avner grabbed the water skin off its peg on the wall and took a swig to clear his throat. He didn't glance at Chava as he handed it to her, too aware of a strange new tension in the air between them he didn't know how to deal with.

THE NIGHT PASSED in a blur of fighting. Avner's legs held steadier on the deck this time than the nights before, but his desire to return to the cell tugged at him, and not from fatigue.

He'd been right. Something *had* shifted down in the hold, even if he couldn't put his finger on what it was. Chava sat beside Felix, her brow furrowed, and her mouth working silently, no doubt in complaining about the night's events. Avner hid a small smile. Chava being her usual self helped him feel like more than just a slave. He glanced toward the hole leading to the hold, longing for another respite, knowing she'd be there with him.

"Avner! Look alive, man! Gavin almost had you there." Felix's voice shot over the deck.

Avner jerked his gaze away from Chava to meet Felix's annoyed glare. Pain registered in Avner's right forearm, and the faint heat of blood trickled down to his wrist. He blinked at the minor wound. Gavin hadn't struck him since the first match two weeks ago.

Avner shook the pain out of his arm and dropped into a defensive stance, but looked back to Chava. Concern knotted her features. *Get it together,* she mouthed.

He nodded numbly.

"Fight with all you're worth, or you won't be able to protect your woman," Felix urged.

Avner forced himself to focus just as Gavin came back at him, his sword raised. The fight continued with no other wounds on Avner's part, though he fumbled far too many moves.

Two more fights went the same way, and Avner did his best to avoid glancing Chava's way, because those intense looks distracted him from the matches more than anything else. When he finally, but barely, won the final round of the night, he staggered too eagerly down the steps to the hold, his mind reeling with a new weakness he never saw coming.

Chava.

21

THUNDER WITHIN AND WITHOUT

Chava

They had a night off. Eloah provided an intense storm preventing anyone from sparring on deck. Chava didn't know what to do with an entire night to herself. Or at least with Avner, locked in their cell. She picked at a loose thread on the blanket as she lounged against the cell wall. She could scarcely believe Avner had covered her with it the previous night, but he hadn't mentioned it, so she wasn't going to either.

Avner sat at his end of the cell, his face stormy. No doubt he was pondering whatever was making him slip up in the matches. Why his poor performance last night? He may have pulled off a win, but he'd been a mere step away from failure.

"You made some...er...interesting choices with your moves last night," she said, immediately regretting it, as his hands stopped wrapping cloth around his wounded forearm. She blurted out, "But you made a good move the night you faced Moises."

He didn't look up. "Had you expected me to attack a child?"

"Of course not. But I've never been more pleased with your moves than when you hit your own foot."

The corner of Avner's mouth twitched into a barely perceptible smile.

Such a small thing, yet Chava's breath wavered.

"I didn't realize you analyzed my moves." Avner lifted his eyes to hers and finished tying the bandage on his forearm with his teeth.

"I don't—I mean it's not that," she stuttered.

"Finally at a loss for words? Never thought I'd see the day."

"It's been known to happen," she quipped.

"I wouldn't have believed it until now." His gray eyes flashed.

Her cheeks grew hotter. Their conversations never went like *this*. "I'm sorry I complimented you, then."

"I'm not."

"Aren't you?" she shot back.

"What?"

"Sorry."

"Why would I want you to take back a compliment when you are so sparing with them?" He eyed her, by all appearances bewildered.

"Because it's from *me*. About fighting."

Avner blinked. He inhaled as if steeling himself, then said, "I'm sorry I ever gave you the impression your compliments didn't matter."

Again, she was breathless. The heat in her cheeks reached the burning point. Avner looked straight at her, and he froze. Chava's breath remained captive in her throat. This couldn't be the end of this moment. She searched for words to keep it going.

"Being in this hold with you isn't as terrible as I thought it would be." Ouch. She floundered for more words, but didn't want to add to her stupidity, so remained silent.

He stared at her, a vein in his neck pulsing, then looked down at the floor.

Perhaps it was for the better. The conversation was only fueling her insanity. She cleared her own throat. "You know, I was thinking..." she trailed off, biting one finger. "Maybe we *should* have Moises steal the knife back from Felix."

Avner's shoulders relaxed, and he looked back up. "Changed your mind?"

"I've heard the crew. We're only two days from Kemet. We won't get another chance, and if it goes wrong, Moises won't be in danger. Felix prizes him, just like you and Horem. He won't kill him."

"I was wrong before. Felix could still hurt him." Avner's voice dropped, "Or you."

A warm tingle moved down her spine. Her pulse hammered in her ears as the torchlight caught the perspiration gleaming on his muscles. Chava looked away before he caught her staring.

But she wanted to look back. To scoot closer, to lay a hand on his knee and let him know things would be all right. She clenched her hand on the bars just as the ship rolled again, making the healed wound from the match in Mereen stand out as a pale line on her flesh.

"Chava," Avner spoke again, his voice still soft.

She whipped her head up, her heart pounding foolishly.

"You don't know how to...um...summon fog, do you?" he asked.

The ridiculous question caught her off guard. "What in the world are you talking about?"

Avner almost looked *embarrassed.* He picked at a loose splinter on the floor. "Leewana summoned that fog—the Orroroo I think she called it—to cover our escape from Curroon the night I went back to get her help to rescue you. It... it listened to her."

"Fog listened to her?" Perhaps constant nighttime exhibition was driving him mad.

"Forget I said anything." He shook his head and stopped picking at the splinter.

Chava opened her mouth to answer, but the stairs creaked, and Dov's shiny black boots appeared, followed by the rest of his mass. He held onto the railing as the boat listed hard.

"Come on, Judge. Felix changed his mind. You're to train the boy tonight." Dov stomped the rest of the way down the stairs and crossed to the cage door. He grabbed the bars just as the ship rocked violently.

"I'm not a manipulator." Avner scowled.

"And I don't have the patience to listen to you argue. Move."

"Why can't the training wait until tomorrow night?"

"Because Felix says it can't. Let's go." The gate squealed as Dov pulled it further open. "Don't forget we were never friends, Judge."

Avner scoffed. "I never thought we were."

"Avner, please. Let's just go." Chava pleaded. The sooner he fought, the sooner they could get back to... whatever this moment had been. She stood up with help from the bars as the ship rocked again.

Dov crossed to Avner and yanked him up. "Listen to Chava now, or Felix will take her out of this cell and into his cabin."

Chava's blood ran cold.

Dov chuckled, low and grave. "That's right. He didn't appreciate that trick in the match with the boy. He's not afraid to force you to do what he wants."

Avner looked at Chava with a mixture of fury and fear.

Chava's knees weakened.

"Felix wouldn't dare touch her," Avner growled.

"You know nothing about me, Avner, but I thank you for that glowing recommendation on my character." Felix thumped down the stairs.

"I'll train Moises, but tell me how much longer this goes on." Avner pushed past Dov and stepped out of the cage.

"Another two days. Then we will be in El-Pelusium. You should look forward to seeing the great pyramid city for yourself. The wine is the finest in the world, which you'll taste if you cooperate." He glanced at Chava, and a sly smile spread across his face.

Chava felt a chill of fear despite her usual warmth. Eloah wouldn't let him touch her, would he? Just as he hadn't with Gidon.

"I see you aren't excited at the prospect of joining me in my chambers even after that moment we had on the deck."

She couldn't stifle a snort.

"Redheads aren't my type, though I would make an exception."

Avner moved so quickly, Chava caught her breath. He

stood halfway up the steps, nose to nose with Felix, his back muscles rigid. "Don't you dare touch her."

Was this the real Avner speaking? Or the one held captive to duty and honor?

Felix chuckled, raised a jeweled hand, and pushed Avner back. "My, my, and here I was believing Dov's claims that you didn't have feelings for Chava."

Avner clenched his fists. For a moment, he didn't move. Chava should stop this before he did something stupid, but before her foot brushed the bottommost step, the ship lurched violently to the right. Chava's shoulder struck the wall of the stairwell, and before she could straighten herself, thunder cracked overhead, followed by a wicked slash of lightning.

"Sir!" A crewman yelled. "We need you at the helm!"

Felix peeled himself off one of the support posts and took an unsteady step toward the stairs. But another flash of lightning flared overhead, and a horrendous crash came from above decks.

"The mast is going!" More frantic yells followed.

Felix cursed and flung himself up the steps, shoving Avner out of the way. Avner slipped and thudded back down onto the floor of the hold. Chava moved toward him, but another roll of the ship sent her flying into the stack of crates. She hit hard, and crates toppled around her, one of them pinning her ankle to the floor. Pain raced up her back.

"Avner!"

He and Dov lay motionless at the foot of the stairs. The boat rolled again, sending Dov tumbling to the right and into the bars of the cage. His head hit them with a resounding *clang*. Chava struggled to right herself, the rough edges of the crates digging into her sides and neck, but another crate shifted further, blocking Avner and the stairs from sight. More thunder reverberated overhead, followed by frantic screams.

The ship continued to pitch back and forth, jostling the crates, and causing her wrenching pain with each movement. With another great heave of the ship, the crate pinning Chava's ankle finally moved, shifting her weight so she flew off the stack and toward the stairs. Her arm struck the bottom step, but she ignored the pain as she caught sight of Avner's golden blood pooling around his head where he lay.

Water poured down the stairs, washing the blood further into the hold. Chava struggled to stand as the sea water rose to her ankles, then her shins, then covered Avner's head. As panic raged within her and her fingers tingled with pain and adrenaline, Chava grabbed Avner's shoulders and hauled him out of the water. He sputtered once, but his eyes didn't open.

"Avner! Wake up!" She screamed as another wave crashed down the stairs, drenching her entirely.

He didn't wake up.

Crying in frustration, Chava slipped her arms under his and grasped his sopping form to her chest. The proximity stirred a new and unfamiliar emotion in her. She heaved him up, only to topple back to the floor with a fresh roll of the boat. More water cascaded down the stairs. No one checked on the prisoners.

Chava stood up, hauling Avner back out of the water, which now lapped at her waist. She staggered beneath him and thudded against the wall of the stairwell. A thunderous splintering split the roar of the storm, and the ship tipped to the side, spilling Chava and her cargo against the far wall. Crates smashed beside her, narrowly missing her head.

"Eloah! Help!" she screamed, taking in a mouthful of salty water. Sputtering, she spewed it back out and kicked until her feet found a solid surface. Another crate hit Avner's back, releasing a thin stream of gold into the dark waters filling the hold.

They weren't going to die here. They couldn't because they hadn't stopped the frost or truly been married.

That latter part of the thought consumed Chava and her adrenaline peaked. She cinched her arms tight against Avner's torso and planted her feet against the wall. Sending up another desperate prayer, she kicked off from the wall and shot toward the now horizontal stairs. Something bumped into her just as Chava released one hand from Avner's floating body to grab the railing.

Dov.

His eyes were open, and dark blood poured from a wound on his head. Dead.

Chava forced her panic back down and tugged at the railing, the water helping to push Avner up behind her. Another wave washed over them, and she choked on the seawater. She began to lose her hold on Avner, but she forced her weakening arms tight again. She refused to lose him after what they'd been through. Not when this life-or-death scenario was making plain what she'd hidden from herself for weeks, if not months.

She was falling for Avner, even if he would never return the feelings.

Mustering every ounce of strength she had, Chava swam over the submerged stairs. When she arrived on the deck, it was clear that the ship had capsized. What was left of the mast lay in splinters against the surface of the dark, raging sea. When she'd asked Eloah to help free them, this wasn't what she had in mind.

A facedown body bumped into her, but she didn't recognize it. Several more bobbed up, then vanished as another wave crashed over the boat, shoving her and Avner under. They weren't on the boat any longer, but beside it, drowning in the angry waves.

Her last thought was how warm Avner was beside her as they floated down into the darkness.

PART II

Many souls lose themselves on the sea, while others find themselves. To know the difference between those two is the journey itself.

-Old Smyman proverb

22

VISIONS OF THE PAST

Shoshanna

"What's our plan if they aren't here?" Tevye's question was just as annoying the seventh time as the first.

Ignoring him, Shoshanna shouldered the pack of goods they'd bartered for at the market before leaving Mereen and faced the massive pyramid city of El-Pelusium rising above them. One side of the pyramid cut into the mountain, and a monstrous waterfall split the city in two as it spilled from the top of the ridge and disappeared into the lower parts of El-Pelusium. A road wound its way up the city, leaving what was inside the center of the pyramid hidden by red sandstone walls. More of the city sprawled below the pyramid. This is where they now stood, among toga-wearing shoppers and commoners going about their day in a market much like Curroon, except that everyone held their noses in the air as if they were entitled to. Reuben had only mentioned this massive place once, and none of what he said did it justice.

Shoshanna hated it.

Twenty thousand people must live within its confining walls. To be near so many... she shivered and drew her cotton tunic closer, almost wishing for Nuri's leathers again to protect her from the stench of the city.

"Where should we start looking for Avner and Chava?" Tevye wore new clothes as his others had been shredded in the games. The thin leather jerkin and pants fit him well, lending him a dangerous look that Shoshanna knew he could live up to if he wanted to.

They had traded work aboard the ship for the clothes, as well as the small knife in Shoshanna's belt. She almost reached for it, but stopped herself. Flashing even an insignificant weapon in a large crowd was foolish.

"It's a pity Leewana refused to come with us," Tevye said as he moved the staff of Doram from one hand to the other.

Shoshanna might not agree, but the woman had helped give them their lives back. The best Shoshanna could do was use the gift wisely.

"We will start with the inns closest to the docks, then go to the slave market," she said.

"They don't have slave markets here." Tevye pointed to a poster hanging on a stone wall on the other side of the street. "Looks like gibborim fighting isn't allowed within ten miles of the city. If Felix brought them here, he must have planned to journey to an arena elsewhere."

"Then the inns are our best bet."

"Unless they've already left. We must locate the closest arena." Tevye frowned at the sign.

Shoshanna caught her breath. There, in the swarming crowd of toga-wearing fools, stood a figure so emblazoned on her mind that it couldn't be real. Thin frame, black hair dashed with silver. Her chest was so tight that her lungs ached. Shoshanna squeezed her eyes shut to clear the image. She was imagining things, just as she'd done back in Curroon.

She hadn't seen Reuben's ghost on the ship in the three weeks it took to reach Kemet, and she couldn't be seeing him now. Her hand fumbled in her pocket, tightening around the pommel stone. Releasing a pained breath, Shoshanna reopened her eyes.

But Reuben remained.

He stood beside a merchant stall, waving a hand as he used to when he paced while passionately arguing.

"Do you see that?" Tevye nudged her elbow.

No. And yes. She saw *him* but Reuben couldn't be there. She looked at Tevye for confirmation that her nightmare vision was real, but he wasn't looking in the direction she was. The vendor stall nearest them held his attention.

When she didn't answer, Tevye pointed to something off to the side, oblivious to her rigid stance and pounding heart. "I'll be right back. Do nothing I wouldn't."

She was vaguely aware of him heading toward the stalls, but she remained riveted on Reuben. She couldn't speak or move, apart from squeezing her stone tighter. Reuben was *here*. In El-Pelusium, in the same market as her. It shouldn't be real, but judging by the rapidly-reddening face of the merchant Reuben was speaking with, the man was very real. The merchant's frown deepened, and he held out a bag filled with unknown goods, his movements tense, as if Reuben had just talked him out of something precious.

Reuben grabbed the bag, saying something she could not hear. He turned, revealing his face. Shoshanna didn't dare move, every nerve tied up in a knot of unusable pain.

The same thin, pointed face, the same brown eyes glowing with satisfaction. The same face she'd last seen when he was begging her to understand that he had killed her husband and wiped her memory for her own good.

He didn't glance their way, but a smug smile settled on his face. Reuben. In the flesh. She barely breathed, and her vision threatened to black out as it had back in Adamah. Even in black and white, Reuben stood out perfectly, every aspect of him just as she remembered. Pristine, fine, egotistical.

Something grasped her elbow and she jerked out of her trance, releasing the stone in her pocket and pulling her arm away. Tevye was back, a leaf-wrapped package in his hand. Whatever he'd just purchased, it paled compared to Reuben's being there.

Shoshanna looked for him again, but he was gone—no! There! He reappeared entering an inn far down the road. Reuben wasn't dead. He was within one block of where she stood. She wouldn't get another chance.

Shoshanna shrugged off her pack and handed it to Tevye. He shuffled his purchase into his other hand and took the pack.

"Go find where any gibborim might be. We stay here until the morning, and if you haven't found any sign of Avner, we leave," she said, curt and breathless.

A look of alarm flashed across Tevye's face. "Are you all right? You're pale."

"I'm going to find us an inn," she snapped. And if she found vengeance along the way, all the better.

"Shoshanna—"

But she jogged away before Tevye could finish. Blood thundered through her ears. Just how had Reuben survived the frost to escape? Hadn't she been on the only ship out of Eder? The journey to Ur would have taken too long, and the chances of surviving the cold were little to none. Yet he'd found a way, however improbable.

Shoshanna cut through the crowd, ignoring the shouts of protest as she bumped into someone and trod on several feet. Her free hand was clenched around the new cloth she'd wrapped around her brand of Zev. She'd take Reuben out as he'd taken out Itzaak.

The inn Reuben had disappeared into wasn't the finest one on the street, but vases of exotic flowers framed the entryway. A woman stood at the entrance holding a bowl of water for hand-washing, with lilies floating on the surface. She held it out as Shoshanna approached, a warm smile on her face.

"Lily water for your hands, madam?"

The greeting stopped Shoshanna in her tracks. No one had ever called her "madam". She stared down at the delicate flowers floating on the surface of the bowl. They were much larger than snow lilies, but they stole Shoshanna's breath all the same.

'I brought your favorite,' Itzaak's voice filtered through the commotion of the street. She could see the flash of his smile and a bouquet of much daintier flowers in his hand.

How did a flower from a distant land bring about such agony? Shoshanna resisted the urge to flip the bowl over, turning away instead. Nuri would have smashed the pottery to pieces, hoping most of the water drenched the poor serving girl. She would have acted before thinking.

"But I am not her," Shoshanna whispered, her throat raw, and she slipped into the gathering room of the inn.

Reuben would select the most exclusive, private accommodations. He couldn't be alone, but with Gidon dead back in Eder, there would only be a few Pack members left to accompany him if they'd made it out. Shoshanna had killed Quartz and Twig at the pools, but Chava said Copper escaped with Reuben. Avner reported the gibborim had killed Dirt, leaving Leaf alive but battered. Meaning two Pack members could be here with Reuben. Nothing she couldn't handle.

Shoshanna waited to draw her knife until she crossed the cluttered room, dodging around a dozen travelers in an array of togas, tunics, and robes. Reuben wasn't among them, but he wasn't the sort to hang around a common area for entertainment. No, he'd be back in his room, going over whatever loot he'd bribed the merchant into parting with. Again, the revelation of how well she knew him hit Shoshanna in the gut.

Curses and ash! Couldn't she go one moment without her emotions taking over? As Nuri or as Shoshanna she had not been so cursed sensitive! Her emotions wouldn't ruin this. She'd find Reuben and gut him before he knew what hit him.

She moved lightly up the steps, knife in hand. No one else entered the hall as she crept past a row of wooden doors and wrought-iron candleholders adorning the adobe walls. The extravagance of cities beyond Adamah sickened her. So far, El-Pelusium reminded Shoshanna too much of Ur, a town which had been dying of its own opulence and self-worth long before the frost killed it.

A voice sounded behind a closed door. Shoshanna pulled up straight, slipping the knife into her belt before anyone could catch her, but the door remained closed. Safe. She pressed on, leaving the knife put away in case she ran into anyone. Her experience with the inns in Ur had taught her that the finest room in an inn was usually at the end of the hall, or at the top of the highest stairs. This place proved no different. A larger door stood at the end of the carpeted hall, the plush fibers running right under it. Light flickered on the other side as someone passed in front of it, then back. Pacing. Reuben *always* paced.

A thrill of anticipation shot through Shoshanna as she crept forward, slowing her steps until her sandals barely brushed the carpet.

"That's it!" Reuben's voice, as clear as the last time she'd heard it, slipped through the cracks of the door.

Shoshanna's hand froze on the hilt of the knife. Desire ached in her muscles, and she could almost smell the coppery tang of his spilled blood. She stood on the verge of avenging Itzaak and the twenty-seven good men who'd died in the ambush at Death's Wall, avenging the loss of her own life to the ice and Eder's service. She'd only dreamed of such a thing for weeks, thinking the frost had stolen revenge from her.

But now, with Reuben's shadow cutting back and forth on the other side of the door, and the knife in her palm, this was finally her moment.

"I'm here, Itzaak," she whispered.

Her dead husband didn't answer, though she knew if he were there, he'd goad her on, demand retribution for his head on a spike, and for her ravaged soul. Another step forward brought the knife another inch up. Shoshanna expelled a breath of nerves she shouldn't be feeling. This was her moment. How many times had she been in the final moments of a mission? It shouldn't cause her palms to sweat or her breath to rattle. Those reactions were Reuben's fault.

"All his fault," she whispered, and placed her free hand on the cool doorknob.

An even colder hand grabbed her shoulder, brushing the exposed, rash-covered skin of her neck. Tevye spoke from behind her, his voice tense. "What are you doing, Shoshanna?"

She stiffened, clenching the knife hilt to the point of pain. "Getting revenge."

"What are you talking about?" Tevye's breath blew across her neck.

"Reuben's here," she whispered, the words scratching against her vocal cords as if they were daggers.

Tevye inhaled sharply, and she half expected him to draw his weapon as well. Instead, his fingers pressed insistently into her shoulder.

"I won't ask how that is even possible. Now isn't the time for this."

No, he was wrong. Now was the perfect time. No other voices had risen from the other side of the door. Reuben was alone.

"Someone is coming." Tevye yanked her back.

Footsteps pounded up the stairs on the far end of the hall. Shoshanna drew in a breath, cursing everything about this moment. For one fleeting second, she considered whirling around and sinking the knife into Tevye's gut so she could continue with this task. But reason stopped her hand. Shoshanna of Doram wouldn't do that. Shoshanna valued allies, and Tevye had been a good one so far.

Cursing inwardly, she pulled away from the door. Tevye spun away into a hall just past the previous door. Shoshanna followed, bumping into him where he stood in a dead-end nook. She pulled up against the shadowed wall, the main hall only three feet away. Tevye mirrored her on the opposite side, his eye glinting with worry as the footsteps pounded nearer. A man with shoulder-length greasy hair walked past their hideout, the sight of his muscled frame knotting Shoshana's gut.

Copper. There was no mistaking it. If she'd doubted she had seen Reuben in the street, this was proof.

Copper passed out of view and his footsteps came to a halt. "Hurry it up, won't you? I'm not staying here a moment longer than necessary."

"Why not? It's finer than our old tents back in the field." Leaf's voice floated down the hall, accompanied by her footsteps.

Tevye inhaled with a hiss and he attempted to pull himself further into the shadow of the alcove. At least Chava wasn't with them. She'd probably trip and fall flat on her face right in front of Leaf.

The only female Pack member crossed into sight. She wore Kemetian clothes, including wrapped toga pants and a loose white shirt with a woven vest over it, but her signature leaf pin was missing. With the two higher-ranking members of the Pack dead, Copper would have become Onyx, as Gidon used to be, and Leaf would be Quartz. Unless Reuben wasn't bothering with those foolish ranks any longer.

"I don't understand what you see in this place," Copper grumbled. "Tomorrow can't come quick enough. I've been dreaming of leaving this filthy city behind and finding open land again, or at least some trees."

Leaf snorted, then disappeared out of view again. A door creaked open.

"Ah! There you are. Did you tell him where to find us?" Reuben's voice echoed down the hall.

Shoshanna's body betrayed her as her pulse quickened and a yearning, sick and twisted, stirred within her. She closed her eyes, but it only made the image of Reuben's face clearer. Expectant, waiting for a full report of her most recent mission. She clenched her fingers and rooted her feet to the carpet, lest they betray her as well, and take her to her former master. The urge to go to him, to talk with him as in old times, overrode the thirst for revenge just long enough for the pain to gut her. This torture was far worse than remembering what Reuben had done. This was a hell of his making, where she was trapped between what she feared and longed for, hated and needed.

A thin groan escaped her lips. Tevye grunted and something touched her wrist. Shoshanna's eyes snapped open. Tevye stood inches away, his face furrowed with concern. Reuben's door closed again, cutting off his cursed voice and breaking the spell.

Shoshanna ripped her wrist out of Tevye's grip, and he flinched.

"Shoshanna—" he began.

"Save it," she muttered. "If you're thinking we are friends, and you can offer me some comfort in this torture Reuben has trapped me in, you're dead wrong. I don't have friends, and don't take comfort from anyone, no matter what we've been through together. Got it?"

His single eye drilled into her. Shoshanna shoved off the wall.

"Let's go."

They couldn't stay in this inn, but she needed to distract Tevye long enough to come back and finish what she'd started, even if it would be triply difficult now that Leaf and Copper had returned. She shoved the knife back in her belt, again almost wishing she could use it on Tevye for what he'd just ruined for her.

As if guessing her thoughts, Tevye said, "If you killed Reuben now, we wouldn't know where the artifacts are. Unless he left them in plain sight in his room, which I doubt. He wouldn't have left them in Eder. We need them, Shoshanna."

Curses and ash, but he was right.

"Let's find somewhere to settle for the night and return in the morning with a plan, okay?" Tevye stepped out into the hall. "You coming?"

Shoshanna took one step after him, but couldn't take another as words forced themselves out. Unspeakable words, impossible to admit, particularly to Tevye. "I miss him."

Tevye stared, and it seemed for a moment as if those words had destroyed a barrier between them, as if she was no longer the Right of his former master, but truly his companion who'd survived the arena with him.

Tevye extended a hand, as if hoping to mend her broken life. "It's all right, Shoshanna. He doesn't own you anymore."

"Then why do I feel like I can't escape him?" Why did she want to run down the hall and throw herself before him? That urge overbore the bloodlust a bit more with every passing second. She shouldn't keep admitting these things to Tevye—weak words from a weak woman.

"You don't have to be defined by his torture. It's your choice. Eloah can redeem your past because he defeated evil. Let him define you, not the evil Reuben follows."

"I don't want to hear about your deity," she whispered vehemently. "Even if he was real, he wouldn't want me after what I've done, and *who* I've been."

"That's not how it works. In his love, Eloah will forget your past misdeeds if you just turn to him, Shoshanna."

Her birth name felt wrong in this place, with Reuben only feet away on the other side of the door. *Nuri. Nuri. Nuri.* The name pounded with each pump of her blood, willing her to take it up again. She had to get away from here, away from the name, and away from Reuben.

"Never talk to me about your god again," she spat and shoved past Tevye, crushing his crippled hand between them. She didn't apologize as she fled down the stairs.

23

SHALE AND WIND

Avner

S omething purple glowed in his vision, blotting out whatever was beyond, *if* anything was. Something dug into his exposed skin, and Avner tried to shift away from the nuisance, but pain stabbed like a scorpion in his left arm, and he lay flat again. He stared harder at the purple blotch, blinking until all fuzziness left, revealing three perfect intersecting circles just below freckled knuckles.

Chava's hand lay on the sand beside him.

Water crashed in the distance, then receded, only to crash once more seconds later. Cold stones and shale registered beneath Avner's side. What had happened? He remembered nothing past Dov telling him to train Moises.

Avner rolled onto his back, gravel crunching beneath him. The meager moon illuminated the dark ocean foaming ten feet away, along with floating debris of what looked like a ship. Craning his neck to the side, Avner tried to take in his surroundings, but the land behind him was dark, giving no clue as to where he'd washed up. Avner shivered. His sea-soaked pants clung to his skin, and the cool wind bit into his bare torso.

Shipwrecked. The word entered his consciousness, too strong to deny.

Chava. Had she survived?

Avner jolted upright. He turned, and his breath cut off. Chava lay beside him on her stomach, her soaked hair splayed over the stoney beach. He leaned over her, panic building at the sight of her lying so still, her eyes closed— her back rose and fell with each breath. Air crashed back into Avner's lungs.

She lived!

Chava groaned and pushed herself up on one elbow. Her clothes were *dry.*

Heat pulsed off her, tempting him closer, but he remained still, refusing to scoot an inch nearer.

Chava met his gaze, and understanding flashed over her face. She sat up all the way. "A-Avner. You're alive."

A rush of gratitude shot through him, and Avner pulled her against him. Her delicious heat devoured him, soaking deep into his bare chest and soaked pants. He buried his head in her miraculously dry hair.

"I thought you were gone," he murmured into her neck.

"I-I thought you were, too." Her voice shook.

Avner stiffened, far too aware of the cinnamon scented skin of her neck so close to his lips. He jerked back, his heart pounding, and released her.

Chava leaned toward him without warning and pressed her warm lips against his cheek. Avner froze, his pulse thudding furiously. But then Chava pulled away. Avner's fingers dug into the beach, and a blush rose on her cheeks.

"We're free," she said, as if that could explain her actions.

"Yes," he whispered.

The moonlight glowing on her hair was enough to bring back the strange emotion he'd felt yesterday when he'd nearly lost a match. Ashes, she was gorgeous.

"We shipwrecked. You were knocked out at the beginning." Chava's words cut through Avner's thoughts.

And just like that, the moment was over. Avner sat back. He glanced behind them again, but the night-cloaked landscape didn't offer any clues to their surroundings. This harsh, rocky, shoreline edged with brambles didn't look like the pyramid Felix spoke so much of. Avner didn't know of any other land in this ocean, although his sea knowledge was limited, at best. A sudden fear overcame him. Anything could be out there. Or *anyone*.

Avner shivered. Chava scooted closer. Her hand came within a breath of his leg, and heat seeped through to his chilled knee. He resisted the urge to groan at the wonderful heat.

"I wish there was a way for me to manipulate this heat around you," she said.

"Or you could move closer," he said without thinking.

Chava tensed.

"I-I just meant... well you're so warm and it's so cold." He was an idiot.

"Right." Her leg pressed against his, followed by her hip, and shoulder. Heat penetrated his skin at every point of contact.

"Th-thank you," he sighed, though he refused to meet her gaze, his own shifting down to his wrist. He gasped, holding his wrist up. The bracelet! If they'd lost it... He could almost see the terrible scenario playing out. A string of dark beads sinking into the black depths of the ocean, never to be found again. The frost never stopped. All of life in Admah, gone forever. Avner's wrongs never repaid.

"Eloah provides. The bracelet is safe," Chava whispered.

"But the knife? What happened to Felix?" The short-lived relief vanished beneath another wave of concern. He should have known finding the knife of Yor had been too easy. Now they'd lost it again.

Chava sank back to the ground and curled into a ball on the rocky sand. "It won't help to stew over the loss now. Let's try to get some sleep and figure out where we are in the morning."

Avner sagged back beside her, careful not to make contact despite how much he wanted her heat. He lay on his side, facing the opposite direction. He closed his eyes, hoping he'd wake to the sun's warmth. Yet something told him what had transpired between them on this beach wouldn't go away with the morning light.

AVNER SHIVERED as sea spray misted over him and he shot up, gravel crunching beneath him. Though the moon was no longer in the sky and the pale light of dawn held the beach, there was a moist fog over everything.

His pulse raced.

The Orroroo?

But no horrible grating noises accompanied the fog, and the gray clouds didn't seethe as they had in Curroon. Of course. Curroon and its curse were thousands of miles away from wherever he was now.

Though sunshine would have been preferable to fog. He tucked his arms across his chest.

"Let's go find shelter—" he cut off as he looked towards Chava's place from the night before.

Empty.

His pulse jumped into his throat. Had something dragged her away in the night? Avner spun around, but the sparse landscape only showed rocks and a few shrubs. Barren and desolate. A low range of hills sat on the horizon, and the rocky beach stretched in either direction, waves crashing mercilessly.

No sign of Chava.

Avner clenched his fist. He'd been right. Daylight would do nothing to stop his erratic thoughts of Chava and his desire to simply *see* her again.

"Avner?"

He spun to the right. She stood beside a rough sign staked into the ground.

"Why'd you wander off like that? I thought something had happened." He resisted the urge to run over to her and shake her.

"I couldn't sleep. I don't know how you did. I can still feel every rock." She scrunched her nose. "Don't worry, I waited until light to search the beach for clues. At least we know where we are now." She tapped a finger on the sign.

He squinted at the engraved words. *THOTH, PLACE OF SECONDS.*

"Thoth? I've never heard of it."

"Me neither. I should have paid better attention to Reuben's maps when I had a chance. Something's been scratched out below that."

True enough. The words *ESHAQ'S DOMAIN* were

gouged out, as if someone had taken a rough stone and tried to erase them.

"It appears uncivilized."

"I bet some would say the same of Doram." Chava raised a brow.

"All I care is if this Thoth has shirts. I'm freezing. Let's see if there is a town." Avner turned toward a small path leading through the rocks beside the sign.

"Do you think this is an island?" Chava said as she stepped around the sign and met him on the path. "And what does Place of Seconds mean? Like second chances, or time?"

"No idea." Avner rubbed the back of his head and winced. He hadn't noticed the cut last night in the chaos of finding himself shipwrecked on a foreign beach. Bandages would be nice in addition to a shirt. His stomach growled loudly "Come on—"

A horrible grating noise cut him off. Chava jumped closer to Avner just as another crash echoed down the rocky coastline. Movement flashed to the side, and Avner spun around, gravel shifting under his bare feet.

A ten-foot-long piece of the splintered mast rose off the ground, followed by a slew of debris. They floated in the air twenty feet away.

Avner's gut sank. They'd found an island with manipulators.

24

THOTH, PLACE OF SECONDS

Avner

Avner shoved Chava behind the nearest boulder and dropped beside her, his heart hammering in his chest. Her frantic gaze met his. A horrid grating sound tore through the air. Chava jumped, flattening herself against him. The boulder they were hiding behind *rose* into the air, smaller pebbles scattering down off it. Avner pulled Chava with him, ducking behind another rock, but it betrayed them as well, flying five feet skyward. There was nowhere to go. More rocks and ship crates hung suspended. Half a dozen men and women dressed in furs stood on the beach, their hands raised, and their eyes glowing in various shades.

Not just one manipulator, but *six*.

Avner tightened his grip on Chava's shoulder, though he'd never felt more helpless.

The nearest man stood at least six feet tall, his eyes blazing a deep green beneath black hair pulled into a top knot. His expression was sharp, wary, as he surveyed the wreckage on the beach. "You came on this ship?"

Avner nodded, his neck muscles tightening.

The man came within a foot of Avner. He dropped his arm and the first boulder crashed to the ground, spraying Avner with bits of shale. He hissed and jumped back, but the man grabbed his arm and yanked him closer. Two fingers and a thumb squeezed around Avner's arm just below his new tattoo. The manipulator was missing two fingers.

"You're a gibborim?" He sneered at the tattoo, his eyes no longer glowing.

Avner pulled Chava closer, panic rising. If these manipulators took her away, surviving the shipwreck meant nothing. The other men and women still held their arms up while their eyes glinted supernaturally. More top knots, and long black hair blowing in the brutal wind.

"I asked if you are a demon-fighter?" The man hissed, gripping Avner tighter.

"Y-yes," he stammered.

The man scoffed and dropped Avner's arm. "Take them," he barked to the nearest manipulator.

"No, wait!" Avner staggered to his feet.

But the approaching man flung his hand out to the side. A rock sang through the air and cracked into Chava's forehead. She crumpled to the beach.

"No!" Avner jumped toward her, but pain burst in his head. The world went black.

PRESSURE PULSED in Avner's head. Thudding. Pounding. Telling him to wake up. Something cinched his arms tight against his body, and twisting did nothing to relieve the pressure. Avner groaned and opened his eyes.

Light filtered through the slats of a partially constructed cabin. The roof was in place, but there wasn't a door or plaster chinking between boards of driftwood. Hammers and iron chisels sat in the far corner. Avner lay slumped against the wall, with ropes around his feet and wrists.

He panicked. Where was Chava? He was alone.

Avner struggled to sit all the way up, his pulse pounding erratically. Chava! Was she all right? Were they keeping her in a separate cabin, or had they done something worse with her? The new inexplicable emotions he'd begun to feel for her rose to the forefront, and he twisted in his bonds. He had to find her!

Light filtered between the unchinked boards, and Avner froze. Someone laughed gruffly. The man from the beach with the top knot stepped inside the cabin. He wore animal hide pants and a fur vest over a woolen shirt. His dark hazel eyes weren't glowing, but Avner pulled back anyway. A hatchet hung from the man's belt.

"Where is Chava?" Avner asked, thankful his voice remained steady.

"You're not the one asking questions here, *gibborim*." The man scoffed. "We might not have witnessed you fighting in the arena, but I've heard what you do. Murderous savage." He spat a wad of saliva on the packed dirt floor. "Where is your master? Were you coming here to capture manipulators to fight with you?" The man's eyes glowed, not with manipulation, but with fiery hatred.

"I was just a slave. Please, just tell me if Chava is okay." Avner tried to stand, but his bound ankles prevented it. He thudded back against the unfinished wall.

The man crossed over to him in two swift strides, his eyes changing to the telltale glow of manipulation. Air whipped past Avner's face, threatening to suffocate him. He couldn't get a breath! Avner tried to squirm away, but the wind followed.

"Don't lie to me, savage! Everyone knows Thoth is an island of manipulators. Tell me where your master is!"

Avner couldn't have answered if he wanted to. The intense wind rammed down his throat, and his eyes watered so much he couldn't see the man trying to kill him. He thrashed against the wall, his head hitting against the wood. His lungs burned, and darkness crept into the corners of his vision.

Then the wind vanished, and Avner sagged to the floor, sucking in blessed air.

"Now, tell me the truth. Who hired you to kidnap manipulators?"

Avner shook his head as he struggled to stay up against the wall. Had this man tortured Chava as well? *Where* was she?

Another man stepped inside the cabin. He'd been on the beach as well. His black hair hung down to his fur-clad shoulders.

"Zosar, she found out about the captives. She isn't happy." The newcomer frowned at Avner.

Avner's attacker pulled back. "Surely, she understands the danger. He's a *gibborim*."

"I told her. She wants to see him."

Zosar reached down and yanked him to his feet. His dark smile didn't spread to his even darker eyes. "Guess you get to be interrogated by the greatest manipulator alive." He turned back to the other man. "When?"

"Ten minutes. She's finishing the lessons."

Avner's breath quickened. Was Chava already with that woman? Was she okay? He should have insisted they got off the beach last night when they arrived. He'd been so foolish.

Zosar sneered down at Avner. "Think on your sins. I'll be back, and if you won't tell our leader where your master is and what you were sent to do, you'll face her wrath. Trust me, it is worse than mine." He turned to his friend. "How is it going with the woman?"

Avner sat rigid.

The other man shrugged. "The redhead won't talk either. Ptol was having to resort to more... interesting tactics."

A rush of fear washed over Avner. "You're torturing her?"

The man shrugged. "It's a pity, too. She's a looker."

"No! I've already told you the truth—"

Zosar's eyes flashed to unnatural green. "Don't make me do something I'll get in trouble for."

"We mean you no harm. Please let her go!" Avner's words had never sounded so panicked. Not even when he'd taken Mikhail's place as a gibborim.

Chava is my weakness. His blood pounded in rhythm with the realization even if he didn't want to admit it. Worse yet, she would let them torture her until it was too late. Avner had never begged before, but for Chava, it came easily. "Please!"

Zosar scoffed and walked out of the cabin behind the other man, leaving Avner alone with the horror of his thoughts. The other man stopped just outside the door, his fur coat showing through the gaps in the planks. He splayed his feet as if preparing to stay awhile, while Zosar continued out of sight.

Avner had to get free. Adrenaline rose with his panic.

One guard and one set of ropes around his ankles stood in the way. He'd faced much worse odds. Reaching those tools without alerting the guard would prove difficult.

Avner slid forward on his rear end, but the gravel moving beneath him was far too loud. He froze, his breath catching in his throat. The guard shifted, but didn't look inside. Exhaling, Avner lay back, stretching his body along the ground, every muscle tense. He waited one minute, then rolled toward the corner with the tools. He froze after one turn. The guard didn't move. Avner rolled again, and cold iron touched his knuckles. Maybe this would actually work.

He settled his hands across the chisel's edge and rubbed the rope against the rusted blade. The guard called to someone walking by. Avner froze again, his pulse pounding in his temples. The newcomer stopped, his feet just on the other side of the planks. His toes were inches from Avner's face.

"I do no' be likin' this. Devil-fighters showin' up again." The newcomer spoke with a strange, lilting accent.

"Zosar thinks we should kill them both." The guard said.

"Aye, but that willna make them be' stoppin' showin' up 'ere. And Miki be on edge abou' them ever since the lad went missin'."

"He left. He wasn't taken by manipulator hunters."

"That' doesna change how she be feelin' about them," the other man said darkly. "I agree wi' Zosar. Be killin' every one o' them who be darin' to step foot on our shore."

The guard 'hmmd' in agreement.

"Be careful wi' tha' one." The newcomer spat, turned, and left. The cabin creaked as the guard leaned against the planks.

Avner's heart beat wildly and he resumed sawing. If he

didn't get free, the only way off this island was death. He only had an hour until they came for him, but he seemed to use a quarter of it to cut the rope. Finally, only a few fibers remained. He jerked his wrists apart, the rope audibly snapping.

The guard pushed off the cabin and ducked through the door. "What are you doing—"

Avner grabbed the man's ankle and yanked him to the ground. He couldn't give him a chance to manipulate, or this attempt to escape would be over. In one swift movement, Avner rolled on top of him and pressed his arm to his throat. The man's eyes bulged, but they didn't change color. His hands flailed, clawing at Avner's arms. Avner snatched a fist-sized stone off the ground and slammed it into the guard's head. His struggles ceased and his arms flopped to the ground.

Avner rolled off him and snatched up the chisel. He sawed through the ropes binding his feet. Then he was out of the cabin and running. A row of finished cabins stood along the path, but there was no one outside. Avner thanked that streak of luck and tore down the path, wincing. He should have stolen the man's shoes. And shirt. The chilly wind cut into his bare skin, but Avner had only one thought.

Chava.

He needed to see her breathing, unharmed. The urge was so raw, so strong, Avner almost continued racing down the path as he entered what appeared to be a ramshackle camp. But common sense overbore his desperation, and he slipped behind a row of boulders on the outskirts of the camp.

Tents and stick structures rose out of the light fog surrounding them. Groups of people sat around several fires dotted between the tents, clutching bowls of steaming stew. Chatter wafted between the buildings on the cook smoke mingling with the fog, and a child shot out between the nearest cluster of tents, clad in animal skin leggings and a fur top. The scrawny boy shot Avner a look, his brown eyes widening, and took off between the tents again. Was he going to find Zosar?

Or did the people here even know about the captives?

The boy looked like Moises. Guilt threatened to overcome Avner. But maybe it was better if Moises had been rescued by Felix instead of captured by these mad manipulators. At least Felix wouldn't hurt him—probably.

Avner crept along behind the boulders until he made it past most of the camp. What if they were keeping Chava somewhere else on the island? His hope wavered. He'd find her. He had to! Maybe he could sneak into every tent below him, one by one—a scream tore through the air.

Chava. The sound he'd know anywhere came from the lone tent at the end of the road. He glanced back toward the camp. The people around the fires weren't looking his way, and Zosar was nowhere to be seen. It didn't matter if the guard had woken up yet. Chava was worth the danger.

Avner pushed off from the rock and sprinted down the path. No one yelled an alarm as he ran like a madman. Reaching the tent, he ripped the canvas flap aside and barreled through.

A thick man with bleeding fists took up most of the interior, except for the support beam where Chava was bound. Blood trickled from her nose and a thin cut ran across her left cheek. Her eyes lit up as she saw him.

There wasn't time to form a plan. It didn't matter if this man was a manipulator. The gibborim inside Avner kicked into gear without warning. He lunged at Chava's attacker, surprised by the guttural growl coming from his own throat. His fists found the man's nose, making it match Chava's with a spurt of blood. The man staggered back, his bulk smashing against the post. Chava screamed as the man landed on her, but Avner shoved him to the ground. His hands found the man's throat. Fingers pried at Avner's wrists, but his muscles wouldn't disengage now. Brown eyes bulged in a red face. Avner squeezed tighter, his pulse pounding in his ears. Chava might have been yelling at him to stop, but there was only the fact that this brute had *beaten* her. Even Felix hadn't done that. Another squeeze, and the fool would leave this life with Avner's face his last sight—pain exploded in Avner's head. He rolled off the man, blinking the lights out of his vision. Chava yelled a warning. The fire ripping through his skull didn't fade, but Avner staggered up through the pain.

The man was standing now, a rock in his hand and a malicious grin on his face. "Yeh must be the gibborim."

Avner roared and flung himself forward. He took the man down to the ground beside Chava. Her legs shot out and wrapped around the man's neck. Avner snatched up the rock and cracked it into his skull. He sagged to the ground.

Avner slid over to Chava and began untying the ropes that held her wrists to the pole. Anywhere his fingers touched her skin, a shock of heat burned up his arm. He avoided her gaze and untangled the last knot.

"Thank you," she whispered, her voice trembling.

Avner's fingers paused for a moment before releasing the rope. Chava's breathing echoed just inches from his ear. He pulled his hand away as calmly as he could, hoping she wouldn't notice it shaking.

Chava looked over his shoulder, and her eyes flared

wide. Before he could turn, his wrists were forced together by something unseen. Dirt rose from the floor and shoved Avner backward. He hit the ground, but it wasn't hard. The dirt *shifted* around him, pulling him into it until he was submerged up to his knees. Avner tried to tear himself free from the dirt, but it held fast, pressing in from all sides. The invisible pressure at his wrists moved—like ropes of air— and slid around his arms, pinning them to his body.

Chava shrieked. Vines had sprouted out of the ground, binding her to the pole once more. Her cries ceased as the vines slithered up her body and around her mouth. Avner struggled with all his strength, but the surrounding dirt didn't budge.

A pale woman stood in the doorway, her almond-shaped purple eyes blazing. A leather belt held her fur tunic in place over woven pants. Black hair hung to her shoulders, framing a thin face. She looked no older than twenty, but Avner knew exactly who she was.

The greatest manipulator alive.

25

FIRE AND DIRT

Avner

As a gust of wind ruffled the woman's black hair, a strange remembrance washed over Avner. Did he know her from somewhere?

Impossible. He'd never been to this mad place in his life.

The woman raised a hand—missing all digits but the thumb and forefinger—and pointed at Avner. *The greatest manipulator alive.* Zosar's words took on a new meaning. This woman could bury Avner while he still breathed if she wished.

Zosar stormed through the tent opening. He helped Chava's attacker to stand, though the man couldn't stop coughing.

"You all right, Ptol?" Zosar asked, turning a dark look on Avner.

Ptol shook his head as he massaged his throat. "Tha' fool be nearly killin' me!"

"You beat her!" Avner strained against the dirt again, but

the woman didn't release it. "Chava wasn't doing anything to you!"

"She wouldna be shuttin' up! She wasna even answering the questions I be askin'."

"And that was a valid reason to beat her?" The powerful woman said, her voice soft and threatening.

"Well, tha' and she be comin' 'ere with a gibborim!" Ptol motioned to Avner. "He be tryin' to kill me!"

"Release me and I'll succeed," Avner growled, heat and anger rising within him.

"I do not hold with beating a woman—or anyone—under any circumstances not decided by Nenet. She has vowed we *will not* return to those days," The woman's raised hand twitched and a flicker of pain flashed across her face. She continued in a near-whisper, "We do not treat our guests the same way Eshaq did."

Zosar had the decency to look ashamed as he mumbled, "I was only protecting the people, Miki."

The woman—Miki—stepped closer to Ptol, her back rigid. Her hand still shook in the air. "We're better than our old ruler. We *must* be. The day's distance back to the mainland won't stop news from traveling. We have peace. Let's not threaten war again."

The knowledge of their location broke through Avner's simmering fury. They might escape, locate a boat, and reach Kemet tomorrow. But when Miki turned toward him, her hard gaze crushed any illusion that escape would be easy.

"I am sorry for what Ptol did, but you've attempted to murder a citizen of Thoth." She looked at the man beside Avner. "You attacked a guest without Nenet's command. The guard will hold you both until she decides your fate."

"I don't have time for this!" Avner tried again to move, but a sharp pain in his ankle stopped him mid-motion.

Miki lowered her hand as she balled her fist. "Your agenda isn't my concern. Thoth is."

Tevye and Shoshanna might leave the pyramid before Avner even got there. It'd be impossible to track them—or the rest of the artifacts—at that point.

"Zosar, take them both to the caves. I'll bring word of this to Nenet. She is busy directing the renovations, but she should have time for them in a week or two."

"Miki, you don't have to wait for that old woman. You can judge this right now. What of the woman?" Zosar asked. "Should I put her in the cave also—"

"No," Miki cut in quickly, her voice shaking, and the torches in the tent flared higher.

Zosar flinched. "I'm sorry, I just didn't think Nenet would want her running free."

Miki closed her eyes and inhaled. Her hands still fisted at her side, as if this was harder than it should be for the greatest manipulator alive. "I'm not the leader here. Nenet is. Bring the woman to her."

Zosar frowned. "You *should* be our leader. If Atsu were still alive, he'd pick you over Nenet—"

The torches by the door flared high as Miki pulled herself a bit taller, though it wasn't much. She was tiny.

"Don't speak to me of what Atsu would want," She whispered dangerously.

Zosar retreated, scowling.

Avner agreed, though for different reasons. Two weeks? He would rot away while Tevye would assume he'd been spirited away by Felix or lost at sea. And what of Chava? He couldn't trust a bunch of savage manipulators to care for her all that time. He *would not* go with Zosar, and there was only one chance to escape. Miki would need to let him out of the dirt.

Avner didn't look away from her glowing eyes as Zosar approached, his footsteps vibrating through the dirt surrounding Avner.

Five, four, three, two, one—Miki's eyes snapped to brown. The air holding his wrists vanished. The ground ejected him, then solidified. Zosar reached for him.

Avner shot up and swiped the ax from Zosar's belt. He yelled, but Avner was already spinning behind Miki. He placed the blade against her neck. "Escort us down to the shore and put us on a boat off this cursed island if you want to live."

He couldn't see Miki's eyes any longer, so could only hope she'd be too afraid that he could slice her throat before she could manipulate. But Zosar's eyes changed to that unearthly green, and the vines which had fallen from Chava jumped up again, tightening more than before. She thrashed against them, and the faintest squeal made it through the one covering her mouth.

"Are you sure you want to do this?" Miki asked in an icy tone.

"We didn't come here to capture you. We just want to get to Kemet, so let us leave." He pressed the ax closer.

A speck of blood rolled down Miki's pale neck, but she didn't flinch as she said, "You have the look of a Kemetian. You should know where you are." Cold. Judgmental.

"I haven't been a Kemetian since your kind sent a seven-year-old boy across the Great Sea alone," Avner spat.

"And yet you've proven how dangerous you are," Miki shot back.

"Yah!" Chava screamed, green juice dribbling down her chin, and bits of vine lodged in her teeth. A chunk of the vine was missing. She glared at Miki. "Tell your beast to loosen this vine."

"You two make a strange assumption that manipulators will obey your demands." Zosar snarled, tightening his fist.

Chava gasped, her face twisting with pain.

"Release her!" Avner clenched Miki's shoulder tighter—but then she moved.

She tore free, the hatchet blade nicking her throat. Her eyes flashed to purple. Dread rushed through Avner. Air attacked him, pinning his arms to his sides again.

Curses and ash!

Miki's black hair rose with the wind, but even as blood trickled from the small wound on her neck, the strange deja-vu overcame Avner again. He tried to throw it off. She was going to kill him, and in front of Chava. Their mission was over. Failed. Everyone back in Doram would die.

Heat flared nearby as flames roared out of the torch hanging on the pole above Chava. It burned toward Avner, just as Homed's flames had on the ship. The fire shot forward, singeing Avner's pants and his skin, but didn't linger long enough to leave burns. He breathed in the fiery air it left behind and staggered to the ground.

Miki raised a hand.

"Wait!" Chava sobbed. "He *is* Kemetian! He's one of you. Doesn't that mean something?"

"He might have the look, but *Avner* sure as shadows isn't a Kemetian name." Zosar scoffed.

The fire moved again. Avner drew in a breath of cool air just before the flames covered him. He was about to meet his end on this cursed island, shunned once more by the ones who had cast him out when he was young.

Chava was screaming something, but all Avner could focus on was the heat devouring the fine hair of his feet. He recalled his conversations with Leewana. Had her brother felt this acute pain as he burned to death? But at least he'd burned for something he believed in—even if it was Eloah—not just because fate had washed him up on the shores of an island full of deranged manipulators.

The heat stopped suddenly, and cool air bathed Avner's painful skin. He blinked, taken aback by the change.

Miki stared at Chava, even paler than before.

Zosar glanced at them, his brows knit. "But I've never heard that name, and I was raised in the pyramid before I was banished."

"I no' be hearin' it either," Ptol gasped, still rubbing his throat.

"I'm telling the truth. It *is* his Kemetian name." Chava said earnestly, clearly continuing whatever arguments they'd been having while Miki was scorching Avner. The remains of the fire behind Miki returned to the torch.

Her wide-eyed gaze slid to Avner as if she'd seen a ghost.

"I know that name," she said, her voice strained. She stepped closer to Avner. Her eyes were brown now, without a tinge of purple. He flinched away from her, but all she did was whisper fiercely, "Tell me again, what is your birth name?"

Why in the name of all things right and true would she care about that when she'd been in the middle of executing him?

But he stammered, working to get words out of his charred throat, "K-kamu."

She stepped back as if punched in the gut.

"W-what is my K-kemetian name to you?"

Miki stared into the distance as she murmured, "I do no' be expectin' this, Atsu."

Zosar shifted on his feet and shared an uncomfortable look with Ptol. If Avner wasn't sure Miki would finish burning him if he moved, he would have run. Was Miki a madwoman? Avner had had enough of them for two lifetimes.

"What is *that*?" Zosar's frightened voice shattered the moment. His three-fingered hand pointed at the blood dripping from Avner's shoulder where Ptol's nails had scratched him as they fought.

Miki raised her sleeve and wiped the blood off Avner's arm. She stared at the glowing fur for a long moment. Avner didn't answer Zosar's question. He owed him nothing.

"Miki? What do you want us to do?" Zosar asked nervously.

She started, as if she'd forgotten they were all there. She cleared her throat and said, "go away, Zosar. Now."

"But that blood... erm, do you still want me to take Ptol and this stranger to the cave?"

"He stays here." Miki pointed a trembling finger at Avner. "So does the girl. Leave, please."

Zosar hesitated, mouth slightly ajar as if he might ask Miki something else, but Ptol scurried out the exit, clearly relieved to escape imprisonment.

"Zosar, let's go!" he called behind him.

Zosar sighed and his eyes dulled to normal. The vines sagged around Chava. She disentangled herself from them and flopped onto the ground. Zosar scowled at her and then followed Ptol out. The cool air their exit let in soothed Avner's skin.

What was happening?

Miki cleared her throat, and when she spoke, her voice was distant. "You left Kemet when you were seven?"

The last thing he wanted to do was chat about his history with this woman, but he wasn't ready to risk death again. "Yes."

Miki exhaled shakily and dropped onto her knees in front of him. He flinched back, but her eyes didn't change back to purple.

"Avner!" Chava cried, unable to see that Miki wasn't manipulating.

"It's okay," Miki said. Her gaze traced the curve of his jaw to the end of his nose. Her hand hovered in the two-foot gap between them.

How could such normal fingers control the elements?

"What are you doing?" Chava asked frantically.

Miki touched Avner's forehead with a clammy hand and brushed his hair back. She inhaled, shaking, and said, "I think you may be my brother."

26

WOMEN

Avner

Avner knocked Miki's hand off his forehead. She *was* mad.

Brother.

But that was impossible. He wasn't related to a manipulator and his birth name didn't mean anything.

But the shock on Miki's face showed she clearly thought so. She no longer looked like a woman intent on burning Avner to death, but like a lost girl. She balled her fists at her sides and released them over and over, like a nervous tick she couldn't stop.

Avner scoffed. The greatest manipulator alive, nervous?

"I've been looking for you for so long," Miki whispered.

"I'm not him." He couldn't be. The chances of stumbling upon his lost family were infinitesimal.

"You're twenty-four, aren't you?" Miki asked, scooting a few inches closer on her knees.

Now would be the perfect time to strike and escape, but

his frozen muscles couldn't get past the fact that she knew his age. Avner's breath came quicker. A coincidence, that was all. He looked his age.

No, you don't, a voice whispered in the back of his mind. A year of gibborimhood had aged him.

"You *are* twenty-four!" Miki gasped. "I-I see it now. You look like my father, only with hair."

She raised her hand again.

Avner dodged it and jumped up. "Stop it! I'm no one."

"I've been wondering what became of you for so long." The words were timid, as if speaking them was a lifeline she didn't want to lose.

"I'm not your brother. I-I can't be."

Chava's warm hand rested on Avner's arm. He hadn't seen her draw closer. "Avner... Kemet has a one-child law. What if your parents sent you away to keep you safe?"

Miki stood up. "My father *did* send Kamu away to protect him from banishment to this very island. When Kamu left, I was only four years old, but I will never forget," she whispered with vehemence.

Avner shook his head, his pulse pounding. "I'm not him."

"I'm not saying I agree, but it *is* almost too much to be coincidence." Chava's logic didn't calm his erratic heartbeat. Neither did the cuts on her face.

Avner didn't want to be related to a manipulator. Either way, he remembered nothing.

"I'm not her brother, Chava. We need to get to Kemet, remember?"

"Yes, of course." Why did Chava look disappointed? Did she want him to be related to this woman?

Miki rose to her feet, her hands still clenching and unclenching. She looked nothing like the woman who'd come storming into the tent minutes ago. "I understand you might need time to consider what I'm saying."

Avner inched closer to Chava. This woman could still manipulate, no matter what she thought of him.

Guilt flashed across Miki's face. "I won't hurt her, or you. I'm sorry. I've only been in this position for a few months. I've no real idea how to lead anyone. Which is why Nenet should do it."

Avner didn't care who Nenet was. He just wanted off this island.

"So if you're not going to imprison or hurt us, do you have a boat we can take back to Kemet?" Chava asked.

Miki frowned. "Yes, but a scout departed on it last week. She should have returned by now."

"Do you have any other boats?" Avner forced himself to ask. He didn't want to engage in conversation with Miki, but they needed her boat to get far away from here.

"We're building more boats, but they won't be ready for at least another week. We were only freed from El-Pelusium a few months ago. There's been so much to build and improve. Getting to the mainland wasn't a priority since so many people were raised here after banishment."

Freed. As if she'd been a slave as well.

While the thought of her having experienced a sliver of what he had as a slave did dampen his anger, it wasn't enough to erase the last few hours on this forsaken island. Yet to look at this woman now, a small, pale thing with eyes wide with hope—for the wrong reason—he would never guess she could manipulate.

He took a step closer to Miki, though a large part of him still screamed no. "What is this place?"

"Thoth is the island all second-born and following children are banished to from the city pyramid of El-Pelusium. I was banished at nineteen, not even a year ago. But it's all different now. We've been liberated." She frowned, a deep crease of sadness between her brows.

Avner exchanged a glance with Chava. Why did freedom bring Miki sorrow?

But she continued, "Thoth is my home now. You're welcome to make my home yours until our boat returns or the others are finished." Miki's intense gaze didn't leave Avner's face. "You look so much like Father," she whispered.

A lump in his throat prevented Avner from speaking. It wasn't fair to put that on him. He had nothing to do with her fantasies.

"Thank you, Miki," Chava said. "But um, are we safe here?"

Miki flushed. "Yes. If I give the word, no one will harm you. I'll explain everything to Nenet. She's like a mother to me. I am sorry, truly." She looked back at Avner, the hope in her eyes too much to bear. "Please give me a chance to show you what this island can be and what I know of you."

His anger dimmed into frustration. He wanted to shout back that she had nearly burned him alive, no matter what she claimed about her intentions or his ancestry. But he caught Chava's gaze again and she gave a tiny nod.

He had no clue what it meant.

Chava waved emphatically, mouthing something indistinguishable.

Equally unhelpful.

Avner exhaled shakily. If they wanted to get off this cursed island, they needed help. With their luck, finding a boat and leaving tonight seemed unlikely. It looked like their only choice was to trust Miki. A mad manipulator who claimed he was related to her.

Great.

"Fine," he said. "But we both need new clothes. And food."

"It's the least I can do after this... incident."

He pushed past her but then hesitated at the doorway. There could be dozens of manipulators on this island.

"I will escort you," Miki said, catching his thought. "I swear no one will touch you."

"Thank you," Avner forced himself to say.

A smile lit up her face and a deja-vu punched Avner in the gut so swiftly and sharply, he staggered back a step as she approached. A foggy memory rose, so hazy at the edges that it could be a waking dream. A woman with black hair and a face just like Miki's, leaning over him, singing. Gray eyes in a pale face.

Avner inhaled, shaking. But Miki's eyes were brown, not gray.

But maybe my mother's were. The thought followed as the memory of the singing woman faded. But Illa, his adoptive mother, had been all he'd known for so long. He couldn't imagine replacing her.

Not replacing, just adding to. Another thought trickled in, along with a warmth building in his chest just like the sensation anytime Illa used to wrap her small arms around him in a hug. The warmth transformed into an ache so intense, Avner blinked moisture from his eyes.

He missed his mothers. Both the one he'd known and the one he never had.

Miki stepped outside and held the tent flap open. "Coming?"

Avner stood frozen. She couldn't be his sister, could she? Chava tugged gently on his elbow. "Are you ok?"

"Y-yes," he lied. He'd never had a memory like that one before.

But that didn't mean Miki knew anything about his past. He exhaled and forced himself to follow Chava out of the tent and into the village of Thoth. Miki led them through the tangle of campfires and tents. Several villagers peered at them, no doubt having heard the commotion with the captives. Avner didn't make eye contact with anyone until he accidentally looked up to find a woman by the nearest campfire appraising his bare chest. His cheeks flushed. Now that his skin had cooled, the brutal wind bit into him. He really needed the clothes Miki had promised.

Especially with Chava right behind him.

Avner tripped on a rock in the path and stumbled two steps. He staggered to the side to avoid colliding with Miki.

Chava caught up. "You ok?"

"Yeah." He waved her forward. These women were going to drive him mad.

They wound through the camp and up a small knoll where several smaller cabins and lean-tos sat. Smoke rose from the nearest one, dancing in the sharp wind. This place was so opposite to the heat in Curroon. Avner shivered as they approached the cabin, clearly newer than other ramshackle structures nearby.

Miki opened the door and motioned them inside. All one room, but homey. Blankets were piled in the corner, no doubt the sleeping area, while a low table with pillows around it sat nearest the door. A warm, heady scent of roasting meat washed over Avner, and his stomach gurgled. He didn't even know the last time he'd eaten.

But worse than that was the nostalgia this house awakened in him. A cozy home, like his had been in Doram.

"Nenet, we have company," Miki said.

An older woman stood up from where she'd been stirring a kettle over a fire in the corner. She turned toward them, and while she looked nothing like Avner's mother, her gray hair was braided over her shoulder just like Illa's used to be. Avner inhaled sharply. He couldn't take any more of these moments.

"Miki, what be goin' on? Zosar just be 'ere complainin' about some slavers." Nenet shrugged off a woven shawl and picked up a stack of wooden bowls from the table.

"He's mistaken. Our guests escaped the slavers themselves. This is Chava and Avner." Miki waved them forward. "This is Nenet, leader of Thoth."

Nenet snorted. "Aye, but I shouldna be. It's yeh, child, who everyone knows be the leader" Then she said to Avner with a twinkle in her eye, "She be too modest to be admittin' it, but no one be carin' what I say. They all be lookin' to the woman who liberated Thoth for answers." She slopped something that looked like stew into the two bowls.

Avner's stomach rumbled so loudly, he was sure they could hear it.

Miki blushed. "It wasn't just me."

"Aye, but yeh are the only one who be comin' back from tha' pyramid after." Nenet set the bowls on the table.

"You know I don't want to talk about him, Nenet," Miki said, her tone final.

Avner shared a glance with Chava. Their host was turning out to be far more than just the greatest manipulator alive.

Nenet glared at Miki, then "harrumphed."

. . .

THIS WOMAN'S bluntness shot down any comparison to Avner's mother. She was nothing like tender Illa. Though she didn't seem dangerous and showed no signs of manipulating the food she was cooking.

Avner shivered as a gust of wind blasted through the single open window. "You don't happen to have a shirt my size, do you?"

"Oh, I'm so sorry!" Miki started. "That's the reason I brought you here. Nenet, can you get them, please?"

"Aye. I suppose he be needin' them sooner than tha' boy." She shook her head, clicking her tongue, and shuffled over to a crate in the corner.

Miki muttered something too low to catch, her hands balled into fists again.

"Are you okay?" Chava asked.

"No. Nenet's grandson went missing over a month ago. I'd promised to teach him to manipulate, but things always came up. A storm ruined half the new cabins, then the adults needed more lessons, not a *child*." She scoffed to herself. "I was such a fool."

"What happened?" Chava pressed.

Miki sighed. "He snuck out on the first boat we finished with the few people who chose to leave Thoth and seek life elsewhere. I don't even know where they were headed, and by the time we realized Moises was gone, it was too late. I had already manipulated them across the back current—the lines of waves ringing us in that force everything back to the island—not knowing the boy was with them. He's known nothing other than this island. I sent a scout to El-Pelusium to hunt for him there, and I've been worried that if I leave before she returns, I will miss out on valuable information. There's been no word from her. I should have started the first day Moises left. The boy could be anywhere by now."

Avner met Chava's startled gaze. Could Miki be talking about the same Moises? Surely the name was common enough in this part of the world.

Chava asked, "How old is he?"

"He will be ten in the fall. I vow he will be home by then." Miki closed her eyes, hands still clenched at her sides as if she could squeeze herself out of existence.

"And he can't manipulate very well?" Avner asked, his throat going dry.

Miki shook her head.

"Avner..." Chava began.

The coincidences were too strong to ignore. If her Moises was the one they knew...that changed so many things. Moises was a good lad, so the woman responsible for him couldn't be evil, could she? Miki did seem genuinely concerned for him, after all.

"I'm guessing he has curly, black hair, about this tall," Avner held his hand above the table.

Miki's eyes widened. She dropped onto one of the pillows around the low table and motioned for them to follow. "Tell me everything."

"While yeh be eatin'," Nenet said, handing Chava and Avner a stack of clothes with two wooden spoons on top.

Avner accepted the bundle while Chava pulled the spoons off. Her clothes were still in good condition, so Avner pulled the thick, woven sweater on. It was a bit snug, but he sighed in relief as it cut the chill. The shutters on the window snapped as Nenet pulled them closed. Finally. He'd have to change into the pants later when there weren't all these women present, but Avner gladly shoved the leather slipper-like shoes onto his feet. They fit perfectly.

"I be pleased they be' fittin' yeh," Nenet said as she set two more bowls of stew on the table.

Miki ignored hers. "What of Moises? Was he a slave with you?"

Chava reached across the table and took her hand. "Yes—"

"Is he all right? What has happened to him?"

"We don't know what became of him after the shipwreck." Avner couldn't hide the despair in his voice.

Miki blinked. "Oh, of course. I forgot how you arrived here."

"The man who bought Moises valued manipulators." He left out that Felix was training Moises to be a gibborim. "If he survived the shipwreck, our previous owner would do anything to ensure Moises survived as well."

"And he was headed to Kemet!" Chava said. "We're only a day away from there, correct?"

Miki nodded, though her face had a hollowed-out look as she glanced at Avner. "And you were a gibborim? Did your master also have manipulators?"

"Chava's right. Felix will protect Moises at all costs."

Miki stood up and wandered to the window. Her hands trembled at her sides. "I be failin' him, Atsu," she whispered to the open air. Avner couldn't see her face, but he sensed her despair.

A hand pressed on his shoulder. Nenet whispered, "She be losin' someone very dear to her. In truth, she be losing everyone dear to her. Except me, tha' is. And a few people back in the pyramid."

"Her hands?" Avner asked.

Miki was clenching and unclenching her hands again.

"Hm. Tha' be an old habit. Bein' raised in a pyramid fearin' for yer life and hidin' in cellars be doin' tha' to yeh. Our Miki be comin' very far."

Avner might have been a slave, but he'd enjoyed a warm childhood, apart from his adoptive father. What had Miki endured? As for himself, he'd done so many things he wasn't proud of because he'd been a slave. Avner inhaled a shaky breath. How much had he done in the name of trying to save his people? He'd murdered dozens to be alive today. Many others had the right to view *him* as a monster, just as he viewed manipulators.

The thought caught him off guard. When did a man become a monster? Was it once a manipulator, or a gibborim, was forced to kill to save the ones they loved? Was *he* a monster then? And if so, was he any different than Miki?

A knot of stress released between his shoulders in an oddly comforting way.

Miki's hands stilled as she flexed her fingers. When she turned away from the window, her face was set. "I will leave for Kemet as soon as my scout returns with the boat."

"Perhaps we should sail together," Chava said. "We need to go to Kemet anyway, and we could point out Felix—the man who has Moises."

Miki glanced at Avner timidly. "I would like that."

Because she erroneously thought he was her brother. But even if he couldn't agree, he did have to admit he *might* have been wrong about Miki. He didn't need to trample her hope, even if it was misplaced.

"It's settled then. You can stay here with us until Clea returns. She's past due already. It's been three weeks. I expected her back in one."

"What of the other boats? The ones you are building?"

Miki sank back onto her pillow at the table. "I could see if the men could finish them sooner. They told me another two weeks just a few days ago. But if Nenet tells them to, I bet they could finish in half that time."

Nenet scoffed. "Be tellin' them yerself. They be carin' more what the savior of Thoth be havin' to say than this ol' bag o' bones." She smacked Miki with a rag.

Miki blushed.

The deja-vu hit Avner once again. *A woman's flushed face beneath tears. Whispered sobs and arms crushing around him, smothering him with the scent of flowers. A bone-deep sorrow such as he'd never felt.*

Avner dropped his spoon into his bowl of stew, the contents splattering across the table. His hand trembled.

Another memory unlike any he'd had before.

"Avner?" Chava's voice was distant.

I love you Kamu. Never forget that. Never forget me and I will never for you, my son. The whispered words from a time long past flowed out of the dusty reaches of his mind, even though he'd never recalled them before. The voice could have been Miki's, as similar as it was.

But Miki sat across from him, not speaking, staring into her own bowl of stew as if searching for answers it couldn't give her. "Yeh do no be havin' to be makin' a mess," Nenet mopped up the slopped soup.

"S-sorry," Avner stammered.

Chava elbowed him in the ribs.

He cleared his throat and ate more soup, though he was far from registering if it was delicious or not. He shot a glance at Miki, who was still frowning at her bowl. The image of the woman flashed in his mind again.

Chava prattled on about something, but Avner couldn't focus on her words. Something about Doram, or maybe Curroon. Miki pushed her bowl away and answered Chava. They continued for several minutes, not bothering to include Avner, which was all for the better. When Nenet finally took his half-eaten stew away, Avner forced a smile. His body felt numb, and foreign.

Could Miki be right? Could they be related? The answer seemed impossible to consider, so Avner avoided it as he followed the women on a tour of the island after lunch. It didn't matter how many tents they passed, how many strange glances he received, or how strange this place felt.

Avner couldn't dodge the feeling that he *knew* Miki, and therefore, this place. Every time she stopped to wave someone over to meet him and Chava, the motion was familiar. Even the moment she hugged a small boy and planted a kiss on his head sent a hollow feeling to the pit of his stomach. Every nod, each chuckle and cock of her head as they wound their way around the island and back to her cabin. The feeling haunted him until he dropped, weary-minded, onto a bedroll she'd procured for him. Maybe sleep would take the haunting and the strange images away. Maybe sleep would put everything right again.

27

PAST LIVES

Avner

The sound of breathing echoed in the dark around him as he huddled in a dark cellar. Footsteps sounded on the floor above, and the two forms huddling beside him scooted closer. Musty air trapped them as well as the darkness, though he knew there was a door nearby that led to freedom. A freedom he couldn't take. Rough letters were carved in it, but he couldn't remember what they were, and candlelight was forbidden.

The footsteps thumped harder above. Louder. Closer. The girl next to him whimpered. The other boy 'shh'ed her too loudly. The ones above would hear. The trapdoor creaked. His heart shot to his throat, and he clapped a hand over his mouth—

Avner shot upright, going from dead asleep to wide awake in a split second. His heart thundered madly. He staggered up off the bedroll, grasping the log wall for support. His legs shook beneath him, threatening to send him back to the floor.

Chava, Miki, and Nenet slept across the floor, each blissfully unaware of the chaotic pounding of Avner's heart. He gasped, drawing in the cold salty breeze, not the stale air of the cellar from his dream.

But it wasn't a dream, was it?

Still bracing himself on the wall, Avner turned and glanced at Miki.

Even in sleep, he felt as if he knew her. Was being here, so near her, pulling at long-forgotten memories from a traumatic childhood? Was she the girl from the cellar in the dream-memory?

Was Miki his sister?

Chava shifted on her bedroll under the window several feet away. She lifted her head and rubbed her eyes, her tangled mass of hair brushing over the ground like a curtain. Her golden eyes popped open and focused on him immediately.

A warm tingle raced down his back.

"Avner? Are you ok? You're pale," she whispered.

Okay wasn't the word. He wasn't sure there was a word to describe what he was feeling. Keeping his hand on the wall, he slid back down to his pile of furs. His legs shook, but he made it. Chava watched with a quizzical look on her face.

"Just a dream," Avner croaked.

She quirked an eyebrow. "The one about your mother?"

He shook his head. Though he almost wished it were. At least he knew what to expect with that memory. He shot a glance at Miki, rolled up in her own furs.

"Did you remember something?" Chava asked, a bit too loudly.

But neither Nenet nor Miki moved.

"Go back to sleep," Avner whispered.

Chava stared at him for another moment, then sighed

and laid her head back down. He pulled the furs up and lay back, staring at the thatched roof.

The cellar in the memory had a stone roof with a wooden trap door. Avner caught his breath. He hadn't seen that in the dream. It had been too dark.

Which meant he remembered that on his own. But did that fact mean anything? Avner closed his eyes, hoping sleep would return easily.

It didn't.

He spent what must have been hours watching the fire burn lower, its shadows receding on the ceiling until pitch darkness overtook the whole interior of the cabin. The sound of breathing and occasional snores disturbed the darkness, accompanied by a few distant howls of what must have been a coyote. Then pale light slipped in through the cracks in the shutters and beneath the door. Avner sat up, pulling himself into the corner, his knees tucked up to his chest and the furs around him. He couldn't see more than the back of Miki's dark head, but he stared at it until a sliver of sunlight cut across it, revealing not a single lighter strand among the black. Like the woman in his memory the day before.

By the time the women stirred around him, he had remembered what the letters were on the door in the cellar in the dream.

And that changed everything.

Miki sat up first, furs piling around her. As soon as those brown eyes met his, he knew he had to ask, though he'd spent the last hour debating it.

"What do MB, BB, and KB mean?" His voice was hoarse.

Miki inhaled sharply, the sound confirming more than

her following words did. "Those are the initials on the cellar door."

"But what do they mean?" Avner pleaded as he pushed the fur off him and rose from his pallet.

"Miki of Bast, Beren of Bast and—"

"Kamu of Bast?" Avner whispered, standing frozen a foot away from her.

Miki nodded, tears welling in her eyes. "You *are* my brother, aren't you?"

"I-I think so." Just stammering those words shifted something within him. Chava was right. Would it be so bad to be related to this woman? She may be a manipulator, but she cared about Moises. About this island. About Avner.

Her arms crushed him in a fierce hug, and Avner staggered back. His head swam as a flood of emotion overcame him and he locked his knees to keep from collapsing. *Sister. Family.* Real and blood-related for the first time he could remember. The world tipped, and he choked on the last of the air in his lungs as Miki squeezed even tighter.

Chava's warm hands rested on his right arm, giving Avner the strength to relax his knees and steady his breathing. He hadn't seen her wake up, which probably meant Nenet was watching this spectacle as well. Though Avner wasn't sure he cared.

"Your brother," he croaked.

Miki's face swam into view as she pulled back. Those familiar almond-shaped eyes, but not the same color as his own.

"What color eyes did our mother have?" he asked.

Miki smiled, her eyes lighting with joy. The sight warmed something deep in Avner's core, and he knew Miki's answer before she spoke.

"Her eyes were gray."

Avner gave a startled laugh. He'd found his family. No matter if it was in the most unimaginable place possible, or if his sister could manipulate. The sleepless night had shown him what truly mattered.

But there was one more test.

He held up his right hand, gripping a nail he'd found on the floor in his left.

"What're you doing—"

But he cut Chava's words off by slicing the tip of the nail across his palm. Golden blood oozed out.

Miki blinked at his upraised palm, unsurprised, but then she'd seen it yesterday in the tent. Her smaller, paler, hands cupped his.

"Your blood was red and normal the last time I saw you. Even though I was only four, I'm sure I would have remembered if my big brother's blood glowed." She smiled sadly.

Even though he'd anticipated her answer, Avner's heart sank. He dropped his hand, struggling to keep his face straight.

Chava took his hand and wrapped a strip of cloth around the small scratch. Her eyes glinted with worry. For him?

Maybe she should be worried. Why couldn't his sister answer the greatest mystery of his life?

"But this only confirms what Felix hinted at, Avner." Chava said.

Avner clenched his bandaged hand. "I don't want to hear that name spoken as if he could be right about anything."

"I just meant he'd suggested your blood wasn't always golden. That's clearly the case, since Miki can confirm it was normal when you were seven. So it changed sometime after you left Kemet, or maybe even on the voyage across the sea, since Mikhail didn't remember it ever being anything but gold."

Mikhail. Another name Avner didn't want to hear. Yet why did a sudden longing run through him at the mention of his own big brother? Avner shoved the thought away. He'd just found his birth family. He wouldn't dwell on his adoptive one.

"What matters is my family. Miki, if you can manipulate, you must be a Second, right? What does that make me? And didn't you mention another brother? Is any of our family still alive?" The words tumbled out before Avner fully comprehended them. None of this felt real.

Miki laughed, grabbed his hands again, and pulled him down onto the cushions around the low table. Nenet busied herself with preparing a simple breakfast of cheese and salted fish. Chava sank onto a pillow next to Avner.

"You're the Second in our family, and my big brother!" Miki held Avner's arm with the hand missing three fingers. She caught Avner's stare. "Part of the punishment when you are banished. Though mine happened a bit differently and I have an extra finger gone." She smiled at her disfigured hand. "People of Thoth bear it with pride."

That explained all the missing fingers, then.

But Miki continued, "Our father is alive back in the pyramid, but our mother passed away many years ago, during a forced murdering of the child within her. Father is helping to guide the new ruler, now that the law against multiple children is ended. Firsts, who controlled the military and held power, banished all subsequent children to Thoth for fear of manipulation. Ironic, because even some Firsts can manipulate if they try. But Father almost died helping me expose the truth of it and free Thoth. It's the reason my—*our*—oldest sister won't speak to him, even now."

"So, I have another sister?" Avner's head was spinning. He'd gone from nothing in the way of family, to so much... He inhaled to steady his nerves and looked over at Chava. She smiled back, and a strange, calm strength came over him.

"Our parents had six children." Miki continued.

"Six!" Chava's golden eyes widened. "That's more siblings than you had back in Doram, Avner!"

Again, Avner's joy dimmed at the memory. He didn't want to think about either of his siblings from Doram. He missed Silas, of course, but Mikhail... The man had betrayed him, no matter how good he'd been to Chava.

The unexpected pang stirred in his heart again. He shook it away and focused on his sister.

"Only half of us still live today," Miki continued, her voice tinged with sadness. "Avner, you are the oldest brother. Beren came after you, but he ran away, was banished and then executed for being a stronger manipulator than the old ruler of this island. I never met him, because he died four years ago when he was eighteen. I would have liked to very much," she added wistfully before continuing, "Isis came next, but she was stillborn. I followed as the Fifth. Then came the sister who died with mother."

"So, we have one other living sister? The first born who doesn't talk with our father." Was she another Mikhail? Driven by her own mission and feelings, rather than by concern for others?

That's not true. Mikhail cared. He died caring. The ethereal voice tickled the back of Avner's mind. His fingers clenched the edge of the table. He shrugged off the thought. He didn't want to dwell on his dead family, but on the one sitting right in front of him.

"Our father will be overjoyed to meet you when the time comes. Would you have time when we go to Kemet?"

"Not really. Every day could see another dozen Adamah-mites dead." Chava's voice jarred Avner out of his thoughts. She quickly filled Miki in on the prophecy and their mission to stop the frost.

Miki accepted their reasoning. "I've seen enough in my twenty years. Will you meet me back here after you've saved Adamah?" She leaned closer to Avner, her eyes bright with hope. "I never really experienced having a sibling. Not with our sister hating me and the others dead."

"I promise I will." He placed his hand on hers. He wanted nothing more.

"Will you no' be eatin' this fine breakfast I be preparin' then?" Nenet grumbled, hands on her hips where she stood above them.

"Nenet! I've just met by brother! You can't blame me for not having an appetite."

"Well I have one," Chava chuckled, and snatched a handful of white cheese off the table.

"I be likin' this one," Nenet said with a smile.

Miki stood up. "Well, we know you are a Second. As strong as I am, you should be easy to teach to manipulate. I can't let you leave here without trying."

"He can't," Chava said. "Felix had him 'read', whatever that means."

Miki shrugged. "Reading doesn't work. If someone has never accessed their power before, they can sometimes read not capable of manipulating. But once they've accessed it, that changes."

Chava glanced over at Avner. He was thankful he had remained seated, as his legs tingled with anticipation.

Reading for manipulation didn't work. Homed could have been wrong.

Which meant Avner *might* still be able to manipulate.

"Miki, yeh do no' need to force everyone to manipulate just because Atsu be doin' it to yeh." Nenet's voice sliced through the small cabin. She frowned at Miki.

Miki blinked, clearly taken aback. "Nenet, that's not what I'm doing. And Atsu didn't *force* me, and if I hadn't let him teach me, Seconds would still be banished to Thoth."

Nenet didn't look convinced, but she held her peace.

"Want to try?" Miki asked Avner, her eyes bright with excitement. "It's not evil, I promise. It's inherited through blood. Curroonians are known for their dark complexions, right? So it is with Kemetians and manipulation. It's not even supernatural if you think of it that way."

It made sense. And manipulation would improve their chances of stopping the frost. No one would ever enslave him again.

"How long does it take?" he asked.

"An hour, maybe less if you're adept, which I know you will be. Everyone here who met our brother, Beren, claimed he was the strongest Third they'd ever met, and I'm the strongest Fifth. Granted, I'm the *only* Fifth many have heard of, but either way, I have no doubt you'll be a natural."

Being a 'natural' at something so *unnatural* didn't seem to make sense. But then Avner had been a natural gibborim, which was unnatural for a pacifist.

Yet his mind recoiled at the thought of gaining another supernatural attribute. No matter what Miki claimed about manipulation being normal, it still felt too *other*. But he couldn't deny his sister—his flesh and blood—what she asked. Avner resigned himself.

"Okay, you can teach me to manipulate." Or at least try to.

Miki took his hand and pulled him after her. "Come on! The class doesn't start until this evening, so we should have plenty of time to show you around Toth. Don't worry, you'll fit right in."

28

THE ONLY ONE WHO UNDERSTANDS

Shoshanna

She had to go back. Reuben was here, within the walls of the city, and knowing that made everything else impossible. For all his good sense, Tevye couldn't understand that. He sat in the only chair in their meager room at an inn several blocks from Reuben's, making a list of all the places Avner and Chava could be, recounting their supplies, and planning to leave at first light.

The faint glow of the moon illuminated the rooftops beyond the open window. It would be so easy to scramble across them and find Reuben's room, stick a knife in his gut, and be done with it.

But Shoshanna's hand shook at that prospect. She'd admitted to Tevye that she missed Reuben. Did that mean her weakness would rob her of revenge? She paced between the window and the bed, passing Tevye sitting at the rickety desk a third time. He jumped up.

"Stop your pacing, woman! It won't help me plan,

thinking you might run off to kill Reuben at any moment and leave me in this blasted city alone."

"Then go back with me and let's end it," she snarled.

Tevye snorted. "I know this city used to banish people to an island of madmen, and I don't care to know what they do to murderers. Besides, that is not Eloah's will. I won't take another life when he isn't trying to kill me."

"Then don't come. If I'm caught, you can flee the city and find Avner without me." Shoshanna crossed the threadbare rug to the door.

Tevye jumped between her and the doorknob. "We have a plan. Follow in the morning and locate the artifacts. Take them. Then leave. Which includes leaving Reuben here, *alive*."

"That's *your* plan," she grumbled.

"Aye, and it's the best one we've got. Getting yourself killed or arrested won't reverse any of your past."

Tevye's words hit home, and she glared at him. But he was wrong about one thing. She couldn't just leave this city and leave Reuben with it.

She crossed to the bed and sat down, her back rigid. "Fine. I will stay here. You go find our route for tomorrow."

Tevye's single eye narrowed. "You think I'm fool enough to leave you alone in this inn, when you'll just leave to kill Reuben?"

"You don't need to leave the inn. Someone down in the common room must know of the closest gibborim arena outside the city. I'll stay right here, as you'd see me slinking down the stairs, anyway."

Tevye surveyed her a moment longer, but then his shoulders dropped in defeat. "True enough. I'll grab us some dinner, too. I'm starving." He pulled the door open and stepped out, then cast another glance over his shoulder. "You promise you won't do anything foolish?"

She only glared back.

Tevye left the room, clearly not the least bit reassured, and shut the door behind him. As if that would keep her in. Shoshanna pelted up from the bed and crossed to the window. Obviously, she wouldn't do anything foolish. She might not be Nuri any longer, but she still remembered how to move like her.

Shoshanna's feet hit the windowsill with a faint *thud* and she jumped out into the night. The roof top caught her fall less than three feet down, and she broke into a sprint before bouncing off to the next one. Two streets over, one up. The path to Reuben blazed in her mind like a map cut out before her. The tangle of city streets, thick smoke, and evening chatter rising from the bars couldn't throw her off.

Crossing a dozen rooftops, Shoshanna nearly smiled at the prospect of what she was about to do.

"I miss him." Her words to Tevye echoed still in her mind hours later. What had prompted her foolish statement? The ache in her chest snatched at her breathing, and Shoshanna stumbled as she stepped down to the next roof. She dropped into a roll, her back scraping against the curved adobe tiles, and popped back up, her cheeks hot with embarrassment though no one watched under the silent moon.

Curses and ash, but she was losing all that made her powerful. Staggering back into a run, Shoshanna crossed the last roof, thankful it was flat, and swung over the side. She dropped to a balcony just beneath it, the railing butting up against an inn. Up on the second floor, the inn's final window was right in front of her. Reuben's. Exhaling, she shoved any emotions deep down to where her love for Itzaak churned night and day, safely tucked away to not distract her from the mission at hand. If she ever let those feelings out... Shoshanna shuddered. She would have been gutted in the arena back in Mereen.

Freeing her knife, she crept toward the window. Laughter echoed in the street below, and doors banged open and closed along the road. Even at night, this city reveled in its stupidity. If Tevye was still in the common room of their own inn, he was no doubt swamped by drunken fools. Shoshanna stifled a scoff. It would take some time for him to return to their room and discover she was missing.

Tonight, there was only Reuben. Holding her breath, Shoshanna slid the knife into the crack of the window shutters and was rewarded with a soft *clink* as the latch fell away inside. No one spoke, though something scraped across the floor. When the windows weren't thrown open, Shoshanna pressed closer to the wooden shutters, keeping her knife between them. Someone sighed, and a tingle shot up her neck.

Reuben. She'd know his sigh anywhere. Her palm slipped around the knife's hilt, but she clenched it tighter. This was it. Jabbing the knife to the side, she flung the shutter wide open and jumped over a small desk beneath the window, landing almost soundlessly in the room. A crackling fire was the only light in the room, illuminating the fanciful swirls engraved in the walls, and curved candleholders mounted on either side of the doorway. Two beds sat at the far end, each erected on its own stone dais. A high-backed carved stone chair sat to the side. Shoshanna held her breath. A shiny boot jutted out in front of the fire grate.

"Still not close enough," Reuben's voice came from the chair.

Shoshanna froze, but he wasn't speaking to her. A hand dropped into view and rested against a leather-clad knee. The fingers clenched, then relaxed. She didn't need to see his face to know he was brooding and upset. Curses and ash. Ash and dust! There wasn't enough air in this stuffy room knowing Reuben shared it.

Shoshanna crept forward, though her legs threatened to give out. How she *hated* what she'd become.

"All your fault," she whispered.

Reuben set down his booted foot and jumped out of the chair to face her, sending a blanket tumbling to the floor. His eyes widened and he went pale. He wore the same clothes he'd worn in the market. The sight of his usual attire sent an almost visceral stab of pain to Shoshanna's chest.

She lowered her knife just a hair, and the air seemed to thicken as his beady eyes met hers, fear etched deep within them.

"N-nuri!"

The name grated on her ears. The room seemed to spin, and she took a small half-step back to steady herself. It would be so easy to throw herself into the chair opposite his and launch into a full mission report, just like old times. Even now, her body betrayed her, wanting to do just that, as her muscles tightened to the burning point.

But gripping the knife tighter, she croaked, "My name is Shoshanna."

Reuben jumped at the sound of her voice. If she'd been surer of herself, she would have smiled.

"Y-you look different. Your hair..." his words faltered.

She should rejoice at his fear, at his shock, but Shoshanna couldn't bring herself to get any closer, or to revel in this moment. The air felt oppressive, the room lavish. He felt...*what?* She couldn't think of a word for him. *Evil* would be too easy, and it didn't sum up what he'd been to her for the last decade.

Reuben didn't move. The vein in his neck pounded. He shouldn't be alive.

"How are you here?" she said, her voice quiet and intense.

He eyed her knife, but she didn't use it to get an answer to her question.

He stuttered, "Y-you know me, Nuri. There was always a backup boat. I wouldn't have let myself be trapped in Adamah."

But she had hoped as much.

"I-I hoped you were still alive. It's good to see you, old friend," Reuben stuttered.

"Friend?" she whispered. "Would you kill your friend's *husband?*" The words came achingly, and she almost wanted to take them back. Each breath she took gave him some sort of perverted satisfaction, but it was too late to leave without her vengeance.

The taste of it rose to her tongue, sharp, bitter, and salty, but she couldn't savor it while Reuben surveyed her with a mix of horror, and strangely, relief.

She forced the next words out, even though each one hurt. "Why are you relieved to see me?"

Reuben swallowed, his eyes flicking to the dagger in her palm, then back to her face. His lips quivered as he inhaled and took a step forward.

"Because I've missed you," he said in a hushed voice, fear still glowing in his eyes. "Have you missed me? We spent a decade together, as a man and his closest friend. Don't tell me that meant nothing to you."

If he was so afraid, why was he acting as if they were back in his study in the pavilion? Like they were still Chief and Right.

Friends.

Bah!

Every moment she spent talking, or listening, she allowed their old relationship to stifle the urge to kill him. Shoshanna's knuckles hurt from gripping the dagger, but she couldn't stab him just yet. She had to know.

"Why did you do it?" she whispered.

Reuben's left eyebrow rose, not even wrinkling his forehead. He had always looked too young for his forty years, even with his salt-and-pepper hair. What would he look like if she carved those eyebrows clean off?

Reuben extended his hand slowly toward the knife. "You don't need that here. We're just talking. Like old times."

An involuntary growl echoed in the back of Shoshanna's throat.

He jerked his hand back. When she didn't jump forward, he smiled, though it was strained.

"You were flawless for so long. Fighting, running, going on missions with only the smallest word from me. A well-trained gibborim operating in the free world without so much as a complaint because you didn't understand that's what you were. "

Shoshanna stifled another growl.

Reuben's gaze left the knife, but his shoulders didn't relax.

"That made it so much more obvious when you started to crack. I knew you were remembering, even if you didn't know what it was you were remembering. It started with the stone from Shoshanna's dagger." Reuben's eyes flashed with their trademark greed. "How did you get it? I looked everywhere for that knife when I captured you at Death's Wall, and it wasn't there. Shoshanna always carried it when she went on missions. It was legend. How did you get the pommel stone?" Point Blank. As if it didn't matter to her.

She stifled the urge to reach for the stone in her pouch. She'd left the dagger at home that fateful day, in such a rush to stop whatever was happening at the Pools. Even Itzaak didn't remind her to get it, as desperate as he was to stop her from going. Ofira must have found the dagger and snuck the stone away before Shoshanna's father claimed it in the aftermath of the massacre.

Then, Shoshanna had killed Ofira for it, and unknowingly reclaimed the pommel stone. She curled her left fingers together to keep from reaching for it. Reuben caught the movement. He'd know, but his gaze didn't move to her pouch. Instead, more of his fear slipped away and he stood an inch straighter.

"Did you even know what the green stone was?" His face softened.

Obviously not, or she would have figured out her identity far sooner. Her legs hurt from standing so rigidly, but she couldn't bring herself to move either toward Reuben, or away.

The sharp lines of fear relaxed from his face. "I shouldn't have sent you for that scroll of Zev—"

"Shut up," Shoshanna whispered.

Reuben stiffened. Even without color, she knew he blushed.

A twinge of anger overrode her horror at her own failure to attack. If she didn't speak her mind now, make him realize what he'd done, she'd never be able to. Her words trembled in a whisper.

"We're *not* friends any longer, Reuben. We never were. You killed my husband. You wiped my memory with the potion. You made me a slave. Made me kill dozens of men for seven years before freeing me." Her voice grew louder, fiercer, until he took a step back. "And what kind of freedom was it? You tried to force yourself on me that first night, knowing I didn't want you, knowing you had killed my husband even if I didn't. You knew I didn't want to be touched, and you only left when I threatened to kill you."

"Nuri, I—"

"And even then, you offered a lie. A freedom I wanted, but only because I didn't know what you had already taken from me. Stringing me along with promises of adventure, though you knew what it was I really wanted, even if I didn't, because you had already killed him." Her right index finger twitched against the dagger's handle, begging to scratch the wandering rash as it slipped under the cloth covering the mark of Zev. If only she could scratch Reuben away as well.

"You were the best of them," Reuben said, his voice shaking. "The only one worth anything. You alone fought back when your own men died so foolishly at the wall. The other gibborim attempted to use you, the woman, as bait, but you turned the situation around and emerged as the sole survivor. When you lasted not the usual year, but three, then five, I knew you were something different. Something worth holding on to."

Another scoff ripped from her throat. *A thing?*

"And then you lasted *seven* years with no sign of stopping. A waste to keep you there. I knew I had to..." Reuben faltered, then cleared his throat. "I'm sorry. I should never have tried to sleep with you. It should have been obvious to me that you wouldn't want to. I saw it that night. A fire of hatred in your eyes, some sign that you knew what I had done to your husband. Some inkling of truth, of memory."

"So, you never tried again because you were afraid of making me remember?"

"And I couldn't live with it," he added, almost as if it took him by surprise. He straightened. "I couldn't see you suffer that way after what I'd made you into. So instead, I kept making you. You became something no one else ever could. My closest friend, and the only person I could talk with. The only one who understood me." He reached out with a pale, gray arm. "And you thrived, Nuri! So much better than if you had remained trapped in the backward Doram, even more than if you had become my lover. Nuri, you became the sister I should have had..." He stepped closer and his index finger brushed her knuckles holding the knife.

Shoshanna yanked her hand out of his reach. "No," she hissed. "No."

He hovered in front of her, not trying to touch her again, but not backing away either. The fire crackled in front of them, far too merry for the circumstances.

"But now the sister I should never have had has ruined you," Reuben muttered. "Do you know what it is, Nuri? Do you know where this supernatural heat Chava possesses came from? What is it?"

Eloah.

Where had that thought come from? It wasn't hers. Eloah didn't exist. Or he wouldn't have brought this upon her seventeen years ago. Itzaak would still be alive, and they would be leading Doram together.

"You didn't even bother to ask if Chava lived," Shoshanna muttered.

Reuben rolled his eyes.

The fool.

"I'd given up hoping she would just die. Apparently, nothing is that easy for me."

"What about Avner?" What made her say that? It wouldn't change anything. Except...

Reuben scoffed again. "Why would I care what happened to a slave?"

"He has an object from the Nameless Tribe."

"What?" Reuben's eyes sharpened, all regret for the past gone. "How do you know this?"

A smile pulled at the edges of her mouth. A revenge of sorts. Knowing he'd missed the object would drive him mad.

"A bracelet from his mother. Chava and the Traitor snuck her to the Pens. I didn't stop them."

The air thickened with the impact of her words, taut as a hide being stretched for tanning. The fire popped.

"You *helped* him? Why?"

"I don't know." Had it been her true self-fighting back? Shoshanna lowered the knife an inch. "But the voice," she whispered. It had insisted she remember something. But surely that had been Shoshanna's voice telling Nuri to remember. Nothing else made sense.

"But where did his mother get the bracelet—" Reuben stepped back with a sharp gasp. "I noticed a bracelet on his wrist, and thought it was out of place. How did a gibborim get it? But I never, not in a thousand years...Oh, I'm such a fool!"

At least they could agree on that.

"I've got to get that bracelet, Nuri!"

"Stop calling me that." She raised the knife again. Enough of this chatter. His answers had changed nothing. They'd only cemented the knowledge that he did this all for his own benefit, which she'd already known. Even his admission that he hadn't slept with her out of respect meant little when he attributed all her good qualities to himself.

So why did the knife feel so heavy?

Reuben answered for her. "You're Nuri, and nothing will ever change that. Nuri is what you're best at. All Adamah knew. They feared Nuri enough to forget Shoshanna. That alone proves what you are. And the fact that you haven't uncovered your husband's brand. If you truly wanted to be Shoshanna again, you'd flaunt that mark."

The cloth stared up at her, and she could still see the flaming 'Z' centered in a sun beneath it. Reuben was wrong about that. She didn't deserve to wear it, no matter how much she wanted to.

"Face it, you are Nuri," Reuben said, too sure of himself.

Nuri. Nuri. Nuri. The name pounded with each fresh thump of blood through her veins. What if he was right? Maybe she couldn't figure out who she was now because it was too late to be anyone else.

"If you won't admit it to me, at least admit it to yourself. You *like* being Nuri. You were far freer as my Right than as Doram's guard dog. You thrived off the role and enjoyed the missions. It didn't matter that you couldn't remember what had happened because you fit in where you were, at my side, as Nuri." A silky, impassioned undertone stirred in Reuben's voice.

She raised her gaze to catch a dull glow in his eyes. A small voice screamed in the back of her mind that she should cut his lying tongue out of his face, but another one said no. Because Reuben was right. If she'd never started remembering, she would have happily gone on being Nuri for the rest of her life, without the truth torturing her every moment, awake or asleep. A fact that made her lower the knife in her grasp all the way to her side.

Reuben smiled his signature oily grin. "So, you admit it?"

"No," she croaked. But her mind didn't agree. Her heart thumped faster, her palms sweating. Why had she come here? She should have listened to Tevye and left Reuben alone. What had become of her new-found clarity?

What if she *wanted* to be Nuri again?

"You missed me, didn't you?" Reuben whispered.

To admit *that* to Tevye was one thing, but to Reuben... She'd never be Shoshanna in truth again.

"I..." she began, then swallowed hard. *Itzaak, help me!*

But he couldn't, because he was dead at the hands of the man pulling Shoshanna in at that very moment. And she couldn't even bear to uncover the brand—the only evidence remaining of him in her life.

Sounds of a struggle erupted beyond the door five feet away. Someone laughed, followed by a smack of skin on skin. The door flew open, revealing Felix, her onetime owner. His eyes lit up as his gaze landed on Shoshanna, but her own went to the pair behind him.

Leaf and Copper. And between them, bound, bruised, and angry, stood Tevye.

29
UNWANTED RENDEZVOUS

Shoshanna

Shoshanna's muscles ached with the urge to run. Curses and ash! What was Felix doing mixed up with Reuben? The dagger burned in her palm. One slash across both necks and this could be over.

Before she could move, Felix stepped into the room, his grin spreading broader beneath his pale eyes. The lack of color in her vision made it worse. Maybe this half-sight wasn't a curse, but a gift revealing people's true nature. Felix's void eyes reflected the void within him.

"Ah, Shoshanna, lovely to see you." Felix clicked his heels together and dipped a bow.

She held back a snarl.

Felix 'tsked' and set a hand on the shoulder of a boy beside him. The boy gave Shoshanna one wide-eyed look and took a step back.

"Copper, take Moises back into the room and lock him safely away."

Copper released Tevye's arm, and relief flashed across his face as he looked at Shoshanna.

Shoshanna smiled back. Good. He still feared her.

Copper yanked the boy down the hall.

"Gentle, my good Copper. He is priceless, after all."

"You don't have to order my Pack around, you know," Reuben said, glowering.

"But they listen so well." Felix motioned Leaf to escort Tevye into the room.

She obliged, not taking care to avoid hitting Tevye's head on the doorframe. He struggled futilely against her grip.

"You two know each other?" Reuben's gaze went from Shoshanna to Felix, his eyes wide.

"Unfortunately," Shoshanna muttered.

"On the contrary, it was quite a fortunate meeting. It was she who introduced me to the golden-blooded gibborim." Felix threw himself into the chair by the fire, his wide sleeves draping over the stone arms.

"Ah. You failed to mention that in your tale, in the weeks we spent together on the boat." Reuben frowned.

Shoshanna held back a smile. He was *jealous*. Whatever brought him pain, let it consume him, no matter how misguided.

Tevye pulled against Leaf, but she yanked him to the side of the room and growled, "Stay put, or I'll do what I should've done back in the pens the night you broke free."

Tevye smiled at the scar gouged into her forehead just below her hair-line. "Never would have thought it would take just one wooden plate from Rivka to bring you down."

Leaf's eyes narrowed, but Reuben cut her off before she could voice a rebuttal. "Tevye! I hadn't noticed you. Still broken, I see."

Tevye's one-eyed glare drilled into him. He spat to the side, the wad landing squarely on Copper's boot just as he reentered without the strange boy. The man growled under his breath and grabbed Tevye's arm.

"I'm assuming he was one of your gibborim as well?" Felix waved a lazy hand at Tevye.

"Still is. I never gave him a letter of freedom."

Felix clicked his tongue. "But unfortunately, I bought him fair at a market, then traded him to get your golden-blooded gibborim."

"But the laws of gibborim ownership state your ownership is void if he is discovered to be a runaway, therefore your trade is also void, and he returns to my possession."

Felix shrugged. "I suppose you are right, though I don't particularly care what happens to him. He's a cripple. That's why I traded him, though he offered interesting sport in the arena."

"Stop discussing me like a piece of meat," Tevye growled.

"Ah! Tevye, I'm surprised at you," Reuben said, turning to him. "You were never one to speak out before. Seems the wild has untamed you."

Again, a burning one-eyed stare. Nuri would have chuckled, but Shoshanna only raised her knife again. She was forgetting why she was here, letting Reuben soothe her, as he always used to. Yes, Tevye's captivity was unfortunate, and Felix's involvement complicated things, but she'd still only come here for one reason. Her foolish hesitation wouldn't ruin this.

She raised the knife. "I, however, *was* freed. Twice."

Reuben didn't pale this time. His trademark sly smile spread over his face. "We aren't alone anymore, Nuri. If you have any rash actions you wish to perform, I'd advise against it."

"You're a coward," she spat. "Leaf and Copper won't save you."

"No, but I will," Felix offered.

"You? Why would you care about him?" Shoshanna flicked the knife's point in his direction.

"Because he's promised to help me reacquire the Golden Gibborim."

"Reacquire? Is he free then?" The hope in Tevye's voice hurt almost physically. Shoshanna refrained from flinching. Hope like that didn't exist.

Reuben snorted. "He's free if he didn't drown, and from what I know of Doramites, they aren't swimmers. Even Felix only survived long enough for me to fish him out of the waves thanks to his proficiency at swimming and a convenient floating scrap of lumber. I doubt the same can be said about Avner and Chava."

"Eloah, protect them," Tevye whispered.

Reuben started, starting at Tevye as if he had three heads. "Not you too?"

Shoshanna's nail dug into the knife handle. This needed to end, or Shoshanna might end up saying a prayer to Chava's deity to get them out.

"Though after what you've told me, Nuri, I need Avner to be alive," Reuben said, looking fearful again for a moment. But then he took in the wooden staff in Leaf's other hand, and his fear was replaced by awe. "The staff of Doram!"

Shoshanna cursed. She hadn't noticed the staff in the commotion either. Tevye being caught was one thing, but the staff being taken was quite another. She could find another witty, one-eyed ex-slave anywhere, but not the only artifact of Doram they knew of.

Reuben crossed to Leaf and pulled the staff out of her hand.

"Finally," he murmured.

Of course. He'd been trying to get the staff for over a year now. Since before he captured Avner. Shoshanna and Tevye both reached for the staff. A satisfied gleam shone in Reuben's eye.

"Ah, no, no. This is rightfully mine, finally. But thank you for returning it to me." He pulled the staff closer.

Shoshanna couldn't stifle a low growl. Reuben started, met her gaze, then laughed. "Do you care more about the artifacts now that you're on the wrong side?"

Sides. Bah. What a ludicrous notion. How could she choose a side without knowing who she was?

Felix crossed his long legs in front of the chair. "As fun as this reunion is, I'd like to state my intent to take the woman gibborim back. You don't mind, Reuben, do you? I don't have the prize I traded her for, and she is the most interesting thing this side of the sea."

"I'll impale you like a pig if you try." Shoshanna took one step closer to his chair, her knife out.

A half smile crept over Felix's face. "*That's* why I like you."

"You won't survive her a second time. She's mad." Reuben stopped caressing the staff and looked up.

Shoshanna stared at him. Had he really reduced his opinion of her to that, despite claiming he thought of her as a sister?

It doesn't matter, a voice whispered somewhere inside her. *Kill him. End this.*

Yes. That's what she should do. But her arm wouldn't slice forward to spill blood from his neck.

"See? She's broken." Reuben dismissed her with a wave of his hand as she stood frozen between him and Felix. So much more confident when she didn't have him cornered and alone. She should have killed him when she had the chance. Even if she tried it now, Leaf and Copper would stop her. Even Felix could, if he wished. She'd seen him fight when he was showing off his prowess the day he bought her.

"I can handle her, Reuben. I'm not the world's greatest gibborim master for nothing," Felix said, still smiling.

Reuben scoffed. "And yet you lost your most prized gibborim."

"As I said, I'll help find your precious artifacts if you help me get Avner back."

"So that's what this is about?" Tevye scoffed. "You won't beat them. We already found another."

His words broke through Shoshanna's indecision and hatred. Yor's knife. Had it been claimed by the sea?

Reuben's expression remained blank, but Shoshanna knew what warred beneath the surface. Jealousy, and anger that he'd been bested to yet another artifact besides the Nameless bracelet.

"Oh? Which tribe?" Reuben asked, with false indifference.

Tevye snorted. "Like I'd tell you. I won't give you even an inch to go off—" he stopped short, staring at Felix.

The man still lounged in the chair as if this encounter was the most boring thing in the world. Tucked into his belt, glinting in the firelight, was the knife of Yor Colebee had given them. The black stone almost blended into Felix's dark belt and pants, so it was no wonder she hadn't noticed it before. He couldn't know what it was, or he would have bartered it to Reuben by now.

The same could be said for Reuben, or he would have found a way to get the knife from Felix. But Tevye's open-mouthed stare would make them both figure it out if he didn't stop being a fool. Shoshanna glared at him, and his mouth snapped shut. He stared hard at his maimed hand.

Ashes, they needed to get out of this ridiculous situation.

"Whatever they found is at the bottom of the ocean, my dear Ben. Your time will be better spent finding another one. And helping me find Avner," Felix drawled, oblivious to the silent exchange.

Reuben's ears reddened, but he waved a hand at Shoshanna.

"Take Nuri then, if you think you can survive her."

Shoshanna stepped back. Reuben should know better than anyone. No one "took" her.

"No, no, my little champion. You won't be leaving here a free woman. Leaf, take her." Felix snapped his fingers.

Leaf paled beneath her scar, casting a sidelong look at Copper. Shoshanna couldn't resist smiling. Those fools knew what she was and what she could do. They'd be even more foolish to attack.

She scoffed. "You tried this before, Reuben. Gidon learned the error of it. Do you want to lose your remaining people to me?" The fire glinted off the blade in her hand.

Reuben shrugged, but fear flickered in his eyes. "If you want her, Felix, it's up to you to catch her. I washed my hands of this madwoman months ago." As if he hadn't just been trying to win her back before Felix showed up.

"Excellent. I'm always up for a challenge." Felix leaped out of the chair, his boots scraping against the stone floor.

Shoshanna took another step back. Reuben would never have confronted her personally. Felix should realize what that meant. A glint of excitement shone in his pale eyes, bringing a strange light to his face. He swaggered forward.

"You should realize it is in your best interest to be my gibborim. This end of the world celebrates a famed gibborim instead of leaving them in a pen to rot. You'll be rich."

Shoshanna wouldn't engage with this brute, no matter how fine his clothes, or how cloying the fruity perfume wafting off him. She couldn't leave here without her revenge, but she also couldn't leave the staff in Reuben's possession and Yor's artifact in Felix's. Reuben would figure it out soon enough once he got a close look at it.

And Tevye... could she leave him to return to the gibborim arena?

Shoshanna backed up as Felix advanced, until the backs of her legs hit the edge of the desk she'd jumped over when she arrived.

Behind Felix, Reuben raised his hand, his eyes widening. "No!"

The back of her neck prickled. There was something behind her he didn't want her to see. Keeping her knife raised, Shoshanna turned. A large chunk of petrified wood sat on the desk, along with a wrapped oilskin bound with a leather cord. Manoach's piece of a ship, and Eder's document. Two of the artifacts Reuben had thus far collected.

Shoshanna's pulse quickened and her breath hovered in the back of her throat. Another, much smaller object sat at the edge of the desk. The small, finger-smoothed knob of wood shone there, reflecting the rising moon in the window above it.

An unintentional sound escaped from her lips. Half moan, half something too personal and deep to express. Itzaak's bit of wood. The good luck gift from their cursed marriage.

Her free fingers twitched, longing to hold it with an urge so powerful, it almost hurt. She hadn't held the bit of wood, or seen it, since before she remembered why it meant so much. As Nuri, it had just been something she'd always had. Something she fiddled with as a source of inexplicable comfort.

Well, now she knew exactly why the smooth ball of wood comforted her.

Take it back for me. Itzaak's raspy voice filtered in on the moonlight.

"I will," she said, quickly stifling a sob. Nuri wouldn't dare cry, and Shoshanna couldn't afford to, especially in this room with *him.*

"Ah, she's noticed your artifacts, Reuben. Probably best to make sure she can't take them," Felix's voice came from behind, and too close.

But Shoshanna couldn't bring herself to look away from Itzaak's bit of wood. *Her* bit of wood. Had Reuben handled it as much as she used to? Polluted it with his finger oil, corroding any bit of Itzaak's that remained? She reached out to pick it up, but Reuben cleared his throat.

"That isn't yours any longer, Nuri."

Her fingers rolled back into her palm and clenched hard enough to squeeze the miserable life out of the man. She'd hesitated to get her revenge, and now she'd pay for it. Half the artifacts of the lost tribes were in one room, counting Yor's knife. No matter what the bit of wood meant to her personally, it still was an artifact of a lost tribe. Zev. Forcing her hand down, she turned from the table.

"Nuri..." Reuben began, only to cut off as her icy stare met his.

Behind him, Tevye gave a fraction of a nod. She didn't return it.

Felix hovered a few feet away, his arms crossed over his chest. "Reuben's told me all about your frost, and I wouldn't have believed it if I hadn't seen the frost-burned toes of a few unfortunate sailors from Ur. But I'd again like to point you can have fame and glory, not to mention as much wine as you'd like, if you come with me, Shoshanna."

The sound of her true name on his lips stung more than her false name on Reuben's. Felix extended a hand, smiling, and strangely, his eyes reflected that smile, as if he truly believed he was offering her all she wanted.

But she wanted the artifacts. And she wanted to kill Reuben, even if a tiny part of her still hesitated. She wanted to free Tevye since he'd done nothing to wrong her. She longed for color and respite from Felix's overpowering perfume.

But above all, she wanted to know what she was, and that wasn't something anyone in the room could tell her. So, she'd have to choose. Tevye, the artifacts and her bit of wood, or revenge.

Reuben took a step back, even as his hand remained extended, trying to protect his precious artifacts. Shoshanna didn't hold back the thin smile pulling at the edge of her mouth. She knew what she'd do, and it would be a revenge all its own. The tingling of the wandering rash shifting warmed her forehead. Felix straightened.

"What in the blazes—"

Shoshanna swung her leg up and rammed him in the gut. He staggered back but she didn't wait to see if he fell. Sheathing her knife, she swung over the table, and snatched up the document. She rammed it between her teeth, then grabbed the rock. It was heavy, but it didn't slow her down as she held it to her chest with one hand and swiped her bit of wood with the other. Cool, blessedly cool. It felt like hers.

"No, no! Stop her!" Reuben shrieked, but too late.

Shoshanna leaped out the window, Reuben's scream of fury mixing with Tevye's cheer behind her. She hit the ground and rolled, her fingers clasped in a death grip around her bit of wood.

"Go! Get them back!" Reuben's order followed her.

Shoshanna jumped up and whipped around a corner, her teeth digging into the precious oilskin containing the document. She slid into a narrow alley and kept running. She had half the artifacts, and half of what Reuben cared about most in this miserable world.

30

SECOND CHANCE

Avner

After a day of exploring Thoth and spending time with his sister, the sun had set when Miki finally led them to the training ground, the meager moon lighting the way. While it had seemed frivolous to wander around while Tevye and Shoshanna waited for them, there wasn't anything to be done until the boat returned. Miki had shown them to a massive tent holding all the washed up finds from shipwrecks, but Chava had immediately pointed out none could be verified as an artifact of the tribes. This had dashed Avner's hope that finding another object would be so easy.

After putting it off all day, the time to learn to manipulate had come.

Now they were half a mile outside of the village. A circle of torches blazed around giant boulders tilted in an array of positions. One boulder lay on its side, one stood straight up, with a white divot in the middle, and another balanced between them.

A group of children and a few adults were practicing the strange power, and Avner's hopes began to rise, but they faded when he noticed Zosar standing in the center, his hand raised, his eyes glowing green, and his face contorted in deep concentration. Avner jumped a little as a small rock flew skyward and cracked into the middle of the white space on the largest boulder. Dust shot into the air, then settled on one boy standing too close.

"Zosar, if you are willing, I'd like to teach my *brother* to manipulate." Miki smiled brightly.

Zosar scowled. "I never heard you had a brother other than Ren."

"Beren was one of two. This is my eldest brother." Miki glowed.

Avner shuffled awkwardly, still not used to the title. He'd never been an older brother in Doram.

Zosar's scowl didn't lessen, clearly not over their initial meeting, but he stepped aside. Ptol wasn't anywhere to be seen. Avner wasn't sure he'd be able to hold back if he saw that man again after what he'd done to Chava.

Miki moved into the open space and beckoned Avner forward.

He paused. The stones and torches were stark reminders of the practice field in Eder and the fighting ring on Felix's ship.

"Go on, Avner," Chava encouraged him. Her presence was strangely comforting.

Miki's face shone with excitement, and Avner's reluctance dissolved. He stepped forward into the ring. This wasn't the same as being forced into the training field. He was *choosing* to do this as a favor to his new-found sister and to help with their mission.

Avner met Miki in the middle of the growing circle of onlookers. A few children elbowed each other and pointed to his hand, then Chava's, the marriage marks glowing gently in the dim twilight. The cool wind skimmed Avner's cheek, and he breathed deeply.

"The first rule is to never think, only feel." Miki's eyes darkened to purple as the wind increased.

Avner's shirt tugged against his torso, and he planted his feet firmly in the dirt to stay upright.

"Once you've tapped into the feelings of the world around you, breathe out, and let your thoughts fade. Then the power of manipulation will flow into you, and you can control it, thereby controlling the elements. Watch." Miki dropped one hand, and the wind died all at once. Her hair settled slowly around her shoulders. She exhaled, and her eyes turned a glowing periwinkle.

Zosar yelled a warning and jumped back just as a spray of ocean water zoomed through the crowd and splattered against the rock. Avner gasped. A quarter-mile separated them from the water.

"Care to try?" Miki took a step back and waved him further in.

Many questions arose, yet he only voiced one. "Do I have to raise my hands?"

"No, but it takes a considerable amount of practice to get to that point. I only raise my hands so others know what I'm about to do, but you're going to need to, regardless. Stand with your shoulders relaxed and let the wind brush your cheeks. Feel it. Relax into it." She spoke the instructions as if she'd given them hundreds of times.

Avner splayed his feet further apart, rolled his shoulders, and took a deep breath. His actions resembled his usual pre-match preparation. Maybe if he felt the thrum and adrenaline of the arena, he could manipulate. Maybe that would be enough. Against every fiber screaming no, he gave in to the memories with a shudder.

Sand, sun, the tang of blood. The strong wind hit him.

"Come on, come on," Miki murmured across from him.

Avner let a gust of wind push him back as if he were a birch tree, feeling its power rush over him. But he didn't feel any other sort of energy flowing into him. No supernatural ability tingling in the fingertips hanging uselessly at his side. Just as useless as they'd been when he had tried to access the power of the Spirit of the Forest back in Doram.

But that was because it didn't exist, where Miki's manipulation clearly did.

"You're thinking. I can see it in your face," Miki chuckled.

"Sorry, there's a lot to think about."

"It takes most people a few times. Can you feel anything when I manipulate?"

Avner frowned. The wind still tugged at his shirt. Nothing else had changed. "No."

Miki didn't seem fazed. "You try this time."

Avner sighed. He tried to let the salt-rich air soothe his mind so he could break away from his past. The torch behind Miki flickered against the star-strewn sky. Like the ones on Felix's ship. The dread of a dozen nights spent fighting overcame him. Avner closed his eyes and gave in to the feeling.

He stood like that, his palms open wide and his eyes closed, for another two minutes. A few murmurs echoed around him, but no one else spoke. Even Chava held her peace.

When his arms ached from holding them out, Avner

dropped them and opened his eyes, scoffing. "This isn't working. I can't do whatever I'm supposed to be doing."

He expected Miki to protest, to insist he try again, but she looked down in disappointment.

"She can't feel anything from him," Zosar muttered. A woman in a fur hood beside him nodded, frowning.

Avner shouldn't have felt ashamed, yet failure stung him.

"Should he try again?" Chava asked.

"I feel nothing from you," Miki murmured. "It's impossible. Even if you weren't manipulating, I should still feel at least a hint of power. Even the youngest second-born children have it." She looked lost, confused. "I don't understand."

Homed had been right after all.

"What does it mean?" Chava asked, glancing nervously from Avner to Miki.

"I suppose it means Avner can't manipulate, despite being a second-born Kemetian. It's unheard of."

The words settled on Avner's shoulders. Another facet of his life that didn't make sense, just like his glowing blood.

Chava squeezed his arm. "It's okay. You've made it this far without that ability. Eloah doesn't need you to have it, or you would."

Avner pulled his arm away, regretting it immediately as Chava's face fell. He hadn't meant that, but not letting her get close had become second nature. He reached for her, thought better of it, and rubbed the bridge of his nose.

"It doesn't make sense," Miki mumbled to herself.

"So, it's just another thing I fail at." Avner started to walk away, though leaving Miki was the last thing he wanted to do right now, even if he'd let her down.

A warm hand grabbed his shoulder and pulled him

around. Chava glared at him. "What in the name of all that is right and good have you failed at, Avner?"

His building tension snapped. "Everything, Chava! I couldn't save Doram when I became a gibborim, and I still couldn't save it when we had to flee the frost, which I couldn't stop. I failed to keep the staff or find any of Reuben's artifacts before we left Eder. I failed Zira, Moss, my mother, and Silas! I'm only valuable to anyone because of my golden blood, as Felix pointed out, and I don't even know why that is. I don't know what I am, and even these Kemetians here can't explain it. I found my sister, but I can't do the one thing she wants me to do! So, you tell me, Chava. What *haven't* I failed at?"

"You didn't fail to save me from Reuben's potion. You got Shoshanna out of Doram and saved me from Felix when I thought I'd die in the arena," she whispered.

He snorted. "All coincidence. None of that was just me."

"You're right. Eloah brought you through, and he can reveal who you are if you let him." The wind tangled Chava's bright curls in front of her anguished face.

"No one can do that. I've tried."

"Avner, please—"

"No. I'm done. Don't talk to me about it again."

Chava snapped her mouth shut, and though he was the one who had failed, she looked as if she might cry. She pushed past Avner and jogged down the dark path without a word. He'd seen her angry before, but this sadness was different. It felt more dangerous. Guilt rose within him, and he almost called her back, but his frustration overbore it.

Miki watched her leave, with a look of deep confusion. "What do the marks on your hands mean?"

Avner cursed the fact that she'd witnessed his outburst, but he couldn't take it back.

With a deep sigh, he ran the marked hand through his hair, then stared at the three purple intersecting rings. "It's a marriage mark."

"Marriage? You and she... married?"

"Kind of," he offered lamely.

Miki frowned. "I didn't think marriage was a 'kind of' scenario."

Avner was silent. If only Miki's words weren't true.

"But that means Chava is my sister-in-law!" Miki's eyes lit up. "Why didn't you tell me that from the moment you knew we were family?"

"I-I don't know."

Miki raised a brow, but didn't press it. Avner turned and trudged back to her house, his answer haunting him the entire way.

31

MIDNIGHT MADNESS

Avner

As the night fell and the camp grew quiet, Chava didn't return to Miki's home. Avner kept telling himself that she was exploring the island or getting some much-needed time to herself after weeks of being forced to spend every moment near him.

Miki slid a wooden plate loaded with roasted meat and fresh cheese across the table toward him. "We normally save meat for special events, but I'd say finding my brother counts."

Avner found he couldn't mirror her enthusiasm. His words to Chava had been true. He *was* a failure. His inability to manipulate was just further confirmation of what he already knew.

Miki frowned at a third plate as she set it on the table. "You sure Chava didn't drop by when I ran out to check for a message from my scout?"

Avner shook his head, and guilt rose up again. Maybe he

should have gone to find her. He could tell himself he hadn't done it because Chava wasn't the kind to appreciate being coddled, but another reason glimmered under the surface—one he didn't want to give voice to. Not the least because he'd shouted the opposite to Miki just hours ago.

"Well, Thoth *is* small. I'm sure she will find her way back." But concern wiped some of the excitement off Miki's face.

Avner fiddled with his fork and glanced out the window. The moon hid behind a row of low-hanging clouds, but some streaks of silver still made it through.

"Chava is more than capable of taking care of herself," he said, more to himself than his sister.

"Thoth is small. She can't get lost." Miki sat on the bench across from him.

Avner glanced out the window again. Chava *was* the clumsiest person he knew. If anyone could get lost on a small island, it would be her. Maybe she'd broken her ankle, and was lying in the brambles, hoping he'd find her. Save her. Hold her.

"So, tell me about your life once you left mine," Miki said, her voice cutting into his spiraling thoughts.

Avner glanced up, dropping his fork. He snatched it back up and cleared his throat. He was being a fool.

"Avner?" Miki tried again.

"Yes?"

"Are you okay? I'm just as shocked as you that you can't manipulate, but maybe once you finish your mission and I find Moises, we can sail for Kemet and do some research in El-Pelusium's library. If a second-born cannot manipulate, those scrolls will address it. And then you could meet Father!" Her voice brightened.

"Father." The title left an acrid taste in his mouth. Avner didn't know how to equate that term with someone he longed to see, after the poor example he'd grown up with.

Miki's fork thunked against the table. "This isn't about manipulation, is it?"

"What?"

"You're worried about your wife."

"She's not my wife," Avner said too quickly.

Miki raised her brow. "You know, I've been meaning to talk to you about her, and I'd rather do it before we are all just feet apart from each other on a boat."

Avner held back a groan. He glanced down at his marriage mark. It wasn't shining without Chava's presence, and for the first time, he longed for it to be brighter.

"In fact, I should have brought this up the moment you mentioned you were married." Miki pushed her food away. "You may be my big brother, but I can still offer you my advice. We have years of catching up to do, but if I had to pick one thing to offer you, it would be about this."

Avner sighed and set his own fork down. "Miki, it's not a normal marriage. That's what I was trying to tell you yesterday. We didn't agree to marry each other. We don't even have feelings for each other."

Liar, liar, his blood pounded in his ears.

"I had someone like Chava once," Miki said softly, balling her hand in what Avner knew was her nervous tick. "I barely got to tell him I loved him before I lost him. Maybe it is because we share blood or because we are both fools, but I don't enjoy seeing you make the same mistake I did."

"I'm not," Avner shot back, stabbing a piece of cheese so fiercely it broke apart into white crumbles.

"You keep telling yourself that, brother," Miki said.

A gust of wind cut through the open window, and Avner glanced out into the foggy night, shivering. Was Chava cold out there? She didn't know this island any better than he did. How could he leave her alone?

Miki's frown proved she wondered the same thing. But she had the grace not to reprimand him as she tied the window flap closed and rolled out the bed pallets, excluding one for Nenet since the woman was spending the night at an expectant mother's house in case the babe came.

Avner kept quiet as they settled down for the night. While there was still so much he wanted to talk to Miki about, he couldn't bring himself to with Chava gone. When they both finally lay on their bedrolls, Miki simply bade him goodnight, as if knowing he needed to be left to his own thoughts tonight.

Avner sat against the wall, his legs under a fur. This morning he had discovered that Miki was his sister in this same spot, but right now a different woman was on his mind. With the window curtain shut, Chava seemed even further away. The mark on his hand was a pale purple, though it seemed to pulse with his heartbeat.

Miki curled onto her side at the other end of the room, and after a few minutes, her breathing evened out as sleep took her. Avner was alone, and Chava... was she okay? Was she lost despite Miki's assurances? He glanced at the sleeping pad Miki had made up for Chava, empty and lonely by the far wall. He should have gone looking for her hours ago. She shouldn't be alone, even on this isolated island.

She should be with me.

Oh, curses and ash.

Avner threw the furs off and stood up. Miki didn't move. Not wanting to disturb her with the creaky door, he crept toward the window and untied the curtain flap. The island's terrain rolled into the foggy night before him, silent and peaceful.

He jumped through the window, a sudden burst of adrenaline cementing his decision. He had to find Chava.

Breaking into a sprint, he gritted his teeth against the pain of rocks jabbing into his bare feet. But he couldn't stop now. He'd been a fool to wait so long. Chava could be anywhere, and he had no clue where to start. But the adrenaline urged him forward, down the path, past dark fires and quiet tents, toward the shore. If she wasn't there he'd go back to the village and search every tent if he had to.

Avner crested the last sloping hill, and the dark ocean spread out before him. The churning line of water surrounding the island, and keeping all the inhabitants stranded, stretched to either side of the horizon.

He didn't slow, racing down the slope to the shore. The sharp tang of salty sea water filled the air, and waves crashed on the empty beach. He kept on running. Maybe Chava was around the next boulder, or the next bend. Each pump of thundering blood through his veins screamed at him to find her.

Tonight. Before it was too late.

Avner sprinted around a massive boulder, clutching his chest. Something jabbed his foot, and he stumbled to a halt, hissing in pain. Bending over with his hands on his knees, he tried to catch his breath.

"Nice of you to join me," Chava's voice came from behind him.

Avner spun around.

She sat against the hillside, her knees pulled up to her chin, and her arms wrapped around them.

He caught his breath in a rush of relief. Just like she had when they first arrived here, Chava looked soft and reserved, the moonlight creating an aura around her. Months ago, he might have thought this side of Chava didn't exist, but now he knew the opposite. It was always there, hiding under her stubborn exterior, protecting her warm core.

"H-hi." Not what he had meant to say. His heart pounded over the crashing waves nearby and his hands trembled. He couldn't stop staring. This side of Chava...something was different. The air was charged with it as Avner stepped nearer to where she sat.

Chava patted the scrubby ground beside her. A thrill of *yearning* shot through Avner. He hesitated only a moment before dropping to the ground. He owed her that much after being so short with her earlier. He sat beside her, unsure of what to say. The adrenaline that had brought him out there evaporated. She was fine. Unharmed and not lost.

Avner grabbed a handful of the coarse sand beneath him. Rough, brittle, just like him.

"I don't blame you for wanting space." The words rushed out. He threw the handful of sand toward the dark water. It scattered in the wind that never seemed to let up on Thoth.

"I didn't want space. Though I figured you'd appreciate time with Miki." Her red curls blocked her face from view, but her words were tinged with a strange emotion. Chava pulled the hood of her fur poncho up and wrestled her curls inside, safely tucking them away from the wind. "Sorry I didn't come back to Miki's. I should have returned sooner, but I hear Eloah louder when its silent."

"I wanted to make sure you were all right." Not just wanted. *Needed.*

Chava nodded and Avner waited for her to say more. When nothing came, he laughed out loud.

"What?" Chava turned toward him.

"I just, well, I caught myself waiting for you to say *more*."

Chava snorted. "I'm sure if I keep speaking I will say something you don't like."

"Probably." Avner smiled. He closed his eyes and pushed his hand into the sand at his feet. There was something comforting about the cool pressure.

"You know Avner, you aren't a failure, and you don't need to understand why you are the way you are to embrace it."

If that was true, he'd never have felt out of place in Doram to begin with, and wouldn't care that he didn't know why his blood glowed. He opened his eyes to a gray shoreline broken only by white-crested waves and weathered boulders. The moon did little to brighten the dark surroundings.

"Maybe I'm cursed." The words rushed out in a whisper. Avner pulled his hand out of the sand and the grains tumbled down like the shattering of his life's hopes.

Chava scooted closer and warmed the gap between their hips. Avner stiffened as the scent of cinnamon floated around him in the wind. Heady, intoxicating. He almost stood up, but the desire to stay beside her was too strong.

"You're not cursed." Chava said softly, and her shoulder nudged his.

"Then why did your Eloah allow me to find my family, only to deny me the answer about my blood?"

A smile tugged at the corners of her mouth. "Are you admitting Eloah is real?"

He frowned. "No, of course not."

"But he couldn't curse you if he's not real, could he?" Chava's smile widened.

"I just meant *if* he's real, he has a pretty cruel way of playing with my life."

"Whatever is going on with your blood must be a gift. And it was a gift to find your sister in the place we least expected to."

"A gift?' Avner scoffed. "How? I'm too late to save my brother who apparently died here years ago, or the sisters who died at birth. I always thought if I found my family, it would explain everything, but it didn't. I'm still a freak."

Chava's hand rested on his wrist. "I'm a freak too," she whispered.

Her fingers pressed his down into the sand, threading between them. Heat snapped in his marked hand. It was almost as if he could feel their heartbeats pounding in sync through her skin on his. He should pull away.

But a strange sensation held his hand in place beneath her fingers as a new revelation brought him up short.

Chava cared for him.

For so long he'd dismissed the possibility because of the circumstances of their sham union, but he'd heard the rumors of matched couples in Eder growing to love each other. The heat in his hand didn't subside, and judging by the blush on Chava's cheeks, she felt it too.

It was too much. Avner pulled his hand away and staggered to his feet to keep from doing something he couldn't take back. He turned to leave, not sure what else to say. This whole interaction had been as unexpected as it was confusing.

"I've always wanted a sister," Chava said softly behind him. "And now Miki is as good as one."

He paused in mid-stride and turned back, despite flares firing in his mind that if he did, they would never go back to how things were. The moon was on the opposite side of the island now, but its glow caught Chava's curls peeking out of her poncho hood, illuminating her features.

She was breathtaking.

"Avner?"

"Y-yes," he whispered. "Miki is your sister-in-law."

Chava inhaled sharply. He'd as much as validated their marriage.

"I'm going to get some sleep," he said, his voice rougher than he meant. "You should—"

What? Come with him? Sitting out here, alone and *touching* had been bad enough. He shouldn't want to share a moon-lit walk with her.

Except he did. He *really* did.

"I'm fine out here. It's so peaceful." Chava saved him from finishing his thought.

"Be careful."

Chava nodded, though a part of Avner wanted her to reach for his hand, to pull him back into the sand and beg him to sit a while longer. He turned and trudged through the sand, his legs like lead. What was he doing? His heart pounded madly. She'd come out here to give him space because she knew what Miki meant to him.

But not what *she* meant to him.

This couldn't go on any longer. He'd been a fool. An idiot.

Avner spun around and strode back to Chava.

She glanced up, confusion flickering in her eyes. "Was there something else?"

"Yes." He sounded far more confident than he should.

He dropped onto his knees in the sand in front of her. She jumped at the sudden movement. Avner grabbed her hand before he could think through this any further.

Chava stiffened, staring at their hands. Purple mark over purple mark. She inhaled sharply as Avner intertwined his fingers with hers and raised their hands. The words he hadn't been able to say moments ago beat more fiercely within him, his blood pounding in his ears.

He leaned in closer, staring straight into her eyes.

"I-I think I love you, Chava of Eder." Though he stuttered, the rest of the words rolled out far more effortlessly than he'd imagined. Relief swept over him as some of the stress he'd been carrying lifted.

She blinked. Twice. Then glanced around as if to make sure he was speaking to her. Wouldn't she say something? Had he taken too long to come to his senses? Would she reject him? Avner fought back a mounting panic. Now that he had voiced it, he *knew* he loved her. Irrevocably.

He tugged her hand gently, pulling her up onto her knees into the gap between them. Their marked hands seemed to glow even stronger, creating a luminous ball of purple light in the dark night. Her heat burned deliciously through him even as the chilly wind tried to cut through his tunic.

Avner summoned courage from the depths of her golden eyes.

"I'm sorry it took me so long to realize you are *everything* to me. I don't just think I love you, I know it. I wouldn't be here now if not for you. Twice. You've also held me through the darkest nights of my life on that boat, and many other times besides."

Her blush showed even in the pale moonlight, building his courage to say the next words.

"Chava, will you be my *wife?*" The title had never sounded so right, so sweet.

Her eyes flew wide open, and for the span of three breaths, Avner waited.

Then Chava smiled until her whole face glowed. She closed the final few inches between them and pressed her lips to his.

Heady, spicy heat flowed over him, and it wasn't just from her. Avner wrapped his arms around her waist and pulled her closer, savoring every second of the kiss. Of her. Of this moment. He'd finally awakened from his foolishness. He finally had his wife.

32

BURN IT DOWN

Shoshanna

The torch in her hand burned with the thick stench of sulfur as Shoshanna slid into the alley behind the inn where Reuben was staying. The place might be made of stone, but the framework wasn't. If the room went up in flames, Reuben would grab the artifacts first and bring them to her. Simple. Straightforward.

She ran a finger over the lump in the waistline of her pants. The bit of wood wouldn't leave her side again, while the stone and document were safely hidden in a coastal cave just outside the city. In five minutes, she'd have all the artifacts but Avner's bracelet.

But Tevye might burn. Itzaak whispered, his raspy voice full of worry.

Shoshanna gritted her teeth. Since when did her dead husband care about the man she'd been traipsing around with? Shouldn't he wish Tevye dead?

Itzaak chuckled softly. *We both know Tevye isn't a threat to me.*

But that didn't mean she needed to save him. He was a smart man. He could escape on his own.

Shoshanna stepped out of the alley and positioned herself at a good throwing distance from the window she'd escaped out of hours earlier. Darkness held the city of El-Pelusium at this hour, and the streets were deserted. Perfect for what she was about to do. The window was still open, revealing flickering light from the fire grate within. Voices rose and fell, but too distantly to make out.

Shoshanna took two steps back and flung the torch straight through the window. Someone yelled. Four, three, two—flames sprang up within the window, aided by the packet of oil she'd tied to the neck of the torch. Shoshanna blinked. It was still so strange to see gray and white flames, when she knew they should be red.

"The water! Leaf, grab the water!" Reuben's voice reached her this time, frantic.

Water splashed inside, followed by a plume of dark smoke churning out the window. Shoshanna kept her smile to herself and dropped into a crouch. She needed to be ready once the time came. Would they take the window or the door?

"The fire! It's reached the door!" Copper's voice.

Window. Excellent.

"It's spreading too quickly! Let's go!" Leaf's head bobbed into view, her braid unmistakable. She hopped up and out of the window, her arms empty.

Of course. Reuben would keep the artifacts himself—Copper followed, holding a satchel. Shoshanna took one step forward behind him, but hesitated at the sight of a bottle neck sticking out of the sack. Provisions, not artifacts. They wouldn't have had time to think of a trick, and Copper wasn't that bright.

Leaf and Copper stood coughing in the street, but neither turned Shoshanna's way. She exhaled evenly, letting the thrum of adrenaline build beneath her skin. Just like back in Eder when she went on missions, and just like when she used to step out onto the ice, ignoring the signs of death from previous matches, focusing only on the next kill.

The street faded into gray around her as only the window glowed above—a fresh burst of gray flame filled the frame.

"Reuben?" Leaf took a step forward, but jumped back as something exploded inside. She and Copper exchanged frantic glances.

Shoshanna didn't share their fear. Reuben was more than capable. He'd survived the pavilion fire, after all. Her face warmed in the heat of the flames, and the burned skin tingled with pain at the old memory. Fire might have ruined her face, but she would never fear it.

An ash-covered boot appeared in the window, followed by a leg. Reuben perched on the window frame, the staff of Doram in one hand. There'd been no mention of Felix since Shoshanna had arrived. If he was in a different room, she'd have to go inside to get the knife. Doing so first would only have alerted Reuben to her presence, something she couldn't afford. Unlike Reuben, Felix wasn't used to her methods.

The thrill of the challenge before her sent goosebumps up her back. Shoshanna smiled. She felt more alive, and more like herself, when *acting*. Doing something in her element.

But wasn't that Nuri's element? Itzaak mused.

Shoshanna gritted her teeth. It was Shoshanna's too. Reuben had only shaped what was already there. She hadn't been known as the hero of Doram without reason.

Reuben hit the ground below the window.

"Reuben!" Leaf started for him.

Shoshanna cut her off from him in three sprinted strides and snatched the staff out of his grip. The wood was cold, though Chava had shot warm light out of it on half a dozen occasions.

"No!" Reuben frantically grabbed for the staff.

Shoshanna whipped it across his legs, and he crashed to the ground with a dull thud. Spinning around, the staff caught Leaf in the gut, then the butt cracked into Copper's skull. He dropped just as Reuben staggered back to his feet, Leaf beside him. The options were simple. Stay and ensure they didn't follow, but risk losing the knife, or go after the knife, whatever may come.

Something exploded in the window above and gray debris showered over Reuben's shoulders. He flinched and batted at a stray flame flaring up on his fur vest.

Shoshanna spun away, sprinted around the corner, and through the unlocked door of the inn. Even at this late hour, a few patrons sat at the bar drinking their brew. She took the stairs three at a time, the carpet shushing under her sandals. Someone yelled behind her, but whether it was Reuben or the barkeeper, she didn't care.

Any room could be Felix's. Unless he'd just been out late. Shoshanna cursed under her breath. Why hadn't she thought of this sooner? If he got away with the knife, all this would be worthless.

Smoke poured out from under Reuben's door at the end

of the hall. The other patrons would notice soon enough—
a door whipped open on her right. A robed woman with
hair piled up on her head screamed at the smoke swirling
around her ankles and ran past Shoshanna. More doors
flew open, including the one beside Reuben's. Felix burst
out of it, his light hair a mess around his shoulders as if
he'd just woken up, though he wore the same clothes as
earlier.

Shoshanna didn't give him time to register what was
happening. She crashed into him, her free hand going to his
belt and her fingers dancing over the cool stone of the knife.
She gripped it, but before she could pull it free, Felix's warm
fingers clenched around her wrist.

"This is an artifact, isn't it? That's why Avner had it." His
breath misted across her ear, far too close for comfort.

Shoshanna twisted, taking him with her, Felix's grip
prevented the knife from coming too. She yanked back, but
his iron fingers didn't relent.

His pale eyes flashed mischievously. "I'm starting to see
why Reuben likes you so much."

Shoshanna released the knife, pulled her arm out of his
grip, and spun around, her foot ready to take him in the gut.

It didn't work.

Felix remained standing with her foot caught in his
hands inches from where she should have kicked him. A
smile pulled at his thin lips. "If the building wasn't burning,
this would be fun."

Scoffing, Shoshanna yanked her foot away and slashed
the staff down at him. Felix staggered to the side a few inches
but didn't overcompensate as she'd hoped and dodged the
blow. Best gibborim trainer in the world, indeed. But even if
he'd earned the title, he wouldn't earn her respect.

Hoping to catch him off guard, she dropped into a crouch.

He hopped around her, impossibly light on his feet. "Again, as fun as this might be, the building *is* on fire and I'd rather live." He strode toward the stairs.

Taking a running leap, Shoshanna positioned herself between him and the topmost stair just as a fresh gust of scorching air slammed into her. Choking, she over-corrected and slid past Felix.

He leaped down the stairs, coughing. Shoshanna threw herself after him. The staff hit him first, taking him in the middle of his back. Together, they tumbled down the stone steps. She landed on top of Felix in a straddle and the staff smacked into the stone floor beside his head.

"Or is this what Reuben enjoys so much about you?" Felix's eyes flashed again.

"Never." Heat burned up Shoshanna's neck.

Felix reached for a fallen brew mug and swung it at her head. She dodged, reaching for the knife again in the same movement. Fingers tasted cool stone and she yanked. The knife came! She jumped up, but Felix matched the movement. He wrenched her elbow so hard, the knife clattered to the ground.

Cursing, Shoshanna dove for it, but Felix beat her, kicking it ten paces away, where it rested in the open doorway at Reuben's feet.

"She's given me an idea for the arena, Ben!" Felix said, his eyes bright with excitement. "One on one tussling over a knife. Place it in the middle and have the gibborim fight over it."

Reuben stared at the knife at his feet, then at the staff in Shoshanna's hand. Then back to the knife. Copper reached for it, but Reuben snatched it up before he could. A look of realization came over his features as the dying torchlight in the room illuminated the strange carvings on the dark blade.

Curses and ash!

"Yor. It must be," Reuben muttered, his voice filled with awe.

Shoshanna took a step back and gripped the staff with both hands. Leaf hovered behind Reuben, fire reflecting in her eyes from the burning shutters overhead. Felix moved in closer, the same wild excitement lighting his fair face. Four on one. This would be the perfect time for Doram's staff to catch on fire, or become a rod of light, or whatever it was Chava did with it.

Shoshanna raised it, and let her breath settle back into a simple rhythm. She could do this. Had done this. She'd taken out eight slavers at once in the Barrens months ago. What were two Pack members, an intellectual, and a crazed gibborim master?

Speaking of gibborim, where is Tevye? Itzaak sounded genuinely worried, though he shouldn't care. He couldn't care. He was dead.

She faced Reuben. "Give me the knife."

"Oh, I don't think so. Give me the staff, and you can have Tevye back."

She scoffed. That was the worst deal she'd ever heard.

"I told you she didn't value him," Felix said with an exasperated sigh, as if they'd gone over this in the hours since she'd stolen the other artifacts.

"Nuri is more loyal than she'd have you believe. Trust me, I know." Reuben stepped closer, holding the knife aloft, but out of reach. "Aren't you, Nuri? You almost returned to me. You were *so* close to abandoning this mission to join me again."

Shoshanna flinched at her old name. No.

Yes. You wanted to join my killer again. You've missed him. There was only sadness in Itzaak's phantom voice this time.

"No," she whispered. No!

"Yes," Reuben said with a smile. "It's not too late. I'll still take you back and we can reunite the tribes together. Clearly, you had luck while you were with Avner and the others." He rotated the knife, his eyes gleaming with greed.

Shoshanna could almost hear him salivating. She scoffed again. She'd been weak once, but wouldn't be again—there was pounding overhead, followed by a chorus of screams. Footsteps echoed, and at least a dozen toga-clad people thundered down the stairs, followed by more smoke, thick and inescapable. Felix, Reuben, and everything else vanished beneath the heavy gray haze.

Shoshanna crouched down low, where the smoke hadn't penetrated yet. Reuben's boots turned from the door but were cut out of sight by the throng of escaping patrons. Shoshanna gripped the staff fiercely. Fire and flame. Light and power. How *had* Chava accessed it? It couldn't be her deity, could it?

But heat tingled beneath Shoshanna's fingertips at the thought. Her right hand jerked away, but she held on with the left. The heat was gone. She'd imagined it and Reuben was getting away with the knife.

There'd been a window to the left. Felix stood to the left. His boots were still there under the smoke. Was he just waiting for her to make a move, or did he have a misplaced hope of capturing her? Either way...

She snapped out with the staff to take him in the legs.

The staff hit air, and the boots flopped to the floor. Empty. Shoshanna couldn't stifle a startled laugh. He wouldn't like trudging through the city barefoot.

More screams, more feet thudding frantically past. Fire roared above. The ceiling directly over the bar was made of wood, not stone. Cursing, Shoshanna threw herself out the front door. The ceiling creaked and groaned, one beam splitting off and crashing to the ground. Someone screamed, going down under it. She didn't stop to pull them free.

The blessedly smoke-free air of the street glowed with the eerie firelight. Shoshanna coughed, clearing the last bit of smoke from her tight lungs. The burned skin on her cheek radiated heat and she hissed, refusing to touch it. Nothing could make her face worse, so it didn't matter if she had re-burned it.

Worse than her painful skin was the absence of Reuben. He could be down any of the half dozen streets intersecting this one, and the throng of people watching the fire devour the inn hid which way he might have gone.

Curses and ash, this was a disaster.

A fresh explosion rocked the street, and the last wooden shutters on the inn blew apart. Angry flames flared through the windows.

If Tevye's up there, he's dead. Itzaak murmured.

Shoshanna turned back toward the street, gripping Doram's staff tighter, but at the last moment, she stopped. Gritting her teeth, she turned and looked back at the inn engulfed by smoke. That alone was enough to kill someone, even without the fire eating their flesh. Did Tevye deserve that?

No, of course not. But she wasn't his protector.

But aren't you his friend?

Friend? That was the most laughable idea she'd ever heard. Besides, if Tevye was still in that inn, he was dead. It was too late to go back and look for him. His corpse wasn't worth her life. But Yor's knife... *that* was worth something. She turned away from the ruined inn just as someone barreled out of it, carrying a half-burned body with them. Exactly. Everyone left was dead.

33

THE MAP

Chava

Approaching Zosar wasn't something Chava had wanted to do, but knowing Avner *loved* her filled her with a giddy courage. Even as she stood beside the campfire outside the largest tent on Thoth, Chava couldn't contain the smile splitting her face so wide her cheeks ached. She would have thought last night on the beach had been a dream, but when she awoke with her neck resting against Avner's arm, to see him smiling down at her, she knew it was real.

They were finally husband and wife, and the favor Zosar was begrudgingly doing for her as reparation for the violence Ptol had inflicted would only cement that fact. Chava wiggled her moccasins in the gravel surrounding the fire, too anxious for Zosar to return so she could go find Avner again.

After they had awakened, he'd gone back to Miki to work on the boats that would eventually carry them to Kemet.

Chava had watched him go, greedily taking in his form with a freedom she'd never enjoyed before. She giggled. She wasn't going to get used to ogling her husband.

"Oi," Zosar's voice broke into her thoughts.

Chava tried to wipe the smile from her face, but not even the sight of Zosar's top-knot and sour look would do it. "Did you get them?"

He stepped out of the large tent where they kept all the things that washed up on Thoth's shores.

"Are these good enough?" Zosar thrust his hand toward her. Two rough metal rings lay on his palm, one smaller than the other. The larger one seemed to be a ring for securing a rope to a mast or holding a fishing net in place. The smaller one was shiny silver, and an actual piece of jewelry.

"They're perfect!" Chava snatched them out of his open palm. It didn't even matter whether they fit. They had their tattoo for that, but she wanted to repay Avner for last night. And offer him something to remember Thoth by in case they didn't manage to return for a while.

"Thanks, Zosar!" Chava leaned forward and pecked his cheek. "I forgive you, by the way! Tell Ptol the same!"

She left him staring after her, open-mouthed. Chava sprinted back down the path to Miki's cabin, clutching the rings in her fist. A laugh bubbled up. "Thank you, Eloah!"

She'd questioned his motives just last night, demanding to know the plan. And like the wonderful Lord he was, he'd revealed it in a more amazing way than she could have imagined. She had Avner, and he had her. Avner might not accept Eloah yet, but he'd said enough to show he wasn't as blind as he'd once been. That hope would carry her wherever Eloah called them.

Chava slowed down just before careening into Miki's home. She slid to a halt and doubled over, catching her breath.

"Okay, that about does it. I can't think of anything else we may need," Miki's voice drifted through the window. "But before we go, brother, have you thought any more on what I said last night?"

"Miki, I—" Avner began.

"No, just listen!"

"But—"

"I don't want to see you make the same mistake I did with Atsu."

"I'm not," Avner laughed. "I almost did, but I'm *not.*"

Chava couldn't bring herself to intrude. She held a hand over her mouth, stifling a chuckle.

"Eventually we're going to be on a boat with nothing to do but talk and get to know each other for twenty-four hours. You realize you will have to share things with me, don't you?" Miki asked sharply.

"And I look forward to it," he replied earnestly. "But you can calm down about Chava. You're right, I was a fool."

Chava suppressed her laugh and stepped inside. "Yes, but thankfully, he's made everything right."

Avner's face lit up. She was never going to get used to that. He closed the two-foot gap and pulled her into a long kiss. She melted against him.

Miki's gasp broke the moment. Chava pulled away from him, embarrassed. Miki was standing behind Avner, her eyes wide. Chava overcame her self-consciousness. They'd wasted far too many months of their marriage to be worried about that now.

Avner turned toward his sister with a sheepish grin. "See? I told you I fixed it."

"Uh, yes, I can see that."

Chava showed Avner the rings. "Wedding bands from the loot tent. I hope this fits you." She held up the larger one. "I know we don't technically need them since we already have our marriage marks, but I like the idea of having a bit of Thoth with us."

"They're perfect," Avner murmured as he slid the metal ring onto his middle finger.

Chava slid hers on her ring finger where it miraculously sat snugly. The marriage marks glowed vivid purple, as if they were finally satisfied.

"Well, then, shall we go work on the boats?" Chava asked, picking up a pack of food and canteens of water from the table.

"Let's go." Miki moved toward the door.

Thirty minutes later, they were back on the beach. The half-finished boats were kept in a cove around the bend, and just out of sight from the main beach where Chava and Avner had spent the night. The beach looked wild in the sunlight, black sand dotted with pitted boulders and lined to the north with surf-carved cliffs resembling faces. They reached the boats just as a man broke over the crest of the hill they had come down, running hard. Zosar.

"Miki!" He waved frantically.

Miki turned back. "What is it?"

He slid to the halt, spraying sand in every direction, and said between gulping breaths, "Clea is back."

Miki straightened. "When?"

"The back current pushed her to shore not thirty minutes ago."

"Where is she?" Miki glanced expectantly back toward town. "Is she all right?"

"Back in camp being filled with tea and soup. She brought word of Moises."

Miki's worry changed her into the sharp woman she'd been when Chava first met her. "What word?"

"He's left Kemet with a gibborim master known for collecting manipulators."

Chava met Avner's gaze and mouthed *Felix*. Avner nodded, clenching his jaw. Even so, relief washed over Chava. Moises lived!

"Where were they heading?" Miki asked.

Zosar's face darkened. "That's the thing. They were heading to Adamah."

Chava and Avner groaned in unison. There was only one reason Felix would head to Adamah, and it barely made sense.

Avner voiced it. "What interest does Felix have in the prophecy? Why would he risk death to go to Adamah? There are no longer any gibborim there."

"It doesn't matter. If that's where he took Moises, that is where we go." Miki bowed before Zosar. "Thank you for the message. Tell Clea I owe her a life debt for this information, and I wish I had the time to visit her."

"She will understand. Her boat is just down the beach." He turned and marched in the opposite direction. Miki fell in line and Chava ran up beside her.

"Adamah is covered in frost. It will be dangerous," she warned as they walked.

"Leaving Moises to die in the frost or as a gibborim isn't an option," Miki said, her voice firm.

Avner caught up. "We still need to go to Kemet and find

Tevye."

"And Shoshanna," Chava added.

"Either way, it looks like we need to take two boats, though we may all end up in Doram afterward anyway."

Miki glanced over her shoulder at them, frowning. "I'd much prefer to have you accompany me."

"I know. Me too," Avner squeezed her shoulder. "But bring that boy home. We've both lost him once. I know you won't let it happen again. I'll either meet you there or back here after we stop the frost."

"There it is!" Zosar pointed down the beach to a canoe-like boat on the sand. He shrugged the bag off his back and handed it to Miki. "Supplies for you. I figured you'd want to leave right away."

"Thanks, Zosar." Miki accepted the bag as they approached the boat, then turned to Avner.

"Tell me what you know about Adamah." Miki pulled the map out of her bag and opened it.

"It's a two-week journey to the southern coast of Adamah, below Doram, from here." Avner traced a finger over the distance from Thoth to the nearest point on Adamah. He inhaled sharply and yanked his hand back.

"What is it?" Chava asked.

"Something bit me—ouch!" He shook his wrist, then froze, his hand hovering over the map in Chava's hands.

The bracelet *was glowing.* Avner pulled his hand back, and the strange golden light dimmed.

"Do that again!" Chava grabbed his wrist and slid it back over the map.

The beads lit up again as soon as the bracelet passed over the image of Adamah.

"What in the..." Avner pulled his arm back again, and

the beads dimmed. He winced and shoved his hand back over the map. "The bracelet stings me every time I move my hand away from the map."

"It wants us to go to Doram!" Chava gasped. *Eloah, is this your plan?*

"It's an inanimate object. It can't *want* anything," Avner grumbled, rubbing his wrist.

"You said that bracelet is from one of your lost tribes?" Miki moved closer.

"Possibly." Avner frowned, still holding his hand out awkwardly over the map. The beads pulsed with light, like Doram's staff when Chava wielded it.

"I'd say it's more of a certainty now," Miki said.

"Maybe it means Tevye and Shoshanna will be there as well!" Chava couldn't say why, but the idea took hold the moment she spoke it.

"We'd be taking a great risk if they aren't. Weeks wasted sailing back and forth, trying to find them. *If* we even could at that point."

"But we'd also be leaving now, instead of whenever we get the new boat finished."

"And you'd be with me," Miki added eagerly.

Chava squinted at the beads on Avner's wrist, but the light didn't fade. The bracelet *wanted* them to go to Adamah. To go home.

"Eloah?" Chava whispered.

Trust me, he spoke on a salt-filled breeze.

"Chava..." Avner began.

"We go to Doram. I'm betting Tevye and Shoshanna will be there. They may have thought that Reuben left something behind, after all. And if not, we will find them once we've collected any artifacts we can from

Eder." Chava threw the pack of supplies into Miki's boat.

"I don't think we can assume anything about Eder at this point," he countered, only to wince as his hand moved away from the map and the beads flickered out.

Chava grabbed the map, folded it, and stuffed it into the pocket in his fur parka. "There. Better?"

Avner glanced down at his wrist. The beads still glowed, but more faintly. "The stinging is gone."

"Because going to Doram is the right move. So, let's go."

"But if we go to Adamah, we must be prepared for the frost. We could die." Avner's gaze burned with untamed desire. "I won't lose you now."

Her knees weakened.

"I think I can take care of staying warm. I can manipulate fire, after all." Miki slung her satchel into the boat and jumped in.

Avner followed, then held out his hand to Chava. She stepped into the boat, making it slightly cramped. They would barely have room enough to stretch out.

"I'm glad you're coming, brother." Miki hugged Avner, melting some of his apprehensions.

Miki's eyes brightened. "Zosar, tell Nenet I'll be back with our boy and that I'm sorry I didn't get a chance to say goodbye. Now, on my word."

"She will understand your urgency." He raised his arms and his eyes started glowing.

"Hold tight. You don't want to go flying once we hit the back current," Miki instructed. "Now!"

The boat jolted forward, the wind cutting into Chava's face. They sped toward the line of waves a hundred yards off —no seventy, then fifty, ten. She barely had time to dig her fingernails into the edges of the boat before they crashed through the back current with a massive jolt. She jerked away from the railing and went flying—straight into Avner's arms. He held her tight against his chest.

"I've got you," he murmured in the roaring wind.

Miki laughed as the boat sliced through the ocean, leaving behind a rippling wake. Chava glanced up at Avner and smiled. Whatever came next, they'd face it as one.

34

REGRETS AND LIES

Shoshanna

*I*tzaac sat cross-legged on the old Judge's rock, the wind ruffling his very shaggy curls. He'd need a haircut before she told her father what they'd done. Though Itzaac's hair would be the least of her worries once her father found out they'd gotten married. Shoshanna raised her painful left wrist. The freshly branded skin was covered in a salve they'd brought just for this occasion.

Itzaak reached out and slipped his hand around hers. "Does it still hurt?"

"Not really."

"Liar," he winked.

Her stomach fluttered. How was she such a fool for him? The three months since she'd met him on the outskirts of Doram had proved that Shoshanna could be more infatuated than she ever thought possible. But she'd known from the start that Itzaak brought a light into her regimented life. She quickly realized that she wanted to be with him until she died, and in the most complete way possible. Claiming wasn't sufficient.

So as of thirty minutes ago, they were married. A trusted squad member had accompanied them as witness, though he'd left as soon as the branding was done so his presence wouldn't be missed back in Doram. They'd opted for the simple witnessed ceremony and the exchange of family marks. She'd heard of another ceremony, invoking the strange deity of Eloah, to seal a different mark on your hands. The parents of Eder's chief-in-training had done it, and they'd both ended up dead. So Shoshanna chose Itzaak's mark.

Now Itzaak raised his much older brand and held their wrists level. Husband and wife. Sealed for life.

She slipped up on the boulder beside him and rested her head on his shoulder.

"To think the Judges don't use this rock for their confirmations anymore when it's so beautiful up here," she mused, looking out over Lake Kefa stretching to the shores of Mount Rachav beyond. The water wasn't frozen now, except for the northernmost end. One of the few months when the ice didn't cover it. Her own father hadn't been confirmed at the rock when he became Judge, and neither had the Judge before him. It had been generations since anyone had taken the oaths out here.

"Why did they stop coming?" Itzaak asked.

"If you can believe it, the Doramites used to be more adventurous than the cloistered people they are now. At some point, the elders ruled that this rock was too far from the center of Doram— and too close to the frost line. They claimed the Spirit of the Forest was stronger in the village."

"That's a shame. They are missing out on so much out here."

Shoshanna murmured her agreement, still dazzled by the sun frolicking on the blue water so far below. They were still miles from the lake, and she'd never been past this point. Maybe one day she'd touch those shores and dip her toes in that water.

"Your people are also missing out on marriage," Itzaak said abruptly, splaying his fingers across hers. "Just don't lie to your father about it. You are a terrible liar."

Shoshanna snorted and punched Itzaak playfully in the shoulder.

Itzaak didn't smile back. "You're lying to yourself even now"

She felt a chill at his sudden change in tone. "What are you talking about?"

"Tevye."

"Wh-what?" She pulled her head off his shoulder. Why did that name seem so... familiar?

"You left Tevye to burn and are lying to yourself about it."

Shoshanna squinted at the sky, her heart racing, but the sky didn't change. This memory didn't shift. She remembered the day they married more vividly than anything since the potion had been reversed. And this wasn't how it had gone.

Yet Itzaak leaned closer, his eyes burning like graying embers. "Tevye would have stayed to save you, and you just ran off without him."

She raised a hand to Itzaak's shoulder and squeezed. Solid. Real. His intense gaze didn't fade. He shouldn't know that name. She shouldn't know it. Tevye only existed in a world where Itzaak had been dead for eighteen years.

"You're a terrible liar, Sho. You always have been."

Waves crashed somewhere outside of the cave where she'd fallen asleep. Shoshanna shot up, nearly bashing her head on the stone ceiling. A sailor called in the distance, followed by the clanging of a bell signaling a ship leaving the harbor. So like the sounds back in the port city of Ur in

Adamah, though any ship bells there were encased in ice by now.

She blinked in the gray light. Her dream had been so vivid, so full of the colors she could no longer see. She hadn't realized how much she missed them. She pressed her palm against her chest, trying to massage the phantom pain away. Itzaak had been talking with her. Alive. Handsome. Real.

And now he was gone.

You are a terrible liar. Itzaak's words reverberated through her mind.

Had she left Tevye to burn? But Shoshanna didn't know anything about herself anymore, so she couldn't answer.

If she ever found Avner, he would want an answer. He was fond of Tevye. Something unsettling stirred within her. Tevye hadn't deserved to burn to death. He'd been a good man. But what could she have done? The inn was on fire.

Excuses, Itzaak whispered, his concern for a man he shouldn't care about thick in his raspy voice. *Tevye was watching out for my wife, and she left him to burn.* He sounded sad now, not accusing like he had in the dream.

"Stop it," Shoshanna whispered back. She couldn't take this from Itzaak, not after the memory of feeling him so close and so real in her dream..

For once, she didn't want to hear her dead husband's voice. It was time to keep going, and to move on from Tevye. She ran her hand against the stone wall, the faint light let in by the crack of the cave entrance just illuminating the gray outline of the bag she'd stolen to stash the artifacts in. Her heart settled back into its usual rhythm, though it hadn't truly been usual since she'd remembered who she was.

It was time to get the knife back, and no guilt over what happened in the flaming inn could slow her down.

Shoshanna shifted a palm frond over the bag of artifacts again, just in case, though no one had poked their head in the cave since she'd first hidden the artifacts there two days ago. Better to be safe—she looked at the fabric wrapped around her brand. It was stained with ash, blood, and who knew what else. She should change the cloth, but that would mean looking at the brand again. The clear image of the fresh brand from her dream flashed through her mind.

You've remembered me, Itzaak whispered. *Why keep avoiding my mark?*

Because she didn't deserve to have it. The fabric could stay ruined for now, just like the rest of her.

Shoshanna stooped down and stepped out of the cave, scattering pebbles. Sunlight glared into her eyes as she shrank against the hillside beside the harbor. Tall grass gave way before the rocky beach and lines of docks jutting out into the ocean. Half-a-dozen ships sat along the docks, with one pulling out. Not Reuben's. She'd made sure last night when she watched Leaf board the ship at the last dock.

Now to get the knife and find a ship of her own.

Are you just going to pretend Tevye didn't die because of you? Itzaak nagged.

Yes, that was exactly what she was going to do. For so long she had cherished hearing Itzaak's voice in her head, but now... Shoshanna scoffed and broke into a jog. There would be time to enjoy him again when this was over.

It was midday, and the docks bustled with merchants loading and off-loading their wares, sailors joining their crews, and toga-wearing fools of all sorts clogging her path. Gripping her knife, Shoshanna hopped off the dock and landed thigh-deep in the warm water. Dark shapes flitted away in the pale gray water, and she ploughed through until the water reached her waist, then her shoulders. Shoshanna slipped under the dock, and sunlight blinked through the wooden slats overhead. Though still able to touch bottom, she lifted her feet and swam almost silently under the dock, passing the first three ships with ease. It wouldn't be long now. She'd scouted this area extensively last night. Though she hadn't seen Reuben, he would be with Leaf. Since their rooms at the inn had burned, they were hunkering down aboard the ship Reuben had taken from Adamah, no doubt trying to wrack their pathetic brains for a plan to get the artifacts back from Shoshanna.

Which they would never do. Surely Reuben knew this, and she hoped he had spent the last day looking over his shoulder fearing that she might come for him, her knife singing. If Shoshanna regretted leaving Tevye behind, which was debatable, she regretted not killing Reuben even more. She'd been weak and was paying for it now.

I know you, Shoshanna. You regret Tevye more. Itzaak's voice held sadness so deep, Shoshanna paused in mid-stroke.

"Copper!" Leaf's voice called out above the noises of the harbor.

Shoshanna stiffened, and her feet sank into the muck at the bottom of the bay, mud oozing between the straps of her sandals.

"Get in here, won't you? He's not cooperating and I'm tired of dealing with him."

Shoshanna allowed herself a half smile. Of course, they were getting sick of Reuben. The man was a pompous fool.

She used to admire that pompous fool.

The smile faded. Not today. She wouldn't let the past stop her revenge today.

Footsteps rattled the planks above her head, cutting out the sun for a few seconds before receding toward the furthest ship. Whatever Copper thought of dealing with Reuben in a mood, he didn't say as he strode up the plank, his greasy hair lying flat in the warm breeze. Leaf must have gone back inside. Excellent. The fools wouldn't be there to see Shoshanna come for them. She stepped out from under the dock, gripped the wooden planks, and swung up onto them, water splashing in an arc around her.

The boards groaned as she sprinted up them and veered right up the plank to the ship. A few sailors loitered on the far side of the deck, scanning crates and checking lists, their white shirts billowing in the wind. The boy Felix had Copper lock up at the inn sat on a crate, his feet swinging as he watched another man move a rock through the air.

Felix's manipulator.

Shoshanna didn't need him to spot her now. She slipped through the doorway to the interior where the cabins were. Colorless flames flickered on torches lining the walls. She tore her gaze away when a yell echoed down the hall.

"Just tell us, and we can stop all this," Copper growled. Skin smacked skin.

Shoshanna slunk against the wooden wall and moved soundlessly down the narrow hall. A doorway stood five feet away, more light spilling through the opening. Someone chuckled mirthlessly inside. She stifled a snort. Copper and Leaf were bigger fools than she had believed if they thought they could talk Reuben out of his hunt to reunite the artifacts. No wonder Reuben had smacked one of them.

"Nuri is one of the smartest people I know," Leaf said. "She won't have left this cursed city without the knife. When

Reuben returns, he won't let us go easy on you anymore, so you'd better talk."

Shoshanna's skin crawled at the compliment. When would Leaf realize she wasn't Nuri any longer? But a curse nearly slipped out at the same time. So Reuben wasn't here. He never would have parted with the knife again, so even if it was Felix they spoke to, this whole trip was a waste. Better to leave and hunt for Reuben in the market, or go back to hiding under the docks and wait for his return. Her fingers tingled with anticipation. She'd lost the thrill of gutting him and retrieving the knife for now, but she'd wait as long as it took to feel it.

Shoshanna took a step back.

"That's not her name," a male voice said, hard as iron.

She froze. It couldn't be.

Tevye.

Copper snorted. "We aren't interested in what that madwoman calls herself. Just tell us how to find her."

"Do you really think she's the type to map out her plan to someone?" Tevye cut back.

He was *alive*. Relief swept over Shoshanna, and she steadied herself against the wall.

Itzaak was right. She'd lied to herself.

"You already know she will do anything to find the knife. Do with that what you will—" There was a thud, and Tevye cut off with a groan.

"Don't get smart with us, Tevye," Leaf spat. "I'll even admit I almost liked you as a gibborim, but that changed when you killed Dirt and your friend Rivka cut my head open with a plate. Tell us where Nuri hid the artifacts, or I'll maim your other hand."

Tevye chuckled. Had he gone insane? Shoshanna didn't

move back toward the door. As she'd said before, he'd made his choice by joining this mission. She didn't have a duty to free him, even if she was glad he was alive.

Yet you've been having nightmares about his death, Itzaak cut in.

Her nails scratched against the wall. She was a fool for caring what happened to Tevye.

But Shoshanna always cared about the men on her squad. That's what made her a great leader, and what attracted me to her.

Yet what could be attractive about her now? She'd been ruined by Reuben.

Only if you let it be true, Itzaak whispered.

"You can't hurt me," Tevye said on the other side of the wall. "Eloah holds me, whatever happens."

"Ha! Chava truly has worked her devil-magic on you. Copper, grab his good hand. Let's get this done," Leaf ordered.

Shoshanna didn't move. She held her breath, waiting for Itzaak's annoying reply, but none came, only the distant cry of a seagull and the lapping of waves outside.

"Hold still," Copper growled. "Are we cutting or breaking?"

"Breaking. Let's make it match the other, and he won't have any healing paste this time."

Oh, curses and ash! There was nothing for it. Maybe Itzaak was right about who she was truly supposed to be, or maybe she was just going soft. Shoshanna slid her knife out of her belt and jumped through the open doorway.

Leaf and Copper stood on either side of the chair Tevye sat strapped to. All three of them looked at her as she burst into the room. Tevye's one eye widened, followed by a brilliant smile contrasting with his torn and muddied clothes.

"I found her for you," he quipped, and yanked his hand out of Copper's grasp.

"Ho!" Copper jumped away from Tevye, pulling out his sword. Leaf followed suit, retrieving her twin daggers.

Shoshanna took a deep breath. Here they go.

Copper came at her first, his sword shrieking. She ducked, danced to the side, and ripped the torch off the wall. She smashed it full into Copper's face. He went down with a blood-curdling scream as Shoshanna spun back to Leaf. The woman was gone, leaving Tevye straining against the ropes holding him to the chair. Leaf had finally wised up? Didn't want to die like Gidon had. Copper still writhed on the floor, clutching at this face. The torch lay extinguished beside him. Shoshanna wouldn't start another fire today.

"Shoshanna!" Tevye cried, and the joy in his voice grated along her spine. No one besides Reuben had been overjoyed to see her in almost two decades.

She slid her knife under the ropes around the arms of the chair, freeing Tevye.

"I didn't think you'd come back for me. I don't have an artifact." So blunt, but so true.

She yanked him up. "Come on."

Copper still moaned from the floor. The burns wouldn't kill him, but she didn't care enough to end him. There'd been enough blood spilled by her blades for a lifetime and more. Shoshanna scanned the room. A simple built-in bed and desk, both empty. Nowhere to hide the knife of Yor.

"I know where the knife is. Let's get out of here." Tevye sprinted for the door.

Shoshanna followed, at the mercy of a crippled, one-eyed ex-slave. She shouldn't feel a twinge of relief that he was alive, but she did, and it might have been even more than a twinge.

Because he's your friend. That is not a bad thing, Shoshanna. Itzaak said, a smile in his voice.

Caring slowed you down. Caring was dangerous.

But she followed Tevye out of the ship anyway. The sailors on the deck glanced up as they burst out of the interior, but didn't call out. Perhaps they were used to torture sessions and escaped prisoners.

Shoshanna sprinted down the gangway. Tevye jumped the last four feet and landed beside her on the dock. He spun around, the gleaming smile back in place.

"We did it!"

"Keep moving." Shoshanna passed him and took off down the dock.

Planks rattled behind her as Tevye followed. "I meant it. I didn't expect you to come back for me. You had what you needed."

Maybe it was the adrenaline pulsing through her system, or the act of saving someone rather than killing them, but the truth tumbled out of her lips, "I didn't think I would either."

Tevye didn't answer, and she didn't look back to see whatever look would replace that brilliant smile. It had been so bright, so full of hope, she couldn't imagine ruining that image.

Finally, the sprint ended at her cave. She ducked inside the slim crack, and the scuffling sounds behind her confirmed there was hardly enough room for a second individual. She snatched up the bag of artifacts and turned to face Tevye less than a foot away.

He spoke first. "You're doing it!"

Well, that didn't make any sense. "What?"

"Remembering who you are!" He grabbed her shoulders.

Shoshanna stiffened beneath the touch, and tension filled the air. Was this what it was like to have a true friend? Not a treacherous Reuben, but an honest, genuine person who cared?

You know it is, Itzaak murmured in the back of her mind. *We were like that once.*

But Tevye was just a gibborim, where Itzaak had been her husband. Still, Shoshanna couldn't stop the warmth she felt inside. "I wasn't going to save you," she said, her voice hard.

Tevye didn't drop his hands. "But you did."

"It was your own fault you were captured. You chose to be on this mission." The words were crueler than they sounded in her mind.

The glimmer didn't leave Tevye's eyes. "Both true, but they don't change the fact that you came for me."

"I came for the knife. You happened to be there."

"True again, but it's what you did when you got there that matters."

"Stop it," she whispered.

"What?"

"Making me out as some kind of hero. That version of me died with Itzaak."

But she doesn't have to.

Shoshanna yanked back from Tevye's grasp. Must both men gang up on her?

"Shoshanna—"

"No, don't. I'm not the person you think I can be. If you

knew what I almost did back in the inn, you'd run as far from here as you could."

Tevye sat back on his heels. "If this is about missing Reuben—"

"No!" Well, yes. Shoshanna couldn't look at Tevye as she continued, heat prickling up her neck. "I almost went back to him."

"What?"

"In the inn. If Felix hadn't showed up with you and the knife, I was going to rejoin Reuben." Shoshanna flung her hands up, striking the rock overhead. She pulled them back, wincing, both at the pain in her hands and what she'd just admitted.

Tevye's silence finally felt right. He understood now how messed up she was, but the accomplishment of that didn't come with the satisfaction she'd expected. Instead, it hurt. The one human who for some misguided reason thought of her as a friend, now knew how evil she was.

The loaded silence stretched on. Tevye studied her with his good eye.

Finally, he leaned forward. "I understand."

The words were nonsensical. Shoshanna scoffed. "You can't. You *don't*."

A pained look flashed across his face, but he didn't pull back. "You're trying to be the woman you once were, but there are seventeen years working against you. It will take time. I might have only been a gibborim for two years, but I know what it's like to have a past where I was someone else, a husband, lover, and then spend two years in hell only to come out of it as someone else."

She balled her hands into fists. His experience was a fraction of hers.

"You don't know anything, Tevye."

He couldn't understand, couldn't know she wanted to miss her dead husband, but the fact that he was dead made it impossible, while Reuben still breathed, making him the only thing she *could* miss.

A small smile tugged at the corner of Tevye's mouth. "Eloah understands. He can help you."

And that is what I was wondering about the day I died... Itzaak murmured.

Shoshanna stiffened again. She should have seen that coming. She shoved around Tevye, the bag of artifacts thunking against the cave wall on her way out. Sunlight bit into her eyes for a moment before a dark mass of clouds covered it. Dark as the mass in her own soul.

"Shoshanna?" Tevye said behind her.

"We must go find the knife. That's all that matters."

"Well, that's the thing." There was an odd tone to his voice. Hesitant, yet amused. "I, well, I have it."

She spun around. "What do you mean you have it?"

Tevye stuck his good hand down the side of his pant leg and pulled out a wrapped bundle. He unwound the gray fabric, and the dark knife flipped into his palm, the etchings curling up the blade and around the handle.

Words wouldn't come. He'd beaten her to it. How was it possible?

Tevye eyed her bashfully. "You were too distracted by Reuben's reappearance in the market. I was trying to tell you, but you wouldn't listen."

"But Felix wasn't in the market." It didn't make sense. He'd only encountered Tevye after that. "You didn't even know Felix had the knife until the inn, just like me. I saw it in your face."

Tevye shrugged. "I'm a good liar."

"But how?"

"We passed a stand that sold ceremonial daggers. They were carved out of onyx, but with a slightly longer blade and less engravings. If you looked at them side by side it would be obvious they didn't match."

"Just tell me this is the real one," she snarled.

"It is. When I saw the merchant stand selling these, I knew it was a great opportunity! I figured it would be wise to have a decoy just in case. I bought one with the money from Leewana. All the money, unfortunately." Tevye blushed. "But it wasn't until you ran off that things really worked out. Felix came out of the inn moments after you entered, with the knife of Yor in his belt."

"You didn't wait for me to help."

Tevye shrugged again. "I didn't think that far. I bumped straight into Felix, yanked the real knife out of his belt and dropped the fake one on his foot. In the moment of confusion, I stowed the real knife in the inner pocket of my pants. Felix snatched up the fake one and returned it to his belt. Then Leaf and Copper grabbed me."

Shoshanna stared. She did vaguely remember Tevye going to a merchant stall while she was panicking over Reuben in the market. Which meant Tevye was telling the truth. It also meant Tevye had the knife of Yor in the room at the inn, and when Leaf and Copper were interrogating him on the ship.

"How did they not find it?" Shoshanna asked, overwhelmed by this new information.

Tevye shrugged again. "Leaf didn't expect me to have it, so they didn't search. They thought Felix had it right up until

Reuben took it from you. Or so I heard, since I was locked up on the ship when you burned the inn."

"And Felix didn't realize he had a fake because he never saw them side by side." Shoshanna muttered as things slid into place.

"I'm guessing. And Reuben thinks the fake is the real one. If Felix studies it long enough, he will probably realize the engravings are far cruder and not covering the blade as they should. They looked more like circles than flowers. I'm sure they will put it together eventually, so let's not wait around for that moment."

Agreed. Shoshanna took a step toward him, to what? Hug him? Thank him? Those actions and words seemed so far removed from her. So, she stood a foot away, her face burning with the awkwardness of it.

Tevye smiled and handed her the knife. "Don't mention it."

She slid it into the bag and ducked back into the cave to pull out Doram's staff. Five down. All they needed was Avner's bracelet.

Tevye seemed to read her thoughts. "Avner could be anywhere."

Or dead. But the men were friends. She didn't need to press the point. Shoshanna handed the staff to Tevye without giving him the chance to protest. The thing held some unknown power she didn't trust. She wouldn't carry it across continents if she didn't need to.

Tevye accepted it without hesitation. "Well, we'd better find another ship. Reuben and Felix will come for us." If he was afraid that Avner and Chava had drowned, he kept it to himself.

"Or we beat them at their own game." Shoshanna

hitched the bag of artifacts higher on her shoulder and headed back down the harbor. She'd only just thought of this new plan, but there weren't any other options.

"What do you mean?" Tevye's sandals flapped behind her.

"There's only one place Reuben and Felix won't be looking for us."

Shoshanna jumped in the water and walked under the dock as before. The splashing of water behind her signaled that Tevye wasn't backing out of her insane plan.

"Hide in Reuben's hold, because the only place he has left to go is back to Adamah, where hopefully, Avner and Chava are going as well," Tevye said behind her. "You're brilliant, Sho."

She'd tell him off for using that nickname once they'd settled into a dark and forgotten hole in Reuben's ship's hold. Shoshanna raised the satchel of artifacts higher to keep it out of the murky water. Her gaze caught the stained cloth wrapped around her wrist. She stared at the ruined cloth, knowing exactly what the brand looked like beneath it. Her fingers twitched, longing to expose Itzaak's mark to the sun again. Her breath caught in her throat.

"You didn't fail Itzaak," Tevye said, no doubt catching her silence amidst the sloshing of water. "You deserve that brand as much as the day he chose you for a wife. He was lucky to have you. You can be free of your past if you choose to. Don't let Reuben ruin that part of you any longer. Eloah can free you of it. Isn't that what Itzaak would want?"

Shoshanna should have scoffed, or thrown an insult back at Tevye, but strangely, his words warmed her core. But daring to hope she could obliterate Reuben from her nightmares and her heart hurt too much. Tevye might offer a sympathetic ear, but he couldn't be right about her, could he?

She didn't look back, heat burning up her neck. The stains on her wrist cloth seemed to tell a story. A man and a woman standing beside a rock, a glistening lake stretched out behind them.

Our story, Itzaak murmured.

Shoshanna inhaled, letting the sea air invigorate her. She'd do this for Itzaak, and for all they used to be. Whether or not they found Avner and his bracelet, she was taking the next step in her journey, and for the first time, she was really choosing something.

PART III

The wind is a liar, blowing a man one way, only to trick him into another. The one who dares to challenge the wind is either a fool or wise enough to surrender and let the wind send him where it wills. Therein is the greatest lie of all. That being found is greater than getting lost.

-Old Smyman Proverb

35

FOG AND ICE

Avner

Chava sat on one of the three benches in the interior of their small vessel with her feet up on another bench and her back resting against the side. The map lay open across her lap, and the wind ruffled her curls as the persistent breeze filled the sail above them.

Curses and ash, she was gorgeous.

They'd been sailing for over a week now, and though the sun beat down on Avner, he refused to remove his shirt and expose his rose tattoo. Just the thought that it was still there, inked into his skin, was enough to drive him mad. So he fiddled with his bracelet. His mother had endorsed his marriage to Chava the last time he saw her before she died. The same night she had given him the bracelet. How he wished he could tell her now that he'd come to his senses. Of course, his mother had seen right through him.

"I wish I could have spent more time with your mother.

She truly seemed like a wonderful woman." Chava's voice interrupted the lapping of the waves on the boat.

Avner started and glanced up. Chava's golden eyes held him.

"Mikhail respected your mother, I could tell."

"Don't talk about that traitor right now, please?" He'd meant it as a request, but the words came out as a command. Cold. Hard. Like the man Mikhail had become before he died.

"He was your brother and my brother-in-law."

"You have an adopted brother?" Miki stepped out of the makeshift cabin.

Avner couldn't suppress a scoff. "I don't count him as a brother anymore." But the same longing he'd felt back on Thoth pulled at him again, hard enough to hurt. Wouldn't this feeling go away? He didn't *want* to miss Mikhail.

"He had two adopted brothers," Chava said firmly. "And Mikhail was a good friend. He changed before the end. You even told me he saw something as he died. I know he is with Eloah."

"Which means absolutely nothing to me. Can we please not talk about this?" Arguing with Chava was the last thing he wanted to do now. They'd already wasted too much of their marriage arguing.

"We wouldn't even be here if not for Mikhail. He gave you the everlasting torch which saved you from dying in the Yocheved match. And the bracelet, Avner!" Chava reached across the gap between them and playfully punched his leg. "He was the one who orchestrated bringing your mother to the pens where she gave you the bracelet. We'd never have an artifact of the Nameless Tribe without Mikhail. Can't you see that?"

"Fine," Avner muttered. "But that doesn't make up for what he did to Silas, and me."

"Perhaps not, but even that set you on this path. Without Mikhail's betrayal, which I'll even say isn't what you think—"

"Chava—"

"No." She squeezed his knee. "Without the events that caused you to offer yourself as a gibborim in Mikhail's place, we wouldn't be here right now." Her marriage mark glowed vibrantly next to his, even in the sunlight.

Something ached deep in Avner's heart, and he wished this conversation would end before he was forced to think of things he'd rather not.

"Apparently there is much I haven't yet asked you, brother." Miki's keen gaze wouldn't leave him as she sank onto the seat behind him. Her eyes turned purple as she took up manipulating again. They had to allow breaks in movement so that she could sleep, but they more than made up for it when Miki was awake.

The boat jolted forward. Avner balled his hand on his knee. There were some things he'd rather not share with his sister. Things that could stay in his old life. He glanced away and inhaled sharply.

"Is that land?" he stood up, holding the mast for balance as he looked around it to the wide swath of white in the distance. The blazing outline cut into the sky in a ray of brilliance. No shapes could be made out in the mass of light and white, but as the shore drew closer, Avner caught his breath. Something else hovered over the water at the shoreline. Fog lay around the edges of the water, so thick nothing could be seen below the frost-encased trees.

"Rather misty here, eh?" Chava met Avner at the side of

the boat. "Probably because the ocean water is warm, and Adamah is, well, not."

Her logic seemed right, but there was *something* about this fog and the way it almost seemed to seethe. Avner's heart beat faster and his breath came in short, clipped spurts.

"Are you okay?" Chava stepped closer.

"This fog doesn't feel right," he muttered.

"What do you mean? It's just fog." Chava squinted at the rapidly-approaching shoreline.

They passed the hundred-yard mark and Avner clutched the side of the boat. He could have sworn he suddenly felt feverish, and it wasn't from the heat rippling off Chava.

No.... This fog couldn't be like the one in Curroon could it? What had Leewana called it? *The Orroroo.*

Avner spun to the side, but the fog extended to either side, leaving no clear place to land. Something flashed within that gray mass ahead, as if it were *alive*. Less than two minutes, and the prow of their vessel would hit the fog.

"Chava, try calling off this fog." If she could speak to it, then the fog was the same as the Orroroo, no matter how impossible it would be for it to come to Adamah, hundreds of miles from Curroon.

"What are you talking about?"

"Remember what I told you in Felix's hold about Leewana and the fog in Curroon?" Avner took a step back as the boat slid uncomfortably close to the pulsating gray mass. They'd be inside it in minutes.

Chava stared at him. "You mean when you asked if I could control fog?"

"All I know is, if you can't call it off and it's the same fog as in Curroon, I'm about to get very sick."

"Why?" Miki asked.

Avner groaned as fever heat rose in his body. This *had* to be the Orroroo! He grabbed Chava's shoulders.

"Just try, please!" His words were filled with desperation.

"I don't know what you mean. It's fog. I can't just talk to it."

She didn't understand, and if he waited for her to see what he meant, it would be too late. Leewana had saved him because she knew what to do, but Chava might not figure out how to call off the fog before the sickness took him. Would the fog eat his flesh? Would the fever burn his life out before Chava understood what to do? Would it take Miki too? He'd brought his sister here. He wouldn't watch her die.

Avner shoved away from Chava and reached for the sail. He pulled the sheet in, then spun around and rammed the rudder arm to the side. The small boat lurched left, coming parallel to the fog, and sliding toward an inlet where a sheet of ice cut into the frosted landscape and led out into the ocean. The river. The fog didn't surround it, leaving clear air and frost. Avner held back a frantic groan. He had to get there before the fog moved in and made landing impossible.

The boat slid into the frozen shore and Chava stumbled against Avner. He caught her with one hand, but his arms were shaking, as if the fog was already weakening him even though he hadn't entered it yet. Even the frozen trees above seemed to whisper a warning.

Chava hopped out of the boat. Avner took a deep breath, half-expecting the fog to lunge forward and devour her, but instead frigid air stabbed his lungs. Ashes, it *hurt!* He'd forgotten just how terrible it was to breathe in this cursed air. It had been months since he'd experienced it.

They shouldn't have come here. Miki's scout may have

found the wrong boy. What if Felix had already been here and left?

"You do have to get off eventually," Chava said softly.

Avner squared his shoulders. He was one of the best gibborim in the world. Frost shouldn't scare him, even with the cursed fog. He'd lived through it once and he wasn't going to let Chava stay on land without him. He grabbed the mooring rope and hopped over the side.

His feet crunched into the frozen river. The fog didn't swoop in to attack. It hovered at the edges of the river, swirling and seething. Avner released a pent-up breath and tied the rope to the nearest rock.

Miki remained in the boat. "I'm going to hide this somewhere in case Felix shows up. I'd rather not let him know someone has arrived. Wait here and stay close to her for warmth."

She sailed around the bend and a fresh gust of icy wind blasted into Avner. Pinpricks of ice and pain stabbed his lungs. He coughed, struggling to pull in more of the freezing air. Chava stepped toward him, and instantly a wall of heat enveloped him.

Yes, he would be staying *very* close to her.

"Do you still want me to 'call off the fog?'" Chava asked, a half-smile on her face.

"No. Forget I said anything." Avner didn't want to explain the Orroroo, because that meant admitting something he wasn't ready to consider. Maybe if they ignored the fog—The gray mist crawled closer, as if sensing him approaching.

No, no, no!

An unearthly shriek echoed from within the fog, and Avner clapped his hands over his ears, though he knew it wouldn't help. "Chava! You must call the fog off! Send it away!"

"Av, it's just—" Her eyes popped wider, her golden irises reflecting the sheen of the fog. "I hear something...a sweet sound, or song." Chava stepped closer to the mist.

Avner reached for her, only to grab his head again. If this fog was the same as the one in Curroon, it couldn't hurt Chava, but it could hurt *him*.

"J-just try—ahh!" Avner fell to his knees, ice cutting through his pants where the river rapids had frozen solid into sharp ridges.

The spine-chilling shrieking increased, grating along his nerves, and down his spine, as if the spiked mace from the Kemetian who almost killed him was still lodged in Avner's flesh. Ripping, tearing, shredding him to his core.

"D-do it, Chav—" his words ended in a moan. His hands fell from his ears and sank into the ice. Gold flecks splattered from his cut knuckles, mixing with the blood from his shredded knees.

And the fog *responded*.

Wherever his blood touched the ice, the gray mist swirled away, leaving the shining, bloodied frozen river clear.

"Wh—" Chava's words drowned under the continuing shrieks of the Orroroo.

Avner should have been shocked. He should have tried to piece together what it meant that the fog moved away from his blood, or why it hadn't done that in Curroon, but heat exploded in his chest as the fever set in, blocking out any logical thoughts. His teeth clamped together, and the first feverish chill swept through him.

There wasn't enough of his blood on the ground to keep

the fog away. Maybe if he released it all, then he would be safe.

But then I'd be dead.

And what of Miki? She needed to stay away. Chava hadn't asked, but Miki never mentioned Eloah. She'd die too. More blood. He needed it to save his sister. Avner tried to raise his trembling hands, offering the rest of his blood if it would satisfy the monstrous fog. Only a few more drops leaked out. The wounds weren't enough.

The world was reduced to swirls of gray and pinpricks of gold. Avner fell forward, his face pressing into the bloodied ice where the air was clear. It wouldn't be enough. The fog still surrounded the rest of his body, the fever wracking him.

He was going to die, not in an arena, but just a few miles from where he'd been raised.

36

HOW SWEET THE SOUND

Chava

A vner held his ears, screaming and moaning all at once, but he couldn't override the beautiful notes stringing along in the fog. They called to Chava, deep and soul-filling. She inhaled the air, but it wasn't frigid. Only sweet. She closed her eyes. Her soul lifted like the puffs of clouds she used to watch through the orange leaves, imagining Eloah in them everywhere. Seeing him in their swirls and careful arrangements. His love. His beauty. His grace. The fog caressed her legs. Holding her tight as he had the day her mother died. A sob caught in Chava's throat, but it changed into a laugh.

Yes! Thank you!

A thousand years of this wouldn't be enough. She stretched her arms out, letting the fog, Eloah, sift through her fingers. He danced around her like light against water. He flitted through her as only light could, illuminating every vein, every artery. Making her skin invisible. Filling her, revealing the true her. Chava laughed again, too giddy to control the rising jubilation.

Avner's scream tore through her ecstasy.

Her heart jumped and she whirled toward him. He lay curled in a ball, his shredded hands pressed to his bleeding ears. Screaming, sobbing. The opposite of everything she felt.

Eloah, no! Save him, please. Chava ran for Avner, the urgency pounding through her so at odds with the blissful melody flowing in the fog. Her husband needed her. He needed Eloah. Tears ran down her cheeks at the cruelty of the evil that didn't let Avner experience the fog the way she did. She was almost to him, one hand out, but her foot caught on a stone and she flew to the sharp, uneven ground of the frozen river. She caught herself with both hands, miraculously saved from shredding her palms. She knelt, praying, crying. Cursing the deceiver for holding Avner's mind like this. The prayer she didn't put into words came out through tears and a song matching the one in the fog. Eloah's song.

Amazing grace, how sweet the sound that saved a wretch like me...

She'd never heard the song before, but it came effortlessly, the way the words to the marriage vows had when she'd needed them so long ago. Something shifted in the fog. Answering, responding. *Moving.*

"I want it to stay," she whispered, even though she knew it couldn't, for Avner's sake. Her heart broke for him, and she knew Eloah would always be there, even without the fog. She pressed her palms flat against the ridges of ice, overcome with regret as the Orroroo drifted away.

Then it was gone. Brilliant sunlight blazed through the trees on the sides of the frozen river, illuminating every swirl of frost and every ice crystal. The frozen landscape only reflected the perfection of creation.

Avner rolled onto his back. He took in a gulp of air, his eyes still closed. Ice crystals clung to his eyelashes, making him look twenty-years older. Chava scooted closer to him and pressed a palm to his chest. He gasped.

"Avner?"

"Thank you," he murmured. His eyes opened and he shivered. His gray eyes reflected the pain in his soul. "You've saved me three times now."

He ran his thumb over Chava's marriage mark.

"I love you," he whispered.

"And I'll keep saving you," she answered softly, "but let Eloah do it. Accept his gift of freedom. He can take away your shame, Avner, and replace it with new life. The Spirit of the Forest never offered that. Doram wanted you to work to be good, but Eloah? He *is* the good. Let him cover you with his love so you can stop trying so hard to be something on your own. Because you can't. That struggle will only bring death and pain, when you can have life with Eloah."

Avner stared at her for so long, Chava held her breath. Was he going to accept Eloah?

But then he said, "Nothing is that simple, Chava, even if I wish it were."

She heard footsteps on the ice a few yards off. Avner jolted upright, and Chava glanced over her shoulder.

Miki stood on the bank of the frozen river where it met the ocean and motioned above them to the frost-encrusted trees. "You weren't joking about this frost. I've never seen anything like this. But I'm glad that fog cleared up." She seemed unaware of the fog's deeper meaning. She had been too far away to be affected by it.

Then, her eyes widened as she took in Avner's bleeding knuckles. "What happened?"

Avner glanced down at his hand. A vein pulsed in his temple. "Nothing," he said half-heartedly.

Oh, Eloah, please let him see! Chava kept her hand from grabbing Avner's. She knew they were past the point where she could say anything to change his mind. It wasn't up to her any longer. She looked around at their surroundings.

The frost covering the forest was thicker than Chava remembered and it glinted deceptively in deadly stillness. No rustling tree branches broke the sound of the waves crashing against the icy shoreline. Adamah was as silent as death. A mausoleum to the lost tribes. Could anyone still be alive?

"The frost is so much worse than I remember," Chava whispered. She leaned closer to Avner and he met her half-way, shivering. "Oh! I'm sorry!"

He only grunted in response. She'd need to stay closer the entire time they were under these trees to keep him from freezing to death.

"We shouldn't stand around," Chava warned, pointing to the encroaching swirls of frost overtaking Miki's soft-soled leather boots. Chava turned and headed further into the trees.

The ice receded everywhere she stepped, leaving brown grass for a few seconds before the swirling frost filled them in again.

"Sometime, you will need to tell me why you can do that," Miki said with awe.

"Gladly," Chava said, smiling.

Avner opened his mouth, a wary look in his eye, but he didn't express his reservations about Eloah to Miki. Maybe the fog *had* made a difference. Chava slid her hand into his, a rush of giddy emotion overcoming her. He was *hers*, doubts and all. She'd walk beside him and continue praying that one day he would understand. Chava took another step, pulling Avner with her. They'd face this frozen land together.

AVNER

ELOAH MIGHT BE REAL, but what Chava claimed about his 'gift' was too easy. And if this life had taught Avner anything, it was that nothing was given freely. Even if Eloah had somehow bestowed Chava with this supernatural heat, *how?* She either got this power from Eloah or somewhere else. It wasn't genetic like manipulation. And she'd been able to call off the Orroroo just like Leewana.

He didn't want to find answers for all of that. He straightened and hurried to Chava's side again, the warmth penetrating the fur Miki had given him.

Miki handed Avner the torch she'd brought. Though it burned brightly with a crackling flame, it did nothing to melt the frost on the nearest bush.

Unlike Eloah's heat in Chava.

That thought was getting harder to ignore. *We're here to find the artifacts, not talk about spirits or deities,* he chided himself.

"We're going to need another one of these. One torch

and Chava's heat won't do it." The pain of the frigid air bit at his lungs again.

"We won't need another torch." Miki's glowing eyes changed to purple.

Ashes, he was never going to get used to that.

Miki didn't move, but the fire from the torch streamed outward. Avner jumped back, his heart in his throat, but the fire kept pulling away, creating a long rope of flame. Miki cocked her head, and the rope *turned*. It raced past Chava, then Miki, then slipped behind Avner and reconnected to the torch again. The flames licked dangerously close to the hair around his ears. Avner jerked the torch further away, and the ring of fire moved with it.

"Hold still," Miki ordered.

"This is very weird."

The corner of his sister's mouth twitched upward, then her face became a mask of concentration. She raised one hand. The flame in Avner's grasp wavered, and air rushed past them. Miki closed her fist. The ring of fire separated from the main torch as if sliced through. Avner watched calmly this time as the ring of fire rose and grew independently of the torch. It widened until it was a comfortable distance around them, but not so far that they couldn't feel its heat.

The torch in Avner's hand continued to burn innocently, as if it'd had nothing at all to do with this.

Miki's hand dropped and she exhaled, letting her shoulders relax.

"I didn't realize you could separate what you're manipulating from the source," Chava said.

"I didn't either, but I hoped so. In theory, if the source is left burning, this ring of flame should live on." She blinked, but her eyes continued to glow.

Avner really liked this sister of his. He raised the torch higher, the flame flickering against the frost-covered leaves above them.

"Let's get going. We landed about a mile west of Doram." He waved with the torch toward the flat swath of ice a hundred paces away. It cut up into the land and vanished between the trees. "If we follow the river, we can find the pools. There will be natural heat there if they haven't been overwhelmed by the frost. Then we can make a game plan for finding more artifacts." And hopefully the warmth of the pools would keep the fog away. Avner shuddered with relief as the last hint of the fever seemed to leave him. It must not have taken hold like it had in Curroon, since he was only in it a short time here. Curses and ash, but he was getting too used to the supernatural.

"We need all of the artifacts, and to verify that your bracelet comes from Nameless Tribe," Chava said with a frown.

And they needed to find Dalea. Avner closed the gap between him and Chava. He grasped her hand.

"Dalea may not be pleased to see us."

Chava beamed. "I don't care."

Avner couldn't help smiling back. Chava was right. He'd barely had a moment to think about seeing his ex-lover again, but the prospect didn't seem as horrible as he would have expected. *If* she lived. If *anyone* lived.

"To Doram?" Chava asked.

"To Doram." Avner waved her ahead. He preferred to walk in her melted footsteps than on the frozen shards of grass. Miki fell in line behind them, and the ring of fire remained centered around their little group. How would they have survived here if he hadn't found his sister?

They crossed under the fence at the back of Doram, and Avner's chest tightened at a fresh thought of Mikhail. The last time he'd ducked this fence, he and Mikhail had come here to spar. A pang of longing rose without warning, and he staggered to a stop just on the other side of the fence. He set one hand on it, imagining Mikhail's beside his. Mikhail's laughter rang out on the frigid air, and for a moment Avner's heart stopped. His brother was gone. They'd never be here together again.

Avner glanced up at Chava's knowing gaze.

He pulled his hand off the fence and pushed forward without looking back. Had he been too harsh with Mikhail? Hadn't Avner made choices that others in Doram considered heretical, evil even, to save someone he cared about?

But Avner hadn't killed anyone other than gibborim. He hadn't killed his *brother*.

Didn't you? The ethereal voice he hadn't heard in weeks whispered on a fresh gust of wind causing Avner's teeth to chatter. *You didn't stop his capture. You rejoiced in his murder.*

No, that wasn't how it happened. Mikhail put himself in a place to be taken and executed.

Because he was trying to help you and Chava.

Bile rose in the back of Avner's throat. He couldn't deny Mikhail had been far better to Avner's wife than he himself had for the past year. But that didn't change anything. Did it?

Avner shoved the question away as they hiked closer to Doram. Silas, though. That brother he could miss freely. The one good thing about the past year-and-a-half was Silas dying before he could see what became of his family and home.

The edge of Doram—of what used to be Doram—came into view. Where cabins used to stand scattered across the clearing, nothing remained but a few foundations.

Chava inhaled sharply. "They took them apart for fuel."

Avner nodded, numb. Had he really left his people like this?

"We *did* try, Avner. They wouldn't come," Chava said to Miki. His sister stared in wide-eyed shock at the decimated village.

Chava's words didn't soften the sight of the haunted, empty town before them. The market clearing was strewn with forgotten wares and piles of old nails, things which couldn't burn. One house just beyond the main clearing remained intact, but was so encased in ice, the Doramites must not have been able to dismantle it.

But at least this meant they lived. Or had lived.

Avner felt a pang for his elk, Yavi. Did the animal live? Or had he been hunted and eaten when food grew scarcer? It had been so long since he'd thought of him, but Yavi had been a better friend than most.

"Where do we go now?" Miki asked.

Where indeed? Avner surveyed the damage again. A pile of something jutted out of the center of the clearing. He moved closer. His stomach heaved.

Bones. Charred and black, but encased in frost.

Had Dalea burned the bodies of those who fell to the frost in a last-ditch effort to remain in the village? And then where had they gone afterwards? Where would a people on the verge of freezing to death find refuge? The frost would find them anywhere, though the pools hadn't been frozen when he was here last.

The pools. If Dalea was anywhere, it would be at the ever-warm sulfur springs.

Avner turned north, the women following. Despite his doubts, Avner said a prayer to Chava's Eloah, asking that the pools remain thawed. If they weren't, Adamah was a graveyard.

37

SIMPLE TIMES

Shoshanna

The day was cold. The day was overcast.

But try as she might, she couldn't remember what day it <u>was.</u> The thin man with bright eyes had informed her that her name was Nuri and she'd had a bad accident in the arena.

"Nuri," she whispered in the dark. The name didn't seem familiar, but why would the man lie about something as simple as a name?

Nuri sat up in the cell she'd awakened in yesterday. There was another cell next to hers, full of sleeping gibborim. The men and women she supposedly shared her life with. She couldn't remember anything before yesterday, but the thin man had said she used to be a gibborim for someone else before he bought her.

Again, why would he lie about the history of a slave?

'Slave' didn't feel right either. It felt as if the man had left out some significant detail, but her memory failed her.

She sat up, pressing her leather-wrapped left wrist into the ground. *Why did she wear a leather cuff on her left wrist, but not her right?*

"Good luck token of your people." *The thin man's voice broke the silence of the early dawn. He stood on the other side of the bars, a sheepish smile on his face, as if he was embarrassed to be near her.*

"My people?" *her voice was thin, hollow.*

"Nomads from the far west. Or so you told me yourself the day I first purchased you. You asked me never to remove that cuff. The least I can do is remind you to do the same now that your memory has been damaged." *He smiled again, as if they trusted each other.*

And if she didn't know something as simple as where she came from, she'd have to believe him.

The cuff would stay on. If she was a gibborim, she would need every ounce of luck she could find.

"Sho?" Tevye's voice broke through her dream.

Shoshanna opened her eyes to the near-dark of the ship's hold. The crossbeams of the floor above them were only three feet away. They'd nestled in this nook at the back of the hold over a week ago and had avoided detection so far.

Tevye held out the canteen of water they'd stolen and refilled at night from the water barrels nearby. Shoshanna took a more generous swig than usual, as if that might wash Reuben out of her dreams. Or memories. Since getting her memory back, she had not thought of these events, of the day after Reuben gave her the potion.

She hated that memory. Her nails dug into the water skin. She'd been too weak to see through Reuben's lies, even though she'd known something was wrong.

Footsteps creaked above her head. Was it Reuben? Shoshanna stiffened, though no one had come close to discovering them, with the water barrels blocking the entrance to their nook. Knowing Reuben could be close by sent a horrid squeezing sensation through her gut.

"We're within sight of land," Tevye murmured.

Shoshanna hissed. "Did you go up there?"

"Didn't need to. Can you feel it?" He hugged his arms tighter around his chest.

Shoshanna sat up, the fur they'd pilfered falling off her shoulders. Cool air, sharp and bitter, slithered over her. The frost still covered Adamah, didn't it? Not that she'd expected anything different. But the last time she'd been here, she hadn't been able to feel its chill.

What if she wasn't strong enough to survive it?

"We will have to sneak out before they stop. I don't want anyone coming down here to unload supplies before we make it safely away." He held up the length of rope they'd found days ago when making this plan.

Sneak back to the deck, run across it and shimmy down the stern using the rope. Run before anyone sees.

The crew couldn't be more than twenty men, but it would only take one sharp-eyed scout to sound the alarm.

Shoshanna peeked around the barrels. With her black and white vision, it was easier to see in this semi-darkness. No one moved through the outlines of barrels and crates. They'd take it in stages, making sure each section was clear before making a run for it.

"Sho?"

She pulled back from the barrels, gritting her teeth. She still hadn't had the heart to tell Tevye not to use Itzaak's nickname for her.

"I'm glad we're in this together. If it had been just me trying to find Avner... well, I don't think I'd have made it this far."

Thank goodness the darkness hid his face. Shoshanna didn't want to admit how she truly felt about hearing that nickname again, let alone seeing the softness of Tevye's words reflected on his face.

The silence stretched between them.

Aren't you going to reply? Itzaak nudged.

Shoshanna cleared her throat. "We should get going before someone comes down."

Tevye chuckled in the dark, apparently not hurt by her lack of response. He couldn't know how much his steady companionship meant to her. Not in any romantic way, but it made her feel human again.

Something she hadn't dared to hope could be possible. In truth, she didn't want the past week in this hold to come to an end. The quiet hours, simply breathing in sync, or sharing a meal of nuts and raisins. Or the few bad jokes Tevye whispered to elicit a small snort from her.

She hadn't experienced such a simple time in years. Decades. She'd cherish it, no matter what happened once they set foot in Adamah again.

"Thank you, Tevye," she whispered.

In the only sliver of pale light coming from the stairs on the far end of the hold, she glimpsed the corner of his mouth twitching into a smile.

Shoshanna turned away before she could say something she might regret and slipped around the barrels. Her feet landed in the hold without a sound. Tevye followed, the bag of artifacts and the staff of Doram in his hand. Shoshanna accepted them and slid the bag over her chest.

Muffled shouts sounded overhead, followed by the scuffing of feet.

"Wait, Sho," Tevye whispered. She turned back and

followed his finger pointing to a porthole on the far side of the hold. They'd already explored it and discovered it only led to a secret stash hole, probably used by smugglers.

"I checked again while you slept. There's a false floor. If we remove it, we can drop down into the water."

"But the frost—"

"I know. I don't fancy being soaked to the bone in the frost either, but at least we're guaranteed a safe exit."

More footsteps thundered above them. The crew was getting ready to berth the ship. There'd be a flurry of activity. Either it would make it easier to weave across the deck unseen, or they'd be spotted the moment they stuck their heads out of the hold.

Shoshanna didn't like those odds. She nodded toward the porthole. Tevye led the way around the pile of crates. He pried the porthole open, revealing a two-foot square storage hole. Tevye rapped his knuckles against the back and it fell inward. Light flooded the space. Shoshanna blinked it back. Bright. White. Glistening. Only frost glowed so intensely, though she couldn't see it from their vantage point.

"I'll go first," Tevye whispered. Grabbing the edges of the hole, he hefted himself three feet up and slid into the hole.

"Well?"

There was a chuckle in his voice as he said, "Eloah leads the way, friend."

Then he dropped out of sight. Shoshanna rushed to the hole and pulled herself up, her heart racing, expecting to see him flailing in the waves below.

But Tevye only smiled up at her from a sheet of ice eight feet below. The ship had mercifully slid near enough to the shore that a channel of ice stuck out directly under the stern.

Shoshanna glanced at the fresh linen cuff on her wrist. A good luck charm indeed.

Or Eloah— Shoshanna cut off Itzaak by dropping the staff down to Tevye. There wasn't time for this conversation now.

She swung her legs over the edge of the hole, then dropped. She landed in a roll and popped back up. The bright, icy landscape gleamed to the north, while the sea lay to the south, and the ship rose above them. No one called out. Reuben and Felix didn't know what they'd delivered to Adamah. The artifacts, and their enemies.

Shoshanna returned Tevye's smile and broke into a jog toward the frost-encrusted trees.

She was returning home, and hopefully, would bring healing to it even if she couldn't manage to heal herself.

38

HOMECOMING

Avner

As they hiked to the pools, the ring of fire around their heads crackled, and the frost-encrusted grass crunched under their feet. Thankfully, the trees were too thick with ice to catch fire. Any ice that melted as they walked by hardened again as soon as they had passed. The trees thinned ahead. Avner didn't voice his fears to Chava or Miki, and they were equally silent. He held his breath as the trees gave way to the rock-rimmed hot pools. They'd last been here fighting Reuben for the objects. It seemed so long ago, and so much had changed.

Chava took a step out of the trees. Avner caught a glimpse of steam ahead, but his relief was short-lived.

"Someone's coming!" Miki hissed, dodging behind a frost-riddled boulder.

Avner grabbed Chava's hand and pulled her back into the trees. The frozen trunks steamed as Chava's heat and the fiery ring melted them free.

"Felix?" Chava hissed.

"Most likely." Which meant they would soon be near Yor's knife, if it had survived the shipwreck.

Avner peered around just long enough to see something dark moving along the river. There was a shout, answered by another. Chava shifted, and frozen twigs snapped beneath her feet. Her fingers dug into the trunk, a warm circle spreading over the tree, eating the spirals of frost.

"*Sorry,*" she mouthed.

Avner placed a hand on her back to steady her, then froze as the voice spoke again, much closer. "I heard something."

A thrill ran down his spine. He knew that voice! Avner stepped out of the trees holding the torch, leaving the ring of fire with Miki. The heat from the torch barely warmed the frigid air, but Avner didn't care.

Tevye stood beside the steaming pools, several furs draped over his thin body, leaning over the figure beside him. Shoshanna.

"Tevye?"

His friend jumped.

"Avner!" Tevye's face radiated relief. He gave Shoshanna a meaningful look. "I told you they survived the shipwreck."

Shoshanna frowned, as if she preferred they hadn't survived.

"Tevye!" Chava scrambled from behind the trees. "How did you know we were here?"

"We didn't—" He cut off, and his hand went to the sling-shot tucked under his furs.

Avner spun around, but it was only Miki approaching, bringing the ring of fire with her. Right. There was so much to tell his friend.

"It's all right, she's with us." He waved Tevye down.

"She's a manipulator?" Tevye asked, wary.

Shoshanna stared daggers at Miki's supernatural fire.

"More importantly, she's Avner's sister," Chava offered.

Miki nodded in greeting. "I'm assuming you are the friends who escaped Adamah—and the gibborim pens—with my brother?"

"Aye, but I didn't know you had a sister, Av—oh!" Understanding dawned on Tevye's face. "You found them, didn't you? Your family."

"Part of them." Avner smiled at Miki.

She smiled back and stepped closer as Tevye shivered. The ring of fire parted to expand around him and Shoshanna. The woman snarled at the fire and ducked back outside of it, but Tevye gave her a look of gentle reproach.

"It's fine, Sho. She's helping us."

Sho? Avner mouthed to Chava. She shrugged, clearly just as bewildered. What had transpired in the last few weeks?

Shoshanna continued to stand outside the ring of fire.

"I'd say you are a much better manipulator than the ones I saw in the arena, Miki." Tevye smiled.

She frowned. "No manipulator should be forced into an arena for sport."

"Are you tired yet?" Avner asked quickly, trying to distract her thinking of Moises.

"No. We need to find Felix."

"Felix brought us," Tevye said wryly. "Stowing away wasn't the most comfortable thing, but it was a lovely voyage." He smiled at Shoshanna, who stared hard at the ground. "Thankfully, the ice gave us a path to shore right under their noses."

There wasn't time to decipher what was going on

between Tevye and Shoshanna. Felix was here. Avner grabbed Chava's hand. "They? Who else is with Felix?"

Darkness clouded Tevye's face. "Felix has teamed up with Reuben."

Avner's fingers clamped tighter around Chava's. "Reuben? But we left him here months ago. Look at this place. He must be dead."

Shoshanna's frown deepened. She glanced at Tevye again and something unspoken passed between them. He moved closer and the fire parted again to include Shoshanna. She didn't balk this time. Tevye placed a hand on her shoulder. *Touching* Shoshanna. That alone was strange, but there was something else about it. Almost as if there was a deeper concern hidden in that movement. Had the weeks together somehow made them *friends?*

But then Avner and Chava hadn't really been husband and wife a few days ago.

Tevye's next words drove all thoughts of relationships away. "Reuben promised to help Felix 're-acquire' you if Felix helps reunite the artifacts."

The words were as cold as the air stabbing Avner's lungs. Reuben. Alive. Avner locked his knees, or he might have staggered back. For once, he understood Shoshanna. To know that the man who'd made them what they were still lived, and worse, was here in Adamah, brought a turmoil of emotion.

"My brother was always too resourceful for his own good." Chava took Avner's hand as she turned toward him. "At least that means all the artifacts should be back here now."

Tevye glanced at their clasped hands. A smile tugged at the corner of his mouth. Avner offered no explanation.

There wasn't an adequate one for his poor behavior over the past year.

"At least Felix is here," he said. "We need the knife back if it survived the wreck."

"We have it." Shoshanna said. Avner hadn't noticed the satchel across her chest or the gleaming, age-oiled wooden staff in her hand.

"You still have the staff of Doram!" Chava stepped closer.

"Aye, and much more besides." Tevye took the bag from Shoshanna and gave it to Chava.

She rifled through the contents as if the items inside weren't hundreds of years old, then glanced up, beaming. "They are all here! We have all the artifacts!"

"How in the world do you have the knife?" Avner asked.

"Eloah provided a way, as usual."

Avner caught Shoshanna's frown and could almost see his own feelings etched in her burned face. If these supernatural coincidences didn't stop, they'd both be forced to accept something they'd rather not.

Chava's eyes went to the staff strapped to Shoshanna's back. Did it call to her the way the bracelet had to Avner when he'd been without it? Shoshanna didn't offer to hand it over and Chava didn't ask, though she sidestepped closer to it.

Either way, Chava's words about the artifacts were only true if the bracelet was really from the Nameless Tribe. Months of searching had led them to this moment.

A woman's shriek pierced the frozen air. Avner dropped Chava's hand and whipped around, wishing once again that he had a weapon. Tevye turned with him, raising his sling shot. The ring of fire burned fiercely, snapping with sparks of heat and energy as Miki raised one hand at the newcomer.

Avner caught his breath.

Dalea, his one-time lover, stood beside the hot pools. Her cheeks were smeared with mud, and her tall frame was wrapped in furs. She stared at Avner and the ring of fire as if they were an apparition.

"I knew it," she whispered. "The Forest has finally sent you to save us."

39

REUNIONS

Avner

Where had Dalea come from? Avner took a step closer to the woman who so barely resembled the one he'd once been paired with. The old Dalea would never have allowed her features to become streaked with mud. Her dark eyes were sunken and haunted. The tip of her nose was gray. Frost bite?

Avner shuddered at memories of Mikhail's frostbitten fingers. They hadn't claimed his brother's life—Nuri had—but the frost had taken much from him.

Dalea stepped closer, eyeing the ring of fire with fear. Miki's eyes still glowed purple. She moved closer, and the fire moved with her.

Dalea shied back. "How did you get the Forest to gift you with such power?"

"It wasn't the forest," Chava snorted.

Annoyance flashed across Dalea's face for the first time.

"I don't know why the Forest would send *you* back to save us."

"Dalea," her name was harsh on Avner's lips, "where are the Doramites?"

Her sunken eyes moved to the boulders surrounding one of the hot pools. Chava gasped. A dark mouth gaping into the earth. Steam rose from it as it did from the pools. Were there caves below the pools? Avner hadn't heard of such a thing, but then they had never needed to explore beneath the pools before the frost.

"Are people down there?" he asked quietly. Surely the whole tribe couldn't fit below ground.

Dalea gave him a fierce look, just like he remembered, but something cracked behind the façade. Dalea shivered, her face taut beneath the dirt on her cheeks.

"The forest should have saved us sooner. Hundreds of us have died, Avner," she whispered. "We only found the caves by chance. The hot pools were the only place that didn't freeze. We found the tunnel after too many people crowded the site and someone fell through. But there wasn't room enough for everyone. More died in the fights." She grew pale. "So many forgot their Oath of Do No Harm so quickly. But now the rest of us live in the heated earth, only venturing out for food, which is scarce. We find frozen game and thaw it, but often the meat is frost-burned. Ice fishing is all we have left, but we barely manage to catch one a day now." Dalea gestured to the still river, marked with telltale axe marks.

Frozen game... *Yavi.* Avner kept from asking about him. What was one elk compared to an entire tribe?

"And the fog... it just showed up one day, covering the frozen forest. Many got sick that first day when we didn't know it was evil. And now we hardly venture out in case the fog is here."

Avner gritted his teeth. None of Doram followed Eloah, so of course the Orroroo hurt them. Another confirmation of what he didn't want to admit.

"Why didn't the Forest prevent this?" Dalia's question hung in the frigid air.

Avner had his own answer, as did Chava and Tevye. But telling Dalea now wouldn't help anything. This woman was a far cry from the fierce stand-in Judge she'd been months ago.

"I was wrong to be angry at you for breaking your vow," she whispered. Her dark eyes held unfathomable sorrow. "I couldn't understand what would make you turn your back on our way of life, but now I know you had to survive. I thought you should have let yourself be killed rather than break your oath, but now I see how horrible death is. I'm sorry."

"I..." Avner didn't know what to say. He would have begged her to say this much long ago. But this whole conversation meant little now.

Dalea stepped closer to him, shivering in her muddy furs, and grabbed his hand. "Avner, I've missed you. I-I'm sorry. I still care for you."

Avner took his hand out of her grasp as gently as he could. Even in the beginning, he hadn't cared as much for her as she had for him. He glanced at Chava. Her cheeks were rosy, matching her hair and bringing vibrant life to her face. Now there was a woman he cared for.

Dalea followed his gaze and stiffened. "Why do you still have that witch—"

"Chava is my *wife*," Avner cut in, "and she always will be.

We will stop this frost together. If you have given up, then fine. I won't. I *can't.*"

He stepped away from Dalea and crossed over to Chava, breathing in the aroma of cinnamon always wafting around her, and took her hand. His fingers threaded through hers as if they'd been designed to fit.

She smiled up at him, and then grew serious. "But how do we reunite the objects of the tribes?"

Dalea's dark gaze didn't leave Avner and Chava's clasped hands. "Did you actually get them all?"

"Everyone, be quiet!" Tevye motioned for silence, as he watched Shoshanna stalk toward Death's Wall—the place where her husband and her previous life had been destroyed —one hand extended, as if her fingers saw something her cursed eyes couldn't.

"Sho?" Tevye asked.

She crept closer to the wall until her fingers trailed against the frozen stone. She'd removed her gloves. Any minute her fingers should blacken with frostbite, but Avner couldn't bring himself to warn her. Something about her deliberate movements sent a tingle of excitement down his back. Did she remember something else the potion had erased?

Avner jogged over to her, still holding the torch. He leaned close to the wall beside her, their warm breath sending more spirals of frost across the stone. Shoshanna's red fingertips traced the mark of Zev engraved in the lower right corner, where frozen blades of grass reached up to meet the stone. But then her fingertips moved away, to another rune. A swirl encased in a square.

The bracelet on Avner's wrist snapped with heat. He yelped.

Shoshanna snatched his hand up before he could protest and pressed the bracelet to the new rune. One bead matched it exactly.

Avner was speechless. A nameless rune on Death's Wall right beside the Mark of Zev. Proof that more than one tribe had been here before.

"It's a map!" Tevye's voice rose with excitement. "I *knew* the runes on the bracelet meant something, I just hadn't been able to piece it together until now. The spiral is a symbol of direction." He pointed to the next bead. A sort of squiggle rune. "This means river. And these vaguely bush-like runes mean forest. The bracelet is directing us across a river through a forest."

"But why?" Avner twisted the bracelet around his wrist until three more runes showed. Indecipherable combinations of 'x's and dots. Squinting did nothing to make them appear more recognizable.

"And those!" Tevye held his hand out. "May I?"

Avner slid the bracelet off and handed it over.

"Hill, maybe. Or burrow. Some sort of natural geographical image, but I can't remember what this extra dot on the third rune means." Tevye's good eye narrowed. He mumbled something under his breath.

"Does it even matter what it means? How does this help us?" Miki asked, her voice strained. The ring of fire wavered.

"We can survive without the fire for five minutes. Take a break." Avner grasped her shoulder.

"I'm fine. Wait—" She straightened, suddenly tense. "I can feel something. Another manipulator."

"How far?" Avner glanced back into the trees, but nothing showed through their frozen branches. Felix must have arrived.

"I don't know. I've never tested how far I can sense another manipulator. All I know is they could be far away still if they are strong, or right behind me if they are weak. Let's hurry this up."

Tevye scowled at the bracelet. "I'd say it says wall, but that isn't in line with the rest of the runes, and the one thing I remember about Nameless tongue is there's a rhythm to it. Only runes in the same family can be used together. The pattern here is geographical, not man-made."

"Death's Wall," Shoshanna murmured.

"No!" Dalea's scream echoed off the stone behind them.

Avner whirled around. Dalea stood framed by Leaf and Copper. Reuben stood to the left, wrapped in fur, and looking far too smug.

Horem, Felix's manipulator, was holding a torch that controlled a much smaller, and still tethered, ring of fire. The fact that Miki was a much stronger manipulator eased some of Avner's rising panic.

Felix stepped out of the trees, his breath misting in front of him. He too was wrapped in fur, as was Moises who accompanied him.

"Miki!" The boy squealed, stepping into the clearing by the pools.

Felix yanked him back by the fur of his hood.

"Don't you dare," Miki said, low and dangerous. The ring of fire pulsed, and a single flame split out, flaring in Felix's direction.

Horem jumped forward and absorbed the flame into his own. He staggered back a step, his eyes flashing a deeper green.

"My, my. Aren't you an interesting one?" Felix stared ravenously at Miki.

Heat burned up Avner's back. This man wouldn't get his sister as he had Avner and Chava. He'd never own anyone again. Avner fumbled at his useless, empty belt too late. A knife whizzed through the air and clattered against Death's Wall behind him.

Tevye shoved the bracelet back into Avner's hands and ripped his slingshot out of his belt. Another knife from Leaf cracked into the stone. Avner yanked Chava away as Copper, his face badly burned, sprinted toward her with his sword out. Avner hadn't come back to Doram to die, and he sure as frost wouldn't let his wife die here either.

Copper's sword sliced through the palm of Avner's glove, and he hissed as the blade found skin. Hot, golden blood trickled forth over the furs.

"Avner!" Chava screamed.

Avner staggered back, tripped over Shoshanna and released Chava's hand, his own braced against Death's Wall to stop his fall. Golden blood smeared against the rock.

Copper didn't finish the attack. He stared open mouthed at the Nameless Tongue rune. Avner held his breath. The rune *sucked* his blood into it. The blood was siphoned away from the rock and into the swirl cut into the stone, filling each line and curve with liquid gold, leaving the rest of the ice-encrusted rock clear.

"Death's Wall," Shoshanna whispered.

Chava screamed somewhere close by. The blood-filled rune began to *spin*. Another scream, accompanied by flashes of fire. Avner tried to stand, but gravity worked against him, crushing him against the wall of vibrating rock. The rune spun faster, brighter, until all he could see was a glowing, spinning circle of gold. Of his blood.

"I can see it," Shoshanna breathed. "There!" She jolted forward, toward the wall.

Death's wall flashed and Avner stared open-mouthed. Instead of frozen, pitted stone, he saw a lush, green valley. He blinked. The stone returned.

What the...

The ground shook fiercely. Avner rolled to his side to avoid cracking his head on the stone wall. He rolled into Shoshanna's legs, and she toppled to the ground. Together, they rolled down a sloping hill. No shards of ice cut into his exposed cheeks, only sweet-smelling, incredibly soft grass. They came to a stop. He scrambled up, his legs shaky, and his body suddenly very, very warm.

Avner drew in a breath, trying to understand the impossible sight before him. He and Shoshanna were no longer at the hot pools, but in a lush, green valley surrounded by mountains and red-leafed trees.

Swaying grass had replaced Reuben, Felix, and the others. Chava's last scream still echoed in the calm air, though she was nowhere in sight.

40

IN THE LAND OF IMPOSSIBILITIES

Avner

E ndless green grass rolled over the small knolls under a brilliant sun. Instead of the bone-gnawing wind, a warm breeze caressed his face. Vibrant red leaves shimmered under the clear sky in a line of trees on the far end of the valley. The scent of an unknown flower wafted in the air, urging Avner to relax, but he couldn't. The landscape was too picturesque, too perfectly serene. Impossible. Supernatural.

He staggered to his feet, sweat already pooling beneath his furs. He turned in a circle, but the scenery didn't change. Death's Wall didn't replace the endless grass, and the brilliant sun wasn't covered with heavy gray clouds.

"W-what happened?" he stammered.

"Your blood." Shoshanna rasped as she stood up.

But how? The rune shouldn't have done anything, let alone respond to his blood, if that was what had happened.

But Shoshana's presence proved this was real. Two people couldn't share one hallucination, could they?

A gentle, deliciously-warm breeze touched his cheeks before swirling through the thigh-high grass to ruffle the red leaves, revealing their dark, vibrant undersides. There was a wooden structure down in the valley, but no one was in sight. The place was untouched and peaceful. It felt sacred. Magical. If not for the panic building within him, Avner might have wanted to stay here forever. As a child, he'd imagined the Summerlands in the afterlife being something like this, but even his imagination didn't do it justice.

And this couldn't be the Summerlands, unless Copper had killed him and Shoshanna. Avner didn't need to check himself to know he had no wounds except the cut on his palm. They had to get back and find Chava. Copper could have harmed her by now.

"How do we get back?" He pulled at the collar of his fur jacket. It was far too warm here for it.

Shoshanna jogged up the hill they had rolled down, then circled back. Her face was strangely calm, despite the bizarre circumstances that had brought them here.

But then, she hadn't left anyone behind. Unless Tevye counted now, odd as that seemed. Either way, Avner wouldn't be the one to bring it up.

"I don't think we can get back this way," Shoshanna said.

Unless Death's Wall and the pools were hidden beneath the hill, there wasn't another way back. They were locked away from Chava and the others with no clue as to how to get back or what had happened.

Avner spun away from Shoshanna. Everything here was too calm. It wasn't right. This place didn't make sense. He sprinted forward, needing to move, to find a way out, panic threatening to choke him.

Inhaling a lungful of the sweet, summer-like air, Avner charged down the hill. The swishing of grass said Shoshanna was following. The cabin in the distance drew nearer. Avner slammed to a halt, his heart pounding, and spun back to look up the hill. Shoshanna dodged around him. The grass was as green and unchanged as when they arrived.

No sign of Doram, or Adamah. Unless this *was* somewhere in Adamah.

Avner breathed deeply, and the warm air seemed to miraculously calm his nerves. Maybe the supernatural air was tamping down his instincts, making him forget the danger Chava, Miki and Tevye were in.

Avner turned back toward the cabin. Maybe the only way back to the pools was forward. Maybe this cabin would hold answers, impossible as it seemed.

That's impossible! Find Chava! His mind screamed with every heartbeat. But how? Where was she? Where was *he*?

"Calm down," Shoshanna murmured as she crept toward the cabin, her knife drawn. "We're here until we find a way out."

Avner took a steadying breath. She was right. He forced the panic back, though he couldn't bury it. Not while he knew Copper was within inches of his wife.

Eloah... if you're there, if you are really with Chava, please protect her!

The irony that he'd said two prayers to a deity he didn't believe was real in the span of an hour wasn't lost on him. Avner stifled a dark chuckle and followed Shoshanna as she approached the cabin. Eloah aside, Avner had to trust that

Tevye and Miki would protect Chava, or that Chava would be able to use the staff to protect herself. She'd never been helpless.

Sweat slicked under his layers. Avner stripped off the fur, letting it drop in the grass. Shoshanna kept her leather vest on, pulling it closer and narrowing her eyes.

"Do you think this is the Summerlands?" Shoshanna whispered. She glanced toward the trees, as if expecting Itzaak to come walking out of them.

"Can't be. We aren't dead." *I hope.*

Avner slowed down at the door of the cabin. A sudden pressing need to see what was inside overrode his desire to reunite the tribes. Foot-wide logs were secured into a frame and chinked with white clay. Bits of it were broken, leaving holes of various sizes. Apart from the holes in the clay, the cabin was eerily like those in Doram.

"It's empty." Shoshanna crouched level with the nearest crack.

Of course. The valley was too serene for anyone to be there. Avner pushed the door inward.

With a screeching crack, the hinges snapped. The door thumped onto the floor, releasing a cloud of dust into the interior of the house. The view out the window presented another three similar houses scattered across the valley.

"Someone lived here," Avner said as he reached for a collection of wooden bowls stacked on the planked flooring. Though, clearly, they had lived there a long time ago. He had never heard mention of a settlement near Death's Wall, apart from Doram, if this place was even in Adamah.

The floorboards creaked as he moved further into the building. A few rolled blankets lay against the far wall, eaten years ago by moths to leave nothing besides a shell. No furniture. Not even a low table as they had back in the tribes. He'd have assumed the frost killed the inhabitants, but the frost clearly hadn't touched this valley, and the blankets seemed much older than a few months.

Shoshanna's shoulder brushed Avner's, and she glanced at his wrist. "Where did your mother get this bracelet?"

"A man gave it to her. We helped him once."

"Where did the man come from?"

"He was a lost nomad. He died shortly after we found him." Avner crossed to a stone tablet built into the wall, with runes etched across it matching the ones on his bracelet. Not that Avner was the linguist Tevye was, but it looked like Nameless tongue. Rotten luck Tevye hadn't come with them. Avner clenched his fists. No, Tevye was with Chava. They needed each other until Avner found a way back.

"Are you sure the man was a Nomad?" Shoshanna asked.

Avner's wrist tingled beneath the bracelet. A lost traveler. A man with no family who happened to possess an artifact of the Nameless Tribe. Avner leaned closer to the runes and they seemed to shift before his eyes, revealing plain, legible text. He blinked and rubbed his eyes with the back of his hands. The letters didn't move again. They must have been tribal tongue the whole time. He ignored the doubt tickling the back of his mind as excitement overrode it.

"They're names!" Avner ran a finger over the etched words. "A list of every generation since the split of the tribes. This is the last generation recorded—the 18th. There are only two names. One is Akaron. Looks like someone tried to slash the other name out," he ran his finger down the deep groove through the runes, gasping.

"Liev." He spoke the name softer than a whisper. The

bracelet warmed Avner's skin, pricking along it with beads of sweat.

Shoshanna moved beside him. "How can you read it?"

"It's right here. Plain as day." He pointed to the wall. "Liev, the nomad my mother and I found, was the last of the Nameless Tribe!"

Shoshanna was paler than usual. Her cinnamon-flecked eyes narrowed at the sign on the wall before flashing up to him. She murmured something he didn't catch. He fought back a shiver and turned back to the wall.

"There's something else here. Did anyone ever know the Nameless Tribe's name?" There was another stone etching in the wall, smaller than the first. Older.

"No, that was the whole reason for calling them the Nameless Tribe. They wouldn't share their true name with anyone outside of their tribe." Shoshanna said, still staring at him as if he were a ghost.

"This other stone plate says 'The Valley of Eloah—'" The bracelet burned hotter, searing Avner's skin as it had in the cave when he almost took the potion.

Eloah. Chava hadn't been here before. How would she and these people know the same deity?

Avner continued, forcing his voice to be calm. "The Valley of Eloah, as settled irrevocably by the Bachir—chosen. Chosen by who?"

Shoshanna glanced at Avner's wrist. "Why does it keep doing that?"

Avner ignored her, while the bracelet continued to glow. *Chosen by Eloah.*

"Ouch!" He shook his wrist, pain and heat gripping it, but the bracelet didn't slip off.

"I told you that was bad news," Shoshanna said, her eyes dark.

"Can you help get it off—" but the bracelet seared him again and Avner cried out. He stepped back, tripping on the stack of bowls, and fell.

Shoshanna shouted something and her knife sang out of her belt. Avner rolled, keeping his burning wrist tucked against him. Her knife clattered against the floor next to a man standing in the doorway. He wore only a loincloth over his sun-leathered skin. Silver-streaked black hair hung in a braid to his waist. His eyes were bright green, and a scar ran down his nose.

The memory which had plagued Avner's dreams since childhood hit him full force. The flash of gold blazed in his memory, and he could hear the nomad's rasping breaths as he lay beneath a tree, his hand on Avner's wrist. The man's gaunt appearance and round eyes were something he'd never forgotten, and now the same face stood before him, impossible as it was.

Avner raised his hand, his fingers trembling. "Liev?"

41

NAMELESS

Avner

The man's spear wavered. His green eyes pinned Avner.
"Liev," he repeated in a thick accent, as if he were
speaking with a mouthful of berries. He lowered the spear
and stepped back, his bare feet encrusted with mud. "How
do you know my brother's name? How did you come to be
here?"

"We fell through the stone wall." Avner stood up, one
hand out to ward off the spear, though it would do little if
the man attacked.

"You cannot walk through stone." The man's left eye
twitched and he frowned, a mixture of confusion and
concern.

"We didn't. The stone vanished." Avner shot a look at
Shoshanna for support.

"What are you saying?" She hissed, edging closer.

"What do you mean? He's speaking tribal tongue—"
Avner cut off at the sight of Shoshanna's glare. The words

he'd just spoken rippled through his mind again. Thick, buttery. Foreign. He took a shuddering breath. Impossible!

He looked back at Liev's brother and tried speaking again. "My blood opened the rock." The words rolled off his tongue, as familiar as the tribal language, yet not. Avner pressed on, his heart pounding in his chest. He held up his hand, the edges still stained with dried red-gold blood.

"The rock vanished and then we were here. Are we still in Adamah?" The bracelet glimmered, but was no longer hot. As if speaking this strange tongue had relieved the pressure.

The man didn't react to Avner's question as he stared at his torn hand.

"Are you Akaron? On the wall?" Avner pointed back to the plaque in the corner and the only other name next to Liev's.

"Akaron is my name." "Liev did this before he left," he pointed one gnarled finger to the scar across his nose, "so I scratched out his name. But this is odd. Very odd. I have not spoken to a human since the day my brother left years ago. Only animals, trees, and Eloah, if he is there, though I doubt it. Now you tell me you rubbed your blood on stone and fell into my valley? A mountain which hasn't moved in six hundred years?" The ornaments dangling from the tip of his spear rattled. Old bones. Tufts of fur.

"We touched a rock wall, not a mountain." Though Akaron didn't seem to know the difference. He'd been alone for fourteen years. He clearly wasn't sane any longer. Still, Avner had to try. "Are you the last of the Nameless Tribe?"

"Aye, I suppose that is what they once called us. Nameless. There is none left now to have a name."

"What happened to them, Akaron?" Avner pressed.

"Do you mind interpreting?" Shoshanna scowled as she moved closer, a murderous look in her eyes.

Akaron started at the movement, his nostrils flaring.

"A woman, no?" he whispered. "I have never seen a woman, though my father told us tales of them, of my mother, before he faded." His eyes didn't leave Shoshanna's face, the vein in his temple throbbing, until he lowered them to take in her chest, and curves, still clear even under her parka. "Like a man, but softer. Like a tree, but she is the color and movement of the leaves," he murmured.

Shoshanna, soft? Avner would have snorted, if not for the bizarre circumstances. She glared at Akaron with a clenched jaw, but he didn't pull his gaze away. Something ticked in Avner's mind, warning him that Chava needed him back at the pools, but he couldn't tear his focus from Akaron.

"Why didn't you leave? What do you mean the mountain refused to move?" Avner asked.

"The mountain has not moved for six hundred years, or so my father told me."

"But it used to?"

"Yes. Or it did at least once when my ancestors settled in this valley in northern Adamah. They commanded the mountain to move and so it did, hiding them from the rest of the world."

They were in Northern Adamah? But Death's Wall was in the south. Supernatural, indeed.

Akaron continued, "But when my ancestors tried to command the mountain to move again, it refused. They tried other passages out, but the mountains are too unforgiving to scale. There are no paths, no passes. The rock walls us in on all sides. Many died trying to leave our valley. So, we bred and survived until, by the time my parents had my brother, sickness took more than half of my tribesmen. My mother died birthing my brother." The words he hadn't used for so long seemed to return full force.

"The tribe dwindled down to my father and my uncles. Then they all died too. Liev promised to leave, that we wouldn't die without wives to continue the tribe of Bachir. I was angry, far too angry. I see that now. I wouldn't let him go because he would die trying to go through the lake and I didn't want to be alone. It's been fourteen years. My brother is dead. The birds, the trees, they are company to a man. But not friends." His gaze finally snapped off Shoshanna and he scrutinized Avner.

His skin prickled under the intense green gaze.

"I met your brother. So you recognize this bracelet, Akaron? Liev gave it to my mother." Avner held his wrist higher, the beads catching the sunlight streaming through the open doorway.

Akaron shuffled forward, sniffing, and inspected the bracelet. "How do you have this? It was my mother's, but Liev took it with him when he left me," he finished with a growl.

"He left? How?" Could they leave the same way?

"He *tried* to leave. He drowned himself in the lake across the valley. Since his body never surfaced again, this bracelet should be at the bottom with him."

Avner shot Shoshanna a glance, only to remember she couldn't understand any of this conversation. The lake might be their way out, though it made little sense. And the bracelet was an artifact!

"Liev can't have given this to your mother. He died in the lake," Akaron repeated.

Avner shook his head. "I swear he lived when I met him, though he died soon after."

Akaron narrowed his eyes. "My father said the other tribes would never understand us. That they hungered for power. You seem the same, coming here with lies."

"The tribes do hunger for power, but we didn't even mean to come here." Avner held a hand to his chest. "I am from the tribe of Doram."

Akaron snorted and snatched Avner's arm, his fingers warm, dirt under each nail. "Doram found me? Of all the tribes? Doram? Ha!"

Avner didn't pull his arm away, though the musty scent of the man nearly overpowered him. "But the tribes aren't under one Chief anymore. They split almost six hundred years ago just after your tribe left. No one knows what happened to many of them."

Akaron nodded. "My father said it might have happened, but we came here to escape them, so it was not a subject we broached often." He dropped Avner's arm. "What of the woman?" He stared at Shoshanna again, unblinking, though his words weren't addressed to her.

She raised her knife.

Avner murmured, "He's the last one, Shoshanna."

Her rash-covered hand clenched the hilt of her knife, but she didn't make any other movements.

"She's Doramite as well," Avner answered Akaron.

"I always wondered," Akaron inhaled, and a smile spread over his gaunt features, "if a woman smelled different."

Shoshanna stared at Avner. "I don't understand a word he's saying, how can you?"

"I-I don't know,"

"And the runes? How did you read those?"

Again, he didn't know.

"Well, he seems mad. I don't think he knows how to get out of this valley."

Akaron stepped closer to Shoshanna, one hand out as if he might touch this enigma he'd never seen before.

Shoshanna jolted forward, her knife out.

"No!" Avner flung himself between her and Akaron.

"He's mad! What good does he do us?" she countered.

"He's. The. Last. One," Avner said, drawing out the words. "He's done no harm." Behind him, the man cackled.

"Feisty, eh? Are all women like this one?"

Shoshanna's face contorted, though she couldn't have known what he said. She darted around Avner before he could stop her and her knife sliced the man's exposed belly. While her blade only left a non-lethal scrape, she didn't strike again. The knife clattered to the floor.

Golden blood seeped from the wound.

Avner staggered against the wall to keep from collapsing.

"Impossible," he gasped.

Even Shoshanna seemed to know the magnitude of this moment. She pointed to Akaron's chest while he wiped the blood off and smeared it on his loin cloth.

"How?" she asked.

Akaron snorted. "You'll have to hurt me worse than that, woman."

"How do you have golden blood?" Avner repeated in nameless tongue, his voice hoarse. He'd given up on this moment after finding Miki. How was it possible?

Akaron shrugged. "Both Liev and I were born with it. A blessing from Eloah. Or so my parents claimed. I don't think Eloah blesses anyone any longer."

A blessing. Avner hadn't ever considered his blood a

blessing. His throat was too dry to speak again so he raised his palm where blood still slightly seeped.

Akaron stiffened. "The *giving*," he whispered, almost reverently.

"What is the giving?"

"A myth. My mother foolishly told my father we could pass our bloodline to someone else when we died if the line hadn't been continued."

Avner stared down at his palm as images of his nightmare memory from childhood flipped one after the other through his mind.

Liev laying beneath a dying tree.

Bony hands on Avner's wrist.

Nameless tongue muttered followed by a flash of light.

The light always ended the dream, but what if there was something else he'd missed that he hadn't dreamed? What if...

He closed his eyes. Hazy images glowed in his memory. Bursts of light, not just one flash. Growing, seeping into his veins. Overtaking his body.

Avner's eyes snapped open. "It's me," he whispered.

"What is going on?" Shoshanna demanded. She stooped to pick up her knife.

Avner waved her off. "I'm part of the nameless tribe," he said, the words practically nonsense to his own ears. He couldn't be, and yet...

"Akaron, what would happen if you did the *giving*?"

"Bah, I wouldn't do it!"

"But how would you do it? Does it require an incantation of some sort? Is there a transfer of the blood right there?" Avner stepped closer, more urgent now.

"Well, yes. Mother made us memorize the words before

she passed. *'I give you my blood, my life. Take the lifeline and spread the fire to all.'"* He scoffed. "But no one ever did it because no one ever had golden blood before my brother and I."

"I think Liev did it to me," Avner murmured.

"But he died!"

"Only *after*. Shoshanna," Avner turned toward her, "there may be a way out of here! His brother left through a lake and made it to Doram. He must have popped up in the river since that is where we found him."

"I don't understand."

"I don't either, but I know why my blood glows." He gave a shocked laugh. It was almost too impossible to believe.

It's not impossible if you know who orchestrated it all, Chava's voice echoed in his ear as if she were there. But it was only his own mind filling in the gaps of months of listening to her ramble on about Eloah.

Avner had ignored coincidences for years, and more recently, during the months since becoming a gibborim. Could Chava really be right about all of it?

"My parents were fools who thought the *giving* would save us, but they died anyway. So did my brother in the lake. I will die and won't give my golden blood to anyone. It is my blessing alone, even if Eloah has abandoned me."

Eloah didn't abandon him, though. He lives still, and has answered the greatest mystery of your life, Avner. Again, Chava's imagined voice. Avner was going to be like Shoshanna if he didn't stop this, but he found he couldn't. He wanted to hear more. To know more.

"Akaron, did Liev believe Eloah had abandoned him?" he pressed.

Akaron scoffed again. "My brother was more foolish than

my parents. He thought Eloah would show him to the other tribes to spread his fire. And he died for it."

But not before finding you and blessing you. Your blood is the only thing that kept you alive in the arena all those months. Chava's logical response came instantly.

Avner had to agree with her. Or himself. He wasn't sure where these thoughts were coming from any longer. Maybe they were even from Eloah. He snorted. Chava would be proud he had that idea.

"How do we get out of here?" Shoshanna cut in, impatiently.

Right. First things first. "Akaron, where is this lake?" Avner asked.

Akaron shook his head. "Do not go in there. You will die."

"That's up to us to decide. You said it is across the valley?"

Akaron pointed the spear out across the valley to the far side where a mountain jutted out of the grass, ringed by red trees. "Do not go there, I am telling you. That is where the legend says Eloah died hundreds of years ago when the frost still held this valley."

Avner paused as he started to step out of the hut. "Wait, Eloah *died?*"

"I do not believe it, but the place is cursed. My father claimed the frost devoured his body but he was filled with life again and drove the frost away."

"But why would he die?"

Akaron shrugged again. "Liev believed the fairytale. Said Eloah died so the frost wouldn't destroy us."

Isn't that what Chava had said? That Eloah took the darkness and shame so people could be free? What if the ice *was* the darkness? Avner had felt that ice inside himself the dozens of times he'd killed in the arena.

I offer you freedom from your past darkness, Avner. It wasn't Chava's voice this time, but a stronger, deeper, ethereal one whispering straight into his soul. The voice from his dream! It had been months since Avner had remembered that someone or something had spoken to him that day when Liev died, but in this moment he knew the voice intimately. It was one and the same. Strong, yet gentle.

"Eloah?" Avner whispered.

Shoshanna groaned. "We need to get out of here."

"Yes." Avner stepped out of the house, grass *shushing* around his legs. He knew they had to get to the lake. It was the way out, improbable as it seemed. Shoshanna followed more than eagerly.

"You fools! Come back! The lake will kill you!" Akaron's cry was muffled beneath the sigh of the shifting grass.

Come, Kamu. The voice—Eloah—urged.

Kamu. The name tingled through Avner's chest, warming him. His legs obeyed the voice, moving quickly for the tree line. The sun set the leaves ablaze, turning them fuchsia. The colors...The warm air...Akaron was wrong. This wasn't Adamah. This was a place which shouldn't exist.

The ray of light slipped between the trees and veered North along the edge of the valley. A few more houses sat just outside the trees, falling into disrepair.

The trees faded, giving way to another valley splitting off the main one. There was no tall grass here, only moss-covered rocks surrounding a lake fed by a waterfall. Small compared to the frozen arena, but ten times larger than the pools at the river outside Doram. Steam rose in spirals, though the air was warm. The bright sun sparkled across the surface, and patches of pink reflected in the water where small clusters of the trees leaned out across the lake. A small mountain rose on the opposite end, marbled white and gray.

The ray of light slipped onto a rock at the far end of the lake. The purple light glowed brighter. It paused, as if waiting for something.

"I never knew such a beautiful place existed," Shoshanna whispered, and there was a softness in her voice Avner had only heard the day she discovered her true identity. She raised one hand, as if wanting to touch the physical beauty painted out before them, before her fingers strayed to the filthy strip of cloth covering her brand. She played with the frayed edges, conflicting emotions dancing on her burned face.

Avner could see the bottom of the lake even fifty feet out, with tendrils of algae hanging immobile from a submerged log. Nothing moved through them, not a fish or stray current. Serene in its stillness, the lake was too surreal to be explained. In a time of its own. The water was so clear there was no color apart from the plants inside it, frozen as if on display.

"Itzaak," Shoshanna breathed his name and stepped up to the edge of the water.

Avner longed to do the same. Something about the water called to him. He had nothing in the world apart from Chava, and this water was a chance to get back to her.

You have more than you know, the voice whispered.

Shoshanna dipped her toe into the water. Still no ripple, not even as the water made room for her foot. Avner leaned over the edge. Nothing moved beneath the surface. Rocks and algae-covered logs sat inches away in the water, preserved perfectly in a lake apart from time.

"What are you doing?" Akaron's frantic cry tore through the air. He'd followed them. "Don't touch the water! It'll kill you," the cry morphed into a sob, but Avner didn't turn to look at the only other person who shared his golden blood. "Please, please, don't go into the water. Don't leave me here alone. Don't leave me." A wail, longing for life. For friendship.

Avner slipped his sandaled foot into water that had no temperature. Ripples shot out this time, circling out in larger and larger patterns as they made their way across the lake. Drawing air through his teeth, he almost stepped back, only to freeze with his foot in midair.

Come... The voice felt like a friend now. Familiar, urging softly.

Shoshanna asked, "Do you really think this lake leads to Doram's river?"

"Yes." He couldn't say why, but the confidence was nearly overwhelming.

Shoshanna gripped the cloth on her brand and pulled. It fluttered down onto the lake.

"I hope you're right about this lake taking us back, but if you're not, I won't die covering Itzaak up. I never should have. He was the best part of me." Shoshanna stepped further into the lake and slipped beneath the surface, yet her body didn't show through the clear water. No rippling form or kicking feet. Just still water and undisturbed grasses.

Avner stepped into the water again and tingles attacked his skin, crawling up his legs, then grabbed hold of his waist and, finally, his torso. For some reason he couldn't explain, only the water mattered.

Kamu, my son, come.

The tingling went away with the whisper, leaving silence and clarity.

"All right," Avner whispered. The impossibility of this working and taking them back to Doram didn't seem to matter. It had worked for Liev. It would work for them. But even more improbable was how real Eloah seemed in this place. Strangely, Avner didn't want that feeling to subside once he left.

I'll stay with you if you ask me. Eloah whispered.

"I'd like that." Why did knowing Eloah was near seem so comforting?

Because I love you, Kamu.

Such simple words with such a simple answer. Eloah loved him despite everything he'd done? To be someone chosen...Not an outcast in Doram, the unwanted adoptee. Not the gibborim with no purpose but to kill, or the failed brother and son.

You are none of those things.

Those few words blasted through Avner, crumbling his years of self-doubt and months of evil deeds. Finally, truth overcame him.

Chava was right.

Eloah was everything.

"Eloah!" Unlike his half-hearted prayers, the name filled his soul as he spoke it. It fit. It was *right.*

You are mine. Now come, Eloah's gentle voice said.

Avner needed no second urging. Arms above his head and clothes still on, he dove.

42

GONE

Chava

An ax pinged against the stone wall, and Chava thrust herself out of the way to avoid losing her arm. She groped around, but came up empty. Avner must have spun the other way. She rebounded and jumped up before Copper could swing the ax again.

"Shoshanna!" Tevye screamed ten feet away, staring in horror at Death's Wall.

Chava followed his gaze, her pulse pounding, expecting to see the woman's lifeless body, but saw only blank rock before her. No Shoshanna. No Avner. Hadn't he fallen that way?

There was no time to ponder, as a rush of air whooshed beside her. She staggered to the left, raising the staff of Doram to block the blow.

Light and heat erupted from the end of the staff, blasting Copper off his feet. He crashed into the stone wall and lay still. Exhilaration swept through Chava and she whooped, but then went silent at the sight of Tevye's pale face.

"Th-they vanished," he stammered, pointing to the place where Chava had last seen Avner. Only frozen grass and ice-covered stone stared back at them.

"That's impossible—" but she was cut off as a gust of ice-cold air pummeled her back and threw her forward.

"No! Release him!" Miki's voice roared.

Chava scrambled back to her feet, her staff raised. Homed held Moises by the scruff, his small ring of fire dangerously close to the boy's face.

"One small boy with a weak skill at manipulating isn't as valuable as the golden gibborim." Felix clamped a hand on Moise's shoulder. "Where is Avner? Return him to me, or the boy dies."

Miki's flames flared with a dozen small offshoots. "It'll be okay, Moises. I'll get you home."

The boy nodded bravely. Chava flashed him an encouraging smile. He looked to still be in good health, even if most of him was covered by furs.

Copper staggered back to his feet, but didn't make a move as all eyes were on Miki and Homed. Chava tightened her grip on the staff. Maybe there would be an opportunity to take the manipulator out of the equation.

One of Miki's flames curled out further, closer to Moises. She raised her hands. Another flame flared higher—then died out. All at once, the entire flaming circle vanished. Something hissed beside Chava's foot.

Avner's torch. Extinguished by the slush at her feet. Miki no longer had the source.

Her regular brown eyes flared wide, only to flicker back to purple again—too late. Homed's own flames snapped out just as he raised his left fist. A chunk of ice from the river soared through the air and cracked into Miki's head. She crumpled to the frozen ground.

"No!" Moises and Chava screamed in unison.

Leaf ran over to Miki and wrapped a rope around her, securing her hands to her sides. More of Felix's men appeared through the frozen trees, surrounding them.

"Don't worry lad. Your special friend will be coming home with us once we leave this miserable place." Felix patted Moises on the head then looked at Chava. "Where is Avner?"

"You saw as well as I," Tevye snapped. "He and Shoshanna vanished into the stone."

Felix snorted. "I certainly didn't see that. Did you, Ben?"

Reuben stared at Death's Wall as if an apparition might burst forth at any moment. Chava looked closer at the Nameless Rune in the corner. Was it her imagination, or did it have a golden sheen?

She heard footsteps beside her. Dalea stared at the rune, ghostly pale.

"What devilry was that?" Reuben demanded, shaking himself out of his trance. He crossed over to Dalea. "Where is Avner?"

"I-I don't know."

"You're lying!" Reuben yanked her away from the wall. "That's all you've ever done."

Dalea's shoulder smashed into Chava's as Reuben thrust her away from him in disgust. He turned toward the others. "Leaf! Copper! Get digging."

"They're not underground," Tevye breathed. "I saw green when the wall flashed open for a split second."

But how had Avner gone anywhere? Reuben and Felix

began arguing the same question, and Chava didn't bother to voice her thoughts. They were outnumbered. With Miki unconscious, only she and Tevye were left to protect the artifacts and Moises.

But between Tevye and the nearest of Felix's men, a two-foot gap remained open to freedom and the frozen forest beyond. Reuben and Felix were arguing again, and the nearest guard was taking too long to pull another set of ropes out of a bag at his feet.

No one would bind Chava again. "Cover me," she whispered to Tevye. "I'll get the artifacts away from Reuben." She didn't wait for confirmation. She turned and ran. Footsteps pounded behind her, but she didn't stop, weaving through the trees and behind boulders, trying to throw her pursuer off. She flung herself into a thicket of frozen brambles. The bag of artifacts snagged between two branches, but Chava yanked and it came, shards of ice slicing into her exposed hands. She wormed her way deeper into the cluster of bushes, ice pricking her.

More cracking sounds followed, and Dalea emerged just behind her, ice shards sticking in her frozen braid, and blood dotting her scratched face.

Chava held up a finger to silence her. The woman would bring Copper and Leaf down upon them the way she was smashing branches. Dalea sank down beside Chava in the center of the thicket and the noise ceased. Shouts echoed behind them, but not too close. Chava dared to breathe again as the voices faded. They were only a few hundred yards from the pools, but hopefully it was close enough.

Eloah, please help us!

Chava didn't dare move again, though Dalea readjusted to pull her knees to her chest and the sound of more snapping twigs was enough to stop Chava's heart. The silence stretched between them. Someone shouted in the distance. Was Avner back somehow? Chava clamped her hands tighter over the staff of Doram, praying he, Tevye and Moises were all right. She should have tried to blast light from the staff again to save them.

But doubt had squashed the idea. There had been so many of Felix's goons, plus Copper and Leaf. Surely, she couldn't have saved the others before someone took her down.

Chava resisted the urge to squirm as the ice turned to muddy slush beneath her. Dalea didn't seem to notice, staring off into the frozen branches blocking them from view.

"Do you love him?"

Dalea's whisper cut through the silence.

Chava froze and faced her. "Really? You're going to ask that *now* of all times?"

"Judging by how cold my fingers are, now is the only time we have," Dalea quipped, her eyes burning. True to her words, the edges of her exposed fingers clutching her knees were already graying.

"Here," Chava tucked the staff into her armpit and grabbed Dalea's hands.

The other woman's eyes widened, but she didn't pull away as she certainly felt the heat spreading from Chava's hands to her own.

"Do you really want me to answer your question? About Avner?" Chava asked.

Dalea cringed. "Are you saying you do love him?"

"And if I do, what difference does it make?"

Dalea's dark eyes filled with tears. What hardships had

this woman endured in the last few months alone, not to mention the year before that, when the man she intended to live with forever had been stolen and changed? For the first time, Chava's heart ached for Dalea.

"Dalea, I'm sorry, but there is someone else you can turn to."

The other woman blinked the tears back. She seemed about to say something. Chava leaned closer. Would Dalea come to Eloah? Chava dared to hope —

Dalea yanked her hands out of Chava's grasp and rammed her forehead into Chava's chest. She ripped the staff out of Chava's unsuspecting hands, and the weight of the bag of artifacts vanished off her shoulder. Branches shattered, raining ice shards down on her until Chava couldn't see.

"Dalea!" Chava scrambled to reach the invaluable items, but pain sliced through her hands as she grabbed at the frozen branches.

Dalea smashed her way back out of the thicket. Chava staggered after her through the frozen forest, blinded by the sun glaring off the ice

"Come back! Don't do this!" She gasped as she untangled herself from the last of the branches, sending dozens of ice splinters flying every which way.

Dalea was already around the corner. Sprinting back the way they had come. Toward Reuben.

"Dalea, no! Please!" Chava wheezed as she struggled after her, each footstep through the slush more laborious than the last. She slipped and landed headlong in the clearing by the pools. She glanced up through watering eyes to see Dalea, muddied, bloodied, and forcing her way through the guards around Felix and Reuben.

"Here! Take them!" she shrieked as she threw the bag at Reuben's feet. "This is all you need to stop this frost, right? So, take them and end this!"

Reuben stared at her, amused. She held out the staff, the same item she'd denied him for over a year, her arm trembling. Dalea, the traitor to the traditions she'd so staunchly defended to the point of letting her own people freeze to death.

Chava tried to stagger to her feet, but the mud worked against her. Tevye grasped her arm and helped her upright.

"Eloah may have a plan yet," he whispered in her ear.

Do you? she pleaded, because she couldn't see a way out of this. Avner was missing, and the artifacts were back in Reuben's grip. Reuben had all he needed. The frost might melt, but he'd receive the power she'd fought so hard to keep him from getting.

Reuben picked up the bag of artifacts, his face alight like a giddy boy. He accepted the staff from Dalea with the other hand.

"My thanks, you wonderful woman."

Dalea let out a sob and sank to the ground, shivering. She'd had warmth on her hands but rejected it for ice. For Reuben's version of power. *Why, Eloah, why?* Chava's question went unanswered as her brother pulled each object out of the bag, his eyes shining, only to frown as he went to pull out the last objects and came up with nothing.

"Where are the ball of wood and the bracelet?"

Chava couldn't stifle a laugh. She'd forgotten! "Wherever Avner and Shoshanna went. You can't do anything without them!"

Reuben shoved everything back in the bag.

"Does this mean we still hunt for my golden gibborim?" Felix lit up.

"Oh, yes. He's going to want his *wife*," Reuben said, his voice as frigid as the ice covering the river next to them. "We'll build a fire here and wait. Avner will return. When he does, we take what is ours and finish this. Take those fools to the river. I don't want them getting in the way, but keep them in the open where Avner can see *her*."

The bodyguards herded her and Tevye onto the river. Miki's still form was dragged to the edge and left there. Her chest still rose and fell. Thank goodness.

"Are you sure about all this, Ben?" Felix pulled Moises with him everywhere he went.

"I told you not to call me that," Reuben snapped. "And of course, I'm sure!"

Their bickering went on like that for a little while, and Chava focused on the mesmerizing spirals of frost beneath Tevye's feet. Her own left a slushy mess in the ice, though not enough to make them fall through. Something flickered within the ice just a few feet away. Chava blinked, but the spot didn't fade.

A dark shape moved *beneath* the ice. She held her breath and took a step closer.

"Where are you going?"

Chava ignored Copper. The closer she came, the more the shape began to look human. But that was impossible—a hand pressed flat against the ice from below and a second one hovered beside it, glowing purple.

Avner was under the ice.

43

LIGHT, ICE, AND FIRE

Avner

"Avner!" Chava dove at the ice. Her burning fists sizzled as she pressed them into the snow, but the ice didn't give way. It had to be at least eight inches thick! Avner's fist hit the ice, but only produced a dull thud. His dark hair floated around his face, and his skin was oddly sallow, cheeks puffed with air. Chava jumped up and spun for Leaf who stood ten feet away, guarding the artifacts.

Chava lunged before Leaf knew what was coming. She scooped up the staff, and in one fluid movement, leaped back to the river.

"Hey! Copper!" Leaf's cry went up behind her.

But Tevye tripped Copper before he could intercept Chava and held him down. "Save Avner!"

She fell to her knees above Avner. His eyes were strangely calm, as if he didn't fear that he would drown and knew she would save him in time.

Chava rammed the staff down. It sank into the ice with a

sharp hiss. Light splintered through the ice in every direction. Leaf skidded to a stop a few feet to the side and staggered back so the tips of her boots were just touching the nearest spike of light.

"Chava! What are you doing?" Reuben's scream carried across on a gust of wind, but a great cracking noise overrode it.

The light spiderwebbed out further, glowing brighter, and whiter. Steam rose out of the cracks as Chava shoved her hand into the strangely warm water. Her fingers groped briefly before connecting with something warmer than the water. She gripped and pulled. Heat snapped in her palm, which could only mean one thing. She'd found Avner's marked hand.

With a heave that tested every muscle in her body, Chava fell backward, screaming.

Then the water rose out of the hole in an impossible movement, *pushing* Avner with it. Miki stood on the bank, her arms still bound at her sides, and her eyes blazing purple.

Avner flopped halfway onto the ice, with only his legs dangling in the water.

Miki balled her hands at her sides. Air whooshed past Chava. Homed staggered away from Moises, clutching his own throat and gasping soundlessly for breath. His ring of fire snapped out.

"Moises! Go!" Chava shouted.

The boy didn't need the urging. He was already halfway to Miki.

"Homed!" Felix screeched.

Miki released her fists and Homed thudded to his knees, hands out on the ice, straining to inhale. A torch held by one of Felix's crew flared higher and the flame shot toward Miki. It licked at the rope binding her, then snapped out, leaving a charred section of rope. Miki thrust her arms out and the rope broke. Her arms flew skyward. The fire turned on Homed, still struggling to catch his breath. His body vanished beneath the flames. The men around him jumped away as the heat roared.

Miki sprinted toward the woods, dragging Moises with her.

Yes! Miki had done it, Moises was free!. Maybe she'd get him safe and come back.

Felix yelled something else, and several of his men took off after Miki. They wouldn't catch her. And if they did, they'd end up like Homed.

Chava leaned back toward Avner and tried to pull him further out of the water. His eyes fluttered open, and she caught her breath. They were still gray, but there was *something* about them. There was a new brightness in the color of his eyes, as if they'd seen something while he was gone.

She didn't need to ask. She knew.

Avner had met Eloah.

Avner

WATER RAN off Avner's face as he lay on the ice, breathing in blessed air. It had worked! Chava's golden eyes looked into his as she leaned over him. The air between them was charged with anticipation. She looked at him with a sort of fierceness, and then a smile spread over her face.

Before he could even begin to touch on all that had happened in the Nameless Valley, Reuben stepped behind Chava and yanked the staff out of her hand.

Chava released Avner's hand, and he shuddered at the loss of heat. Avner pulled himself up on his elbows and brought his feet all the way out of the water just as another head broke the surface. Shoshanna stared at them all with her mahogany-flecked eyes. Avner hadn't seen her under the water, but she'd come up right behind him even though he'd entered the lake in the Valley of Eloah after her.

"Shoshanna, take my hand." Tevye leaned out over the water.

She stared at it, but didn't make a move to take it. Had she met Eloah too?

Tevye leaned further over the cracked ice and pulled Shoshanna's hand out of the water, revealing the brand of Zev. Avner joined him, grasping her other hand. Together, they dragged Shoshanna up onto the shelf of ice.

Avner glanced around. A strange, charred form lay ten feet away and the ice beneath it was now slush. His heart leapt as he realized that Miki and Moises were nowhere in sight, unless one of them was the body... "Where is Miki? Moises?"

"Safe," Tevye whispered. "She got him out."

Which could only mean the body was Homed. Miki had proved she was stronger after all.

"Well, this was unexpected," Reuben said, clapping his hands together.

"Yes, but what about that Manipulator? I need her and the boy back now that we don't have Homed." Felix complained.

"But you have your Golden Gibborim back," Reuben

waved his hand dismissively, "*and* I believe we have all the artifacts now."

Fingers closed around Avner's wrist as he sat back from Shoshanna's prone form.

"No!" He tried to pry Copper's hand off, but the bracelet went with it.

Copper's burned face contorted, and his fist rammed into Avner's forehead. He careened into the ice beside Shoshanna, staring straight at the gray sky swirling unnaturally above. He missed the blue sky of the Valley of Eloah.

Trust, Kamu. Eloah's voice rushed through him, driving out the chill and the damp in his clothes. Avner was still. He caught Chava staring at him. She gave the slightest nod, and he returned it. Eloah must have a plan. His own bizarre life proved that to be true. He had to tell Chava about his blood, but didn't want Reuben to overhear. Although the revelation that he was the last of the Nameless Tribe dimmed now that he was back to real life and not in the Nameless Valley. He wasn't sure what significance it held.

Copper handed the bracelet to Reuben, who slipped it over the top of the staff where it rested securely in place.

Leaf yanked Chava back. "It's too late. You've lost. You can stop struggling."

"You only say that because you don't want me to head-butt you again."

"Again?" Leaf scoffed.

"I'm sure I've done it at some point."

Avner laughed despite the circumstances. Leaf scowled and yanked Chava toward the bonfire. Copper's hand dug into Avner's armpits and hauled him off the ice. The chill didn't cling to him since Chava had touched him, but he could still feel the cold in the air.

"Your clothes aren't wet." Copper paused and stared at Avner.

Avner smiled, and Chava flashed him a knowing look.

"I've done it. I've found all the tribes." Reuben's gleeful voice broke the moment.

Shoshanna held her legs up against her chest, her quivering chin pressed into her knees. The greatest fighter in history, crying? Even Reuben cast her a sidelong look as he arranged the objects in a pile by the bonfire.

"I guess you did break the greatest gibborim in history." Felix clapped him on the back.

"Did he, or did someone else?" Chava murmured, her eyes flashing with meaning.

Avner almost asked Shoshanna if she had met Eloah as well, but something stopped him. There was no joy in her face, like what burned in Avner's heart. Something was off. The tear tracks on her cheeks only spoke of shame. Had she met him, but not accepted him?

Felix stepped around Shoshanna and waved Copper away from Avner. "As your master said, I have *him* back now."

"If you can handle him," Copper muttered under his breath, releasing Avner's arm. He set about starting the bonfire.

"My dear man, I've owned him for a month now. I'm more prepared than you could imagine." He grabbed Avner's sleeve and ripped the shoulder open, exposing the flower tattoo of Felix's ownership. He grinned maliciously. "See? He will always be mine."

Avner clenched his marked hand. This couldn't be the end of his freedom. He wouldn't go back into any arena. He wanted to get to know Miki more. He wanted to return to

Kemet and meet his father. He wanted to build a life with Chava. He needed to learn more about Eloah and spend endless hours listening to him.

But none of it would matter if the frost wasn't stopped. It took Copper five tries to light the pile of icy broken branches he'd collected. Even then, the frost swirled up to the fire, only inches away.

Avner almost crept closer to the warmth of the bonfire, but he preferred Chava's heat. She still stood in Leaf's grasp on the opposite side of the circle of people. Her face was a study in contrasting emotions Relief. Joy. Worry. If they survived this, Avner would take her where Reuben and Felix would never find her, and they'd finally live as they should have for the past year. As husband and wife.

"Ironic, isn't it?" Reuben said as he removed the artifacts from the pile and set them in a line. "We're right back where we started. At the pools, with my men holding all of you."

The fact wasn't lost on Avner, though many things had changed. Namely, he'd learned the truth about his blood and about Eloah.

Reuben stepped back and turned toward where Shoshanna still sat clutching her knees. Seeing the once great hero of Doram and greatest gibborim of all time looking so vulnerable was disconcerting, but there was no way to get close to her and ask if Eloah had spoken to her in the valley as well.

For once, Chava was stone silent, and that fact alone added to the gloom of the moment. Even Leaf seemed to share the thought as she jerked her hand off Chava's arm with a start. Steam rose from both.

Leaf shook out her hand, cursing before wiping it on her fur coat. Chava didn't try to run now that she stood free, but stared hard at the objects as Reuben pulled a burning stick out of the fire. Dalea stood beside the hot pool, still shivering, but riveted on Reuben's every move.

"Nuri, I haven't forgotten about your bit of wood. I know you have it." Reuben turned toward her.

Shoshanna didn't move. Reuben stepped up to her. She kept shaking, her teeth biting into her knees, leaving behind little half-moon indents in her leather leggings. Reuben leaned over and hesitated for one second, his hand hovering above her. When Shoshanna didn't move to stop him, he plunged his hand into her belt pouch and pulled the bit of wood out. He jumped back, stumbling over his own feet, until he stood beside the line of artifacts.

Still, Shoshanna made no move to get back the most precious object of her life.

Avner wasn't sure if that was a good sign or a bad one.

A look of relief spread over Reuben's face as he set the bit of wood at the end of the line. Doram's staff, the petrified ship chunk from Manoach, the document of Eder, Yor's knife, Nameless—Bachir's—bracelet, and Zev's ball of wood. A shiver ran down Avner's spine. This was it, wasn't it? Reuben would either save the world and inherit untold power which he would then misuse. Or he would fail, and they would all die.

Avner wasn't sure which option was better. but it was out of his hands now.

"When the falls thaw, when the lake is water again, then will the tribes be reunited. Then will the power be given to those who returned." Reuben intoned, his voice trembling into the silent air. The torch wavered in his grasp. The flame bent and touched the document of Eder. Another flame flared, jumping onto the staff. It fizzled and died.

Frowning, Reuben pressed the torch harder against the document until it caught fire. Flames engulfed it. The document popped and exploded, giving off a burst of acrid smoke. A few of the ship's crew members jumped back.

"Uh Ben, are you sure you are supposed to burn the objects?" Felix asked.

"I have done extensive research about this, so yes. Fire brings the tribes together as it did hundreds of years ago when they were first established." Reuben walked down the line of objects, holding the torch over each one until they all caught fire. Chava groaned as the flame licked out at the staff of Doram. Avner held his breath as the flames were lowered to the trinket which had seen him through so many events in the past year.

But it was just that. A trinket. Eloah mattered, not the beads. They caught with a pop and the wooden runes went up in flames, just like the document of Eder and now Shoshanna's bit of wood. She didn't even look up as the object she'd once killed for was charred black. Most of the flames soon died out, leaving sooty marks on the gravelly ground where the heat had melted the frost away. The bit of wood only flared a minute longer before sizzling out. Eder's document shriveled and burned, red lines of fire eating the years of history it had seen.

Then it too, burned out.

Gone. Eaten.

The river did not melt. No light flashed across the sky. Reuben stood frozen, still bent over Zev's wood as if expecting something else to happen. But nothing did. It hadn't worked.

44

UNDESERVED

Shoshanna

Colors moved in front of her. The ground was painfully cold beneath her, the ice stabbing through her pants. As she watched, the rash receded from the back of her hand. Shoshanna held her breath, ready to feel its tingle somewhere else.

It didn't come.

The torch Reuben held flickered orange and red. Color. Shoshanna held her breath. She could see color, and the rash wasn't returning. What was it about these pools?

Eloah.

A short distance away, Reuben was saying something in a voice filled with despair, but she couldn't focus on him when so much had just happened. When the colors she hadn't seen for months danced before her.

This is what I offer, Shoshanna, the voice caressed her mind. Gentle, calm.

She pulled her knees tighter to her chest, unable to look

away from the colorful flames in front of her though the ice beneath her was making her body numb. Such an unfamiliar sensation, but she deserved it. She should have been feeling every bit of cold from the moment she took the potion and while she committed every heinous crime against her people.

She blinked, but her sight didn't fade back to grayscale.

Impossible. Undeserved.

Shoshanna hung her head and let the sobs come.

45

BROTHERS

Avner

Dalea fell to her knees as if all hope had been snuffed out of her.

Standing beside Avner, Copper let out a slow breath. All around Avner, swirls of frost were growing *thicker* and inching closer. His fur boots were coated in frost now, but something about the way the swirls writhed and spread sent a fresh shiver down his back. The frost hadn't been stopped by the objects. It was getting *worse*.

Felix clicked his tongue. "Is that it, Ben? Shouldn't this insufferable chill go away now?" He glanced out at the frozen branches beyond the river as he pulled his fur closer. Every twig was encased in ice.

"It has to be the bracelet," Reuben muttered. He dropped the torch and it hissed against the frozen ground. "Where did you get it?" He spun on Avner.

The bracelet sat in the lineup, its runes burned beyond recognition. The sight should have stung, but instead, the charred object only looked pointless lying among the other ruined items. They might be hundreds of years old, but they hadn't stopped the frost. After all, how could they? They were just things.

The thought reverberated through Avner's mind.

They are just things.

Why would a prophecy care about trinkets when it was *people* who went missing? The tribes had once comprised six groups of people, not six groups of objects.

"Is this bracelet from the Nameless Tribe? Answer me! You're still my slave," Reuben said, standing very close.

"If I remember correctly, Ben, he is *my* slave. That was the deal. I help you track the objects down, and I get him back." Felix stepped closer. Something black glinted in his left hand.

The knife of Yor, looking no worse for wear after being lit on fire. After all, stone didn't burn.

Reuben bristled. "Put that back. You can have Avner, I don't need him, but that's my knife."

All this time, everyone had fought over possession of Avner, but what if there was something, or *someone* else who also wanted him? Not just to own him, but to know him? Someone he'd just met an hour ago. What if all Eloah wanted was for the tribes of Admah to know him again, as they used to in the days before the tribes split? What if *he* was the fire that united them?

"Put the knife back." Reuben hissed.

"This knife is worthless." Felix shook it as he spoke. "You can't reunite any tribes. You can't save us. I saw through your posturing weeks ago, Reuben." His face twisted, his usual joviality gone. He raised the knife, and his circle of crew members tightened, pressing toward the frozen river.

Ice cracked beneath Avner's feet as Copper inched him back, eyeing Felix's men nervously.

Leaf pulled Chava onto the ice as well to avoid the javelin tip of the nearest sailor. Frost swirled off the ice and crept up Avner's boots.

"Chava," he whispered.

Her head whipped up.

"This isn't about objects," Avner said, his voice shaking. As soon as he said it, he was certain of it. It all made sense! How hadn't they seen it?

"Silence!" Reuben screamed, though it wasn't clear if he was talking to Avner or Felix.

The latter still held the knife aloft as he circled Reuben like a gibborim around his fallen opponent. "Adamah will remain under the frost. No one cares about it. You folk were always a weak breed. And I don't need your promised power. I will conquer the arenas elsewhere through cunning, and thanks to you, my Golden Gibborim."

"No," Reuben spat. "*I* will end this!"

Felix laughed, cold, and mirthless. "You won't even be remembered in the scrolls of history from the time before Adamah was destroyed." He danced two steps forward before Avner could even blink and ran the knife of Yor across Reuben's throat.

"No!" Chava screamed, trying to rip herself out of Leaf's grasp. "That's my brother!"

Reuben didn't even try to clutch the wound in his neck as he dropped to the ground. Copper's fingers loosened on Avner's arm, but he did not rush to help his master.

"Seems I did you a favor, Chava." Felix wiped the ancient blade on Reuben's shual-fur vest. "Killed by his own obsession. Ironic, isn't it?"

Chava's brother lay dying right in front of them, and a sudden understanding overcame Avner. A sob tore at his chest, but not for Reuben. For Mikhail. *Mikhail.* He'd wasted so much time hating him, he'd never had a chance to mourn him. So Avner sobbed with Chava as she tore free from Leaf's grasp and ran to Reuben's side. Blood pooled beneath him, freezing as the frost crawled over it, more potent than the heat of Reuben's life running out of him.

"No, no, no," Chava sobbed. "Reuben, I forgive you! Let Eloah forgive you!"

But Reuben couldn't speak. His fingers stopped flailing on the ice as he took his last breath. Dead.

Reuben. Mikhail. Brothers. Dead and gone. Both forgiven, but only one had received Eloah's forgiveness.

Avner glanced at Shoshanna sitting near the fire, her knees up to her chest, staring at Reuben. She didn't show any signs of relief that her enemy was finally gone.

Something flashed on the other side of Reuben's body as Dalea yanked a knife out of the belt of the nearest sailor. He tried to grab it back, but Dalea was already sprinting away.

Toward Shoshanna.

Avner couldn't be seeing this. Dalea with a *knife.*

"This is for all the Doramites dead because of you!" she shrieked and plunged the knife down toward Shoshanna.

The woman made no move to deflect the blade. It sank into her shoulder, all of Dalea's anger driving it forward, shredding Shoshanna's flesh as well as Dalea's vow to do no harm.

"No!" Tevye shrieked and rammed his shoulder into Dalea's chest.

Both fell to the ice and the swirls of frost hungrily leapt on their clothes. Tevye staggered back to his feet, but Dalea collapsed into a heap, her body convulsed with sobs. Shoshanna's blood covered her right hand. Dalea stared at it, then shook her hand, screaming, as if that might undo what she'd done.

"I broke the vow, I broke the vow..." she sobbed. She tried to wipe the blood off on the ice beneath her and only succeeded in shredding the side of her hand on the jagged shards.

"Well, at least we won't need to bother with that broken one any longer," Felix said, watching both women with a crooked smile.

Shoshanna lay on the ice, trembling. Tevye ripped off the outer layer of his fur and wadded it up against her wound, murmuring words Avner couldn't hear.

Shoshanna's reply was loud enough for all to hear. "I deserve this."

"He can erase it all, Sho," Tevye sobbed.

"Get rid of the others," Felix barked to the nearest of his men.

Avner started to pull away from Copper, only to realize the man had vanished in the chaos. Leaf must have realized this at the same moment, as she turned from Chava, her eyes wide and her arms extended to stop the closest javelin. Too late. One of Felix's men speared her clean through the shoulder. Leaf staggered back. Avner turned his head, unable to watch, but he couldn't block the sound of her groan and gurgle as the sailor struck again.

"You, Avner, will go back to being my golden-blooded champion. I'll keep your wife alive if you don't struggle. I'm sure I can find a way to use her heat in the arena. Maybe I'll take a page from Reuben's book and have you fight on ice again." Felix grabbed Chava's arm and dragged her away from Reuben.

But taking in all the death and destruction around him—Reuben, Leaf, Shoshanna and Dalea—drove home the strange realization kindling in Avner's heart so that it couldn't be overridden by Felix's threats.

"It's not about objects!"

"You're right. It's about me using you to become the richest gibborim master in the world."

"Chava!" Avner staggered after her and the man dragging her back down the river. "The frost isn't about objects!"

Her brows knitted in confusion. Couldn't she see this wasn't about worthless things? Two of the sailors pointed their javelins at Avner and he stopped trying to move toward Chava. Instead, he dropped beside Shoshanna's trembling form as he passed her. Her mahogany eyes were hollow, and for once the flecks of cinnamon were still.

"What did you hear in the valley, Shoshanna?"

"Bring my golden gibborim!" Felix shouted back. He and Chava were twenty feet away now. "Quickly!" He side-eyed the creeping swirls of thickening frost as he backed away.

Come on, Come on! Avner needed just another minute with Shoshanna. He shoved another guard back and grabbed Shoshanna's shoulders. "Did you meet Eloah?"

She had stopped sobbing, but the somber silence hanging over her was worse. Blood pooled beneath her, already frozen. She wouldn't die like this. She couldn't, not after all Eloah had brought her through!

The tip of a javelin pricked Avner's arm. "Move."

He took Shoshanna's hand, only to yank it back. She was as cold as the ice beneath them. "Shoshanna, please. Accept Eloah's gift."

"There's no gift for me. He can't want me after what I've done," she croaked.

"But he does, Sho." Tevye took her other hand. "He wanted me, and I've killed dozens of men. Same with Avner—" he cut off as a guard hauled him mercilessly to his feet and dragged him away. "Listen to us, Shoshanna! Please!"

"Move!"

The javelin pricked the back of Avner's leg this time, cutting through his thick leather pants.

Avner had no choice but to back up as the sailors herded him closer to Chava and Felix. Tevye was thrust out after them, leaving Shoshanna alone on the ice, bleeding. Dying. Dalea still lay sobbing against Death's Wall, the heat from the bonfire alone protecting her from the life-stealing frost. Avner couldn't help her, even if he had been free to do so. Dalea was in a prison of her own making.

"Chava," Avner said as soon as he was within earshot, "Reuben had it all wrong, so no one else saw it, because you were the only one who believed in Eloah."

"See what? Is Shoshanna going to die?"

"She's in Eloah's hands now." Avner might have wished for her death weeks ago, but now he ached for her loss if she went without meeting Eloah. He had to trust that Eloah would provide a way for her. Yet his most recent revelation overrode thoughts of Shoshanna, even though she was a part of it all. "But the frost isn't about artifacts! It's about people. It's about the tribes returning to Eloah."

"The tribes? But they are gone."

"No, they aren't—"

A ball of fire exploded out of the trees to the left side of the river. It crashed into the ice in the middle of a group of

Felix's men. Screams erupted. Javelins hit the ice as they scattered, some clutching singed appendages.

Miki was back. She stood on the shore of the river, her eyes blazing purple. Beside her, eyes glowing blue, Moises held his arms over his head. The air shivered around Avner. Moises clenched his fingers. Heat from the fire ball expanded outward, making the air thick and hot. Avner choked and staggered away from it as the ball continued to burn on the ice. The frozen river turned to slush, and three of Felix's men fell in, their screams cut off by the frigid waters. One pulled himself back out, but a rock flew and crashed into his head. He slipped back under the surface and disappeared.

Tevye whooped.

The guard escorting Avner urged him forward with the javelin. "Hurry!"

But he didn't want to hurry away from his sister, standing like a powerful siren on the opposite bank. More fire rained down, and the guard beside Chava fell with a cry as his clothes began to burn. Felix dodged, pulling Chava with him, and stumbled to the ground. Chava ripped her arm out of his grasp and spun back, dodging another ball of fire.

Curses and ash, was Miki trying to hit his wife? Avner spun around, but Miki wasn't on the bank any longer. A thunderous cracking shook the ground, and a boulder larger than the dingy they'd arrived in tumbled through the air. It struck the ice a few feet away, splintering it into dozens of chunks. More guards screamed, climbing onto the chunks, trying to find safety. Only a few succeeded.

Blazes, his sister was a force to be reckoned with.

"Oh no, you don't!" Felix grabbed Chava's leg as she fled, but fell back with a cry, clutching a burned hand.

"Avner!" Chava leaped around another flying rock.

"Moises! Watch your aim!" Miki yelled.

Avner jumped back up and grabbed Chava's hand. Felix yelled behind them. On his feet again. Closing the distance with the remaining half dozen men. Avner yanked Chava behind the chunks of boulders. Something crashed on the other side, shaking the ice beneath them. Avner yanked her up again. He pulled her between two of the guards just as one swung his sword. Chava spun around and kicked him in the chest, sending him flying into his comrade.

A thrill of pride ran through Avner, but then a spear flew toward Miki fifty yards away.

"No!"

The spear froze in mid-air. Moises's arm shook as he held his hand out, his face tense with concentration.

"Good job!" Miki shouted with a laugh, before knocking the spear away with a flick of her wrist.

Something cinched around Avner's ankle. He tried to jerk back, but Felix held the rope firmly in his fist. A wild smile played on the man's face. Two of the remaining guards closed in beside Chava.

"You're both coming with me," Felix said, giddy with delight. His disheveled hair and blood-smeared clothes were a far cry from the man who'd bought them in Mereen. "Let's move—"

"Yaaah!" The man holding Tevye screeched and staggered back, jerking Tevye with him. Frost curled up his neck, creeping closer to his face. It had already frozen each strand of the fur on his boots. The man shrieked again and tried to kick his feet, as if that would send the ice crystals away, but all it did was lock his legs to the frozen ground. He writhed but couldn't step either way. The frost on his face traveled to his nose, then his mouth. His shrieks stopped.

Tevye jumped back, but the frost had already leached onto his pants.

"No!" Avner lunged toward him and the rope popped out of Felix's grip. The man stood with his mouth open, horror on his face. Avner staggered closer to Tevye.

But the frost moved quicker. The dazzling, glowing crystals spread over him, covering his torso. Tevye swatted at it like a swarm of bees, but it made it to his face and even slipped under his eye patch. With a cry, he thudded to the ground.

"Eloah, help us!" Chava screamed.

Avner made it to Tevye. Too late. His friend was a statue of ice, one eye open wide, unseeing, as if it were made of glass.

"Tevye!" Avner tried to shake him, but the icy form of his friend was too heavy to budge. His chest didn't rise and fall. His pulse didn't beat. Tevye was frozen. Avner couldn't think the rest. Just as Tevye was unable to breathe, Avner could not utter a word.

Eloah, no!

Avner glanced up, tears freezing against his cheeks, to meet Chava's intense stare.

"No," she whispered, and she clenched her fists.

They weren't going to win. They hadn't stopped the frost, and now it had claimed the best of them.

Chava's knuckles whitened as she clenched her fists harder. Steam seemed to radiate off her like a ray of sun.

The frost churned beneath Avner's knees, and he felt the sharp sting of it as it grabbed hold of his legs. He inhaled, for what might be the last time.

But then the frost slowed down and pulled away. Avner let loose the captive breath. He glanced at Chava again. Her eyes flared brighter and her fingers clenched tighter. The frost moved faster. Was she *controlling* it?

The frost veered left. Toward Felix. The swirls slithered over the ice, refreezing the holes Miki had made, trapping one soldier permanently underneath. Felix's boots turned white. He tried to stagger back, but his feet wouldn't move. Frozen to the river.

"No, no, no!" He yanked and pulled, but nothing happened. "Get me out of here!"

The remaining soldiers exchanged glances, then turned and fled.

The spirals swirled their way up Felix's foot, then to his knees. He inhaled with a hiss which ended in a scream as he yanked again. His feet separated from the ice, but only enough for him to fall over with a thud. His frozen appendages met the solid river. Before Felix could scream again, the swirls encased his body, slipping into his open mouth and covering his terrified eyes with glistening frost. His chest rose, but didn't fall. His fingers splayed out for help, but didn't find anyone. Frozen.

Chava's hands unclenched, and the frost *stopped moving.* It didn't creep any further, but it didn't recede either. Chava snatched the charred staff off the ground where Reuben had left it and sprinted for Tevye's frozen form. "No, Eloah, please." She reached out with the staff and touched Tevye's eye patch.

For the span of two breaths, nothing happened. Hope burned in Avner's heart

Then white light burst out of the patch, spreading across his face, peeling the ice away to reveal perfect pink skin.

Avner lifted his hand off Tevye's chest as the frost vanished off Tevye's clothes. As if the rest of the world wasn't frozen beyond repair inches away. As if Tevye stood apart in a thawed land of eternal summer.

Chava sobbed in relief beside Avner. Then she offered the staff to Tevye.

Avner didn't dare to hope his friend would reach out—

He did. Tevye's left hand rose, without any sign of the maimed and bent fingers he'd had for the past year, and grasped the staff. Tevye sat up, his chest moving again. Breathing. Warm and alive. He released the staff and reached his healed fingers, trembling, to the eye patch.

It can't be... Avner held his breath. His friend had never shown him the scar where his eye—

In one fluid motion, Tevye pulled the patch off. A healthy golden eye twinkled where the scar tissue should have been. Dazzling. Brilliant, brighter even than Chava's. He stared at his healed hand with one green eye and one gold. Then threw his head back and laughed.

46

BEAUTIFUL IN DEATH

Shoshanna

A face flickered in the darkness. Black curls swayed as Itzaak bent toward her. *'Here my love, your favorite!'* Bright pinpricks of light reflecting off white snow lilies. She reached for them, her 'z' brand matching her husband's.

Cool air brushed her face. Itzaak and his lilies vanished. Everything hurt, everything was cold. Or nothing hurt and had no temperature. Shoshanna could no longer tell. Everything had stopped making sense the moment she found herself in the Nameless Valley. And she had a feeling it wouldn't make sense for the rest of her very short life.

How long did she have? Moments? Seconds?

She tried to sit up, to press a hand to the wound on her shoulder, but her body wouldn't respond. Maybe she'd frozen and would never move her limbs again. She kept her eyes closed because opening them seemed impossible. She'd failed to stop Dalea from stabbing her. A woman who'd never hurt anything, yet she'd dealt Shoshanna a mortal blow.

Was that how weak she was?

Yes.

But the voice in the valley had said Eloah covered her weakness.

What did that mean? Her weakness only got her killed, and Itzaak, along with all her men so long ago. Her weakness was her biggest failure. She couldn't save anyone, least of all herself.

But the voice whispered that it didn't matter. That he still wanted her. She wanted to believe it, but it couldn't be true. She was worthless. Corrupt. Ruined.

Not to me, Eloah—if that was who this was—whispered back.

Shoshanna tried to groan, to shake her head, to insist he was wrong.

"Sho?" Tevye's voice pierced the heavy darkness. A weight pressed against her arm. Warm. Comforting.

She savored the touch for a moment. Too long. No one touched her. Tevye knew all she'd done. Why would he want to comfort her?

"Shoshanna? Can you hear me?" he pressed.

Answering would mean she was still alive. She wasn't sure she wanted to be alive.

"Reuben's gone. Felix too. No one is going to harm us again," Tevye whispered. He sounded close. Too close.

But she couldn't find it in herself to pull away.

"Tevye?" she croaked. Ashes, her throat hurt. She winced, and the motion sent shooting pain through her shoulder. The stab wound.

"Don't try to move. They haven't been able to heal your

shoulder. There isn't any healing paste left, and even the staff didn't work. It seems to have a mind of its own—or at least only answers to Eloah's plan." His next words came with sorrow she didn't deserve. "You've lost a lot of blood."

In other words, she was dying.

She would have cried if she had the strength. Killed by a pacifist after years of being the best gibborim in history and the lone survivor of the massacre at Death's Wall.

"Sho?"

She grunted. "Water." The word grated her parched throat.

Something scraped nearby. Then the sound of water. A hand tipped her head forward.

"Drink," Tevye ordered.

She tried. Cool moisture sloshed across her chin. A few drops made it into her mouth. Shoshanna laid her head back and forced her eyes open. A dark ceiling faced her. Flickering torchlight revealed roots meandering through dirt. Underground.

"Dalea's people let us in after what happened. There's a remarkably large cavern under Death's Wall. There's a few hundred Doramites left."

Shoshanna's people.

"Dalea's been restrained for the time being. None of them want a leader who broke the oath," Tevye continued, as if Shoshanna cared what became of her murderer.

She deserved this. It was Eloah's judgement on her for all she'd done. She couldn't deny he was real after all she'd witnessed in the lake and beyond, but he'd lied about wanting her. He taunted her with love she could never have.

"Avner, Chava, and Miki are trying to figure out why Reuben couldn't reunite the tribes. They think the prophecy isn't about artifacts, but *people*. But since we have no way of knowing how to reunite people, we're taking all these Doramites back to Thoth on Felix's ship. Adamah will be left to the curse of the frost."

Why was he telling her all this? She'd be dead before she witnessed what became of Adamah. Of her homeland and the place where her husband died.

"They've made sure the boat is still there. We found the remainder of Felix's men frozen—"

Shoshanna found the strength to flop her arm to the side and grasp Tevye's. Warm skin. A tingle of heat ran through her. When was the last time she'd felt someone's skin? Been close enough to?

Wanted to?

Tevye inhaled sharply. His hand covered hers on his arm. "Sho?"

She craned her neck an inch to the side, pain shooting through her shoulder. She hissed, but didn't draw back. She needed to see Tevye's face. Her breathing ceased for a second.

He had *two* eyes. One green, one gold. The gold one sparkled in the firelight

Impossible.

A small smile touched his face. "Eloah gave it to me."

There was so much Shoshanna wouldn't live to understand. The new eye brought life to Tevye's face. He'd always had a kind look, but now, he was whole. Handsome. He deserved to have a new life without his past as a gibborim haunting him. He was a good man. The best of men. Though he was deluding himself that they were anything more than friends, or that she could accept this gift of Eloah as easily as a good man like him had done. No, she was going to die.

"The rock," she croaked.

"What?" Tevye leaned closer.

"Take me. Promise me. Before I die. Not much time."

"I don't understand, Sho. What rock?"

"She means the old Judge's rock." Avner's voice cut through the stifling air of the underground chamber.

Relief swept over Shoshanna. Yes. Avner would know.

"She married Itzaak there," he continued, his voice drawing nearer.

A shadow fell over her, but Shoshanna couldn't bear the pain of turning to look.

"Then we take her," Tevye said, his voice firm.

Shoshanna let out a sob. She didn't deserve this friend. She expected Avner to fight back, to refuse. It would be a long way from the river, and the frost still controlled Adamah.

Instead, arms slid under her back. She rose. Pain split her shoulder, and she cried out. Darkness crept to the edges of her vision, but not like it used to. This was death coming.

A hand slipped into hers.

"It'll be okay, Sho," Tevye whispered. "We'll take you there."

She could have sobbed with relief. To be where she'd been united with Itzaak, the only man who'd ever understood her.

Tevye leaned over her, panicked worry on his face.

Itzaak was no longer the only man who understood her. Shoshanna would have bothered to untangle what that meant if she wasn't going to die in a matter of days. Or hours.

"Forget me after this, Tevye," she whispered. "You're a good man."

He squeezed her hand. "I will never forget you."

Her body swayed as Avner moved along the dark tunnels. Voices rose and fell as they passed what must be the cavern Tevye had mentioned. Shoshanna didn't bother to look at the remainder of the people she'd failed. Soon, they'd be free of her.

"Where are you taking her?" Chava's voice.

"The old Judge's Rock," Avner responded. "Grab supplies and more furs. Let Miki know to wait for us for two days. If we don't return, she can leave without—"

"I'll wait until you return, brother. No matter how long that may be." The strange manipulator stepped up beside Chava, a stark contrast. Both pale, but with features and hair to rival each other. Red and black. Blood and death.

Shoshanna scoffed, but it only came out as a thin groan. She was delirious. Would she even know the rock by the time they arrived there? It was at least a day away, if not more. She hadn't navigated to it in so long.

"Don't worry, I'll watch out for these people. Moises has been sharing fire with everyone he can. He's getting stronger every minute." Miki placed a hand on the shoulder of the curly-haired boy beside her.

He held a torch in his hand. He raised his other hand, and fire siphoned from the torch to fill his palm.

Shoshanna was too wounded to be shocked. At least death would mean she didn't have to face a manipulator ever again. She squeezed Tevye's hand still wrapped around her own.

"We need to go," he said.

Yes. His words brought such relief. Shoshanna's heart felt weaker with each beat.

"I'll get the supplies and meet you out there." Chava spun down into the cavern.

Shoshanna moved again as Avner made for the exit. He barely fit with her in his arms, and she cried out as her shoulder struck the frozen dirt wall.

"Sorry," he mumbled as he squeezed through the exit. Frigid air blasted into her. He gently lowered her to the ground. Tevye helped guide her onto a stretcher.

"They used this to carry the weaker Doramites from the village. Since Dalea isn't in charge any longer, no one will object to us borrowing it."

Tevye gave Avner a meaningful look. Shoshanna would have scoffed at one time, but all the things she hated for so long seemed so pale and insignificant in the face of her looming death.

"I'll go get Chava and the supplies." Avner ducked back inside the crack in the rocks.

The icy air overrode the heat from the pools at this distance, and the cold nipped at Shoshanna's exposed face and hands.

She gave a half chuckle.

"What is it, Sho?" Tevye asked. He crouched beside her.

"For so long I couldn't feel the change in the air, the wind or temperature."

"And now you can, when it's too cold," he said somberly.

"No," she swallowed, her throat still hurting. "It's more wonderful than I remember."

Tevye rested a hand on hers again. "Shoshanna—"

"No. I don't deserve your pity, Tevye. You'll be better off with me dead."

He squeezed her tight. "That is a lie. Don't listen to it. Eloah wants you. He loves you. Please believe that before it is too late."

She didn't have the heart to scoff in his face any longer.

Her own heart yearned for his words to be true, but how could they be? She looked away, tears welling in her own eyes. Death was making a weakling of her. Though she found for once, she *wanted* to be weak. To admit she couldn't do it all alone. To let someone carry her.

But no one could.

I can, Eloah whispered.

But why would he want to?

"Shoshanna?" Tevye grabbed her other hand. "Please."

She didn't answer. Her throat hurt too much. But more than that, she was afraid of what she might say if she did.

Better if she died now and didn't have to feel this any longer. The pain, the hopelessness, the ruin of her pathetic life. But not until she touched the rock and felt the last bit of Itzaak again. Not just her hallucinations of him, but something real, solid.

Avner emerged from the tunnels with Chava close behind.

"Are we ready?" she asked.

Tevye pulled away from Shoshanna's hand, but slowly, reluctantly. His mismatched eyes begged her to listen.

She looked away, her heart aching.

Tevye reached for the stretcher handles behind her, but she never felt his gaze leave her. Avner picked up the front. They set off on Shoshanna's last journey, Chava's heat keeping a bubble of warmth around them. Shoshanna stared at the trees going by overhead. Frozen, yet beautiful in death.

Would that she could be beautiful as well once life left her.

47

THE JUDGE'S ROCK

Avner

"It is only by Eloah's grace Shoshanna is still alive," Avner muttered.

"And I thank him for it," Tevye said, his voice heavy with emotion. As he walked behind Avner on the other side of the stretcher, Avner wished they had a moment to talk about all that had transpired between his friend and Shoshanna. He supposed they would do this on the journey back to Thoth —which seemed the only place to go since they hadn't been able to stop the frost. It wasn't the warmest place, but if Miki was there, it could certainly become a home.

Avner glanced at the silent forest as they made their way northeast. He would have loved to see these trees alive again. The frozen leaves had long since fallen off, leaving glistening white trunks. He missed the vibrant orange foliage and the sound of the wind moving through it like a sea.

"You miss it, don't you?" Chava said softly. Over the last few hours, she'd stayed further back, near Shoshanna's head, to keep her heat around her so she didn't freeze to death after losing so much blood.

Avner helped Tevye lift her sleeping form over another patch of frozen bushes. He glanced at his wife.

"The things I miss wouldn't come back even if we stopped the frost."

"Illa?"

"Yes, and Silas." Avner couldn't hold back a sad smile. Had Silas known the truth of Eloah as he died? He'd hinted at something outside of the Spirit of the Forest only moments before Shoshanna killed him.

For the first time, it struck Avner that Shoshanna had killed both of his adoptive brothers. He tightened his hands on the stretcher, but didn't turn to look at her fading form. How many brothers had *he* killed in the arena with full cognition, whereas she'd been blinded by the potion?

Avner cleared his throat. "And Mikhail. I miss Mikhail."

Chava breathed in sharply.

"I think I'd been missing him for a while, I just wouldn't admit it. I admired Silas, but Mikhail was the older brother I needed. He understood me in ways not even Illa did. I know he didn't intend for Silas to die, or for me to become a gibborim..." Avner's words failed him as Mikhail's face swam in his memory. A wide smile under mischievous, but good-natured eyes. The image faded to the horror on Mikhail's face when Avner offered himself as a gibborim in Mikhail's place.

"It broke him, what happened with you," Chava whispered.

"I know."

But Mikhail had seen Eloah. Mikhail had lived his last year trying to correct one anger-driven mistake. Eloah had accepted Mikhail despite his flaws, just as he was accepting Avner now. Mikhail hadn't deserved to be forgotten by Avner. The pang of longing for his brother Avner had felt at the fence beyond Doram rose again, twice as strong, pulling so hard that tears pricked Avner's eyes. Mikhail, his brother. His best friend. Dead, unforgiven.

"I miss him," he whispered. The ache in his heart doubled, and Avner almost glanced over his shoulder to see if Mikhail would come striding through the trees, a wide smile on his face, begging Avner to come spar just one more time.

But Mikhail wasn't there, because he'd died. And Avner had rejoiced in it.

"I'm so sorry," Avner whispered. He'd have given anything to erase the memory of the last time he saw Mikhail and the feeling of his hands around his brother's throat.

"We will see Mikhail again one day," Chava said with such raw faith that Avner choked back a sob.

He had to believe it.

Avner stepped around a frozen shrub and hissed as the end of a branch cut through his glove. Golden blood leaked out.

"It still doesn't make any sense," Chava mused, staring at the blood. She caught up to him and wiped it off with a corner of her sleeve. "If the prophecy is about reuniting people and not artifacts, how does giving you the Nameless —Bachir—bloodline solve anything?"

"I'm as clueless as you, but knowing Eloah, there is a reason."

"One I can't figure out either," Tevye muttered. The prophecy never mentioned blood, right?"

"Right," Chava sighed. "Maybe Eloah knew the glowing blood would keep you alive in the arena. How many times did the sight of it stop another gibborim from killing you?"

She had a point. Avner sent a silent prayer of thanks to Eloah and hefted the stretcher over another bush.

They traipsed forward in silence for another hour. Their breaths misted into the air, including—praise Eloah—Shoshanna's. Her color was worsening. Near gray. They had to be close, but Avner had only ever heard Silas discuss the location, and hadn't been there himself to recognize the signs. He knew they were headed in the right direction because the frost was thicker—older—up here.

"I'm not as versed in Doram lore as you both," Tevye said. "Why did Shoshanna marry Itzaak at the rock?"

At least he was speaking again. He had grown more silent as Shoshanna's color continued to fade.

"Because her father didn't approve of her claiming Itzaak. And of course, marrying him was a sin far worse," Chava said, as if quoting some memorized text. Avner had forgotten how much Chava used to obsess over Doram's lost hero.

How long ago that seemed.

Shoshanna groaned. Avner glanced behind him. Her arm flopped off the stretcher. They paused and Tevye leaned over, gently replacing it. She opened her eyes. Glazed, red. Dying.

"Shoshanna? We are almost there," Tevye whispered.

"I can feel it," she murmured, scanning the trees feverishly. "Is the lake...?"

The lake? They weren't near Mount Rachav. That would take another day.

"Yes!" Chava gasped, pointing east. "That's it!"

Avner spun around. Sure enough, the frozen expanse of the lake he'd fought on for over a year stretched out in the distance. It was no doubt miles away, but their vantage point on the hill they'd just climbed made it visible through the leafless trees.

Shoshanna let out a rattling chuckle. "I-ironic, isn't it? Married within view of the lake...that later stole my soul—" She gasped for breath and fell into a coughing fit.

Tevye's face fell. He grabbed her hand. "We will get you to the rock."

"T-top of the h-ill," she wheezed.

Avner grabbed the stretcher pole again and resumed the hike up the hill. His calves burned. It had been over a week since he'd done any training, and his lungs struggled against the frosty air. Tevye helped to keep the stretcher level as they made their way up, while Chava melted the ice before them, making the trail less treacherous.

At last, they crested the knoll. The lake spread out in the distance. White, innocent, giving no sign of the hundreds of lives lost on it.

"Yes," Shoshanna breathed out in relief.

The old Judge's rock sat in what must have been a meadow on the top of the hill. The trees surrounded the four-foot boulder, the bright orange color of their leaves perfectly preserved in ice, and every blade of grass was frozen in time, telling of something grander that had existed here once. Even covered in frost, Avner *knew* this place.

But from a dream, or a memory?

He didn't take his eyes off the frost-covered rock as they lowered Shoshanna to the ground.

"Easy," Tevye cautioned.

Avner released the stretcher pole and stepped closer to

the rock. They had used a boulder closer to Doram to swear in judges for the past century.

"I just want to touch it," Shoshanna whispered, her voice weaker. The scars on her exposed hands stood out like purple tattoos against her deathly pale skin. "Hurry."

Sнoshanna

Tнe нeat of spreading infection kept the chill away, but Shoshanna still shivered violently. She hadn't been to this place in eighteen years, yet why did it seem so...familiar? An itching crept up her palms, tracing the lines of her scars. Each one. All hundred and twelve. From the pinkie tip she had almost lost in her first gibborim match to the fresh wound in her shoulder. Oldest to newest, they hummed with anticipation. Of touching the rock. Of dying.

"I want to touch it," Shoshanna whispered. "Please." Her whole body ached for the rock to be beneath her fingers as it had the day she married Itzaak.

"You will," Tevye said.

The aching subsided for half a moment. There was something else... A breeze, soft and cool, licked the nape of her neck, curling the short hairs to tickle her skin. She pushed up on her good shoulder, crying out in pain.

"Sho—" Tevye tried to guide her back down.

"I need to see it!"

There it sat. The boulder was just as she remembered, apart from the glistening swirls overtaking it. Even with the deadly ice, it was breathtaking and beckoned her closer.

With a gasp, and stabs of pain through every inch of her torso, Shoshanna fell back onto the stretcher.

"Closer," she croaked. Her trembling fingers just managed to trace the brand of Zev on her left wrist. She hadn't done that in almost two decades. But then her hand stretched out on its own accord. Reaching for hope that wouldn't come, for the death that surely would. For remembrances of the last truly good thing in her life.

AVNER

SHOSHANNA'S FINGERS WERE BLACKENING, just as Mikhail's had so long ago. But the frostbite wouldn't matter. Avner exchanged a glance with Tevye, whose whole face was pulled tight with the somber truth.

Shoshanna wouldn't live to make the journey back to Doram.

Tevye's eyes glistened with unshed tears. Shoshanna's fingers stretched further. So close to the rock now. They should move the stretcher closer, so she wouldn't have to move so much. Avner coaxed it closer to the rock.

Rock.

...Only when the tribes return to their rock will power be given and Adamah saved. Only then will a new order be established under the one who reigns.

A rush of understanding blew through him. "The *rock*," he breathed.

He turned toward Chava, pulling the stretcher.

"Easy!" Tevye tugged the stretcher back to the rock. "Get it closer, mate."

The sight of Shoshanna's hand stretching toward the rock froze Avner in place. As if her fingers were slicing through years of misunderstood notions about a prophecy given to those who followed Eloah, but misinterpreted by those who didn't.

"It's us returning to Eloah," he whispered.

SHOSHANNA

AVNER'S VOICE droned in the background, filled with excitement, but Shoshanna only had eyes for the rock before her. It was not smooth, but old and pitted. Marked with the divots of a harsh life.

Like her.

The breeze shifted, but instead of the mind-numbing cold, it was warm, gentle. Speaking to her life, to her ruined past, touching it with a flicker of love. As if Itzaak himself were here, guiding her hand closer to the stone.

But not Itzaak, someone else. Someone who, if she believed it, loved her even more than her husband ever could have.

Shoshanna choked out a sob, her heart aching more than the life-stealing wound in her shoulder. She longed for it to be true. She longed for so much more than this pale life she'd lived.

"Eloah," she breathed out as her scarred fingers touched the pitted rock.

AVNER

AN ECHOING boom shook the forest around them the moment Shoshanna's blackened fingers brushed the rock. A rush of warm air hit Avner first. Soothing and absorbing. It wrapped his limbs with light and color. It tickled his ears and chin.

Chava shouted as she flew backward with another gust of warm air. Avner's feet flew out from under him. The stretcher beneath Shoshanna tipped. He hit the ground amidst earth and melting snow.

Avner's palms dug into moss, fresh and green between his fingers. Craning his neck, he looked around the glade. Shoshanna lay beside a flowering shrub. Her shoulder... blood-free. Only smooth skin showed through her ruined shirt.

His head throbbing, he rolled to the side. His hand touched warm skin.

Chava groaned and sat upright, her eyes gleaming in the sunlight. Perfect. Beautiful. Avner's hand lingered on hers. Her fingers curled over his. There was no need to say anything.

"The lake! The lake!" Tevye yelled, standing in a patch of lush, green grass and pointing to the east.

Just over the next knoll, the expanse of the Frozen Lake, the lake where Avner had fought and killed, where he had been lost and found, stretched into the distance.

He caught his breath.

Blue, glittering water, without a trace of ice.

48

HOME

Avner

Doram was in chaos. Joyful chaos.

Children running to and fro, squealing in their delight to be out of the muddy cave and in the sun again. Men and women dug through the rubble left behind by months of frost, exclaiming as objects were found. Others still wept openly at the loss of all the houses, and the lives of the unfortunates who didn't make it through the long cold. Piles of muddy, filthy ruined parkas lay in the center of the village, ready for a jubilant bonfire.

No other sign that the tribe had been under the frost remained. The maple rows stood as they had in the days when Silas was Judge and Avner helped him tend the trees. Some men were already hoisting their tapping tools onto their backs, ready to begin their lives again. Others still wandered, dazed, staring at the lush orange foliage as if they'd emerged from the underground into a dream world above.

Avner understood their confusion.

If he hadn't put all the pieces together and seen Shoshanna's hand touch the stone, he wouldn't have believed it himself.

The Doramites who'd stepped in to fill the vacant elder roles tried to organize the chaos, but many were too overwhelmed to listen, staring wide-eyed at the summer scene before them. Dalea stood, hands still bound, at the edge of the village clearing, staring in disbelief. She met Avner's gaze and hastily looked away. Shame written all over her face.

"What will become of her?" Chava asked.

"It's hard to say. In the days before the frost, she would have been exiled for breaking the Oath of Do No Harm. But seeing as so many who are here broke it to survive, they can't banish the whole tribe. I'm guessing they will pardon her eventually, though she will never again be given a leadership position."

"But for now, can we please get Shoshanna to a healer?" Tevye frowned at her still form on the stretcher. Her wounds had been healed when she touched the rock, but she hadn't awakened. Thankfully, she was still breathing.

Avner motioned to where a lean-to was already being erected for the wounded from the cave. Tevye helped him carry the stretcher the rest of the way.

"You go rest, Tevye. I'll stay with her until she wakes."

"No." His knuckles were white as he gripped the stretcher, crouching beside it among the other wounded. "You go. I should be the one here when she wakes."

Avner stepped back. "All right. Let me know if you need anything."

Tevye only nodded, not taking his eyes off Shoshanna. Avner smiled to himself and turned back to where Chava stood, handing out rations of food from Felix's abandoned ship to a gaggle of muddy children.

"So, tell me." Chava handed the entire basket of provisions to the nearest lad. The children swarmed him, cheering. "How did we reunite the tribes and stop the frost without finding someone from each tribe if it was about people?"

"I don't think that was a good idea," Avner warned, pointing at the children.

They had sprinted after the food basket, screaming and giggling.

"Don't avoid my question. How did you know it would work?"

"Because we *did* find someone from all the missing tribes. And it wasn't about being at the old Judge's rock. It was about returning to Eloah, our rock."

Chava cocked her head. "How, exactly? To both your points."

"Remember, *I'm* the last of the Nameless Tribe. Eloah transferred the bloodline to me from Liev when he lay dying, giving me glowing blood in the process..." he trailed off.

Miki stood with Moises on the other side of the village center, manipulating rocks to clear a path for new homes to be built.

"My blood is the reason I can't manipulate, Chava! I'm no longer Kemetian. I don't have the genetic material required to manipulate."

"But then how can you be the tribe of Manoach?"

A valid point. Yet the frost was still gone, and the tribes reunited.

"Because... because I'm still from Kemet. My parents are

still descendants of Manoach, no matter if I still have that blood. Just like Shoshanna is Zev through marriage. I don't need to have the physical blood to be grafted into the tribe."

"And Shoshanna is Doramite as well! So, with both of you we have Manoach, Nameless, Zev, and Doram. I'm Eder. And Yor..."

"Leewana," they said in unison.

"It doesn't matter that she wasn't at the rock," Avner continued. "That was coincidental. But Leewana and her husband already knew Eloah, meaning they brought the tribe of Yor back to him."

Understanding finally dawned on her face. "Which means Shoshanna believes in Eloah now!"

Avner smiled. He'd figured out as much the moment the frost had melted, but they'd been too busy trying to make sure Shoshanna still lived to press the issue. He nodded.

"I have to tell Tevye!" Chava turned and sprinted to where their friend still sat with Shoshanna.

Avner watched her go, the smile still on his lips. Then he took in the celebration and the work going on in his home. Dalea could never banish him again, and no matter what, there would be plenty of room in Adamah now that most everyone had fled or died. Perhaps he and Chava could resettle Eder. Or somewhere else entirely. Maybe Tevye would take them to the Barrens and show them the beauty he saw there.

The warm breeze caressed Avner's exposed shoulder beneath his torn shirt. The rose tattoo showed through, but as Avner stared at it, the irreversible mark struck him differently. Felix never had a chance to fill in the petals. Eloah had carried Avner through without further harm. The rose wasn't a curse, but a blessing. A sign of where Avner had been, and where Eloah had brought him.

He looked away from it, smiling, and caught Miki's own wide smile as she watched Moises frolic with the other children. He'd get the time to know the sister he had yearned for. She noticed him looking and winked. *Sister.*

Then he glanced back at Chava, and the trees beyond her. Neither Thoth nor Doram was his home. They were.

SOMEWHERE IN THE GRASSLANDS

Shoshanna- Two months later

The grass and weeds shushed around her knees as Shoshanna hiked up the knoll. The warm wind rippled through it, so unlike what she had seen the last time she had been here as Nuri. A year ago, this had been north of the Frost Line. Now it was just another part of Adamah under an unseasonably warm sun. No sign of the snow from the past six hundred years. No snowmelt or runoff. No floods. No marshes. Just gone.

A miracle.

A pang of longing pulled at Shoshanna. The beauty of this place paled in comparison to the valley where she had met Eloah. She'd tried to return to it as soon as she woke up after touching the old Judge's rock, but the nameless rune had vanished from Death's Wall.

She wasn't surprised. It had accomplished what Eloah intended. Though what of Akaron? Was the lonely man trapped forever in that valley until he perished? But he'd made his choice not to believe in Eloah, as she once had. Avner had agreed they wouldn't be able to find the valley in the north even if they tried. Eloah had brought them there for his purpose, which was now accomplished. Akaron would die, and Avner would continue the nameless—Bachir —tribe here in Doram, then on Thoth once he and Chava returned there with his sister. Eloah's grand plan.

Shoshanna's knees almost buckled at the relief that Eloah had pulled her out of such darkness.

Shoshanna's hair blew in the wind, and she brushed it away from her face. Out of habit, her eyes scanned the skin on her arms and hands. The rash was still gone.

She slowed down to watch the wind on its journey north. Curling in the grasses and shaking the purple and blue ferns at the bottom of the small hill. The sky was no longer gray with the weight of snow, but blue and clear.

Like her vision. She'd been able to see in full color since diving into Eloah's Lake. That hadn't been what changed her mind about him, but it had helped. He was the Lord of miracles, and he'd worked a miracle in her.

The clay pot with Mikhail's ashes warmed her fingertips as she pulled it out of the satchel across her chest. Still. Silent. Shoshanna had found the ash pile where the few surviving Doramites had burned any bodies after they thawed. It might be Mikhail, or it might not, but this gesture was more symbolic than anything, since Shoshanna knew where Mikhail really was. Mikhail wasn't just a pile of soot in a jar.

Shoshanna blinked as a tear stung her eye. Even after all the tears she had shed since she accepted Eloah, she still wasn't used to it.

Eloah, the Lord of all, Lord of her life, despite all she had done as Nuri, had healed her. Not just from color blindness and the wandering rash, but from her past. He had healed Adamah. The falls—melted. The lake where she used to fight and kill—deep blue water as it hadn't been for six hundred years. The stand-in elders in Doram claimed the Spirit of the Forest had done it, and most of the few hundred remaining Doramites believed them. They were all blinded by the lies they followed. Now they continued on as if the months of frost hadn't happened. Still believing Eloah wasn't real.

But then, Shoshanna had done the same for forty-three years.

She glanced to the East, past the towers of stone where she and Reuben had once fought the Yocheved. Another lifetime ago. She set the jar of ashes on the top of the hill.

"I'm sorry. But I suppose you know more of Eloah and his glory than any of us here below." She chuckled and pulled the small green flecked stone out of her satchel, careful not to crush the snow lily nestled in the outer pocket.

She smiled. Itzaak had been curious about Eloah in those final days, and she'd brushed it off. But now she held a strong hope that it had been more than curiosity, and that she'd see her husband again. If only she'd listened to his musings back then. Maybe things would have been different. *I have already made amends for you.* Eloah's voice whispered in her ear.

"I know," she said softly. The green rock glinted fiercely in the sunlight, and she squinted as she set it by the jar. "Ofira, I am sorry I robbed you of the chance to know Eloah. I am sorry I took your stone in this place. And your life."

I forgive you, Shoshanna, Eloah whispered again.

She knew, oh how she knew. The heat of the power of

Eloah sizzled along her fingers. It snapped out, sparking against Ofira's stone. The power Reuben hadn't understood. It wasn't a physical power for the uniter of the tribes to inherit, but a spiritual one. Shoshanna, Chava, Avner, Tevye, and any of the Doramites whose eyes had been opened in the last two months since the frost vanished. They possessed the power. She would never get used to it.

And she didn't want to.

Shoshanna stepped away from the jar and the rock. If not for Mikhail's woman she'd murdered so long ago in this very place, Shoshanna would still be lost within Nuri.

But she wasn't. She was found in Eloah.

Shoshanna turned and jogged down the hill, smiling. It was time to join Tevye and journey across the continent with their combined purpose.

It was time to spread the news.

ACKNOWLEDGMENTS

This book wouldn't have been possible without Jesus, Yeshua, my savior and friend.

To all my fearless friends who I surprised with a second book in this series, thank you for putting up with my nerdiness.

As always, thank you to the The Kindlers and Story Group for fielding my incessant questions and offering sometimes totally ignored advice. You are all amazing yet again.

Thank you to my diligent and inspiring editor, Nicole. This book wouldn't be in the world without you. And to Grace, for catching the best typos and plot-holes. You're a champ!

Thank you to Libby and the Roastery for letting my sit endlessly in the back room typing away. Sorry I drank all the tea and strawberry protein smoothies.

This series also wouldn't have happened without Johnny, Ruthie, Charlie and Penny. Thanks to the most supportive family ever.

ABOUT THE AUTHOR

Abigail L. Wilkes writes New Adult Fantasy grounded in her savior's truth and believes that if there isn't a character having an identity crisis, something is very wrong. Dark chocolate and earl grey fuel her candle-lit writing sessions before the sun and her three kiddos are up. She lives with her mountain-man husband in the snowy Rocky Mountains of Colorado and finds inspiration hiking, traveling, and contemplating the Sting replica on her book self.